"DO YOU WANT
TO KISS?"

*

Jericho looked down at her hands folded primly in her lap. "Yes," she said.

Lounging on his side on the mossy stream bank, Lord Dove smiled gently. "Come here, beauty. . . ." She moved, bunching her skirts, walking awkwardly on her knees until she knelt beside him.

"Dove, I don't think we should kiss lying down."

"Certainly, certainly," he said. "Real kissing is done lying down. Ask anyone."

"Dove—"

"We are only going to kiss, Jericho. I give you my word." He reached up and drew her down into his arms.

"Dove, I don't think we should—"

"You don't mind if I lie partly on top of you, do you? Like this?" With a twist of his handsome shoulders he showed her, and she found herself lying under him, her breasts softly crushed to his warm chest. Her heart pounded.

"Dove, I think we had best kiss only once."

"Then let's make it a good one," he said, and brought his mouth down to hers . . .

*

The Golden Dove

Jo Ann Wendt

POPULAR LIBRARY

An Imprint of Warner Books, Inc.

A Warner Communications Company

POPULAR LIBRARY EDITION

Popular Library® and the fanciful P design are registered trademarks
of Warner Books, Inc.

Cover art by Gregg Gulbronson

Popular Library books are published by
Warner Books, Inc.
666 Fifth Avenue
New York, N.Y. 10103

 A Warner Communications Company

Printed in the United States of America

First Printing: November, 1989

10 9 8 7 6 5 4 3 2 1

This one is for my mother, Lola Mueller, back home in Oshkosh . . . and, for listening and listening and listening some more, my boundless thanks to Dorothy, Joan, Marion, Trish.

PART ONE

DOVE

1658

Chapter One

England, January, 1658 . . .

Snow fell softly against the casement windows of Blackpool Castle. It fell with slow grace, whirling snowflake drifting down upon whirling snowflake, and slowly gathered in the crevices of the stone window ledges where it grew into mounds of cold radiance that glittered, catching and reflecting the firelight within.

Inside the castle, in a great hall hung with tapestries, with ancient weapons that gleamed in firelight, and with life-size portraits of silken lords and ladies who seemed to breathe in the glow of a blazing, crackling winter's afternoon fire—there—words fell softly. Words colder than the crystalline snow.

"Find her and kill her."

"Ay, Your Grace."

"I desire it be accomplished at once."

"Ay, Your Grace. I understand."

"I want her obliterated. Leave no trace of her. She never existed. She does not now exist. She *shall* not exist."

"Ay, Your Grace. I understand. I'll start tomorrow."

Alerted by the sudden rasp of silk, and a hiss of rich chair leather, the three wolfhounds who had been sleeping before the fire opened their glassy eyes.

" 'Tomorrow'?"

His Grace, the duke of Blackpool, shifted his slim elegant body in the sumptuous depths of his Russia-leather chair and contemplated his steward with cold unblinking eyes. " 'Tomorrow'?" His Grace repeated faintly. "Surely I misheard?"

On the hearth, the wolfhounds lifted their immense heads and haughtily contemplated the steward too, as if they too had misheard.

Fox Hazlitt, the steward, squirmed and eased a thumb between his thick neck and his lacy shirt collar. Although the shirt was new, bought only yesterday at Cheapside in London, it suddenly seemed too tight. "Milord, I misspoke," he offered quickly. "*Today*. Naturally I'll start *today*. I'll write me agents *today*."

"Ah. So I thought."

A satisfied silence. Fox Hazlitt relaxed. But he continued to watch his master with wary eyes. Cold bastard, he thought. As cold as your castle. Stifling a shiver as a stray draft curled up his spine—the castle was colder in winter than the sheets under a two-shilling whore—he made to inch his chair closer to the fire. He was checked by a low throaty growl. Goddamn dogs. Scared a man half to death. Great ugly beasts. They had jowls that could snap a sheep in two and long skinny bodies that tapered to nothing. He could smell their wolf shag. Fox cleared his throat in the unnatural silence. The snow was falling faster now, hitting the windows like fine shot.

"Where would Your Grace have me begin the search?"

The unblinking eyes of man and dogs stared.

"Surely it's your task to decide 'where,' is it not? Unless, of course, you deem yourself no longer capable of serving in my employ?"

Fox flushed and the collar tightened still more. He'd grown rich in a decade of the duke's employ. He owned a fine house of timber and plaster in Westminister. He dressed his wife and his children in silk; and when his wife went out, she went in style, riding in her own sedan chair, carried by two catch-farts. He kept his mistress, a Drury Lane actress, in even finer style.

Quickly, he made haste to dash water on his burning bridges.

"Your Grace, pray overlook. Milord, I misspoke. 'Tis me own task, to be sure. Depend on it, Your Grace. I'll dispatch me agents today. Today, milord."

The dark eyes, eyes like burning coals, contemplated him for a long and uncomfortable moment.

"Better . . . much better." The duke managed a frosty smile. "Excellent."

With that soft sibilant murmur, the duke leaned forward over a low, lion-footed table on which stood the remains of a casual repast: a cold joint of mutton, bowls of Spanish olives and Jerusalem almonds, pickled onions, bread, wine. Taking a gold-handled dagger from the sheath at his waist, he neatly carved pieces from the cold joint. He tossed them to the dogs piece by piece. Like crocodiles, the hounds snapped them down.

Fox watched warily. A breed bred to hunt wolves, wolfhounds seldom found such prey in these forward, modern times. But he'd seen them bring down a stag. He knew that at a signal from His Grace, the hounds would attack a man and leave nothing behind but coat buttons and bones.

When the duke finished cosseting his pets, he wiped the dagger clean on a dainty lace and linen napkin, then leaned back in his chair and crossed one slim leg on the other. He hooked his elbows on the chair arms and toyed with the dagger, turning it over and over in his slender fingers as he spoke. It was an unnerving habit, and, after years of service, Fox still was not used to it. For though the duke spoke with exquisite softness, never raising his voice, he gestured with the dagger as he spoke, underscoring a request here, emphasizing a point there.

Abruptly, the duke looked up. His dark eyes flashed. "Listen and listen well," he ordered softly. "Need I say it would make me unhappy to have to repeat this story? Or . . ." The dagger gestured. "—if the story were to return to my ears, carried back to me by other lips?"

Fox drew a careful breath. "No, Your Grace. Me lips are sealed."

"Excellent . . . excellent."

With that, the duke gazed about, as if in annoyance, as if to delay the telling for a few moments longer. At last, drawing an irritable breath, he plunged in.

"The brat I wish obliterated . . . was whelped here, here in Blackpool Castle, eleven years ago. In my absence. During my three-year sojourn in France, you understand?" Fox didn't understand, but nodded anyway. "When a trusted servant sent me word, warning me there would be a secret birth, I dispatched a bag of gold to the castle midwife. I instructed her to drug the mother into unconsciousness during the birthing. I ordered her to break the whelp's neck 'ere it came from the womb. She was to bury the brat and later, when the mother regained consciousness, she was to tell the mother her brat had been stillborn."

The dagger flashed, catching firelight. "A month ago I learned the old hag had played me false. She took my gold. She obeyed all of my instructions, less one. She did *not* kill the brat. Instead, she padded her purse by selling the whelp. On the auction block. At St. Katherine's Docks in London."

Fox's heart began to thud in dismay. "St. Katherine's Docks, Your Grace?"

The duke shot him an irritated look. "I have just said so, have I not?"

"But—but, Your Grace! Ships of every nation put in there. If the brat was sold there, she could be anywheres in the world."

The dagger came around and pointed. "Precisely."

Fox felt the ground shift under him. Suddenly, this was not a mission he fancied. It smacked of failure. Failure didn't fill a purse; success did. Shrewdly, he considered how to avoid the assignment. "Your Grace. Pray consider. Few infants survive infancy. Doubtless the brat is dead."

The duke eyed him coldly. "Then bring me proof of it."

His heart beat with alarm. "But, Your Grace. Pray consider. If I cannot tell me agents where in the world to search? If I cannot even tell 'em what the brat might look like? Milord, I beg. Milord, I need—"

The plea died in his throat, for the duke's eyes flashed. With a movement as swift as a cat, the duke leaned forward in his chair and viciously pointed the dagger at a portrait that hung upon the near wall. Fox looked at it, befuddled. A familiar portrait, a familiar lady. Beautiful! Pale skin, delicate bones, hair like a mantle of soft brown velvet. Eyes so sad a man was in danger of weeping if he looked into them too long. Fox blinked in confusion. Across the low table, the duke's gaze burned.

"You understand, of course, that the brat might look . . . like . . . my wife?"

It was a jolt, a shock. Her ladyship? Why, her ladyship was as loved and respected in the parish as the duke was disliked and feared! Fox felt as if he'd suddenly stepped to the edge of a precipice.

"Then again," the duke murmured in his soft way, "you understand, of course, that the brat might also resemble—"

With a vicious and unexpected movement, the duke turned in his chair, whipped back his ruffled wrist and hurled the dagger. A streak of gold and firelight, it shot across the great hall to pierce home with a powerful thunk, tearing into the painted throat of a handsome, buoyant young lord who had carrot bright hair and merry blue eyes. The blade buried itself in the portrait's backboard, vibrating, humming in a stillness broken only by the crackling fire and the peck of snow at the windows.

"My beloved cousin," the duke murmured. "Aubrey de Mont."

Lord Aubrey? That bold, respected soldier?

Now Fox was truly scared. For a moment, he was afraid to speak, afraid to move. Afraid even to raise his eyes to the duke. Dry-mouthed, he stared at his own boot tops. He didn't need a tree to fall on him to know he was privy to a dangerous secret. Fail the duke in this mission, and he was a dead man!

His thoughts galloped wildly in every direction. Find this illegitimate brat? Sniff out a trail eleven years stale? Impossible! Easier to find your own spit in the ocean.

How then to save his neck, his lucrative post? Outfox the duke? *Pretend* to find the brat? Pluck any redhaired orphan off the streets of London and kill her? Possible, possible. But great care must be taken. The duke was nobody's fool. Still, the possibility served to steady his nerves.

The duke was awaiting a response. Fox cleared his throat.

"Ah, Your Grace. I understand. I b'lieve I see me duty clear."

"Do you?" The tone was unexpectedly dry, amused. With an elegant graceful movement, the duke slung himself out of his chair and sauntered across the great hall toward Lord Aubrey's portrait, his high-heeled, red-lacquered shoes clicking leisurely on the richly polished parquet flooring, his jeweled shoe-roses gleaming.

"Allow me to help you see even more 'clear'. My source tells me the brat was born marked. She carries upon her body three red birthmarks, the size and shape of strawberries. The first is on the inside of her right wrist."

Fox drew a startled breath. Birthmarks, by God! A clinker in the clockworks. Brats with red hair he could find by the dozen. But brats with birthmarks? He thought quickly, his mind coursing to and fro. On the wharves in London he'd seen foreign sailors who tattooed themselves. Surely three simple strawberry birthmarks . . .

He carefully licked the inside of his lip. "And the second and third birthmarks are located where, milord?"

The duke smiled thinly. "Come, come. Do not trifle with me, Fox. The location of the second and third are *yours* to describe, are they not? When you've found the right brat and killed her?"

Fox breathed unevenly, knowing he'd backed into a snare. In a leisurely manner, His Grace resumed his stroll to Lord Aubrey's portrait. When he stood before it, he reached up and retrieved the dagger. But he did so in a way that slashed Lord Aubrey from throat to testicles.

Then he turned, eyes widening in feigned surprise. "Dear me. See what has happened. It seems my cousin's portrait has met with an accident. A bungling maidservant, no doubt. Careless with mop or broom. Or perhaps some lout of a lackey, clumsily snagging spider webs." The ingenuous gaze widened. "You *did* see it happen, did you not?"

Wits addled, for a moment Fox could only nod and swallow thickly. "Ay, Your Grace. I seen it. 'Twas a lackey done it."

"Then hadn't you best go and report it?"

Fox swallowed again, his voice a clot. "Ay, Your Grace. I'll go at once. I'll go to the castle steward."

He was checked by a thin smile. "Dear me, no. That will not do. Do not report it to the castle steward. Report it directly to . . ." The duke's cold gaze traveled across the hall to the portrait opposite Lord Aubrey's. "Report it directly to the duchess . . . to my faithful and beloved *wife*."

Fox lost his breath. Such a cat-and-mouse game.

"Ay, Your Grace," he said thickly.

The duke's posture changed, signaling the interview was at an end. Glad to go, glad for time to be alone and think of a way out of his quandary, Fox was already bowing himself out of the room when a soft knock came at the door. After a discreet moment, the arched oaken door with its iron bands and fittings of brass yawned slowly inward.

For a moment it seemed to Fox the portrait on the near wall had sprung to life and stepped down from the wall. For there, standing frail and lovely in the doorway, even more beautiful than her painted likeness, was her ladyship, the duchess of Blackpool. Clutching a shawl of brown wool and framed by tall, arching corridor windows that were curtained with falling snow, she looked like a delicate moth that has lucklessly hatched out of season and is doomed.

"My lord?"

"Angelina, my love, come in!"

"My lord, might I have a word? I would ask a boon."

"A boon?" His Grace smiled and gestured extravagantly, wrist lace billowing. "My love, ask what you will. I am yours to command. Ask any boon you will. It is yours. Enter, my love, enter."

She neither returned his smile nor entered. Her eyes skittered to the hearth, to the dogs who now sat on their haunches, alert, watching, eyes a glassy green in the firelight.

"You know I am afraid of the dogs."

"My puppies?" His Grace looked about expansively, as if the very idea were absurd, humorous, amusing. "My puppies are harmless."

"They are not!" she said with a rare show of spirit. "I often fear they will do someone harm. Some innocent child perhaps. Or some peasant gathering windfalls in the orchard. My lord, I have seen them bring down a hare in the gardens.''

The duke smiled indulgently. "My love, *you* are not a hare. You are, and have ever been, my . . . beloved and faithful wife.''

Did she falter? Fox thought so, but he hadn't a moment to savor it, for the duke wheeled suddenly. "Fox! The leashes. Leash the dogs and take them to the far end of the room. The dogs are frightening Her Grace.''

Fox jumped to obey, but burned inwardly. Make him a kennel keeper, would he? He found the leashes and gingerly applied them to the powerful, sinewy necks. As he led the dogs away, their nails clicking over the floor, he strained to catch every word.

"My lord, I pray you will reconsider old Bess's dismissal. She did not mean to drop the vase. Her poor hands are crippled and twisted. Her joints ache and swell painfully in this cold weather. My lord, she is *old*.''

"And useless.''

With her soft pretty voice, the duchess tried again. "My lord, I pray you. Bess has served Blackpool Castle for nearly thirty years. She served here in your father's time, your grandfather's time. She has always been a faithful and devoted servant. My lord, Blackpool Castle is the only home she has ever known. If she is turned out she will have nowhere to go. My lord! She has no way to earn her bread.''

"Then let her beg for it.''

"My lord. Husband. Show mercy. I implore you!'' Forgetful of herself, her ladyship stepped forward, her shawl dropping away as she lifted her palms like pale supplicating lilies. Oh, she was a beauty all right, standing there pleading her case so prettily.

The duke strolled to his begging wife, retrieved her shawl and with slow sensual movements draped it around her slim shoulders and knotted it at her breast. His hand lingered there, touching her familiarly, the way a man has a right to touch his wife. She didn't like it. That was plain. Even so, she stood her ground. "My lord, Bess?''

"Your boon is granted, Angelina. Did I not say so?''

Her ladyship flushed, startled as a bird that has been tossed an unexpected crumb. Then, gracefully, she sank into a curtsy. "Thank you, my lord, thank you," she murmured quickly. "And Bess thanks you. She thanks you with all her heart." Backing away, she turned to leave, then evidently changed her mind. Throwing a scanty glance at Fox, she said, "My lord, is there any war news from London? Did your servant bring any word of the war?"

Servant! Fox heated. He wasn't a servant, he was the duke's righthand man. He was the duke's chief steward. He was important! He narrowed his eyes at her. Oh he could see through her all right. She didn't give a tinker's damn that England lay bloodied and torn asunder by a dozen years of civil war. She didn't give a damn who won, Oliver Cromwell or King Charles. She was worried about only one soldier. Lord Aubrey de Mont.

The duke saw through her too. For he smiled thinly. "War? Is that what you call it, Angelina? I do not. I call it a rabbit hunt. The king's ragtag band of cavaliers in hiding, fleeing like rabbits from burrow to burrow. Cromwell's army of Roundheads hunting them down, dragging them out by the ears, hauling them to London and chopping off their luckless heads. And the king himself? Penniless as a pauper, living rabbit-poor in exile. War? Really, my love. How droll. You should thank God I had sense enough to swear allegiance to Cromwell and save Blackpool Castle from this farcical rabbit hunt."

"Nevertheless," she persisted with quiet dignity. "Is there any word?"

The duke took his own sweet time answering. "Nothing fit for your gentle ears to hear, my love."

Instantly, worry pinched her lovely features, but she knew better than to press. She knew her husband. With a soft murmur, "Thank you, my lord, thank you for sparing Bess," she again curtsied, then swept gracefully to the door.

She hadn't even once looked in the direction of Lord Aubrey's portrait. She had carefully avoided it. A sure sign of guilt, Fox thought shrewdly. But suddenly, as if she couldn't bear to leave without a hasty glance at the man she loved, she cast her eyes there. Aghast, she stood stark still.

"What happened?"

The duke shrugged elegantly. "An accident, my love. A careless lackey damaged my cousin's portrait with a broom handle. Fox, there, saw it happen." Fox nodded obediently. "More's the pity. For it's likely the last portrait to be painted of Aubrey. Considering the dire news Fox has just brought . . ." Fox glanced at him, curious.

The blood faded from her ladyship's face. Her skin paled. Her eyes grew large and dark. "What news?"

"Alas, my love. Cromwell's army has captured Aubrey's band of cavaliers. Aubrey has been caught, tried for treason and beheaded."

It was not true. Fox had brought no such news, but its effect upon her ladyship was delicious. Fox had never seen the life drain out of a human being. He did now. Her ladyship grew ashen. Lips a stricken blue, she stood as still as death.

"When?" she said in a faint whisper. "Where?"

"My love! The details are too gory for your gentle ears. Let it suffice to say that I intend to write London and protest on my cousin's behalf. The state *must* hire better executioners. These stupid, bungling woodchoppers. Ever forgetful to grind their blades to a sharp, merciful edge. It quite brings to mind Queen Mary."

Even for Fox, this was too much. He swung horrified eyes at the duke. Mary Queen of Scots, great-grandmother to the present exiled King Charles, had been sent to the block seventy years earlier and had suffered what no human being deserved to suffer. Her executioner had bungled. Failing to kill her with the first stroke, he'd grown rattled and hacked her to death.

Fox swung his eyes to her ladyship. For a moment he thought she would faint, drop like a flower. But she didn't. Her chest gave several enormous heaves. Bright tears, brighter than candlelit crystal, sprang up. She stumbled backwards in shock, then picked up her skirts, turned and fled, forgetful of curtsying to her husband, forgetful of shutting the door, forgetful of everything. She fled down the long, echoing corridor, past windows curtained with falling snow. When her footfalls had faded, the duke turned with an amused smile and strolled to the dogs. He petted them one by one.

"Dear, dear. One should not believe *every* rumor that comes leaping over the hedgerow, should one, Fox."

Fox cleared his throat, a bit shaken himself. "No, Your Grace."

"I wonder, Fox, if you would be so kind as to send us a letter from London in a week or two? Saying you'd erred? Saying Lord Aubrey de Mont is *not* dead as reported, but is alive?"

"Ay, Your Grace."

The duke's voice grew colder, crisper. "A month after that, you will write again. You will tell us Lord Aubrey is grievously ill. At death's door in fact. Dying painfully of a putrified sword wound."

"Ay, Your Grace." Shaken by the cat-and-mouse game but wanting to please, Fox added, "And write in me next letter that I was mistaken, that Lord Aubrey is reported in good health?"

The duke's eyes brightened like candles. "How clever of you, Fox! I like a clever man. But I would warn you. Do not become *too* clever."

Fox quickly backed off. The meaning was all too clear.

"Nay, Your Grace."

The duke looked at him, musing, then sauntered to the window and stared out into the falling snow, his eyes hard, his expression intense. Fox knew at what he was looking, even though it lay six miles distant, not visible from Blackpool Castle. In his mind's eye, the duke was "seeing" Arleigh Castle, the de Mont family seat. The duke had long coveted it. Old rumors said he'd once coveted the countess of Arleigh, too. But Lady Glynden had despised him. She'd wed his rival, Lord Royce de Mont, Lord Aubrey's older brother. Unwilling to wed and bed Blackpool, she'd willingly wed and bedded Lord Royce, giving him four sons: Lords Hawk, Raven, Lark and Dove.

Sequestered now, seized by Cromwell, Arleigh Castle was no longer the home of proud lords and ladies. Now it quartered a regiment of wintering Roundheads, Cromwell's crass soldiers who urinated where they pleased and who passed the long boring winter whoring and scrawling obscenities on the once-proud walls.

As for the de Monts? Gone. Scattered. Lord Royce, dead. His widow, Lady Glynden, in France. The four de Mont sons, Hawk, Raven, Lark, Dove? *Their* once-proud names now topped the list of those wanted by the axman, right under their uncle's name, Lord Aubrey de Mont.

Finished perusing the falling snow, the duke swung around. His eyes flashed irritably. "Surely, you have work to do."

Startled out of his wool-gathering, Fox nearly jumped. "Ay, milord, surely, surely. I was just running me plans through me head."

"Do it elsewhere."

"Ay, milord, of course." He was bowing his way out of the room, giving the duke the fawning, boot-licking treatment he liked, when he was checked by an impatient gesture.

"One additional request."

"Of course, milord."

"When you comb St. Katherine's Docks, tracing the brat, delve into the sailings of one particular ship, a merchant vessel. My informant tells me that eleven years ago the midwife's brother was a crew member aboard her."

"Ay, milord. A ship sailing under what flag?"

"Dutch."

"And the name of the ship, milord?"

The duke raised a disdainful brow. *"The Jericho."*

Chapter Two

May 1658 . . .

To the eye of an eagle soaring at rarified heights, soaring high above the forested coastline of the New World, the tiny settlement of New Amsterdam might appear to be no more than a dot on the edge of a vast wilderness, a speck on which humans built their strange nests.

But to eleven-year-old Jericho—sitting scared and anxious on the stoop of a noisy New Amsterdam tap house, holding a bundle that contained all of her earthly possessions on her small lap—New Amsterdam seemed a great, huge city. A metropolis of ceaseless noise and activity.

New Amsterdam boiled with sights and sounds! Richly dressed merchants conversing in loud booming voices rushed up and down the narrow dirt lanes, hurrying to and from the Exchange that met in the field at the foot of de Heere Graft Canal. Hollanders, Englishmen, French Walloons. Spaniards with oiled beards and a gold earring a 'shine in one ear.

Buckskin-clad fur traders tramped by, and then came Mohawk sachems in feathers and savage finery. To the loud cadence of kettle drums, Dutch West India Company soldiers marched past, the tramp of their boots shaking the ground, their lobster-tail helmets flashing in the bright May sunshine.

Dutch goodwives clumped past, wearing starched white coifs and gowns with crisp white collars and cuffs, their wooden shoes protecting their beautiful embroidered Dutch stockings from street mud. Geese flocked everywhere, hissing and honking. Pigs wearing collars and little tinkling bells wandered the lanes at will, eating them clean of garbage.

Tap houses abounded. Amidst them, winter-snug dwellings of plank and plaster rose thick as trees in a forest. Each house had its own cow shed, 'its own wall of grinning wolfheads nailed up in neat tidy rows.

Built to keep out wolves and unfriendly Indians, a stout wall with watchtowers and gates bounded New Amsterdam on the north, stretching across Manhattan Island from the East River to the Hudson.

To the south, on the tip of Manhattan, stood the fort, a formidable complex of bastions and barracks, shops and warehouses, built by the Dutch West India Company. At the southmost tip, a battery of cannons kept iron eyes trained upon the harbor entrance, guarding it from foreign invaders. Each day at dawn and at dusk one cannon was fired, to scare the Indians and remind them to behave.

Between the wall to the north and the fort to the south, lay all of New Amsterdam——its tap houses, its dwellings and, best of all, its intricate honeycomb of natural canals. And the whole of it knitted together, as neatly as a Dutch stocking, by little wooden footbridges!

Jericho was awed by all of it. As she sat on the tap-house stoop, she sent scared, hopeful looks at each passerby. But no one paid her the least attention, and as the day wore on and her polite nods drew no returns, she felt the pain of being ignored. She slumped and merely sat. Like a bird that has run out of song.

She'd been sitting on the tap-house stoop all day, ever since dice cups had begun to rattle inside, and men had begun to whoop and holler and crow. Still, the games showed no sign of ending. Master showed no sign of coming out. Voices grew louder and drunker with every passing hour.

Jericho knew that when the gaming came to an end, her indenture would belong to somebody new. And so would she. For that was the way things went.

Her spirits slid lower. She'd been gambled away before. She'd been sold too, and once she'd been swapped for a sheep. All in all, she'd had more masters than she could count or remember.

Dejected and hungry, feeling suddenly cross, she drummed her bare heels on the porch skirtboards, then watched for a while as the sun dipped to the west in a blaze of glory, lying upon the canal like a golden lily. Idly, she rubbed at the ugly birthmark on her wrist.

"*Duivel* mark, devil mark," Master's nasty son had taunted her. She'd fixed him. He was bigger than she, but she'd gone at him, fists swinging. She'd knocked him down in the muck of the cow shed and, her cheeks wet with fierce angry tears, had pummeled him until Master had come running and yanked her off him.

She tugged her sleeve down, covering the shameful thing. She had two other birthmarks, one on her chest and one on the nape of her neck.

Maybe I am a *duivel*, she thought despairingly. Then she thought, I don't care!

Gloom filled her. She looked at the boy's breeches she

wore. She thought about her *duivel* marks, her faceful of ugly freckles, her stupid stutter. She thought about the only nice feature she'd had. Her hair. It had been long and red and as thick and curly as rope. Master had cut it off. A punishment.

Tears sprang up, hot and salty. For a moment her chest heaved perilously. Then she knuckled the tears away and sat defiantly tall.

"I don't care!" she said to the dog who slept at her feet.

The dog didn't care either. He went on with his snooze in the warm patch of sunshine, lazy as a rug. But he thumped his tail to assure her he'd heard, and when he did, Jericho bent down and gave him a powerful hug. He tolerated it, groaning only slightly, to tell her she was spoiling his nap.

After hugging Pax, she felt better. But the shine was off the day. Subdued, daunted, she gathered her bundle on her lap and sat. Her spirits ebbed. Hungry and utterly discouraged, she followed Pax's example. She curled around her bundle and fled into sleep.

Rich, young, and full of himself, eighteen-year-old Lord Dove de Mont leaped lightly over the sleeping ragamuffin on Dieter Ten Boom's tap-house stoop, sent the tap-room door whacking inward and stepped into the noise and revelry. His smile was bright, eager.

He was a sociable young man by nature. He loved fun, he loved action. Loved? Demanded! Whenever fun and action failed to present themselves, he'd been known to go seeking them with a reckless gusto that was the despair of his friends.

And today, especially, Dove longed for action. Today was a milestone. His birthday. His eighteenth! And God's soup, a man should celebrate coming of age, shouldn't he? Eagerly, he swept the loud roistering room with a glance. The action he most wanted today—his birthday!—was a roll in the hay, a bounce in bed with a warm and willing wench.

Hell's bells, forget that! Governor Peter Stuyvesant ran his

Dutch West India Company colony tighter than a prioress of an abbey of foresworn nuns. Wench, tart, loose woman? There wasn't even a girl with loose drawer strings within three thousand miles. Governor Stuyvesant, the sour old puke, didn't tolerate them.

Second best then? Plunged into gloom, he brightened. A rousing good sword fight! Nothing definitive, of course. He didn't want to mark his birthday by sending anyone to kingdom come. He just wanted some exhilarating play—a few nicks, a gash here or there, a spurt or two of the old scarlet . . .

Juices rising, he swept the room with another eager glance, only to have his spirits drop again in disappointment. Not a swordsman in the lot. No one but fur trappers, sutlers, and merchants, not a one of whom would know a sword from a sausage. He sighed gustily and swung around to his best friend, John Phipps, who should've been right behind him, following him in.

But John, being John, had paused to look pityingly at the sleeping boy on the stoop. Dove hadn't given the brat a second glance, except to note in a lightning quick, transitory way how homely it was. God's soup, if he hadn't known the mess on its face to be freckles, he'd have sworn it had wheat blight.

"John, I'm going berserk! If I have to stay in this godforsaken colony one more day, I'll be fit for Bedlam. There's nothing *here*. Mud, pigs, Dutchmen? A billion pine trees? And behind every tree a silly painted savage? Savages so stupid they think the windmill's alive and sneak down the canals at night to shoot arrows at it?" Without pausing for breath, he said, "John, my mind's made up. I'm going back to England. On the first ship that presents itself."

John stepped into the tap house with a wry smile. "Fine, go. Your handsome head'll look right pretty stuck up on a pike at Southwark Gate in London. All the females in the city'll flock out to swoon over it and snip off them pretty, golden locks as souvenirs."

Dove heated: "Hell's bells, I need to *do* something. Thunderation! I should be in Scotland helping Uncle Aubrey raise an army to fight Cromwell—I should be with Raven and

Lark, privateering against Cromwell's fleet—I should be in the Caribbean with Hawk, fighting for the king's cause *there*. I should be anywhere but *here*."

"You've got a mission here, Dove, and you know it. So shut up and stop whinin'."

"Mission?" Dove snorted. "Since when is feeding sweetmeats to a baby a mission? I can't think why King Charles wants to court these dullards. I can't think why the duke of York covets this colony. Manhattan isn't worth piss. What's here? Rocks and rattlesnakes, wolves and savages . . ."

Across the room, a rum-swiller bellowed, trying to entice gamesters into putting up high stakes and gambling for a bondslave's indenture. Dove swatted at the blue hazy air to clear it. An abominable habit these Dutchmen had! Stoking weed into clay pipes, setting fire to it, and puffing the smoke like chimneys. Tobacco they called it. They'd adopted the queer habit from the Indians. The air stank!

"And furs," John put in placidly.

Dove stopped swatting the smoke, glanced at John, and conceded with a smile. "And furs. I'll grant that."

Inspired afresh, Dove got down to business. Whipping a purse out of his doublet, he winged it over the loud, roistering room with a high toss. It landed on the serving counter.

"Drinks for the house," Dove shouted above the boisterous noise. "Today's my birthday! Drink up. Drinks compliments of me, Lord Dove de Mont, and—as always—" he shouted louder, "drinks compliments of His Majesty, King Charles the Second, of England, and His Majesty's royal brother, James, duke of York!"

Men cheered and whistled and drummed the plank floor with their hobnail boots until the room reverberated in thunder. Dove grinned, enjoying it. Though New Amsterdamers were Dutchmen, they hated the Dutch West India Company. The Company ruled them with harsh, brutal laws and backbreaking taxes. England, it was well known, treated its colonies more fairly.

Amidst the uproar, one table did not cheer. Pointedly, a group of Dutch West India Company directors, including Director Verplanck, a sour bulldog of a man, rose from their card game, sent glowering looks at Dove, and humped out a side door, probably going straight to Governor Stuyvesant. Dove shrugged, unperturbed. Stuyvesant didn't dare touch him. Neither did the Company. He was an Englishman, an aristocrat.

But John turned on him with exasperation. "D'ye have to do everything without a whit o' subtlety? D'ye have to be forever skatin' on thin ice?"

Dove flashed him a smile. "Solid is boring."

"Boring! They know what you're up to, Dove. They're not ignorant. One more fiasco and Stuyvesant'll bounce you out of the colony."

"Hallelujah. My lucky day."

"Don't be flip, Dove." John warmed. "And while we're on the topic, there's one woman in this colony *you* better not be skatin' on thin ice with. Great day, Dove, have you lost your mind? Hildegarde Verplanck is the *wife* of a Company director."

"I'm only flirting with Hildy."

"Flirting? Is that what you call it? Taking her fishing and bringing her home with kiss marks on her neck? Slipping love notes into her prayer book at church? Playing foot-patty games with her right under Stuyvesant's banquet table, while dinner's going on, right there with the whole blessed Company assembled and dining?"

Dove threw him a good-humored look. "So it was you who kicked me, eh? Now I feel better. I'd feared it was Hildy."

"Kicked you? I wanted to bash your brains in. If only you had any, that is."

Unworried, Dove folded his arms across his chest, tossed happy nods at the men still cheering him, and let his eyes roam the room, sizing up the action. He was popular with New Amsterdamers, if not with the Dutch West India Company.

"I'm only trying to put some fun into Hildy's life. And into mine, too. Hildy's but seventeen. Verplanck? A graybeard. A lard bucket to boot. Hell, John—" Dove threw him a playful grin. "In bed he probably needs a winch to get his pecker up."

"Damn it, Dove!"

Dove's grin faded suddenly, his temper changing like quicksilver, as was the way with de Monts.

"Keep it!" he ordered abruptly.

John kept it. He shut his mouth and said nothing more. He watched gently as Dove's bored, restless glances roved the room. John understood. Behind that brassy mouth there lurked a festering anxiety. Dove was worried sick. That's why he was behaving more wildly than ever. He'd had no letters from his family all winter, and here it was May already. Hawk, Raven, Lark? Lord Aubrey? Were *their* heads already on a pike at Southwark Gate? John felt bad he'd even teased Dove that way.

John was just opening his mouth to say something soothing when the uproar brought Lizzie popping out of the kitchen. John's chest lightened. He and Lizzie were stuck on each other. Lizzie wasn't Dove's sort of girl; she was too common for Dove. And she was plump. But she had eyes as blue as the sky and a sweet manner. John was satisifed.

When she spotted them, Lizzie's blue eyes lighted first with delight, then with alarm. She plunked down her beer buckets with a slosh, then came flying through the crowded, smoky room, drying her hands on her hips. She lit into Dove. Tickled, John leaned a shoulder against the wall and watched.

"Lor' Dove, ye cannot come in here," she said breathlessly. "Ye cannot. Herr Ten Boom, he's at the fort but he left strict orders. 'Lor' Dove, he's not t'be admitted. Not under no circumstances. Not never again.' "

Smiling, Dove reached out and tucked a wayward wisp of curl under Lizzy's coif. "Lizzie, I ask you, is that fair? This is the only decent tap house in New Amsterdam. The others aren't fit to swill a hog in."

"I know," she agreed sweetly. "But them's my orders, Lor' Dove. So you'll have to go." When he simply kept smiling at her, she threw an appealing look at John. "John! Tell 'im to go."

"Go, Dove."

"There now," she said hopefully. "Y'heard John, Lor' Dove."

Peeling off his plumed, broad-brimmed cavalier hat, his

coat, sword, and buckler, Dove absently suspended them in space. With a sigh, John caught them and tossed them aside. Dove had been born with a silver spoon in his mouth.

"Lizzie, be fair," Dove coaxed. "Have I ever failed to pay for anything I've broken? Have I ever failed to make restitution if I got a slight bit foxed and a scuffle broke out?"

"No, Lor' Dove."

"Then I ask you, sweetheart!"

Frustrated, Lizzie tossed her head and shook it. "Y'do bring to mind a bee's hive, y'do, Lor' Dove."

"Hell's bells, John!" Dove stooped. "Take a close look at Lizzie. Why, she's the spitting image of King Charles's sister. They've both the same fair, silky hair. Lizzie! Are you sure you've not been deceiving us? Are you sure there's not a drop or two of royal blood in your veins?"

John bit back a smile as Lizzie's hands shot up like a shield. She staunchly refused to look at Dove.

"Don't you go sweet-talkin' me, Lor' Dove. Nor givin' me that heart-meltin' smile. John! Tell 'im to go."

"Go, Dove."

"Lizzie, it's my birthday!"

"Y'told me that *last* week, Lor' Dove."

"But this week it's true. I swear. God's soup, Lizzie, today's my birthday and it's John's birthday, too. We're both eighteen today. You trust John, don't you? Ask John."

Taken aback, she stared at them, startled. John pushed off the wall and verified it. Suddenly uncertain, she shot wary looks between them. Then, her mind made up, she staunchly folded her arms on her bosom. "I don't believe you!"

John and Dove glanced at each other and burst into laughter. Of all the tales they'd fed Lizzie, this one happened to be true. On the same day, almost in the same hour, Dove had exploded into the world in an elegant Arleigh Castle bedchamber that belonged to the earl and countess while John had been born downstairs in a room off the scullery that belonged to a footman, William Phipps, and his wife.

Affronted by their laughter, Lizzie drew herself up with sweet dignity, and John and Dove quickly sobered and apologized. Then John coaxed on Dove's behalf, vouching for him.

Sweet on John, Lizzie's anger dissolved like wet sugar. "Well, you can stay," she decided in a rush. "But only for one hour, Lor' Dove. And you got to be gone b'fore Herr Ten Boom comes back from the fort. I'll tell ye true, Lor' Dove. Herr Ten Boom, he's gone to the fort to lodge a complaint against you. *With Governor Stuyvesant*," she added in an awed whisper.

Dove flicked a speck off his immaculate, snowy white shirt sleeve. "Gracious. I'm trembling in my boots."

"And so y'should be," she scolded breathlessly. "I'll tell you true. The Company's not forgave you for what you done y'very first day in New Amsterdam. Land alive, sir! Leapin' up on the gallows wi' your sword and cuttin' down that runaway negro they was fixing to hang?"

Dove's easy smile faded and the de Mont temper flashed. "For God's sake, Lizzie, the first rope broke under his weight! They were going to hang Black Bartimaeus a second time. There isn't a man in the world who deserves to be hanged twice. Especially not for the minor crime of running away from a whipping."

"I know," she said with genuine feeling. "But y'cannot go tweakin' the Company's nose, Lor' Dove. 'Twill get you in terrible trouble."

"Dove, calm down."

Ignoring him, Dove was making a suggestion as to where the Company could stick its trouble when tankards began to pound table tops, and Lizzie had to rush back to her serving.

When she was gone, Dove smiled in amusement. "So you'll vouch for me, eh?"

"Against my better judgment."

But as Dove's restless glances raked the room, John had misgivings. There was a fever in Dove's eye. He couldn't even stand still today; he twitched a shoulder, tapped a foot. Dove was spoiling for a brawl. John knew all the signs. He'd known Dove from the cradle. Damnation, he thought! How to distract him? One day the beloved reckless fool would hand his own head to Cromwell on a platter.

Across the room, the rum-swiller who'd been trying to gamble his bondslave was still at it. "*Kom, Kom*," the loud-mouth barked, spewing beer and wiping his greasy beard with a coat sleeve. "Who'll play me fer the big strappin' bondslave what's out there on the stoop?"

John glanced out the open door. "Big and strapping"? He shook his head. Luckless lad, having a rum-swiller for a master. The boy's freckled cheek bore an ugly bruise. John angrily glanced at the lout's table, then at the lad again.

An idea flickered. If Dove had something to distract him for the afternoon . . . And he would likely win. John touched Dove's sleeve. "Dove, look at that bruise on the lad's cheek. He didn't get *that* falling out of no tree."

Dove didn't look. He wasn't interested. "Hell's bells, John!"

"Look."

Irritated at the request, Dove made do with a brief, hostile glance. As he did, the child stirred uncomfortably on the hard floor boards. The sleepy eyes fluttered open for an instant before drifting shut again. The eyes startled Dove. They were wonderful eyes. A deep cobalt blue. So dark a blue they glowed purple. Velvet eyes. Feminine eyes.

"If that's a lad," Dove snapped, "I'll eat my shirt."

"All the more reason."

Dove winged a glance at John. "Meaning what? No, don't bother to say it. It's written all over your face, plain as boot tracks in jam. The answer is no."

"You wouldn't have to keep her," John countered reasonably. "You could sell her. At the bondslave market in the fort. To a decent master. Not to the likes of *that* scoundrel. Dove, a little girl . . ."

"*No.*"

" 'Twould be a mercy . . ." He'd pressed too far. He saw it as Dove's bright hazel eyes filled with glacial frost. The de Monts were not the kind who could be pushed. Dove gave him a cold look.

"I'm not in the mercy trade." And strolled off into the revelry.

Having planted the seed, John had to let go of it. He looked at the luckless child. If he himself had money . . . But he hadn't. Even if he had, he'd lose it quicker than a cat's wink at a gaming table. He was no gamester. He wasn't like Dove, lightning-quick of mind and hand, an expert in every god-damn game he sat down to play.

An enormous dog crept up the stoop step and plunked down beside the child, resting its muzzle protectively on the child's hip. The dog was so ugly it made John smile. It had a coat like a porcupine's and one empty eye socket, which was ringed with black fur. Like a one-eyed pirate.

John drew a regretful breath, then thrust dog and child out of mind. He'd done his best. More he couldn't do. Grabbing a tankard from a peg on the wall, he headed for the kitchen. With luck, he and Lizzie could steal a few minutes to go out back and kiss.

Dove decided on skittles. Batting away the smoke, he slung a booted leg over a stool at the rowdiest table and shoved a skittles board at the best player there. Then, he slapped his wager down and applied himself to mastering a Dutch game that was as odd and pleasant as two other pastimes he'd discovered in New Amsterdam—bowling and skating. He especially liked skating, flying over a frozen pond in winter, flying faster than the wind, pitting his speed and nerve against others . . .

He was soon absorbed in skittles and forgot about John's brat. That is, almost. Now and then, when his conscience pricked, he glanced at the child. A big ugly moose of a dog had curled up beside the brat. Dove shuddered and applied himself to skittles. He liked dogs even less than he liked children. In fact, he hated dogs. Children he merely loathed.

He took two games, his opponent took two. Irritated at the noise from the rum-swiller's table—his obnoxious crowing as he won at cards—Dove's concentration broke and he lost the deciding game and the wager, five Dutch florins. Instantly, he cleared the board, slapped out another wager, and challenged again.

Incensed with the whole situation—with John, with the braying of the rum-swiller, and, most of all, with being stuck in this backwoods hellhole on his eighteenth birthday—he

stole another hostile glance at John's brat. Late afternoon
sunshine was creeping across the porch. It had come to
rest on the child's freckled cheek. As he watched, the
sun highlighted a bruise that was the size and shape of a
man's fist.

That did it. Gathering his coins and his full foaming tankard, he got up. When his skittles partner raised a quizzical
brow, Dove jerked a nod at the rum-swiller.

"Watch 'im, Lor' Dove. He's a cheat."

"Is he!" Dove gave him a dazzling smile. "Thank you.
You have just made my birthday."

Eagerly, Dove wove his way through the noise and smoke
to the drunk's table and stood watching the play. The fellow
was plainly a cheat. Dove knew it at a glance. Not for nothing
had Dove lived two years, two of the bloodiest Cromwell
years, in Holborn, a criminal sanctuary in London, hidden
there by thieves loyal to the monarchy—cardsharps, pickpockets, coney catchers, countesses of the trade.

Dove's lip curled in scorn as he took in the coat the lout
wore despite the heat in the stuffy smoky room. An amateur's
ploy, hiding cards up a coat sleeve. No self-respecting Holborn cardsharp would stoop to using such a simple, unimag-
inative trick.

In addition to the rum-swiller, a half dozen noisy drunks
occupied the table, some playing cards, some simply getting
drunker. Dove chose the drunkest one, wedged a booted toe
under his stool and upended it. The startled sot crashed to
the floor and bellowed in surprised outrage, but when Dove
slapped his own full tankard into his drunken paw, the lout
was well-satisfied to go on drinking on the floor.

Grabbing the stool, Dove righted it and straddled it. He
eyed the rum-swiller coldly.

"Are you as able at dice as you are at beating your bondslaves?"

The caustic remark did its work. The man's head jerked
up like a bull's. He was a swarthy, unkempt fellow. He stank
like a shoat. Disgusting tufts of black hair quivered angrily
in his nostrils.

"You've a big mouth for a young pup."

"Stop farting into the wind. Do you want to play dice or not?"

Dove wrenched his money pouch from his doublet and shook out a shower of Dutch guilders and florins. The rogue's greedy eyes took in the coins and pouch. Folding his cards with a hairy paw, he slung them away and bellowed for the tap-house runner.

"Bring the house dice," he bellowed. "*Kom.* Bring dice!"

A cheat himself, he eyed Dove warily. "I warn ye, young pup. Ye better not have flashy fingers."

Dove grinned at the other men. "Flashy fingers? How could you tell? You're so drunk you wouldn't know your finger from your pecker. Even if it peed."

The men hooted, spraying mouthfuls of beer, and drew their stools closer, watching with anticipation. That was fine with Dove. The more watching, the better.

Caught without a retort in his witless skull, the scoundrel hotly shoved forth his first wager. A single cautious guilder. Dove coolly matched it, then raised the wager, adding three guilders, dropping them one by one with separate silvery chinks. His opponent blinked, hesitated, then matched it.

Dove had a plan. He prayed it would work. Already, his beloved "birds of Holborn" were hidden in his palm, tucked under his thumb while his hand appeared to rest casually on the table top in plain sight, fingers relaxed, casually tapping. His beloved "birds," which he carried in his pocket as a good luck talisman, had been a farewell gift from the people of Holborn.

The house dice were brought on the run. Dutch West India Company rules decreed only house dice could be used in gaming houses, lest some cheat use loaded dice. As the tap-house runner tumbled the dice on the table, the rogue reached. But Dove was swifter and snatched them up in a flash.

"Courtesy, rumpot. Mind your manners. *I* am the challenger. Challenger throws first."

"Watch yer mouth, pup!"

"You watch it. I'm occupied." Dove brandished the dice and shook them showily. He tossed. Smoothly, the house dice vanished up his sleeve and his "birds of Holborn" went rolling out over the pine table. He held his breath. Sweat prickled in his hairline. Would the switch be detected? He'd purposely grabbed the house dice fast, before anyone could get a good look at them.

But dice were dice. The rum-swiller saw nothing wrong and gathered them up with an eager growl. Dove resumed breathing.

"If it's a lesson ye want, ye mouthy pup, ye shall have it. I'll learn ye a lesson ye shan't forget."

"Throw the dice, windbag. If I want a sermon, I'll go to church." Everyone laughed.

"By *Gott*!" Incensed, face flushing an ugly color, the scoundrel took an angry swig from his tankard, shoved it aside and leaned forward. He smote the dice to the table top, concentrating on the roll with all his might.

Dove leaned forward and concentrated too. He needed all the concentration he could muster. Controlling loaded dice was a difficult matter. It required a deft touch, a steady hand, and steel nerve. So as not to appear contrived, the number of dots appearing face up had to vary, had to appear random. And hell's bells! Each dice toss had to appear casually thrown, lest someone grow suspicious.

It was hard work. Dove buckled down. Intently, he concentrated. Not on winning, but on losing. While the rum-swiller crowed like a cock, taunting him, jeering at him, Dove deliberately lost guilder after guilder, florin after florin. When the lout confidently pushed forth the bondslave indenture, Dove lost thirty guilders at a whack.

Pretending to explode with frustration, Dove jumped up, kicked over his stool, wiped his brow, righted the stool and sat, then angrily grabbed his coin pouch and dumped the remainder of his guilders on the table.

"Play, rumpot! My luck's sure to turn."

The rogue sneered and patted his winnings. "So you ain't had enough, eh, pup?"

They played on. When Dove had lost his last coin, he leaped to his feet in an explosive show of excitement and temper.

"Bring a hammer! Runner, bring a hammer," he shouted excitedly at the top of his lungs. "Bring a hammer. This sot's playing with loaded dice."

"The *duivel* I am!" Incensed at the accusation, the rogue lunged to his feet, his stool crashing. "I beat ye fair 'n square, ye mangy pup. Ay, bring a hammer," he shouted to men who'd abandoned their games and gathered to watch. "Bring a hammer. By the Virgin's tits, we'll test the proof o' *this* pudding. I beat 'im fair 'n square, I did. These dice be house dice!"

The hammer was brought with speed, for this was a serious charge, a grave accusation. Men crowded around, murmuring. As accuser, Dove was awarded the hammer. He took it, sighed once for his beloved "birds of Holborn," then positioned the hammer head above one die and smartly tapped it. The die split in two, revealing a tiny telltale bead of lead artfully embedded in one wall.

Murmurs rose to angry mutters. Utterly astonished, the rum-swiller stared at the dice, his eyes bulging. He looked stunned as a newborn babe. "But, I dinna. I swear I dinna!" As blank as a felled ox, he looked about for support, but found none. Men growled loudly.

"The house dice probably are in his pocket!" Dove shouted over the growing tumult. With a swift, unexpected movement, he leaned across the table, plunged his hand into the dazed man's coat pocket. His hand emerged brandishing the house dice, which he'd smoothly shaken from his own sleeve. "The house dice!" Dove shouted, tossing them to the taphouse runner for confirmation.

"Ay," the runner confirmed excitedly. "They's them. I 'member this wee scratch on one o' em." The crowd exploded in anger. Cheats weren't liked in New Amsterdam, nor in any decent tap house anywhere in the world.

"You forfeit, rumpot," Dove snapped. "Company rule." Snatching up the indenture, he stuffed it into his shirt, then quickly swept all of the money into his pouch.

For a moment, the rogue stood dumbfounded, slack-jawed. When comprehension sifted through, the color drained from his swarthy face, then rushed in again, as purple as grape.

A growl curled deep in his throat and built to an enraged howl.

"I'll kill ye," he thundered. "Ye damned coney catcher, ye conned me. I'll kill ye!"

Dove had only a fraction of an instant to react, to kick the table over and use it as a shield. For the rogue came lunging with a knife.

Chapter Three

Jericho awoke to a savage howl. Hard on its heels came a crash that shook the stoop. She reared up, dazed with sleep. Tables crashed. Men snorted and bellowed like bulls. Bodies slammed into walls, shaking them, bringing down bits of roof thatch on her head. Inside the tap house, the tap room was being knocked to smithereens!

When a stool came hurtling through the small four-paned window and glass flew like rain driven by a hurricane, she snatched up her bundle. Leaping from the stoop, she ducked behind a woodpile in the sideyard and grabbed Pax. Just in time. The tap-house door shot into the wall like a musket crack, kicked so hard she heard wood splinter. Someone stooped through the low doorway, and for a moment Jericho forgot to breathe. For stepping out into the blazing sunshine, and outshining it as easily as day outshines night, was the handsomest young man she'd ever seen.

Gold! was her first confused thought. For he seemed to be made of it. Golden hair, golden-tanned skin, tawny eyes. His eyes blazing with anger, he strode across the stoop, jumped to the lane—knees almost buckling under the load he shouldered—and marched straight to the footbridge. Men came tumbling out of the tap house, laughing, hoisting tankards, egging him on.

Only then did she see what he carried, and the sight made

her pop up like a cork. For slung over his shoulder was the
limp body of a man. It was dressed in greasy buckskin and
a green serge coat Jericho had brushed only that morning.

Master!

Pax barked wildly.

Without missing a beat in the cadence of his step, the
goldenhaired man marched up the footbridge and out into the
middle of the canal. The sharp bang of his step woke Master,
made him stir. Master looked about, dumbfounded. When
he saw where he was, he began to writhe like a snake.

"*Stoppen! Stoppen*, ye young fool! I dinna swim!"

"*Learn*," the young man snapped. Then, with an enormous grunt, he crouched and hove Master over the railing
and into the canal. Master hit with a splash and sank like a
stone. Stunned, Jericho stared at the whirlpool. Collecting
her stunned wits, she ran to the canal.

Master bobbed to the surface shouting, flailing his arms,
and spitting water. "Hulp! I dinna swim! Hulp!"

Her heart pounded wildly. She didn't like Master. But he
was her master! He *belonged* to her and she *belonged* to him.
Bystanders laughed, and Pax galloped back and forth, barking
merrily, thinking it a game.

Meanwhile, Master was in terrible straits. Air had billowed
under his jacket, lifting him just enough to keep his nose out
of water. But the tide had turned! Slowly, slowly, ever so
slowly he was floating down the canal toward the river. Like
a great croaking bullfrog riding a lily pad out to sea.

Feeling the tide, Master shrieked. "Hulp—hulp!"

The bystanders only laughed harder and strolled along the
canal bank, accompanying him, watching him go. Jericho's
throat constricted violently.

"Dove, that's enough!"

She whirled. A brawny young man with angry brown eyes
came running across the tap-house yard hand-in-hand with a
servant girl whose eyes were huge with fright.

"Damn you, Dove!"

"Lor' Dove, ye promised, ye promised—" the girl wailed.

"*He* started it," the goldenhaired man shouted back at
them, and Jericho whirled.

"I don't care!" the brawny young man shouted back,

dropping the girl's hand and barreling up onto the foot-bridge. "Fish him out! Damn it, Dove, one more fiasco in this colony . . ."

The man called Dove didn't like it. But he gave in. "All right," he snapped crossly. "I'll put the creature out of its misery." In his lightning-quick way, he loped from the bridge to the tap house yard, halted, and looked around. Heart pounding, Jericho thought he was looking for a pole to fish Master out. Instead, he pounced on the woodpile ax, grabbed it and loped back to the canal.

Jericho's pounding heart rose to her throat. Master spied the ax coming, and his weak, watery yelps grew to shrieks of terror. "*Neen! Neen! Stoppen* ye young fool!"

Strolling along the bank, keeping pace with the tide, buck-skin clad sutlers and trappers threw back their heads and loosed roars of laughter. Jericho clutched her bundle. Wasn't anybody going to do anything?

Positioning himself at the edge of the canal, Dove hoisted the ax. Master screamed. So did the frightened servant girl. Dove hove, and Jericho squeezed her eyes shut, flinching, waiting for the awful thud. It didn't come. Instead, the flat of the blade cracked water and droplets flew like a rain shower. Laughter roared. When Jericho's eyes flew open, Dove was leaning out into the canal, grinning, extending the axe handle to Master.

After a dazed moment, Master thrashed toward it. He was hauled up the steep bank and dumped there, like a gaffed fish. He heaved and gasped for air. Jericho felt faint with relief.

"*Stoppen, stoppen*," Master begged pitifully, crawling away as fast as he could, sodden clothes trailing in the dirt, his boot tops spurting canal water. As bystanders howled and the golden Dove grinned, Master twice tried to find his feet, fell, tried again and at last went careening down the lane as fast as his weaving pitching steps could carry him.

Jericho clutched her bundle and bolted after him, glad to go. Pax came galloping, too. As she ran, she threw a scared look over her shoulder. Dove? He wasn't any "dove," he was a hawk, a vulture.

She caught up with Master at the bottom of the lane. Feeling sorry for him, she gently reached for his elbow to steady him, but he wheeled in his squishing boots and cracked her so hard her ears rang. "Begone, wart," he growled.

Holding her smarting ear, she backed away with a scared pounding heart. "W-w-what?"

"Begone," he thundered. "Ye stupid, stuttering brat. Ye be goldy hair's problem now. And good riddance!" He cursed her, then humped his shoulders and stomped off. He didn't look back. She watched him go.

For a long while, her heart beat painfully. She'd belonged to Master for a whole year. She'd begun to think he might keep her. She'd begun to pretend he was her father. Sudden hot tears scorched her cheeks. She knuckled them away.

"I don't care," she said shakily. "I don't care."

Sitting at her feet, gazing up at her with curiosity, Pax cocked his head. She put her bundle down, knelt, and hugged him. She hugged him for a long time, burying her face deep in his coat. She cried. When she felt better, when the pain had dulled to a throbbing ache, she wiped her eyes, picked up her bundle, and stood. Heart pounding, she slowly made her way up the lane to her new master.

With the spectacle over, the gamesters had drifted back into the tap house. Only the golden Dove and the brawny, brown-eyed young man stood in the lane, and they were arguing.

"Thank you very much, John," Dove snapped, his bright, irritated eyes sweeping her in as she gingerly approached. She halted at a cautious distance; she couldn't swim, either. Pax kept his distance, too. He crouched in the lane, his perplexed eye on Dove, his battle-scarred ears curling up and down like flags on a flag pole each time the curt voice spoke. "Do you have any other wonderful ideas to ruin my birthday?"

Jericho swallowed uneasily.

"Don't whine, *milord*. It don't become you. Great day, have a little patience, can't you? It's only until the bondslave market opens tomorrow. Though why you can't play a simple game without bashing a tap room to shambles is beyond me,

Dove, it is. Sometimes I think you're insane. Gimme your purse.''

"He came at me with a knife!"

"Do tell!" John grabbed the pouch handed him, yanked it open, shook coins into his palm and angrily flung the pouch back at Dove. "You know a hundred ways to take a knife away from a man without starting a brawl. I've seen you do it. No, Dove. You brawled because you just plain wanted to. And now there's Lizzie cryin' her eyes out, hiding in the kitchen, scared for Dieter Ten Boom to come back." He gave the coins in his fist an angry shake. "I'll try 'n make it up to her. And I'll *try* 'n make it up to Ten Boom. Though prob'ly he'll prefer your scalp to your money."

Bondslave market? Was she going to be sold again? Wasn't this master going to keep her either? She anxiously pressed her lips together.

"And in the meantime, what do I do with *that*?" Bright hazel eyes scorched her. The eyes were as bright and roily as a bucket of minnows.

"Great day, use your common sense. Take it home and feed it. The child looks starved."

"This is my birthday!"

"So, natal day felicitations, *milord*. It's *my* natal day too, if you'll but stop to give it a second's thought. And you've done precious little to make it a happy one."

With that, but with a gentler glance at her, John tramped up onto the stoop and disappeared into the tap house. Jericho watched him go with anxiety. She wished he would stay. She liked John. He had a kind face. She whipped scared eyes back to Dove. He was sighing gustily.

"This is the *worst* birthday I've ever had in my life." He suddenly winged a glance at her. As if looking for sympathy. Was she supposed to feel sorry for him? *She* had never had a birthday. She didn't know where she'd been born or when. She only knew the year.

"Do you speak English?" he demanded. She nodded hastily, hoping it would please him. She'd had English masters as well as Dutch. But nothing pleased him. "Is that ridiculous moth-eaten bear rug yours?"

She followed his glance to Pax, swallowed anxiously, but
nodded firmly. Pax was *hers*. She wasn't going to part with
him. Not even if the golden Dove took a stick and beat her.
Pax *belonged* to her. He'd *belonged* to her ever since the day
she'd found him in the woods, a puppy in pain, his eye gouged
out, probably by mean vicious boys who'd thought it a prank.

"This is the *worst* day of my life."

It was a low moment. Her soul seemed to drown in misery.
She felt miserable and anxious and unwanted. This master
wasn't going to keep her, either. She knew by the disgusted
way he humped his shoulders. She bit her lip and concentrated
on a trail of ants that were heading for a damp spot near her
toes, where someone had spilled beer in the lane.

He sighed and studied her disspiritedly.

"Look, sucker, are you hungry?"

Her eyes flew to his in startled surprise. Although the words
were mean, the tone wasn't. The tone was civil, almost friendly.
She gazed at him with rising hope. "My-my-my dog is hungry, too."

"Oh, hell! Somehow I feared he would be." He sighed,
then sighed again, this time in resignation. The golden Dove
was a constant sigher. "I'll get my coat and hat. Wait right
here, understand? Don't move an inch. I don't want to have
to hunt for you all over the whole damned settlement."

In his lightning-quick way he was in and out of the tap
house in seconds, emerging as he buckled on a sword, his
coat and hat slung over one arm. He swung off down the
lane with long rapid strides and was across the footbridge in
a flash. She breathed anxiously. Was she supposed to follow?
He'd ordered her not to move. Maybe he only meant to send
food from his house, by servant.

He was halfway down the lane on the other side of the
canal when he looked back, halted in exasperation and draped
his hands on his slim hips. "Well, what are you waiting for,"
he shouted. "A written invitation?"

On the walk to his house, Jericho tried her best to please
him. But it was impossible. Nothing pleased him. Whenever
she didn't walk fast enough, he turned and said, "What are
you, a snail? Hustle!" And if she broke into a trot, trying

to keep up with his rapid strides, he said, "Where's the fire?"

Pax made his own judgment. He slunk along in the rear, tail low, his perplexed, glowing eye on Dove. Each time Dove glanced over his shoulder, Pax bounded to a tree and hid behind it.

At one point, Dove glanced at her with bright, irritated eyes and wrenched her bundle out of her arms, slinging it over his shoulder, carrying it along with his coat and hat. It was a nice thing to do, and she was surprised. Still, he didn't think much of her. That was plain. Whenever he glanced at her, his glance dismissed her with disgust. But by and by, he got used to her and grudgingly began to talk.

"What's your name? Your indenture's written in Dutch. Hell, I can't read Dutch."

"Jer-Jer-Jericho." She took care not to slacken her pace.

He shot her an impatient look. "That's not a *name*."

Startled, she looked up and nearly tripped on a gnarled tree root that was working its way up through the hardpacked dirt surface of the lane. "It-it-it isn't?"

"Hell, no! It's a *place*. You know. *Jericho*. The trumpets blew, the walls came tumbling down, Joshua fought the battle, all of that?" She didn't have the least idea what he was talking about, and it made her nervous. "It-it's my name," she said firmly.

He shrugged. "Have it your way."

They skirted a pile of pig droppings. Squashed, the droppings sent up a rank odor. Black flies glittered in the muck like the bits of shiny black obsidian that Indians prized and used for arrowheads, when they could find it.

"What's your last name?"

"I-I-I don't have-have one," she said softly. It was a deep hurt, not having a last name. Other bondslaves had last names. She didn't. Her mother, whoever her mother had been, hadn't liked her enough to give her one. Her mother had sold her at birth, nameless. It was the birthmarks, she'd long ago decided. The ugly birthmarks. And the ugly freckles.

Dove studied her with those bright, keen eyes.

"Well, hell," he said, "that's nothing to be so down-in-the-mouth about. It's easily solved. There're a million names in the world. God's soup, just pick one! Take it and make it yours. There's no need to mope like a ninny about a problem that's easily solved.''

Her head popped up and she nearly tripped on another tree root. She gazed at him with gripping interest. The sun was starting to go down and goodwives were out in the lanes, performing their last task of the day, sweeping their stoops.

"W-which-which-which name?"

Dove shrugged. "Hell, *any* name. Why ask me? Use your head. You don't want a fancy name, of course. You want something plain. Something in keeping with your station in life. Smith, Brown, Jones. One of those."

She drew an excited breath. She walked along, her gaze intently on the ground. She silently mouthed each name, saying it to herself. She tried "Smith" and stuttered. She tried "Brown" and stuttered. She didn't stutter on Jones.

"Jones!" she said excitedly.

"Jones, it is," he agreed. "You're Jericho Jones now." In an unexpected spurt of generosity he added, "I'll write it on your indenture tonight, if you like. Make it official, eh?"

For a moment, she forgot she was scared of him and gave him a happy smile, and, for a fleeting moment, he returned it. "You've a nice smile, grubworm," he said. "Now, you can stop moping like a gutless ninny, eh? Hell's bells, what are you, a man or a mouse!"

She was a girl, she remembered in a scary flash. If he found out, he would throw her into the canal. A girl's indenture wasn't worth anything. That's why Master'd made her dress like a boy. Nervous, she edged away from the golden Dove and walked on the outside of the lane. But she walked a little prouder now. Now she *was* somebody. She wasn't a nobody anymore. She had a last name. It was going to be written into her indenture. She was Jericho Jones.

"Are you a boy or a girl?"

She almost jumped out of her skin. Tripping over a tree root that jutted up in the lane, she caught herself and threw him a scared look. He was a *duivel*. He could see into minds.

"A b-b-boy," she said quickly.

"Well let me tell you, Pansy Eyes. You're the queerest boy I ever saw."

They trod along in silence, Lord Dove brisk and easy and flirting with goodwives who batted their eyelashes and called greetings, Jericho treading on eggs, every muscle tight, tense. But when he didn't flush out her secret, she breathed easier.

"Lor-lor-lord Dove?"

"Give over! If you can't say 'Lord' without carrying on like a chittering squirrel, then call me Dove. Holy Mary, you sound like your tongue is caught on a washboard."

"Dove." She tried hard not to stutter. "Dove, are-are y-you going to keep me?" She had to know. Not knowing was always the worst part. It made every day a worry.

"Hell, no," he said cheerfully. "I'm going to sell you. The very first chance I get."

"Oh."

She didn't know if she was sad or glad. She stole a glance at him. Queer? *She* wasn't queer, *he* was. He was the queerest master she'd ever had. Knocking tap rooms to smithereens. Throwing people into canals and fishing them out with axes. Carrying bundles for bondslaves. She stole another quick glance at him. She'd never known a master who would carry a bundle for a bondslave.

"Besides," he said, slamming the door on hope, "you stutter. It would drive me stark raving mad."

Jericho drew a glum breath. Nobody wanted a stutterer.

The sun had just set. Light was being leached from the canal, leaving an afterglow. Twilight had descended, and shadows were gathering in the lane like velvet, hiding the tree roots that twisted up in gnarled loops, trying to trip her. Dove's pace didn't slacken. Nor could hers. Hurrying in his wake, she followed him around two grunting sows that were bedding down in the lane for the night, hollowing out cozy sleeping places with their snouts. Just as she picked up her pace, hurrying to keep up, a hairy tree root snaked out of nowhere and brought her down. She hit the ground hard.

Shock was the first thing she felt. Then, pain. Dragging herself up, she crouched in the lane and clutched her knee.

"What now!" Lord Dove called. "Holy Mary, but you're a lot of trouble."

Her chest heaved. "I-I-I fell."

"Oh, hell." He strolled back to her and disgustedly draped his hands on his hips. "I suppose you're going to cry about it."

She had been. But not now. Now she wouldn't cry even if he poked her with a sharp stick. Blinking hard, she shook her head no, and when Pax came nosing she shoved him away.

Dove sighed. "Let's have a look."

Unbuckling his sword, he tossed it aside along with coat, hat, bundle. He squatted and they examined the wound together. Beneath the torn breeches, the skin lay as scraped and pink as a peeled peach. Tiny pinpoints of blood were rising.

"What should I do?" Dove asked uncertainly, and she looked at him in surprise. She'd thought he knew everything. But suddenly he sounded young and unsure.

"Do y-you have-have a handkerchief?" Her knee burned.

"Of course! What do you think? I wipe snot on my sleeve?"

"I mean may-maybe we could tie it a-around my knee."

"Oh." Generous, he produced the handkerchief at once. But when she worked clumsily, he wrenched it out of her hands. "Oh, for God's sake, let me." He sat down in the lane, Indian fashion. "I don't believe this," he muttered. "The fourth son of the earl of Arleigh, sitting in a lane full of pig shit, playing nursemaid to a grubworm."

She braced herself for rough treatment, for rough hands and pain. But to her surprise, Dove's touch was as gentle as a kitten's. Even when he had to flick bits of pebble and dirt out of her scrape, he did so with featherlike touches and concerned glances, demanding over and over again, "Did that hurt? I didn't hurt you, did I?"

She watched him in utter wonder. Queer? He was the queerest master in all the world. She didn't know what to think of him.

Twilight deepened all around them, descending like a soft, glowing blanket. Sounds faded. The sharp distinct outlines of trees and houses blurred pleasantly. It was cozy huddling in the lane with Dove as the day throbbed to a close. In the tree branches that arched overhead, birds twittered frantically, having one last conversation before tucking head under wing and going to sleep. Pax yawned and curled up in the lane, too. All of New Amsterdam seemed to pause, waiting for the last stroke of day, waiting for the cannon boom that would signal it. Even the tap houses grew peaceful. So did Lord Dove.

"Better?" he murmured.

"Y-yes. Much b-better."

To show him she meant it she smiled, and to her surprise, he smiled back. Not an impatient one this time, but a peaceful one. He's very handsome, she thought softly. His clean golden hair possessed a life of its own, glowing even without the sun in it. She liked his sweaty smell. He smelled young and healthy.

The cannon boomed down at the tip of Manhattan Island. Sleeping birds awoke and screeched as if their tree were afire. A moment later, the boom rolled upward over the island, over the rivers, and then out into the wilderness, echoing.

"Day's done," Dove murmured to himself. "Another day gone without hearing from them, without knowing . . ."

She didn't know what he meant. But she knew enough to be silent. The words had been private. He bound her knee. She helped. When he was done he caught her wrist. "Hell, you skinned your wrist, too . . . ah, no, it's only a birthmark."

She jerked her wrist back, ashamed he'd seen. He was so perfect. Ashamed, she blurted, "Some-some people call-call it a *duivel* mark."

"Do they? Then they're jackasses," he stated flatly. "Hell, my Uncle Aubrey has a birthmark. Birthmarks run in the de Mont family line. I'd like to meet the man that dares tell *me* my uncle is a devil. I'd run him through with my sword. He'd meet his Maker in two seconds flat."

She smiled at that. And felt a ripple of envy. She wished she had Dove's boldness. She wouldn't have gone at Master's nasty son with tears and fists; she would've run him through with the butter-churn pole. It was a nice moment, a quiet moment. They shared a smile. Then, quite swiftly, in his quicksilver way, Dove's mood changed.

"Don't get ideas!" he warned, springing to his feet and gathering up their things.

But Jericho already had an idea. A very good idea. Lord Dove should keep her.

Chapter Four

Jericho was summoned to Dove's chamber that evening. She went with her heart in her mouth, too nervous to enjoy the novelty of climbing a staircase. Dove knew she was a girl. Daisy, the friendly, witless kitchen maid who'd fed her and helped her wash up, had cheerfully blabbered the news all over the house. Now Dove would never keep her.

And she longed to stay. The instant she'd stepped into Dove's kitchen her quivering senses had swiftly tallied everything—the food, the abundance, the servant chatter. Bondslaves weren't beaten in this house; no one went hungry here!

Clutching her bundle, she crept up the dark stairs. She wished Daisy were with her. Or the others—Goody or Cook or Samuels, the young Negro who wore a red shirt and a gold earring and was always grinning at Daisy. Or Black Bartimaeus, the shy, ebony-skinned giant who was so tall his head nearly brushed the rafters. Or even Mrs. Phipps. Mrs. Phipps was stout and stern. But stern wasn't mean. Jericho knew the difference.

Most of all, she wished Pax were with her. But Dove had hotly refused to allow him in the house. He'd ordered Pax fed and tethered in the backyard, where he was now howling at the top of his lungs. Another black mark against her.

Dove's room was at the end of the hall. The door stood open, spilling bright light into the dark hall. For a moment she was startled. Dove didn't burn just one candle as most people did; he burned a dozen at a whack. The waste astonished her.

She tiptoed to the door and saw another astonishing sight. A bedstead. It was as big as a cave. In the breeze that wafted in through the window, blue silk bedcurtains rippled like blue water. Most people slept in a Dutch cupboard in the wall.

"All right, grubworm! What's the proper punishment for a person of the inferior sex who impersonates a person of the superior sex? Eh?"

She jumped. Half-hidden by a rich mahogany wardrobe, Dove was standing at a looking glass, changing his shirt. Though why it should need changing, she couldn't guess. It looked spotless to her. He'd been watching her in the mirror.

"W-w-what?"

" 'What'! Get in here. You're a girl pretending to be a boy, that's what. Don't you know that's against the law?"

She swallowed anxiously. "It-it-it is?"

"Is it! Holy Mary, yes. It's a crime of the highest degree. It ranks right up there with highway robbery and murder. Hell, it's so bad you might as well've gone ahead and committed blasphemy. So you'll have to be punished," he finished flatly.

Her throat constricted. It wasn't a crime in New Amsterdam. But Dove was from a country called England . . .

"H-h-how?"

His smile flashed in the mirror. "That's the spirit, Pansy Eyes! Attack the problem direct. I like that. 'How' is the question, all right. Black Bartimaeus suggested thumb screws. Daisy and Mrs. Phipps said boiling oil." Brushing his hair now, he gestured with his hairbrush. "Sort of cook you, you know? Like a codfish? But I say the rack. Then again, why not please everybody, eh? Punish you with all three."

She blinked several times. He was jesting, wasn't he?

Tossing the brush to a table, he shouted, "Mrs. Phipps, prepare the rack. And a side dish of boiling oil, please!"

For a moment, her heart leaped to her throat. Then, from downstairs, from the bowels of the house, came a shrill retort.

"Master Dove, behave yourself! I vow. I rue the day Lady

Glynden made me your wetnurse. And I rue the day I followed you to New Amsterdam. You haven't the sense of an oyster. Stop tormenting that child or I'll take a broom to you." Dove chuckled and swung his golden head, inviting her to laugh, too.

Jericho nervously clutched her bundle and decided that if Dove changed his mind and kept her, she would take care to give him a wide berth. She would stay out of his way. She would stay in the kitchen. With Daisy.

He gave her an annoyed frown. "Oh. No sense of humor, eh?"

When she could breathe steadily, she wet her lips and said, "Sh-should I-I-I dust y-your room?" If she could show him how useful she could be, he might keep her.

"I don't want my room dusted."

"I-I c-c-could polish your boots."

"Black Bartimaeus does that."

Her eyes skittered over the rich room. On one wall, handsome swords glittered in the candlelight. "I-I-I c-could go through your wardrobe and find sh-shirts that need mending and m-mend them." This annoyed him more than any of the rest.

"Do I *look* like a man who would wear a mended shirt?" he demanded.

"N-no."

"Well then!" Slightly mollified, he looked her over with those bright impatient eyes, as if he didn't know what to think of her. He glanced at her bundle. "What do you carry in there, anyway? The crown jewels? Your diamond tiara?"

Hoping to make friends with him, she knelt on the silky, white pine floor and untied her bundle to show him. He didn't exhibit any interest until she held up a black arrowhead that glittered wickedly in the flaring candlelight. It was obsidian. Then he came over and squatted. She'd known Dove only hours, but she already knew how brief and fleeting his interest could be. So she made good use of the time, quickly putting arrowheads into his palm one by one, naming the tribe: Mohawk, Seneca, Ute, Cherokee, Huron, Algonquin, others. Dove fixed bright, intense eyes on her.

"How can you tell?" he demanded.

She sat back on her knees, astonished. Everybody could identify a tribe by its arrowhead. There wasn't anybody she knew who couldn't. Even little children could. It was the first thing you learned. How else could you know which Indians—friendly or unfriendly—were hunting the woods near your dwelling?

But she couldn't insult him. She answered politely. "W-well-well, y-you s-see, each tribe sh-shapes its arrowheads in-in a different way. And-and uses different s-stone." She showed him a flat arrowhead made of quartz and a three-sided arrowhead carved of deer bone. She showed him how some tribes notched the edges while other tribes left the edge smooth.

"Well, hell," he said generously, "that's interesting!" Her heart swelled with delight. Nobody'd ever told her she was interesting before.

She offered, "W-w-when In-Indians go on the w-warpath, they dig up a n-nightshade plant and rub the root on the arrowhead."

"Why?"

She gazed at him in disbelief. England must be a very ignorant country. "Well-well, n-nightshade root is-is a poison. When-when the enemy is-is s-struck by the arrow, the-the poison gets-gets into the bloodstream. He-he dies a painful death."

"Oh."

He was looking at her arrowheads with such interest that she offered, "Do y-you want-want to keep them?"

"Hell, yes!" He whipped out a handkerchief and scooped them into it. "I'm obliged. I'll show 'em to my Uncle Aubrey someday. He's a military man. He'll be intrigued. I wish I had a ton of that nightshade root, too. I'd use it on my mortal enemy."

"On-on Crom-Cromwell?" There'd been kitchen talk about a wicked man called Cromwell. He'd cut off a king's head and wanted to cut off Dove's head, too. Daisy had told her. Daisy loved to gossip. Mrs. Phipps spent half her time scolding Daisy.

"Cromwell!" He gave her a look that told her she was an idiot. "Dunce. Cromwell's my enemy, but he's not my *mortal* enemy."

She was mystified. "Then-then, w-who?"

She was sorry she'd asked. For Dove's face changed. The brightness left his eyes like a snuffed candle. His features hardened and his voice changed, too. Flat, toneless.

"I do not yet know his identity. But when I find out, I will kill him." He gave her a glittering look. "He killed my father."

He sat back and wrapped his arms around his knees. "I was three years old. Father had taken me hunting in the forest near Arleigh Castle. That's my home—at least it was until Cromwell grabbed it. I was riding on his saddle, cradled in his arms. We came to a snare we had set. He dismounted to check it, leaving me in the saddle. I heard a man's voice. Then snarling dogs came hurtling. Father had only enough time to smash his fist into our mount's rump. To send the mount bolting. To send me to safety." His voice trembled. "Everyone says I do not remember a'right. That I was too young to know dogs from wolves. That it was a remnant of a wolf pack that used to inhabit Arleigh Forest. That it was wolves tore Father to pieces before my eyes. But I know. I saw. It was dogs."

"Oh, Dove," she breathed after a long moment, "that's terrible." To have a father and then to lose him. She wanted to weep for Dove.

"It is worse than terrible," he said softly. "It is beyond bearing."

He stared straight ahead, through her, through the wall behind her. She knew what he was seeing. He was seeing something that had happened far away, a long time ago.

She sat still and quiet. In the silence she could hear the night sounds of New Amsterdam. A whippoorwill trilled, making its nightly demand to whip poor Will. Tap house roistering echoed on the canals. Down in the lane in front of Dove's house, pigs grunted, bedding down for the night. There was the faint tramp of boots as the *kloppermen* began their night patrol . . .

But Dove's moods, she was learning, changed in a flash. He suddenly gave her a demanding look.

"Have you ever seen a swordsman?" She shook her head. "Well, get out of the way. You're going to see one now."

He sprang up and headed for the array of swords on the wall. She swiftly scooped up the forgotten arrowheads, put them on his beautiful writing table, then got out of the way, taking refuge in a corner.

Dove selected a thin, long, pointed foil that had gold work in its silver hilt. Unsmiling, graceful as a panther, he struck a deadly pose, then lunged. The swordsmanship began. His movements came so fast the flashing steel was a blur. Thrust, parry, whirl! Thrust, parry, whirl! The foil whistled through the air, sinister, frightening. He was all over the room, leaping stools as if they were twigs, landing light as a cat, leaping atop a brass-bound trunk and fighting there. Sweat damped his shirt, spreading in ever-widening rings. His brow was beaded with sweat, and the golden hair clung moistly. This wasn't play. This was a fight to the death. She knew who Dove fought. He fought the man with the dogs.

Just as he lunged near the bedstead, he made a misthrust. Jericho cringed at the unmistakeable sound of ripping silk. Dove's sword fight ended instantly. He sighed and tossed the foil aside. "God's soup! Mrs. Phipps'll have my head. That's the third set of bedcurtains this year."

Jericho crept forward to see the damage. The beautiful blue bedcurtains. They exchanged a look, Dove's was of disgust, Jericho's was full of worry.

"I-I c-could m-mend it for you. I c-could go down to Daisy's i-ironing table and get n-needle and thread."

"Mrs. Phipps is down there. She'd tumble to it."

Jericho thought. "To-tomorrow, then," she offered. "I-I c-could get thread when-when s-she's n-not in the kitchen and m-mend it for you. To-tomorrow."

"Yes! That'd be—" His brightened eyes narrowed. "Nice try, grubworm. But no dice. Now go sit in that chair by the window and be quiet. I've letters to write. When John Phipps comes back from the tap house we'll put our heads together and find you a new master." Flinging himself into a chair at his writing table, he pushed the forgotten arrowheads aside, slung open the lid of his letter box and pounced on paper. "Hang up my fencing foil. And close the door. The draft makes the candles flare."

As she did his bidding, something salty and stubborn rose in her. She'd done her best to make him like her. He wouldn't even try. He was mean. She was irked that she'd felt sorry for him.

"I don't care if you keep me!"

"That makes two of us," he said calmly. "Now sit. Settle. Be quiet. I've a love letter to write. To the girl I intend to marry. I can't make paper-love to Marguerite if you're going to chitter like a squirrel."

She gave him a black look, but he didn't even glance up to notice it. So she settled in the window chair and thought black thoughts. Marguerite. It was the ugliest name she'd ever heard.

Outside, a half-moon had risen in a clear sky. Its light stretched upon the canal like a band of silver. She watched an Indian canoe glide down the canal, gliding down the silvery watery path, and a few minutes later, she heard the harmless ping of arrowheads hitting the windmill. The Indians did that at Fort Orange, too.

She looked at Dove, resenting the way his hand leaped effortlessly over the paper. He made writing look as easy as planting corn. She watched jealously. A clock ticked on a shelf. She studied its puzzling face. She'd seen a timepiece once, but never a clock. Master told time by notching his north window sill and glancing out the window to see how many notches lay in sunlight, how many in shadow.

Tick, tick, tick. The ticking clock and the steady scratch of Dove's quill pen lulled her, made her eyelids droop. The day had been long and worrisome. Her heart still ached from Master's words. Her head nodded sleepily. Snapping her eyes open, she fought to stay awake. She wanted to be awake when John came home. If Dove wouldn't keep her, maybe John would. Maybe John would keep her forever!

But, one by one the candles in the wall sconces burned down and guttered out with a faint hiss. Shadows sprang up

in the corners. The candles on Dove's writing table burned
brightly, bathing his golden head in a halo of light. Bone-
weary, she made a cushion on the chair arm with her arms
and laid her head down, watching him. She was so tired that
she felt dizzy.

"Dove?"

"What?"

"You-you really are very handsome."

He looked up with a lazy grin. "Keep it up, grubworm.
Flattery can get you anywhere."

"W-what?"

"Nothing. Go to sleep."

She nearly did. She fought it. She had to stay awake for
John. John was going to keep her. Tick, tick, tick. The pen
scratched steadily. She felt dizzy. Thoughts whirled.

"Dove?"

"What now!"

"Dove . . . why-why . . . do mothers sell-sell . . . their
babies to be bondslaves?"

"Because they don't want them," he said bluntly, hoping
to shut her up. But when it accomplished exactly that, his
conscience stung. He glanced up. A single teardrop, bright
as crystal, glittered on her red lashes. Hell, he thought, and
lay his pen down.

"Look," he said, "don't take it personal. Holy Mary, it's
a wonder *any* mother keeps a baby. What do babies ever do
but puke and shit? And usually at the most inconvenient time.
In Lord's Day worship, for instance. Or when a man is sitting
down to a fine meal. Hell, I can't think why any female
would keep one. *I* wouldn't."

"I w-would."

She had amazing eyes. Much too pretty for that ugly duckling face. A deep royal blue, rich and vivid. Whereas the iris
of most people's eyes was ringed with gray or black, her's
were ringed with purple. He grabbed a fresh quill. "That
only proves you're a witless female."

A second crystal teardrop formed. *God's soup!* The last
thing he wanted was to start a deluge. If she started in, she'd
probably bawl up a flood and he'd have to build a damned

ark just to get out of his room. He tried to think how to make her feel better.

"Look," he said, "your mother was probably a whore in a brothel. Whores *cannot* keep babies. Hell, it's bad for trade! What man feels comfortable stripping off his drawers if he hears the 'consequences' squalling in the next room, eh? Use your head. Now be quiet. I'm writing letters."

He went on writing. To his irritation, she sleepily interrupted him one more time. "Dove? All-all those wolfheads on-on the wall outside y-your privy. Did-did you shoot all-all of them?"

"No! I talked them to death, as you are likely to do to me."

That shut her up, and Dove worriedly finished his letter to Marguerite. Would Marguerite's guardian force her to marry someone else in his absence? He kissed the letter, folded it, and sealed it with wax he had warmed in the candle flame. He stamped it with his signet ring.

Next, he wrote his mother in Paris. This letter he wrote in code, directing her to pass the letter on to "Those Two Highly Esteemed Gentlemen." In code, he reported the number of Dutch West India Company ships in the harbor and estimated the value of the cargo they would carry, a fortune in furs. He reported on the vulnerability of the fort. Most important of all, he reported on the temperament of New Amsterdamers. He doubted New Amsterdamers would lift a finger to defend the Company if England should sail in and take the colony.

Now and then, he glanced at the child. She was asleep. Her long eyelashes were as obnoxiously red as her hair. His conscience pricked. But hell's bells, he was too young to saddle himself with a child! He had his wild oats to sow. How in hell could he sow them with a corncrake hanging on his shirttails?

Midway through the letter, as candles in the wall sconces guttered out and shadows stole heavily into the room, leaving him in an island of bright candlelight, he worriedly raked a hand through his hair and wished he could write his brothers, wished he knew where they were.

Across the room, in dark shadow, the door latch clicked.

Dove swung his head and watched. The latch dipped awkwardly up and down. The door inched open. A black nose and scruffy muzzle pushed into the room, a frayed, chewed tether-rope dragging.

Dove put down his pen and glowered at the intruder. "Did she teach you that trick, you ugly, one-eyed, flea-bitten, miserable, godawful hound? Or did you learn it by yourself?"

Knowing a cold welcome when he heard one, the dog slunk in, hightailed it to the child's chair, crawled under, and lay there, his wary eye trained on Dove.

"Shit," Dove said, and returned to his letter. When he finished it a few minutes later, ending with a cranky demand to go privateering against Cromwell's fleet, he sealed it and rose. He would carry the corncrake to the kitchen. Daisy doubtless had a pallet ready.

He took one step and stopped in his tracks as a growl menaced. Hackles stiff as spikes, the enormous dog halfrose, teeth bared, guarding the child, daring Dove to move.

Dove's heart began to pound. Sweat broke out on his forehead, gushed cold and clammy in his arm pits. He obediently froze. Dizzy, he reached out and steadied himself against his writing table. Blood, there'd been so much blood. His father's blood spurting, dogs snarling and tearing and howling . . .

He shook his head to clear it, his heart banging like a three-year-old's. "Jericho," he whispered shakily, fearing to rile the dog with loud talk. "Jericho?"

But she was dead to the world. If he shouted to the crew downstairs, the dog would likely spring. It was unmanly as hell to fear dogs, and the shame of it made him flush with anger, even as he stood there trembling. He glanced at the wall where his swords hung. On the table before him lay the dagger he used to pare his quills. But his hands were shaking too badly to use any of them.

Unsteady, sick, dizzy, he reclaimed his seat. He sat there, treed like a possum, his heart ticking faster than a babe's. It was a twenty-minute eternity before John's footsteps sounded on the stairs and he finally looked in. John's mild brown eyes took in the scene, and his face spread in a grin.

"Get him out of here," Dove snapped, courage resurging.

"And if you ever dare say a word about this to anyone, I swear I'll pound you to pulp!"

With difficulty, John reined in his grin. "Mum's the word, *milord.*"

Then, to Dove's deepening disgust, John stooped and whistled softly. The stupid moose crawled out from under the chair, went bounding to John and happily licked his face.

Chapter Five

A brilliant spring morning had descended upon Manhattan by the time Dove swung out of his house and headed for the fort. The wind was fresh, the canal sparkled, the sky overhead was a dome of sunny blue, and his mood was uglier than a warthog's.

John, the lousy traitor, had refused to do the dirty work. He'd refused to take the grubworm and sell her. Now, Dove was obliged to do it. Striding along with black thoughts, he stopped under a wild plum tree in a shower of falling blossoms and spun around in the lane.

"Hustle!" he shouted.

A hundred feet to the rear, she stubbornly continued to trudge at her own pace. Her stupid dog trotted behind. "An appealing child," Mrs. Phipps had said. Appealing? As appealing as a plague. She might've fooled Mrs. Phipps, but she hadn't fooled Dove. Underneath those pansy eyes she was tough as a turnip. She had a stubborn streak a mile wide.

Dove drew a frustrated breath. He didn't know how to handle her. He didn't know how to make her behave. He'd never dealt with a child before. Much less a girl-child. He couldn't wallop her. It wasn't seemly.

He strode to the bridge, sat on the stile, and waited for her to catch up. She took her own sweet time. He felt like bouncing her on her head. He watched a canoe go by. It was heaped with furs. Riding low in the water, it glided toward the fort, paddled by two sleek, oiled Mohawks whose heads were plucked bald, save for a long hair tuft. Their heavy clam shell and lead-bullet earrings stretched their earlobes almost to the shoulder. The earrings clicked rhythmically as they glided by. When the brat finally stood before him—stubborn, sullen—he sighed.

"All right, grubworm, let's hear it. Spill."

"I-I th-think you're mean."

"Mean!" He sat back, genuinely surprised. "Mean? Why, there's not a mean bone in my body. Let me tell you, brat, I've been called a lot of things, but *mean* isn't one of them." He drew a frustrated breath. "Hell's bells! I went to a peck of trouble for you yesterday. To save you from that rum-swilling master of yours. The same damned master, I shall point out, who gave you that whopping bruise on your cheek. Holy Mary, aren't you the least bit grateful?"

"No."

"Why not?"

"I want-want s-somebody to keep me. For-forever."

Dove's conscience twinged. He hastily looked away. When he'd carried her down to her sleeping pallet last night, it had startled him to discover that a child could weigh less than a sack of chicken bones. It had bothered him that a little girl whose bones were as delicate as wren's wings should be saddled to an indenture. *But, hell!* He couldn't save the whole world. He'd do well to save his own neck. He'd do well to keep dancing two steps ahead of Cromwell's axeman. He glanced at her.

"Why in hell pick on me? Why are you so set on staying in my house? Do you like me for a master that much? Is that it?"

"I-I like Daisy."

"You like Daisy."

"And-and I like Mrs. Ph-Phipps."

"You like Mrs. Phipps."

"And-and S-Samuels and Black-Black Bartimaeus and Goody and Cook. And J-John." She gave "J-John" special emphasis. As if he were a frigging saint. It vexed Dove that *he* hadn't even made her list. He glanced at her.

"Stop that," he ordered sharply. She was digging at the dirt with her toe. She stopped, but not before giving the dirt one more gouge. Holy Hannah! No wonder the brat had had more masters than a centipede has legs.

He tried reasoning with her. "Look. It's not that I don't like you. Hell, I like you fine. You're not half as terrible as most children. You've got spunk. Hell, you've got nerve! I like that. But I *cannot* keep a little girl. I'm only eighteen, for God's sake. I can't saddle myself with a child. According to England's child-indenture law, I would be obliged to keep you until you turn twenty-one. I can't do that. I don't want to do that. I'm sorry." There was a long empty silence. "Thank you for the arrowheads."

"Y-you're w-welcome," she responded softly.

He wished she hadn't said that. He truly wished she hadn't. Drenched in guilt, he lunged to his feet. "Let's get this over with, eh? The sooner the better. Believe it, I'm not enjoying this any more than you are. So hustle. This is ship-day. A good day to find you a decent master." Taking her by her skinny neck, he hurried her across the bridge and down the lane.

Just then, a movement upstream caught Dove's eye. Out in front of the Verplanck house, Hildegarde Verplanck was being helped into her rowing boat. A black slave took the oars, and a Dutch West India Company soldier, her guard, climbed in at the stern. Hildy! Dove sprang back to the bridge, loped to the middle of it, and waited, his smile eager.

"Mrs. Verplanck, good morning," he called, as the boat came spurting sedately down the canal, plowing a path through the sunny sparkling water.

Hildy glanced up with delight. "Lord Dove, *goeden morgen.*"

The black, to whom Dove had slipped many a coin, stopped rowing and stabbed an oar into the canal bank to hold the boat against the mild tug of the current.

"A beautiful day to go boating, Mrs. Verplanck!"

"*Ja*, Lord Dove, most beautiful." She lifted flirty eyes to him. Hildy was the prettiest woman in New Amsterdam and knew it. She was a trifle vain, but Dove liked her. She had a wild streak. So did he. They were suited.

"Where are you off to? May I inquire?"

"*Ja*, my lord." She blushed slightly. His attention always flustered her. But she took pride in it, too. He was a lord, a feather in her cap. She pointed at the woodsy little island in the East River, a few hundred yards away. "We go to dig wild violets. I fancy a bed of violets in my yard, come next spring."

"A violet bed! What a coincidence. That's exactly what *I* planned to do today. Might I join you?" He added hastily, "You and your servants? I could help you dig."

"Well . . ." The furtive glance she threw at her house spoke volumes. Lard-bucket Verplanck obviously had issued his bride orders: stay away from Lord Dove.

Ignored, feeling cross, Jericho stood on the canal bank with Pax and sullenly watched Dove make a fool of himself over the lady in the boat. Mrs. Verplanck. It was the ugliest name she'd ever heard. Uglier even than "Marguerite." And what was so wonderful about butter-colored hair? Nothing!

"I won't ride out in your boat. I'll row out and join you later," Dove was suggesting to the lady, a silly smile on his face. "First, I've a trifling matter to deal with at the fort."

The lady glanced warily at her house, but agreed, and Dove's smile grew even sillier.

A trifling matter! Jericho gouged at the ground with her toe, dislodged a dirt clump and flipped it over the edge. It went cascading down the bank. Most of it hit the water with sharp, musical pings. But some of it landed in Mrs. Verplanck's blue linen lap. She glanced up, startled. Dove glanced too.

"Stop that!" he ordered. Jericho stopped, but went on working the dirt with her toes. Ignoring her, overlooking her as if she were no more important than a worm, Dove went on flirting with the lady in his silly, smiley way.

Jericho thought, I don't care. I don't care!

Dove felt guilty as sin, consigning the grubworm to the bondslave sutler. He couldn't even look her in the eye. But, hell! He couldn't keep a skinny little ugly-duckling corncrake.

His friends would laugh. He would be the joke of every tap house in New Amsterdam.

Besides. Hildy was waiting, and Dove had the feeling this was going to be his red-letter day. Today, he and Hildy wouldn't just kiss. Today, they'd go all the way to the stars!

So he left the fort without a backward look and sprinted all the way home to get his rowing boat. Ten minutes later, he beached the boat on the pebbly shore and sprang breathless through the pines, following the sound of voices. Hildy, the soldier, and the Negro were on their knees in a patch of purple flowers, trowels in hand, digging. Hildy wore lacy gardening gloves.

She looked up with a mischievous smile. "Lord Dove."

"Mrs. Verplanck. What a surprise to find that you and I share a favorite flower. The violet!"

"Indeed, Lord Dove. Fancy you being a lover of violets." Her blue eyes teased, and Dove faltered a little. Blue eyes, pansy eyes. The grubworm, sitting slumped on the auction platform, upset and mad as a wet hen. He pushed the image away.

Hildy sparkled up at him. "Did you get rid of that terrible child?"

Dove winced. "She wasn't so terrible."

"No?" Hildy giggled. "You are too large-hearted by far, Lord Dove. I would not put up with a bondslave like that."

He smiled to rid himself of the guilt that came washing in, then enthusiastically crouched and took the trowel from her hand.

"Allow me."

"My lord, I am honored." The polite talk was for the sake of her servants. Not that they were fooled. Behind her back, the Negro grinned, anticipating his coin. The soldier rolled his eyes. Dove shot them a stern look and began to dig. If Hildy wanted to preserve her reputation, it was her right.

Unaware, Hildy giggled. "That is a weed, Lord Dove."

"Is it?" Dove looked at it mystified, then smiled at her. "I have an idea! We could dig twice as many violets, Mrs. Verplanck, if you and I dig *here* while your servants stroll to the far end of the island and dig *there*."

"That is true, Lord Dove."

Hildy flushed and grew breathless. The last time they'd kissed in Dieter Ten Boom's dark, windowless fur shed, she'd let him unlace her bodice. Hildy jumped to her feet and turned with a whirl of her skirts to haughtily dispatch her servants. When they'd gone trudging away, she whirled back to him.

"Well, Lord Dove."

"Well, Mrs. Verplanck."

"Violets, indeed," she said with a playful nervous laugh. "I wager, Lord Dove, you do not know a violet from a tulip."

"Oh, but I *do*." He smiled and leaned against the trunk of an oak tree. "I also know a passably pretty woman from a beautiful one. And you, Hildy, are a beautiful one. Standing there with the sunlight dappling your hair and your gown, you are as stunning as a fairy princess."

"Pretty words," she scoffed, but in a breathy way that told him she got no pretty words from the pompous tub of lard she was married to.

"Pretty is as pretty does, Hildegarde. Come here, and I will prove my words."

Her breath caught. A lovely flush rose on her throat.

"And how—how will you do that?"

"Come and see."

"Lord Dove—Lord Dove, we had best dig plants." She was having second thoughts. She wasn't a bad girl. She was just a bold young girl who hungered for romance.

"Come? Come and see? Allow me to show you?"

She wavered. Then, her hesitant, light footfalls softly snapped the pine needle carpet. As she came into his arms, her heart pounding, the fragrance of pine and violets enveloped the two of them.

"I will show you like this," he whispered, kissing her with exquisite gentleness, brushing her flushed, warm cheek with his lips, kissing her brow, her nose, her fluttering eyelids. "Like this, Hildy, and like this . . . and like this . . ."

They were lying in a bed of violets *en dishabille*, half undressed, half-dressed, kissing, petting, hearts pounding in a wild prelude, when a queer thing happened. A hair's breadth from making his conquest, Dove looked down and saw not Hildy's love-drugged blue eyes, but vivid, angry, pansy blue ones.

He drew back, jolted. His passion fizzled as effectively as if someone had thrown a bucket of cold water on him. That which had been a firm, hard commitment—wilted.

Hildegrade looked up, stunned. "What happened?"

"You won't believe this."

She rose up, her breasts slick from his kisses.

"Lord Dove, what's wrong?"

"I have to go."

"Go? *Now?*" She uttered a breathy little laugh. "Lord Dove, you tease. You are not serious."

"Alas," he said, fastening his codpiece, "I'm serious as hell. It's a matter of a grubworm."

She jerked up, sitting bolt upright, clutching her gown to her breasts. "You have worms? *Mijn* God!"

"Not worms, Hildy, one worm. Only one." Swiftly he kissed her shocked mouth, grabbed the rest of his clothes and hauled them on.

"Lord Dove! What are you talking about?"

"I'll tell you tomorrow."

"No, you shan't, you shall tell me now. This moment!"

"Hildy, I'm sorry."

He hauled on his last boot, jumped up, and hit the ground running, sprinting down the mossy river bank and into the pebble strewn mud. He'd forgotten his hat, but he didn't go back for it. The keel of his boat crunched over pebbles and rocks as he shoved it into the water and jumped in.

"Lord Dove!"

"Hildy, I'll be back—"

"Do not bother!" Hildegarde shouted, her vanity injured, her anger ringing through the woods. "Do not ever come near me again, Lord Dove. Do you hear? Do you hear? Never again!"

Hot and sweaty from rowing like a galley slave, Dove abandoned the boat at Dieter Ten Boom's tap house and ran the rest of the way to the fort.

It was ship-day, and everyone in New Amsterdam crowded into the fort to buy. The fort was in chaos. The noise deafened. Housewives bargained shrilly. Dutch West India Company officers argued loudly about newly arrived consignments of wine, candles, linen, spices—even chamber pots. Mohawk sachems gabbled among themselves and childishly gave a fortune in furs for cheap bead necklaces. Newly arrived livestock mooed and baahed and clucked and bleated, vying with all this noise. Dove's foot slid in sheep manure. He swore.

Grubworm, you'd better be worth this!

He pushed his way on. But when he reached the auction platform his heart sank to his feet. He was too late. The auction was over. No bondslaves remained on the platform. Instead, casks of Madeira and untidy piles of tradegoods heaped the sagging platform, arranged to catch the buyer's eye.

He felt a queer inner sting. As if he'd lost a minor but favorite possession, one he'd scarcely noticed while he owned it, but sorely missed when suddenly it was gone.

He swallowed. Well, she was gone, and that was that. It wasn't his way to entertain regrets. Hell, life was full of regrets! It was full of missteps, wrong turns! You couldn't brood about every damn one of them.

Just then, something caught his eye up on the platform. A movement in the shadow of a wine cask. He shaded his eyes in the sunlight. Red hair. A freckled face. Jericho. Unwanted, unsold, she sat on the platform, arms wrapped around knees. Her dog slept at her feet. When she spotted him, her eyes grew bigger than pansies.

He was so relieved, he almost smiled. But that would be a mistake. If he was going to keep her, she would have to learn her place. So he glared. She flinched, but continued to stare with those scared, hopeful, vivid eyes.

"Get over here," he said crossly.

She was at the edge of the platform in a shot, scared, blinking. Her dog scrambled forward, too. Dove gave him a withering look, then turned his attention on the brat. It was damned difficult to growl into eyes that were the exact color of June bluebells, but he gave it a try.

"All right, grubworm. Let's get a few things straight, eh?"

"Y-y-yes, Dove." She nodded nervously.

"This may be news to you, but *I* am the master and *you* are the bondslave. If I tell you to sit, stand, drop dead, or roll over, you will do it. Without backtalk. Understood?"

She nodded, eyes huge. "Y-yes, Dove."

"You will *not* sulk, you will *not* make me wait for you—ever!—and you will *not* kick dirt into ladies' boats just because you're jealous. Is that clear?"

"Y-yes, Dove," she whispered, nodding.

For a moment, Dove shut his eyes and held his hand to his forehead, foreseeing the headache she was going to be, foreseeing year after year of a grubworm kicking dirt at the ladies he wanted to make love to. Holy Mary, he'd have to keep her a decade! He would be an old man—nearly thirty, for God's sake—before he could hope to be rid of her. He opened his eyes a wary slit, hoping she'd somehow vanished, disappeared, vaporized, gone up in smoke. But she was still there, still nodding, her eyes huge and dark and sweet. He sighed in disgust.

"Well, then, grubworm, I guess we're stuck with each other."

She stared at him for an instant, stunned. Then she startled the hell out of him. She threw herself at him, a sprawl of skinny arms and legs. It was catch her or let her drop. But he felt damned foolish standing in the middle of the fort with a sobbing child wrapped around him like a maypole ribbon. To make matters worse, the one-eyed pirate leaped down and barked at him nonstop, making him a complete spectacle. Onlookers gaped. He felt like a street-corner puppet show.

"Stop it," he demanded. "Stop crying. Not one more tear or I'll wallop the tar out of you. Jericho, do you hear? Stop, damn it."

"Dove," she sobbed, "K-k-keep me? Don't ever s-sell me!"

It pierced him. Sliced into his heart like a knife. His throat thickened, and his own eyes were in danger of growing moist. He thought of her indenture certificate. Worn, soiled, tattered, scrawled with countless signatures. So many masters, so damned many masters. Not knowing how to comfort a child, he thumped her skinny back so hard her sobs rattled.

"I'll keep you," he vowed gruffly. "Hell, I promise."

"T-truly?"

"For God's sake, what do you want, my vow written in blood?"

"N-n-no."

"Well, I should think not!" Chafing under the amused smiles of passing spectators, he bounced her to the ground, yanked out a handkerchief and commanded her to mop up and stop leaking.

"Do you remember how to get to my house?"

"Y-yes, Dove." Tears dried, she returned the soggy wad.

"Then make tracks for it."

"M-my bundle, Dove."

"Hell, yes. Don't forget the crown jewels." Vaulting up onto the platform, he found the dilapidated bundle and chucked it down to her. She caught it, then grabbed her dog.

"Come on, Pax. Dove is going to k-keep us."

"I didn't say the dog," he objected crossly. "I won't keep the dog. Jericho, the dog cannot—"

Either she didn't hear in all the noise, or she was damned selective in what she listened to, for she and the stupid hound went happily leaping into the ship-day throng and disappeared.

When he reached the island, Hildegarde was gone. In her place, on the spot where their love bower had been, he found a neat, tidy little pile of rage. The valentine he'd written her on St. Valentine's day was torn to shreds. The ballads he'd written were ripped to smithereens. She'd left the gold locket and the lace-edged handkerchief, his love gifts. She'd even savaged his hat. The plume had been wrenched off and torn, the silver cockade was smashed, and the crown had been trampled flatter than a Shrove Tuesday pancake.

Yet all of it lay in a neat pile. He grinned. Leave it to the Dutch, he thought, to rage tidily.

Chapter Six

In December, New Amsterdam vanished under a blanket of snow. Overnight, the tiny settlement disappeared. By morning, the world had become a white wilderness. All that remained to be seen of the little colony was the fort, looming stark and bleak in the vast unending whiteness, and a scattering of cheerfully smoking chimneys. Here and there, a roof poked through. There and here, a windswept wall emerged. But everything wore white. Even the wolfheads wore crowns of white.

When New Amsterdam dug itself out, two pigs were found frozen to death in the lane in front of Dieter Ten Boom's tap house. The minor tragedy was converted into a festive winter picnic. The pigs were immediately butchered, spitted, and put to roast over crackling fires in the tap-house yard. All of New Amsterdam was invited to the celebration. In a rare burst of magnanimity, Governor Stuyvesant and the Dutch West India Company contributed a barrel of beer to the outdoor feast. But Dove outdid them. He contributed rum, two casks of it.

In a lighthearted speech to the cheering celebrants gathered around blazing fires in the tap-house yard, Dove toasted King Charles and the duke of York. He urged citizens to eat, drink, and be merry. For the rum, he shouted with infectious enthusiasm, was a gift from Their Royal Highnesses, who highly esteemed the industrious settlers of New Amsterdam and thought them the cleverest, bravest, most intelligent colonists in the world.

"Huzzah!" the crowd cheered, stomping their boots on the frozen, snow-packed ground. "Huzzah!"

At the conclusion of Dove's speech, the governor and the Dutch West India Company directors, who had been standing on the tap-house stoop, exchanged narrow looks.

"Is the rumor true then?" Director Verplanck demanded. The air was frosty. His breath rose like steam. "If the English Parliament restores King Charles to the throne, he will turn on Holland and declare war?" News had come in summer that Oliver Cromwell had died. A worry. It was in Holland's best interest to see England's internal strife continue.

A second director lifted a cynical brow. "True? Do not be obtuse. 'Tisn't true, 'tis as certain as sunrise and sunset. England has lost her sea trade during this foolish civil war of hers. We Dutch have captured it. England's treasury stands empty, depleted. If King Charles is restored to the throne, he *must* refill England's coffers. He *must* recapture the trade routes. War is not a possibility, it is a certainty."

Governor Stuyvesant's sour face grew sourer. "England shan't take New Amsterdam. Not while *I* govern."

"*Ja*, that is certain. New Amsterdamers will fight to a man," Verplanck agreed.

The cynic's brow lifted sardonically. "Will they? With Lord Dove winning their hearts, buying them rum on every occasion, and inferring that Dutch colonial rule is harsh and that England would treat them more fairly? Man, use your head! The duke of York covets our fur trade. He intends to seize this colony and make it a 'new' York. Lord Dove is his agent."

Verplanck burst out heatedly, "We should rid the colony of de Mont. Banish him."

The lines in Governor Stuyvesant's face became etched more sourly. "Do not be a fool, Verplanck. The de Mont family has high connections in Holland. The Company will have our heads if we trifle with a de Mont. My hands are tied. Unless, of course, the young pup does something overt. Then, I can expell him. And with pleasure."

Verplanck burst, "We should put a watch on his house!"

The cynic chuckled, adjusting the lace cuffs of his gloves, preparing to stroll into the festivity. "Were I you, Verplanck, I should set a watch on my own house."

Verplanck reared, nostrils flaring. "And what shall that mean?"

"Take it to mean what you will." The man drifted down the stoop step and into the revelry.

Ruddy color rose in Verplanck's jowls. He swung his head, searching the crowd for Hildegarde. He found her. She was the picture of merriment, a vision of beauty in her red wool cardinal cloak lined with dark mink. Her eyes sparkled and her cheeks glowed, nipped by the frosty air. He watched her destination as she made her way through the noisy, imbibing crowd. Though she might pretend to be drawn to the right or to the left, stopping to chat with this group or that, she didn't fool him. She was making a beeline. Straight to Lord Dove.

The day after the feast, slaves and soldiers were sent out of the settlement to shovel the snow off Collect Pond. By midmorning, the frozen pond glowed frostily, cleared of snow, and New Amsterdam's skating season had arrived. By noon, Collect Pond rang with such gaiety that soldiers in the guard towers on the wall watched the distant pond wistfully, wishing they too could go and join the fun. As December deepened and the skating season began in earnest, all of New Amsterdam flocked out to Collect Pond. Those who didn't go to skate, went to watch.

Jericho went to watch, too. She went to watch Dove, her heart in her eyes. She stood at the edge of the pond, shivering in her warm cloak, hoping he would pay her some attention.

In the seven months she'd lived in his house, she'd all but broken her neck trying to please him, trying to gain his attention. But he'd paid her scant notice. She knew he considered her a pest.

Yet he was good to her. When she'd cried at his order to get rid of Pax, he'd given in at once. "Oh, for God's sake, keep him. Anything to prevent the Second Flood." Dove still glared at Pax, but at least he put up with the dog.

He'd also sent her to school, and when the dame schoolteacher's drunken husband had caned Jericho black-and-blue, trying to beat the stutter out of her, Dove had been so incensed he'd gone tearing to school, yanked the man up from his dining table and caned *him* black-and-blue. Jericho had never been caned again. Now, she loved school. She especially loved sitting next to Maritje Ten Boom. Maritje didn't mind her stutter at all. She and Maritje had agreed to be best friends.

Her eyes aglow, she watched Dove skim around the pond as fast as lightning, as graceful as a bounding deer, his steel skate-blades flashing, his long golden hair streaming in the wind. The sixth time he circled the pond he threw a snowball at her. She grinned happily. She didn't care if he threw a whole snowbank at her, so long as he noticed her. The next time around, he looked as if he might skate over and talk to her.

But just then, a group of ladies glided out onto the ice. Instantly diverted, Dove glided up to the laughing, velvet-cloaked ladies. Smiling his bright smile, he reached out and plucked Mrs. Verplanck from the group, taking her gloved hand. Jericho's stomach twisted jealously, as the two of them glided off over the ice like a pair of matched swans.

"Dove? Can-can I borrow your s-skates?"

"No. My skates wouldn't fit you. Hell's bells, Jericho! I told you that yesterday."

Thwarted, her chest throbbed. Three days had passed since she'd watched Dove whirl Mrs. Verplanck around the pond, and in those three days, she had grown fiercely determined. She was going to learn to skate. She would skate even better than Mrs. Verplanck. Then Dove would notice her.

"Y-yes, they w-would, Dove. They'd fit me, they w-would."

Ignoring her, Dove stomped snow from his boots. The kitchen door opened again and a gust of cold wind swept John and Leonardo d'Orias in. Mr. d'Orias was Dove's house guest, an Italian who'd arrived in November with letters and trunks of fine things from Dove's mother, Lady de Mont. A tall, broad-shouldered man, he had black hair that hung knife-straight to his shoulders. Jericho liked him. Though he looked fierce as a Mohawk, he was gentle and soft-spoken. And he had a birthmark! On his wrist. Like hers. She'd glimpsed it when she'd taken hot wash-water to his sleeping chamber one morning.

The three of them had just returned from hunting. They'd shot a deer near Collect Pond and dragged it home on a sledge. They'd shot a wolf, too. Its head was already on the privy wall, bloody and grinning. Bundled against the wind and cold, Black Bartimaeus and Samuels were out in the yard now, butchering the deer. D'Orias and John shucked their cloaks and headed for the mulled ale.

"I could w-wear two pairs of-of w-wool stockings, Dove," she argued. "Then-then the s-skates w-would fit."

"No. For God's sake! You'd trip and break your neck."

"No, I w-wouldn't. I w-wouldn't, Dove."

Dove slung off his cloak and coat. Jericho hung them on a wall peg. He drank deep of the steaming tankard cook brought him, then looked around the kitchen with renewed spirit. While other men might sink in exhaustion from such a day, Dove thrived on it. The more vigorous the day, the higher his spirits.

"I-I w-wouldn't, Dove."

He frowned in exasperation. "So that stubborn brain of yours is set on learning how to skate, eh?"

"Y-yes!"

He looked at her for a moment, took a swallow of ale, went to the kitchen money-box, grabbed coins, and slapped them into her hand.

"Run to the fort, pest. Buy yourself a pair of skates."

She stared at the money, overwhelmed. Skates? She'd never dreamed of owning skates.

"Do-do y-you mean it, Dove? R-really?"

"No," he said impatiently. "In fact, pester me one more minute and I'll take the money back."

That was all she needed. She flew for her cloak and mittens. While she dressed, Dove snapped instructions. She was not to get cheated. She was to get value for the money. She was to warn the sutler that Lord Dove would wring his neck if he sold her rubbish.

"Make haste, Jericho," Mrs. Phipps called sharply as she flew out the door. "Run. 'Tis winter. 'Twill soon be dark."

She didn't need to be told to run. She was too excited to do anything but run. She ran all the way to the fort, her breath like pipe smoke in the frozen air, her feet slipping and sliding on the icy footbridges. Pax ran with her. By the time she got to the fort, daylight was already draining from the winter sky and tallow candles burned smokily in the sutler's shop.

Excited, she was forced to wait while the sutler served adult customers, serving even a group of three untidy, rough men who tramped in after her. They were newcomers to New Amsterdam and they transacted their business with maddening slowness and asked strange questions. Were there many children in the settlement? Say, of the age ten, eleven, or twelve? Any with dark brown hair? Any with red hair? The men loitered in the shop, warming themselves at the fireplace, sampling the sutler's Madeira.

When it was her turn, she took Pax by the collar and stepped to the counter. "*P-plezier*," she said politely. "I w-want to buy s-skates."

"Do you have money?"

She showed the sutler the three guilders. He sucked at his curved, long-stemmed clay pipe. The smoke smelled pungent.

"You are in luck. I have just one pair left that will fit you. By coincidence they cost exactly three guilders."

"Lord Dove s-says y-you are not to cheat me!"

He made a sound like air being squeezed out of a pig bladder, glared at her, but clumped off to rummage in his shelves and crates. The three men at the Madeira cask strolled forward, tankards in hand. She didn't like their looks. They made her uneasy. Pax didn't like them either. He growled, but the men only laughed. One of the men had lank, greasy hair. The second had pitted, pock-marked skin. The third was powerfully built, thick-set, like a bull. All three smelled of sweat and strong drink.

"That there one-eyed pirate don't cotton to us, men."

The bull-like one laughed. "One kick o' these hobnail

boots and he'll be wearin' his ribs inside out.'' Jericho tugged
Pax close and cuffed him to stop the growling. She glanced
over her shoulder. She wished the sutler would hurry.

"How old are you, girlie?"

"E-e-eleven.'' She didn't want to answer. But she was a
bondslave; she was used to obeying. The men exchanged a
look.

"Who're your parents, girlie?"

"I-I-I don't have-have any.''

"Well, well. You a bondslave?''

She nodded. She didn't like the way they were eying her.
It made her nervous.

"Red hair . . . blue eyes . . . eleven years old. Fox said
the hair might be red.'' They looked at each other.

Alarmed, but determined to wait for her skates, she took
a firm hold on Pax's collar and tugged him to the opposite
side of the room, closer to where the sutler was rummaging
through his crates. Pax didn't want to go. He wanted to stay
and growl at the men.

"She don't go for our charm, men,'' the bull-like one said
with a laugh.

"Let's check and see if she's got a . . .'' Their voices fell
to a whisper and she couldn't catch the rest of their words.
New customers tramped into the shop, stomping snow from
their boots, filling the air with pipesmoke and ordinary conversation. She was relieved. The men made her uneasy with
their questions and their talk about a fox.

But she forgot them when the sutler came back with her
skates. Awed, she took the skates as if they were holy, holding
her cheek to the fragrant new leather, to the cold blade. Oh!
She could see herself. Gliding over Collect Pond with Dove,
gliding like a pair of matched swans . . .

When she'd paid the sutler and got her change, she tied
the coins in her handkerchief and stuffed the handkerchief in
her mitten. She picked up her skates, grabbed Pax by the
collar, and hurried to the door.

Suddenly, a hairy arm snaked out of the shadows and
grabbed her arm. "Is that a birthmark on your wrist, girlie?
Have ye two other birthmarks on your body, eh?''

Pax growled and lunged. The man kicked him, and Pax

went running out the door, yelping in fright. Terrified, Jericho tore free, cradled her skates to her breast, and ran. With Pax running along at her side, she ran out of the fort, ran all the way home, casting scared looks over her shoulder, her heart pounding, fear thundering in her ears.

The kitchen was warm and steamy and cheerful and smelled of supper when she slipped in the back door, breathless, trembling. Everyone was at table. Dove, John, Mrs. Phipps, and Mr. d'Orias sat at the head of the table, above the salt. Daisy, Samuels, Black Bartimaeus, Goody, and Cook sat below the salt, eating quietly, listening to Dove and the others discuss the day's hunt. Her heart still pounding, Jericho hung up her cloak, then quickly slipped into her place on the bench beside Daisy. She cradled her skates on her lap. She wished she could tell Daisy about the men. Or Mrs. Phipps. Or Dove. But she couldn't. That would mean talking about her ugly birthmarks. She was too ashamed.

That night, snuggled safely against Daisy's broad, warm back, listening to Daisy's comforting snores, she tried to push the scary happening out of her mind. She concentrated on her beautiful skates. She thought about skating. Sleep came eventually. With it, came dreams. She was Mrs. Verplanck. Dove had his arms around her, and they were gliding over the ice like a pair of matched swans . . .

Jericho threw her heart and soul into learning how to skate. Skating was the answer. The key. If she could skate like Mrs. Verplanck, Dove would notice her.

So she went to Collect Pond as often as she could. Mrs. Phipps forbade her to skate alone, so each time she went she had to stop at the gate in the wall and inquire of the soldiers in the guard tower, asking if there were skaters on Collect Pond. Always, there were. All Hollanders loved to skate. They were always skating. They were good at it. They didn't fall all the time the way she did. They didn't bang their knees or bump their crazy bones so hard that tears sprang up. And they didn't wobble like ducks. They sailed like swans.

But she improved. To her delight, Black Bartimaeus came to watch her progress, standing at the pond's edge tall as a tower, shaking his old head, smiling at what he considered a foolish sport. Daisy and Samuels came to watch her, too. But Daisy and Samuels were in love, and mostly they stood with their hands in each other's cloaks, kissing. Even Goody and Cook came once. Jericho felt loved.

Once, she thought she saw the three men who'd frightened her so badly that time in the sutler's shop. Were they watching her? Maybe not. Maybe they were just watching the skaters. But it gave her a scare, and immediately she'd taken off her skates and walked home with Black Bartimaeus, stealing nervous glances over her shoulder.

Dove had promised to take her skating on Christmas Day. She'd badgered him into it and had her heart set on it. She wanted to surprise him, show him she could skate backwards, just like Mrs. Verplanck.

As usual, he forgot his promise and forgot *her*. When Christmas Day worship service ended in the fort, Dove went springing after Mrs. Verplanck, gave her his arm, and escorted her to Governor Stuyvesant's quarters to eat the Christmas feast.

Betrayed, let down, Jericho tramped home from church in an angry mood, walking well behind the others, unwilling to share their Christmas gaiety. Muskets were shooting all over New Amsterdam, saluting the Christchild. But Jericho took no joy in it. He'd promised! For a moment, she hated him so ferociously that tears stung her eyes. Feeling cranky, mulish, she broke into a run and caught up with John. He was walking behind Mrs. Phipps and his two brothers, who'd come down from Fort Orange.

"John, take me s-skating today!"

"No. I said no at the church, now, didn't I? Jericho, I'm losin' patience with you. I'm sorry Dove forgot. But that's the way he is, and you know it. He'll take you skating tomorrow."

"I don't w-want to go tomorrow. I w-want to go today."

"Now you're bein' a brat."

"Then I'll go by m-myself."

"Nay. 'Tis Christmas Feast Day. Collect Pond will be empty. All New Amsterdam will be feasting." The air was so cold that the snow squeaked underfoot. Their breath steamed.

"I can s-skate alone. I can."

"Nay, Jericho. There's always the chance of wolves."

"W-wolves never come in the daytime."

"No. 'Tisn't safe."

"Th-then I'll take Pax. Pax isn't afraid of wolves."

John lost patience, turned around in the lane to block her and rammed his gloved hands on his hips.

"I said *no*, now, didn't I."

To show him she hated him too, she stayed where she was and let him walk on alone and annoyed.

I'm going! she decided.

Christmas Feast was a lengthy merry affair, starting at noon. There was an abundance of food and drink, and as the merriment went on and on, Jericho quietly slipped away from the table. No one noticed. Or if they did, maybe they thought she was going to the privy.

Her cloak, wool coif, and mittens hung from a peg near the door. Earlier, she'd tucked her skates and her fur-lined moccasins under a bench. She dressed quietly, then eased up the door latch, and let herself out. At the table, the laughter and happy talk went on. Pax slipped out with her. When she closed the door without being caught, she drew a gleeful breath. Then, she ran like the wind, flying down the empty Christmas Day lanes to Wall Street. Only a few hours of light remained. She mustn't skate long.

At the wall, soldiers in the guard tower were celebrating Christmas in their own way, passing a flask amongst themselves, laughing, singing. With a scarcely a glance, they waved her through the gate. Pax went bounding ahead. She ran fast, her skates under her arm.

When she reached Collect Pond, she had a moment of anxiety. She'd never been here alone before. She'd never seen Collect Pond so deserted. So empty. So silent. It was eerie. The only sounds were the distant singing of the soldiers and the occasional plop of snow dropping from tree branches. The tall pines that encircled the pond stood silent and dark. Out on Collect Pond, the ice lay like window frost, its surface etched by skate blades into whorls, swoops, lines, slashes.

It was so . . . quiet.

If Pax hadn't been with her, she would've turned tail and run home. For she felt as if the trees had eyes, as if they were watching her. But that was silly.

Determined to skate—that would show Dove she didn't need him!—she sat on the log where ugly old Mrs. Verplanck always sat, and she shed her warm moccasins and shoes and pulled on her skates. She stuffed her belongings into her big, roomy cloak pockets. Pax could be wicked with shoes. When she skated out onto the ice, she felt better. The sound of her own skate blades cutting ice was a familiar sound, and Pax's loud, cheerful bark as he romped was familiar, too. She forgot her uneasiness. Still, she kept one eye on the wall. As soon as the soldiers lighted a lantern in the guard tower, she would stop skating, take off her skates, and run for home. Nightfall came quickly in winter.

While Pax barked and romped, clumsily chasing a rabbit across the pond and into the pines, she practiced skating backwards. One, two, three, four strokes. She fell.

"Fiddlesticks." She picked herself up, brushed the ice crystals from her skirts and tried again. One, two, three, four, five—a bump on the ice foiled her and she fell hard, banging her knee. She sat a moment, holding her knee, then pushed to her feet and tried again.

Off in the pines, Pax went on barking. But his bark sounded different now, wilder. Had he trapped the little rabbit? She hoped not. She didn't want him to hurt it.

"Pax," she shouted toward the woods. "Pax, you come back here. You leave that rabbit alone."

He didn't pay any attention. He went on barking. She concentrated on skating backwards, holding her arms and her head the way Dove did when he skated backwards. In the midst of a furious tirade of barking, Pax gave a sharp yelp. Then he was suddenly silent. She stared at the motionless pines.

"Pax?" she shouted.

She waited for him to come bounding. When he didn't, her heart started to pound. Sometimes trappers set out steel traps. But not near Collect Pond. People skated here. She sat down on the ice and tore off her skates, then swiftly pulled on her shoes and moccasins. Jumping up, she ran across the pond toward the trees, slipping, sliding. Bunching up her skirts, she plunged through the snowbank and into the pines. Icy snow spilled into her moccasins, melting into her wool stockings.

"Pax?" she shouted. "Where are you? Where—"

A pine branch moved.

"Pax!" she started to scold, furious with him for scaring her. But it wasn't Pax. A man jumped out and leaped at her. Too startled to cry out, she whirled to run, but a man jumped from the other direction, too. They were the men from the sutler's shop. The third man leaped forward with a leather sack, as if he were going to sack her like a market hen.

"Don't!" she cried out, but the cry went nowhere, trapped in the thick, suffocating sack. Terrified, she blindly fought and struggled. She lost her mittens and clawed. But rough hands caught her wrists and bound them. She was picked up and thrown over a shoulder. Her neck snapped. The hard shoulder jounced her stomach, knocked the wind out of her.

She couldn't breathe! She panicked. She kicked and fought. The men cursed her. Somehow she dropped free, dropped into the snow, and found her feet. But when she tried to run, she couldn't. Her legs were bound too. She couldn't see! She pitched wildly.

And then, amidst their curses, a fierce blow cracked her head. She gasped at the shock of it. For a moment her head rang like a bell. Then, her head seemed to separate from her body and float away. Uttering a soft, surprised sigh, she drifted down into the soft snow. Inside her head, the world whirled and grew dark. She faintly smelled blood. And then she smelled . . . nothing at all.

Chapter Seven

"Dove, Jericho is missing," John said.

"I know she's missing. She's missing a few brains, she's missing tact, she's missing decent manners. Do you know what the brat said to Hildy the other day? At Collect Pond? Hildegarde told me she said—"

"I mean it, Dove. She's missing."

Dove swung around abruptly. He'd just arrived home from Stuyvesant's Christmas feast. He was in high spirits. Though Stuyvesant and his cronies had been as dull as Dutch cheese, he'd sat across from Hildegarde at dinner. During the dull conversation, they'd sent messages with their toes: one tap for *A*, two taps for *B*, three for *C* and so forth.

He glared at John. "What do you mean, 'missing'?"

"Just that. We can't find her."

"Then find her stupid hound. Find Pax, or whatever it is she calls him. Wherever he is, she is. They stick closer than oats to the bottom of a cookpot."

"Pax is missing, too. Dove, I'm not joking. I'm worried."

Dove glanced out the kitchen window. He rubbed his jaw uneasily. "Hell, it's almost dark! She belongs at home. The grubworm belongs at home. When she gets here I'm going to wallop the tar out of her. Scaring us like this. Did you check with her fat friend? The Dutch butter-box she's so crazy about?"

"Maritje Ten Boom," Mrs. Phipps put in in a worried voice, bringing Dove a hot posset drink. "Yes. We sent Samuels to the Ten Booms'. He just returned. The Ten Booms haven't seen her."

Dove's heart began to pound. She was a nice little girl, a good little girl. He hadn't paid her much attention, but he liked her. He did.

Daisy came rushing down the hall stairs and into the kitchen, her heavy step thumping, her plump breasts bouncing.

"Lor' Dove? Her skates are gone! Always when she be done skatin' for the day, she cleans 'em up pretty and puts 'em on the shelf. She's that fond of 'em, she is, sir. They're gone, Lor' Dove, gone."

He and John exchanged a worried look.

"She wouldn't," John said. "Dove, I forbade it. I told her she could *not* go to Collect Pond today. She wouldn't."

"Oh, wouldn't she!" Dove grabbed the cloak he'd just shucked. "Black Bartimaeus! Get muskets, pistols, powder, shot. Load the guns. Samuels? My sword and buckler. Get it. Goody? Goody, you prepare lanterns. Then run to Governor Stuyvesant's quarters. D'Orias is there."

"Ay, Lor' Dove. Ay, Lor' Dove." Everyone sprang into action.

"Will you quick change your suit, sir?" Daisy asked, her eyes big and weepy. " 'Twill be the ruin of it. In the snow."

"The hell with it. It's almost dark."

Hauling on his clothes, John put in quietly, "Daisy, get blankets. Cook? Get us a flask of rum. If she's hurt herself, she may be half-frozen in the snow." Daisy stared at him, then burst into tears, and ran to her task.

"Hurry, John, hurry." Mrs. Phipps dispensed mufflers, wool caps, mittens. "Master Dove, hurry."

John put his arms around her and hugged her. "We'll find her, Mother. Don't worry."

"We'll find her," Dove vowed, "or we'll not come back."

Dove and John led the way, sprinting through the darkening lanes, running for Wall Street. Firelight glowed in cottage windows as they sped past. Black Bartimaeus and Samuels trotted behind, encumbered with gear and lanterns. Dove reached the gate just as the soldiers were pulling it shut for the night. With a shove, he went charging through while John halted to explain, panting.

"Did you—see a—little—redhaired girl?"

The soldier tugged at his ear. "She what comes skatin' every day?"

"Ay! Lord Dove's bondslave."

"*Neen*. Ain't seen her today. But I only come on watch this very hour. There be nobody on Collect Pond. The pond, she's clean as a whistle. You can see it plain from the guard tower."

John clattered up the wooden steps to have a look. Nothing. Collect Pond lay as empty and frozen as glazed glass. The only figure on the rocky path was Dove's. Running. He clattered down the stairs.

"Leave the gate unlocked," he shouted as he ran.

"*Neen*. Cannot," the soldier called. "Governor Stuyvesant's orders."

"There's five guilders in it," John promised in a shout, thundering down the path after Dove. The soldier's response echoed in the cold, frosty air.

"In that case, the gate, she's unlocked all night!"

"Jericho!" Panting, Dove stood on the edge of the frozen pond and shouted into the silent emptiness. "Jericho, are you here? Answer me! It's Dove!" As he listened fruitlessly to the echo of his own shout, his throat constricted. "Jericho, answer me! Answer me, damn it. Answer me, or I'll wring your neck!"

His threats rang out over Collect Pond and echoed in the silent pines. But nothing returned to him. Nothing but silence. Dusk was fast deepening. The dark pines were growing darker, the fresh snow brighter, more luminous. A frigid winter night would soon descend. His heart gave an uneven beat. Where in hell was she! Out upon the ice, out in the middle of the pond, something glittered and caught his eye. Slipping, sliding, he went sprinting over the ice.

When he reached the middle of the pond and saw what it was, his innards twisted. Her skates. He stooped. Picked them up. She'd loved her skates. She would never leave them behind. Not willingly. He swallowed rising panic and sprinted back toward the bank where John was beating the bushes, searching in the pines for her.

"Dove," John shouted. "Did you find anything?"

Dove brandished her skates aloft as he came running. John paled. They wasted no time in talk. They plunged into the stands of silent pines, searching frantically. Dove kept swallowing back the words, swallowing back what had to be asked. Finally he forced it out.

"Wolves? Did wolves get her?" As he uttered the words, the old horror flashed so vividly in his skull that he had to shoot out a hand and steady himself against a tree. His father's blood, spurting, spurting, covering everything with red . . .

John grabbed him, shook him. "Nay, Dove. Nay! Don't think it. There's no blood. No blood! Not wolves. And not dogs. It's not what happened to your father. Dove! *Not wolves*."

After a moment, the sick dizziness passed. Gritting his teeth, he cursed himself. It was so damned unmanly! Angry at himself, he shook off John's steadying hand. They plunged on through the dark silent pines, through the snow. They searched side by side, cursing in frustration. The snow was trampled with footprints and told nothing. All of New Amsterdam had tramped around Collect Pond. Beyond the pond, toward the wall and the settlement, lanterns came swinging down the steep path, the bright candlelight trotting through the darkness. Black Bartimaeus. Samuels. He beat the bushes with John, his jaw taut, tight.

"I promised to take her skating today. I promised."

"Dove. Don't blame yourself. Jericho wouldn't. There's not a resentful bone in her body. She's salty sometimes, but she don't mean it. She adores you."

"I know that! Damn it, shut up. I know how sweet she is."

John shut his mouth and searched silently. When Black Bartimaeus and Samuels trotted down to them, out of breath, panting, their black faces glistening with sweat in the lantern shine, Dove snapped orders. Then he sprinted back to the middle of the pond, back to where he'd found the skates.

The clue had to lie here. The ice glaze lay brushed in swirls, as if swept by a gown. She'd sat down on the ice to take off her skates. Why? Why would she take off her skates in the middle of the pond?

Because she'd heard something. And wouldn't it be natural

to sit facing the sound? Which way had the skate tips been pointing? He racked his brain. He swiped a mitten over his hot brow. East. The tips had pointed east. He scanned the east bank. It was thinly populated with trees, except for one thick copse of dark pines. Had she heard something in the copse?

He sprinted toward it, cursing his slippery leather boots. He reached the bank and plunged into chilling, waist-deep snow. He flung himself through it. Even before he reached the copse, he heard the faint whimper. His heart slammed into his ribs.

"Jericho?" he shouted. "Jericho?" He bellowed to the others and gestured frantically. They came running from all directions. Samuels reached him first. "Give me the lantern." He wrenched it from Samuels's hand. "This way! Over here!"

He went crashing into the stand of pines. Samuels followed. The pitiful mewling grew louder, and suddenly he was upon the sound. He pushed back a pine branch and held the lantern forward.

"Pax!" Pax lay under the tree. He raised his head, the fur dark with congealed and frozen blood that had oozed from a wound. He tried to stand, but toppled. Dove rid himself of the lantern, knelt in the snow, and strained to lift the heavy, shivering dog into his arms.

"Easy, boy, easy," he comforted. "Where is she, Pax? Where's Jericho, boy? Where's Jericho?"

But Pax only whimpered and pitifully laid his wounded head on Dove's shoulder. When the others came charging through the snow, Black Bartimaeus draped the dog in a blanket and took him into his big arms.

"Savages, Lor' Dove?" Samuels asked, breathless.

"No." Too upset to say more, he pointed at the trampled snow, the tracks left by three men.

"Boots," John murmured. "White men."

"Let's get going! Whoever did this—I'm going to kill them."

With grim swiftness, Dove grabbed the lantern and sprinted on, setting the pace, following the trail of boot tracks. The others followed. Dove steeled himself, prepared himself to find her body along the trail, dumped, discarded, like so much garbage. A clot the size of his fist rose in his throat as he remembered his broken promise to her. "Take me skating, Dove?" I promise. Pansy Eyes . . .

Sometimes they trotted, sometimes they tramped. But they remained silent, the snow crunching underfoot, their boots squeaking on ice. The only voice was Pax's. He whimpered in pain, though Black Bartimaeus carried him as gently as possible. The boot tracks led away from Collect Pond, and sloped downward to the East River. They cut an icy, soggy, miserable half-mile through a frozen hunting marsh where ice-encased cattails jutted up, tearing the men's clothes. They followed the tracks down to the river and halted on its frozen shore, cursing in frustation. Skid marks of a rowing boat were plainly imprinted in the snow, the keel-rut shining in Samuels's lantern light.

"Do you think they took her across the river? Into the wilds?" John panted, lungs heaving for breath. Dove had set a killing pace.

"Possibly. But they might be in New Amsterdam. They may have used a boat to avoid the gates, to avoid being seen from the guard tower."

"Then it was planned?"

"I don't know." Dove flared, "Christ, who would plan a thing like that! A child who never did anyone harm—a grub-worm who—" His throat muscles constricted violently. "Let's get going."

Dove flew, retracing his own trail, charging back through the frozen marsh, back through the forest of pine, back across Collect Pond and up the steep rocky path that led to the wall. He reached the wall first and curtly shouted the situation to the guards and made demands. The guards responded at once. They fired a three-shot musket salvo. The sound of the gunfire cracked the frozen winter air like timbers splitting. Hearing the signal any other day of the year, New Amsterdamers would've come on the run, ready for Indians or wolves or whatever else threatened the colony. But this was Christmas. Musket fire had saluted all day long. A few evening musket shots generated no alarm. Dove paced the guard tower in frustration.

"Have you a drum?" he demanded. "Try your drum!"

A soldier produced one at once and beat a loud tattoo. At last, New Amsterdamers popped out of their cozy cottages, curious. But when another three-shot musket salvo followed the drumming, they grabbed cloaks and guns and came at a run. Dove ran to meet them and tersely shouted Jericho's plight. The word was passed swiftly from house to house, man to man, and soon, every male in the settlement came running, warmly bundled for a night of searching, armed with musket, rum flask, lantern. Dove was ashamed to see the very men he'd openly despised and made fun of: Verplanck, all of the Dutch West India Company directors, even the dame schoolteacher's husband. Governor Stuyvesant came too, hobbling on his wooden peg leg. Every soldier in the barracks turned out.

Dove was further humbled. How often he'd laughed at the Dutch penchant for organizing everything they did. Now he was humbly grateful for it. In less than five minutes the search had been organized and begun. After agreeing on a signal— whoever found her would fire a three-shot musket salvo to call off the search—the men swiftly separated themselves into cadres of ten, divided up the settlement, and marched off to search every inch of it. Other cadres of men marched off toward the frozen Hudson River to the west, to trek into the wilderness and search the land toward the Swedes' colony. Others ran to prepare boats for the East River search. Even braver Dutchmen volunteered to man those boats, knowing the river was full of ice chunks as big as their boats.

With this last group, and with John and Black Bartimaeus and Samuels, Dove swiftly crouched in the snow and drew the outline of the opposite shore, dividing it into search segments. Men spoke up, quickly pinpointing hunting paths and Indian trails that might have been taken, marking the locations of hunter shacks, crude shelters that both Dutchmen and Indians used when caught in bad weather. Then, separating into pairs, they ran to their boats.

Dove was at the river, hauling an overturned rowboat out of a snowbank, struggling to right it, when, suddenly, strong, black cloaked arms reached out to help, and the boat sprang upright.

"I go with you."

Dove swung around and felt immense relief. D'Orias. Blunt, handsome features. Black hair straight as a sword. Trustworthy eyes. He'd liked and trusted Leonardo d'Orias from their first handshake.

"There's danger," Dove felt compelled to warn. "Ice. When the tide sends it shooting, the ice could poke a hole in the boat. You'd be safer searching on foot."

"I do not ask for safety." Grateful, Dove nodded curtly, unable to speak, a knot in his throat.

D'Orias was no slouch. For when they'd launched the boat into the slushy freezing water, he got in and seized the oars, leaving Dove free to direct and stave off the huge floating ice chunks with his musket butt. Some of the chunks were as big as outhouses.

"Tell me where. I row."

Dove pointed. "Line up the bow with that rocky promontory on the long island. That's my search segment. We'll beach the boat there, search the shore in both directions. If we find nothing, we'll row on to the next point. And to the next. Until we find her."

D'Orias nodded. He stroked like a galley slave, his powerful shoulders sending the boat surging into the hazardous waters. Icy spray flew, and slush sheeted off the oars, freezing on contact, making them grow heavy as iron. But d'Orias didn't slacken. The lantern swung in the stern, and in the bow Dove strained to divert the drifting ice chunks. When they reached the promontory, they leaped to shore and hauled the boat in over the ice and snow. They worked well together as they combed the shore for footprints; d'Orias swiftly tracked north while Dove tracked south.

When the search netted nothing, they met at the boat, launched it, jumped in, and pressed on, rowing to the next point to repeat their search there. This then became their silent, arduous, exhausting pattern as the night deepened and the bitter cold descended. Splashes of slushy river water turned the oar locks to ice, but d'Orias made no complaint. He rowed on, hour after hour. He was as staunch a comrade as Dove could hope for.

They were both chilled half to death. The flagon of rum was small solace. Their breath steamed, their faces grew ruddy with cold. Ice crystals formed on d'Orias's black mustache, and Dove's hands grew stiff. As the boat spurted on, Dove slipped his sword hand out of his fur-lined mittens, slipped it into his cloak, into doublet and shirt, and warmed it on the hot skin of his belly. A swordsman with stiff fingers was no swordsman at all.

"We will find her. Do not despair, de Mont." D'Orias broke the long silence, his breath steaming, his low Italian voice soft with compassion. Dove couldn't speak. He nodded mutely.

"We will find her, de Mont. Do not give in to despair. Despair clouds the mind. A man cannot think when he despairs. So do not despair. Only think. Only search."

Dove's throat thickened. "She's so . . . young. She's only a child. When I imagine what those bastards might be doing to her . . . doing at this very moment . . ."

"Do not imagine. Only think, *si*? Only search, *si*?"

Dove nodded bleakly. By the fourth hour, clouds drifted away and stars came out, twinkling as coldly and starkly as diamonds. A quarter moon rose in the sky, shedding cold light. Moonglow glazed the endless miles of snow. On the river, Dove could see the distant lanterns of other search boats. Pinpoints of light. Glancing across the waters toward New Amsterdam, he could see the outline of Hildegarde's house. For the first time, he glanced at it without interest. In the settlement, moving lanterns flickered everywhere, even out on the rocky shoals at the tip of the island. Everyone was out searching, despite the bitter cold.

"They are good people, the Dutch, *si*?"

"Yes." Dove was ashamed he'd ever thought otherwise.

The boat scraped bottom once again. Once again, they leaped out, hauled the boat ashore and began the sickeningly familiar pattern, d'Orias trekking north, Dove south. But he was losing heart. There wasn't much more logical shore to search. Desperate that the search not end, he followed the Indian tomahawk hashmarks on tree trunks and trekked up an unlikely Indian hunting trail. The trail lay covered in waist-deep pristine snow, the topmost layer delicately crusted, glittering like iridescent mica. The snow was unbroken. No one had traveled this trail. But he pushed on anyway, forging breathless to the top of a low slope. He stood panting, breath steaming, his eyes desperately searching the empty wilderness in all directions. Except for the pines that stood dark and thickly branched, the leafless ash and elm trees looked like skeletons, and he was filled with despair. Jericho. Would someone stumble upon *her* skeleton when the snow melted away and spring came again?

He turned to retrace his steps, to charge on with the fruitless search, when suddenly a scent made his nostrils quiver. Smoke! Just the faintest trace of it. So fleeting that it was gone in an instant. Had he imagined it? Heart thundering, he wheeled and ran, retracing his steps, plunging down the trail he'd broken. He reached the boat. D'Orias wasn't back yet. Abandoning his musket and powder tin, leaving them in the boat—the thirty-pound musket would slow him down—he took only his sword and ran south along the shore, searching for a hunting trail. The smoke *had* to have come from a hut.

He nearly missed it. The trail was well-hidden. The rogues had been clever, chinking the hashmarks on the trees with packed snow, hiding them. They'd also used a broom to sweep away their footprints. Dove intensely studied the shore. He saw an unnatural snow mound between two bushes. He ran to it, drew his sword and tentatively inserted it, testing. Steel clicked against wood. He frantically brushed the snow away.

Their boat!

Common sense told him to wait for d'Orias. But, *Jericho*. At the mercy of brutes, perhaps suffering—at this very moment—what no child should ever suffer.

He made his decision.

Plunging into the waist-deep snow, he leaped forward and followed the disguised trail. D'Orias was smart. He would put two and two together, follow Dove's tracks. He plunged along a trail that led deep into the wilderness, past thickets of leafless hickory trees, past tall, dark stands of pine, over frozen creek beds, past frozen springs. A dozen times he lost the trail and retraced his steps in a frenzy of frustration. Overhead, in the dark sky, the stars twinkled with cold indifference. The quarter moon rose higher, the snow grew brighter. Once, a white rabbit leaped across his path, startling the hell out of him, leaving a delicate trail of cloven prints in the snow's slight shimmering crust. Now and then, a wolf bayed distantly or a tree limb cracked in the deepening cold. But mainly, there was stillness and silence, only the labored sound of his own breathing, only the dogged trudging of his boots, the sound of his scared heart beating. Jericho. Would he be in time? He was her master. He ought to have taken better care of her.

At a distance he judged to be a hundred yards from the river, the rogues had confidently abandoned all attempts to conceal their trail. Three separate sets of boot prints emerged in the snow. In one spot, where they'd set her down for a moment, he found a smaller set of moccasin prints. She was alive!

Elated, he leaped into a steady trot, following the trail through a windswept trough of broken snow. The smell of woodsmoke came again. Grew distinct. Then, suddenly, forging breathlessly to the top of a low rise, he looked down through the pines and saw the hut just below. He was almost on top of it. His heart hammered in his throat. Sheltered by snow-covered granite outcroppings, the crude hunter's hut had no window, no chimney—only a door and a smoke hole in the center of the thatched roof. A pine branch had cleverly been laid over the smoke hole to disseminate the rising smoke from the warming fire inside.

His blood surging, he shucked his cloak. He wrenched his glove off with his teeth and thrust his sword hand under his doublet, under his shirt. His hand was so cold, his belly ached from the touch of it. He warmed his hand until his fingers grew supple. At the same time, he warmed the icy silver sword hilt in his arm pit. He made his plan. Three men. It would have to be a lightning attack. Give them no chance to get to their weapons. Catch them unaware. Make every thrust a death blow. Kill or be killed.

His heart hammered. He wished he could wait for d'Orias.

But Jericho! What was happening to her? He drew a long, scared breath of cold air, then gripped the sword hilt in his warmed hand and ran full speed down the rise, snow flying from his boots. He flew at the hut, kicked the door in and sprang into the room. The flimsy door crashed into the wall. In less than a heartbeat, the scene before him burned into his brain. The room was smoky. A crude fire crackled on the dirt floor. Thrown upon a blanket on the floor, stripped naked, bound and gagged, lay Jericho. The two men squatting there wheeled, startled. He saw the terror in her eyes, and then he saw red. He exploded like a volcano.

"Get 'im—'tis her master—get—"

Dove sprang. The shout was still coming forth when the rogue's head nodded at an unnatural angle, like a limp ribbon. A single slash all but decapitated him. Jugular blood spurted to the rafters, spraying the smoky room with a fine, slick spray that glistened in the firelight. Dove whirled and lunged for the second rogue, who'd gone springing for a pistol that lay upon a stool. The rogue grabbed for it. Dove slashed. Hand and pistol remained on the stool. With a scream of shock, the rogue backed away, blood pumping from his stump. Hot with anger, Dove advanced on him.

"Nay! Nay! Mercy—I beg—"

Dove thrust. Anger carried the belly thrust into the soft pine-log wall behind. Blood surged out of the man's mouth like vomit, and for a moment the wretch hung impaled to the wall, still alive. Gagging in disgust, Dove wrenched the sword free. Dying, the rogue melted to the floor. Panting, revulsed, Dove threw the bloody sword aside and leaped for the bed. The dirt floor was slick, slippery.

"Jericho?" He was just kneeling, swiftly covering her shaking body with a man's cloak when a voice cracked from the open doorway.

"Nicely done, milord. You've saved me two purses o' gold. Now I shan't need to split wi' them two."

He swung his head. He looked straight into a brass-bound pistol barrel. God. Three, not two. He'd forgotten.

"Stand up, milord."

Heart hammering, he covered Jericho, hiding her face so

she wouldn't see. He stood slowly, unsteadily. He swallowed and eased away from the bed. If the pistol went off, he at least was determined that Jericho not be hit.

"Easy, milord, easy. None o' your tricks." Dove's eyes swept the man. A thick-necked, brutish man. Built like a bull. Cold, indifferent eyes.

"Let the child go," Dove demanded.

"Nay. Indeed, milord, this exceeds me fondest expectations. Two at a blow, so to speak. I don't wonder but this'll earn me a extra purse o' gold."

"If it's money you want . . ."

The rogue laughed softly, and Dove jettisoned all thought of bribery, negotiation. This was a madman. He was not to be reasoned with. His thoughts flew to escape. Were it not for Jericho, he would risk a rash move, take his chances on the pistol misfiring. Pistols rarely fired straight. They were chancy, unreliable weapons. And he could leap like lightning. But what if the lead shot hit Jericho?

Taking care not to move and anger the rogue, he swept the room with furtive darting glances, calculating. The door stood open, framing the snowy wilderness and cold sky. The quarter moon hung low in it. The air stealing into the room was bitter cold, freezing the spilled blood into pale ruby crystals of ice. The dirt floor would be as slippery as Collect Pond. If he could somehow anger the madman, induce him to come close, induce him to lash out with a fist . . .

He gazed at him with cool contempt.

"What sort of cur kidnaps and rapes a child? Only the sort who cannot succeed with a real woman."

The pistol's aim grew deadlier, shifting from Dove's head to his heart. At least its sweep did not now take in Jericho.

"Careful, milord. Your life is measured in minutes."

"And your manhood could be measured in a thimble."

"Be silent," he growled. "Be silent!"

Just then, Dove saw a shadow steal across the snow. D'Orias? It had to be! He prayed it was. To cover the sound that even d'Orias's stealthy step would make in snow, he burst into an inane, loud, blustery tirade. Heart pounding, he ranted at the man.

"You lamebrain! You imbecile. You think you can get away with killing me? Fool. I am a de Mont. My brothers would hunt you down to the ends of the earth. And when they found you, would they kill you immediately? Oh, no, you dark cull. You would not be so fortunate in the hands of my brothers. What they would do to you, you miscreant, would not be pretty. There would not be enough of you to feed to carrion!"

The pistol came closer as the rogue extended his arm.

"Bid the world farewell, milord." The brute took pleasure in torture, Dove noted. Smiling an ugly smile, the brute took his time squeezing the trigger. He watched Dove sweat. D'Orias, for God's sake!

A dagger flew through the air, flashing past the low-hanging moon. Hurled powerfully, it struck with the speed of a musket ball. The rogue screamed and Dove dived to the floor, avoiding the discharge as the pistol dropped and fired wild. The shack rang, the loud reverberation caromming off the walls. The rogue fell heavily to his knees, clutching his bleeding shoulder.

Leonardo d'Orias leaped into the doorway, black cloak, black hair, black eyes glittering, assessing the situation at a glance.

"What took you so long?" Dove demanded crossly.

D'Orias smiled gently. "*Mi scuza*, de Mont." The smile faded as worry replaced it. "The little one? She?"

"Alive," he snapped. "On the blanket. But first—" Dove crawled to his feet and gestured at the rogue. Retrieving his sword, groping for it, his hand shook. The room swayed. Blood. So much blood. His father's blood spurting. The smell . . . the sweet sickening smell . . .

He swayed for a moment. D'Orias leaped forward. Dove stopped him with an angry head shake.

"This—is my duty, d'Orias. Remove your dagger."

"As you wish." Without mercy, d'Orias went to the moaning man and ruthlessly wrenched out his dagger. The rogue screamed in pain and fell forward. Unmoved, d'Orias wiped the dagger clean on the wretch's clothes, then sheathed it. "He is yours."

Dove stepped forward to finish him. Jericho. Jericho stripped naked, bound and helpless. With the toe of his boot he flipped the heavy, moaning man to his back and held his sword tip to the man's frantically thudding throat.

The small, crafty eyes opened wide, terror-struck.

"Nay! Nay! Mercy! I beg! Mercy! Mercy, milord, mercy!"

Dove felt dizzy. His sword hand shook. Gently, d'Orias's hand closed over his and took the sword. Dove backed away, grateful. The rogue's screams rose to shrieks.

"Mercy! Mercy!"

"*Si*. I grant mercy. The same mercy you granted the child."

D'Orias thrust.

Dove fought dizziness as blood gushed again, as the dying creature on the floor writhed and emptied his bowels. He staggered to the open door, drew in a breath of cold air, then went to Jericho.

"Jericho?" He gathered her up and carried her to the fire. He clawed the cloak from her face. Beneath her red freckles she was white. She shook like a terrified animal. Blinded by fear, the pupils of her eyes had constricted to pinpoints. For an instant, she didn't know him. She tried to lunge away. A pitiful testimony to the treatment she'd had. His anger boiled. He wanted to kill them all over again.

He shot an angry look at d'Orias, who grabbed blankets and a flask of rum, then squatted beside them.

"I killed them too quick," he snapped. "I should have sliced the flesh from them inch by inch."

"It is not your way," d'Orias said softly.

"Jericho, it's me! It's Dove. You're safe now. You're safe. The bad men are dead. I'm here. You're safe."

Then she recognized him and began to sob, sobbing through the dirty gag they'd stuffed in her mouth, trying to say his name. While d'Orias bundled her in blankets, Dove gently worked the gag free.

"Dove," she sobbed. "Dove, don't look. I don't have-have cl-clothes on. They-they took off m-my clothes. I-I don't have any cl-clothes on. Don't l-look, don't l-look."

He was touched. He held her close and let her sob, his cheek on her soft throbbing temple. "I won't. I won't," he promised. "I won't." He already had. As he'd bundled her into the cloak, he'd looked swiftly for signs of rape, for blood on her straight sturdy thighs. None, thank God. He conveyed that to d'Orias in a glance. Except for the bump on her head, she seemed to be untouched.

"Is-is Pax all right?" she sobbed.

"He has a bump on his head, as you do. But he'll be fine. Black Bartimaeus took him home. Daisy and Mrs. Phipps are tending him."

"I w-want to go home, Dove!"

"We'll go home in a minute, grubworm. But first, let's get you warm and dressed. Can I unbind your wrists now? Your ankles?"

She nodded tearfully, her scared eyes as huge as pansies.

"B-but don't l-look."

"I won't. I promise."

While he tended Jericho, d'Orias quietly moved about the room, doing what needed to be done, closing the door, building up the fire, dragging the bodies out of sight and throwing a blanket over them so she wouldn't see them. Taking a dead man's musket and powder, d'Orias went outside and fired the signal. The thunderous musket cracks reverberated through the frozen wilderness. A few minutes later, a distant three-shot salvo answered. The search was over. The searchers could go home.

Jericho burst into tears. "D-Dove? They-they w-were go-going to cut off my h-hand. To get my birthmark. They-they w-were going to cut off my-my hand and g-give my b-birthmark to a fox. To a fox. They w-were go-going to give my birthmark to a fox."

Dove stared at her, astounded that she could imagine such a thing. He and d'Orias exchanged a look and shook their heads.

"No, grubworm, no," he said quickly. "They were not going to do that. They were not. No." The men had had no such intention. What they *had* been going to do was rape her and sell her to the Indians. But, hell, he couldn't scare her with that. "They probably meant to hold you for ransom. They knew you were my bondslave. They knew I would pay."

She shook her head, refusing it. "N-no. They-they w-were going to give my birthmark to a fox."

He assured in every way he could think of, but she wasn't buying. Her tears flowed, her sobs erupted. When she was calmer, he hunted her clothes and brought them to her.

"They-they tore my gown," she said, bursting into a new freshet of tears. He knew she wasn't crying for the gown. She was a tough little bondslave. She didn't cry over small potatoes. He seethed. He wanted to kill the bastards all over again.

"Daisy will make you a new gown. I'll tell her to make you ten new gowns," he said, squatting at the fire. "Do you need help dressing?" He didn't have the least idea how to go about it. His experience lay in undressing females, not dressing them.

But she shook her head with dignity. Carrying her clothes into a corner, she dressed modestly under the cloak.

Finally, they were ready to start out. When d'Orias turned to close and latch the hut door behind them, Dove swung around.

"Leave it open."

D'Orias gestured. "The bodies, de Mont. Wolves . . ."

"Leave it open!"

Chapter Eight

"I cannot fathom it. I cannot puzzle it out," said Leonardo d'Orias, swirling tawny rum in a pewter cup that caught the firelight in Dove's parlor. "My understanding fails me, de Mont. Why should three men steal a child? A bondslave?"

"Rape." Dove glanced at the ceiling. Upstairs, hours ago, Jericho had been petted and cossetted and tucked into a feather-erbed. Pax slept in a nest at the foot of her bed.

The parlor finally stood empty of people. Dove felt relieved. As the searchers had returned, group by group, they'd come tramping in to refresh themselves with well-earned food and drink. Dove had been glad to feed and thank them. But it had been a strain telling and retelling the story of Jericho's rescue. He felt glad to sit alone at the fire, alone with d'Orias.

Reaching for the rum pitcher, Dove leaned forward and topped d'Orias's cup. His hand still trembled from the night's events, and he tried to hide it from d'Orias. But he suspected those compassionate, watchful eyes missed nothing.

"Perhaps." D'Orias sipped his rum. "Yet I feel there is more behind it. There must be more."

Dove frowned impatiently. "What more could there be?"

D'Orias shook his head, his hair so black in the firelight it looked blue. "One does not know, yes? One cannot even guess. Yet, so bizarre the story the child told! Cut off her hand? Cut off her birthmark? Give it to—how say you the animal in English—to, to a fox?"

"She was overwrought. She imagined it."

"Perhaps." D'Orias was reluctant to agree. "Perhaps."

They sat together, sipping rum. Dove glanced at the big, broad-shouldered Italian. He liked him more than ever. He was staunch, reliable. No wonder his mother had trusted d'Orias to bring money and letters to New Amsterdam. And though he would rather jump off a cliff than admit it, he was grateful d'Orias was sitting up with him. Dove was shaken by the night's events.

When the clock struck the hour of three, bonging mellowly, d'Orias put his cup aside and rose. "Now, my young friend, I must take my leave of you."

"Of course," Dove agreed quickly. "You've earned bed."

D'Orias smiled gently. "You misunderstand. I must leave New Amsterdam. The last Company ship of the season sails today at dawn. If I am not to winter in New Amsterdam, I must be aboard her. The Hudson already is frozen hard. If bitter weather continues, the East River will freeze, too, and the harbor will be locked in ice until spring."

"Leave?" Dove felt a genuine pang. In the short weeks he'd been acquainted with d'Orias, he'd grown damned fond of him. There was something familiar about d'Orias. It stirred a vague, unaccountable remembrance.

D'Orias buttoned his doublet and drew on his coat.

"*Si*. I must leave. Your mother will be anxiously awaiting my report. She will be eager to know I found you well and safe. No, no, do not get up. My trunk already is aboard the ship. I have the letters you entrusted to me, the letters to Lady de Mont, the letters to your brothers and to Lord Aubrey and to Lady Marguerite. If you wish to send aught else, dispatch it to the ship before dawn."

"I will. Thank you. Hell, d'Orias, I'm sorry to see you go."

The Italian's eyes lighted with affection. "I am sorry to leave you, de Mont. Much pleasure have I felt, meeting you."

Unwilling to part with d'Orias, reluctant to let him go, Dove strolled with him to the kitchen door.

"You never told me. How did you come to be acquainted with my mother?"

D'Orias gave him a wry, whimsical smile. "She put her dagger into me."

"She what!"

D'Orias stayed his gloved hand on the door latch. "It happened in a flower market in Paris. Lady de Mont was purchasing flowers, accompanied by her servants." D'Orias's eyes took on a a soft glow. "Lady de Mont is a very beautiful woman. She looks much like you, yes? The same golden hair. The same bright, intelligent eyes. I fear I was so taken with her beauty that I did something foolish. I approached her." D'Orias gestured ruefully. "My English, it is lamentable. My French? Worse. I fear my lady takes me for a *banditi*, a highwayman. She stabs me. Just so." He tapped a spot dangerously near his heart.

"Good lord! What happened then?"

"I fall down in the stones and mud, bleeding. Certainly, I am dying. Your mother, she gathers up her silk skirts and stalks off. A moment later, she comes stalking back, a fiery Juno. Scolding me without ceasing, she rips her petticoat to bind my wound and she commands her servants to carry me to her house, to put me to bed and fetch a surgeon." D'Orias's eyes glowed with amusement. "I do not know which was worse, my lady's tongue lashing or my wound. From that unlikely beginning came a friendship I shall cherish for the rest of my life."

D'Orias looked at him with quiet challenge.

"I am devoted to your mother."

Came the dawn! Finally it dawned on Dove. He'd been deaf, blind, and thick-headed. The hushed reverent tone d'Orias used whenever speaking of his mother. The glow in his eyes. The concern that was as plain as sunrise and sunset. Protective of his mother, jealously protective of his father's memory, he bristled. He grew hostile.

"And *she*? Is *she* devoted to you?"

D'Orias raised a gloved hand. "No. Do not think it. No. Lady de Mont is a widow of impeccable character. She makes of widowhood a noble calling. She is devoted to your father's memory. She is devoted to her sons. She is zealous and tireless in her efforts to regain Arleigh Castle for her sons. She cares for nothing else."

"But *you* care for her," Dove charged, unsatisfied.

"*Si*," D'Orias admitted with steady calm. "Since the day I set eyes upon my lady, other women have ceased to exist for me. Is that a crime? If so, accuse me. But know this, de Mont. I worship your mother. I would lay down my life for her. And know this, too. I am not ignorant. I am aware that Lady de Mont is highborn. My mother, whom I loved with all my heart, was a peasant girl."

Dove's heat abated. He didn't know what to say. He glanced at the snapping kitchen fire. He glanced across the room at Samuels and Black Bartimaeus, deep in sleep on their pallets, snoring, sawing wood.

"Take—take care of my mother," Dove blurted awkwardly. "Until my brothers and I can return."

"Be assured of it." A good-humored man, the ghost of a smile flickered once again in the dark eyes. "In so far as she will allow it. Now, my young friend, I bid you farewell. Take care of the little flower." His smile grew oddly enigmatic. "She will make someone a magnificent wife some day."

"Wife?" Dove was astounded. "She's but a child."

"Children grow up."

Dove had trouble picturing it. The grubworm grown up. Did skinny, flat-chested little girls grow up into women?

D'Orias thrust out his hand. Yanked back to the moment, Dove took it. They shook hands. A warm, firm clasp.

"I owe you my life," Dove summed up.

D'Orias refused to hear it. He adamantly shook his head. "No. Not so. Had I not been there, you would have thought of a way to save yourself. And to save the child. I have confidence in you, de Mont."

D'Orias opened the door. A gust of frigid, arctic wind swept in, curling around Dove's legs, bringing back vivid and horrible memories of the cold night's work.

"We worked well together, d'Orias."

"We worked well."

"We will meet again someday, I hope?"

"Be assured of it."

With that and with a swing of his black cloak, the tall Italian stepped out onto the stoop, descended the wooden steps and strode into the wind, into the darkness, into the shadowy lanes of New Amsterdam.

Dove couldn't sleep. Killing a man, he discovered, was not conducive to a night's sleep. Killing three men? He probably would never sleep again. He roused Black Bartimaeus and requested a hot bath in front of the kitchen fire. He scrubbed every inch of his flesh. He put on fresh clothes. Still, he smelled the blood . . . the blood . . .

He prowled the house, restless. Rouse John? Have a game of cards? No. John was exhausted. He too had tramped miles through deep snow, searching.

He went up to his room. He started to write a letter, then ripped it up, half-finished. Blood. Even the ink smelled like blood. He went downstairs and prowled the house, moving from window to window, rubbing the accumulating frost off the inner pane with his shirt sleeve. He watched the kloppermen tramp by, patrolling, their lanterns swinging, boots crunching the hardpacked snow, pipesmoke rising like steam.

Restless, he went to the kitchen and stood motionless, hands on hips, looking at everything, looking at nothing. Blood. Blood. He returned to his sleeping chamber, built up the fire, lighted a candle, and selected a book at random, any book. He willed morning to come. But this was winter. Darkness would enshroud New Amsterdam until nearly eight of the clock.

He was trying, unsuccessfully, to read a French novel when his door latch clicked. The door opened, and Jericho stood there. Beneath the russet freckles, her face was whiter than her nightrail.

"Dove?" she whispered. "Can-can I-I c-come in?"

He sprang up. "Yes, of course." Jumpy, he was glad for company. Even a child's. He slung a second chair to the fireside and grabbed a goosefeather quilt from the bed. When she'd settled into chair and quilt, she said, "Dove? They-they w-were go-going to c-cut off m-my hand. They-they w-were g-going to cut off m-m-my birthmark. They-they w-were go-going to give it to a fox."

"No, Jericho, no." He put another log on the fire. Sparks whooshed. "Hell's bells, grubworm, you imagined it, that's all."

"N-no, Dove. I-I-I h-heard th-them s-say it. They-they w-were go-going to g-give m-my birthmark to-to a fox."

"Then you misheard, eh? No one would do such a thing." Her eyes told him she wasn't buying.

"Can-can I-I s-stay h-here w-with y-you for a-a w-while?"

"Yes, of course. Do you want some rum?"

She looked at him in surprise. "I-I th-think I-I'm too y-young to drink r-rum, Dove."

"Hell, that's right. I forgot. Sometimes you seem young, sometimes you don't. Then I'll drink it." He retrieved his rum cup. A log rolled in the fire. He kicked it back. The fire hissed and crackled. The night was so cold that the room was frigid. The windows were solidly frosted.

"W-well, may-maybe I-I c-could h-have a s-sip, Dove. Th-then may-maybe I-I w-won't dream of foxes."

Dove went to the window, rubbed a shilling-sized hole in the frost and looked out. "Believe me, grubworm, rum's not the solution. I've dreamed the same nightmare since I was three."

The fire crackled. In the distance, a wolf bayed.

"A-about the-the dogs kill-killing y-your fa-father?"

Dove swung around, surprised. She was an intelligent thing. More intelligent than a lot of adults. Perceptive. This time she'd certainly put two and two together.

"Yes. It is."

"I-I'm s-s-sorry y-you dream th-that, Dove."

"I'm sorry, too."

He smiled a little, feeling better about the night, and lightly bopped his rum cup on her shoulder as he strolled past and sank comfortably into his chair. They sat quietly, staring into the fire, mesmerized by the dancing flames. Her pansy eyes grew darker and darker, her pale eyelids heavier and heavier. At last she gave in. Exhausted, she fell asleep. When her head lolled back and banged into the chair frame, making her whimper in her sleep, Dove picked her up, quilt and all, and tucked her into his bed. Weary himself, he lay down beside her and curled into the goosedown quilt.

It was Mrs. Phipps, rising first in the morning and tiptoeing past the open door of Dove's room, who found them like that. Her first thought was to scold. Jericho had no business being in Master Dove's bed. Master Dove had no business permitting it.

Her second thought was kinder. What a pretty pair of children! Dove's thick sprawl of golden hair covered the pillow. His long, dark golden lashes were knitted in innocent sleep. His mouth was lax. He'd done a man's work last night. But just now he was an eighteen-year-old youth, deep in slumber.

And Jericho. She was nestled in his arms, her curly red head on his shoulder. Pax had sneaked in sometime in the night. He slept upon the foot of the bed. Without moving a muscle, the dog opened his eye and stared warily. Mrs. Phipps wagged a warning finger, and, with a long-suffering sigh, he reluctantly jumped down. His nails clicked on the cold, drafty floorboards. He obediently padded down the stairs to the kitchen. Mrs. Phipps closed the door.

The faint click of the door closing woke Dove. Sleep drugged, he blearily opened his eyes and got the shock of his life. Nestled in his arms was a beautiful woman. She had witch's hair, red as flame. She had long, sweeping lashes of the same color. Startled, he blinked. His head shot up. Then he saw. He expelled a breath. God's soup, it was only Jericho. Carefully, he laid his head back down on the pillow. Don't wake her. She's had a bad night. Crying out in her sleep. Always the same cry. A fox, a fox.

Queer. Very queer. He breathed quietly. He watched her, reassessing her. She *was* a decent-looking little thing. She didn't strike him as homely anymore. Were the freckles beginning to fade? He lifted his head. Hell's bells, they were. Someday she might be a pretty woman. Perhaps even a beautiful one. The thought surprised him. He tried to imagine her grown-up. He couldn't.

His thoughts drifted. He should *do* something for her, provide for her. D'Orias was right. She wouldn't be a child forever. She would grow up someday. She was his responsibility. What good thing could he do for her? Thoughts came and went. He turned them over in his mind. A dowry, he decided. When she came of age, and her indenture ended, he would settle a dowry on her. Not a large dowry that would attract scoundrels. A small dowry. But enough—certainly!—to save her from having to marry a wood chopper or a chicken plucker.

Jericho, grown-up and married. Somehow, the thought irritated. He'd become used to having her fetch and carry for him. He'd become used to her unpredictable, ornery moods. He'd even become used to her stutter. Hell, he liked it! It was . . . charming.

Jericho, grown-up and married. It irked. It irritated. Irked and irritated, he rolled away and got out of bed. The jiggling of the mattress made her stir. He stood beside the bed and watched her wake, half-scared to see what she'd be like this morning. Had what she'd gone through scarred her, destroyed her pluck? He held his breath, wondering what she would say.

But what she did say, when she opened those pansy eyes in annoyed vexation, made him smile broadly. He needn't worry about this brat. She was as tough as old barrel staves.

"Dove? W-where are my skates!"

For a week, Jericho found herself the center of attention in New Amsterdam. She reveled in it. She'd never been the center of attention before. She told the story of Dove's rescue to everyone who asked. Maritje Ten Boom and the other girls at school grew jealous. She liked that, too. She'd never had anyone jealous of her before.

But as the excitement faded, the gravity of what had happened seeped into her, became real to her, and left her shaken. This had not been make-believe. This had been real. Men had died! Dove had killed for her! It was a sobering revelation, and she grew quieter after that. Overnight, she grew up.

Dove grew up, too. He seemed older, nicer. He showed more patience with her. He took her skating on Collect Pond three times that winter. They were happy romps. At least they were, until Dove would suddenly spot Mrs. Verplanck and his eyes would brighten, and he would go gliding off, leaving her behind as if she were a warty old potato.

She had a few nightmares that winter. Frightening dreams of foxes chasing her on Collect Pond. But the dreams gradually went away. In the end, the experience left two marks upon her: a deep distrust of strangers and renewed anxiety about her birthmarks.

She dealt with both. She gave strangers a wide berth, going nowhere near them. As for her birthmarks, she took scraps from Daisy's sewing basket and sewed pretty wristbands to hide the one that showed, the one on her wrist. Mrs. Phipps thought the wristbands nonsense. Daisy and Cook and Maritje teased her. Jericho didn't care. She grew happy again.

Then, one cold windy day in March, her world fell apart.

*   *   *

"Daisy, where's Dove! Is he dining w-with us today?"

Dashing into the kitchen for the midday meal, she hung her cloak on a wall peg, grabbed the box that held the wooden trenchers and spoons, and swiftly set the table, her noon task. "Where's Dove, Daisy!"

It was always her first question. Waiting for Daisy to answer, she sniffed eagerly at the delicious smells. Rabbit roasted on the spit, well rubbed with herbs and pork fat.

"I want to tell Dove, Daisy. I w-was fastest adding four-digit columns of sums today. Even faster than the boys. Robert Ten Boom got angry. His face got all red. Robert is used to being fastest. But I'm fastest now. I want to tell Dove."

Daisy didn't answer. Instead, she sank to a cricket stool and burst into tears. Jericho froze. She set the trencher box down with trembling hands, suddenly aware. Everything was different this noon. Goody sat in a corner weeping, wiping away tears with her sleeve. Tending the kettles, Cook was grim, her eyes red, swollen. Black Bartimaeus sat on a stool holding his head in his black hands. Samuels smiled, but wanly.

"Where's Dove?" Jericho demanded. Nobody answered.

"Jericho, come here," Mrs. Phipps said softly. Mrs. Phipps was sitting in a chair by the kitchen window. Sitting! Mrs. Phipps never sat in the daytime. She was was always busy, always bustling about, checking things, doing things . . .

She felt dizzy. Sick with dread. "W-where's Dove?"

"Come here, child." Mrs. Phipps gently held out her hand. She looked older than she'd looked this morning, older by years.

Jericho's heart hammered. "W-what happened? Where's Dove, Mrs. Phipps? W-where is he?" She looked around wildly. "W-where's John?"

Daisy screwed up her face and burst into fresh sobs.

Mrs. Phipps rose wearily and took Jericho's hands. "Child, Master Dove is gone. And John has gone with him, to companion him."

Jericho nodded. "Gone-gone to-to the tap house. Or-or to the fort. Or-or-or m-maybe he w-went to Fort Orange." She nodded desperately, wanting it to be true.

Mrs. Phipps sighed tiredly. "Jericho. Child. You are too young to understand this, but Master Dove has been banished from the colony. Soldiers put him aboard ship two hours ago. The ship just sailed. For the Caribbean. John went with him."

"The Car-Car-Caribbean? Not-not Fort Orange?" She went numb. Then, slowly, she began to shake her head. "N-no. N-no, it-it's not true! He w-went to Fort Orange, Mrs. Phipps. He did, he did, he told me." She turned to the others. "Daisy? Samuels? He w-went to Fort Orange, didn't he!" They wouldn't look at her. Daisy sobbed with fresh despairing sobs. Samuels knelt and hugged her.

Mrs. Phipps gently squeezed her hands.

"Jericho. Child. Listen to me. Wicked things will be said about Master Dove, but you are *not* to believe them. For they are *not* true. If I live to a hundred I shan't believe!"

"Dear life," Daisy wailed, lifting red weepy eyes from her apron. "Mr. Verplanck found him in bed wi' her, Mrs. Phipps. He found the two of 'em doin' it."

"Daisy, be silent!" Mrs. Phipps snapped. "Say that again and you forfeit employment in this house. Lord Dove is your master, you wicked girl. He is a good lad. He would never behave so!"

Jericho listened, swallowing. Tears gathered in her throat, choking her. She tore out of Mrs. Phipps's grasp.

"Jericho? Where are you going? Child, stop!"

She was out the kitchen door in a flash, flying down the lane, through the cold splattering March mud, her wooden clogs forgotten, her cloak forgotten. Barking, thinking it a game, Pax galloped with her. She swatted him away. Tears choking her, she flew through the lanes, scattering geese and irate merchants. She flew over the footbridge, past the tap houses, past fur warehouses and finally clattered onto the Dutch West India Company wharf in the East River. She ran out to the very end of it, her shoes thundering on the rotting timbers, her lungs heaving.

The ship was already far out in the harbor, past the rocky shoals on the tip of Manhattan. A small sailing boat, a red-sailed pilot boat, guided it. Boat and ship were already di-

minishing in size. She could see sailors scrambling in the
rigging, their monkeylike figures small, indistinct.

"Dove," she screamed. "Dove, come back. Take me with
you. You promised to keep me. You promised!"

Pax whimpered and nosed her cold, mud-spattered skirts.
She batted him away. The ship continued on its impersonal
course, plowing out to sea, leaving nothing behind but a
lengthening stretch of plowed water that lay gray and turgid
under the slate March sky.

Heart pounding with hope—He would come back for her,
he *would*, if he saw her!—she screamed and waved frantically, jumping up and down. But to no avail. Safely past the
shoals, the ship's main sails unfurled and caught the wind.
The ship bucked and danced, meeting the ocean current.

Throat pounding, she watched the ship grow smaller and
smaller, dropping lower and lower in the water, the hull
disappearing first, then the windfilled mainsails, then the topmost flag on the crow's nest. She watched until there was
nothing to see but gray water and sky. Then, her knees weak
and wobbly, she sat on the wharf and watched some more.
She didn't cry. She was too shocked to cry. She simply
watched. If she kept watch, she assured herself, Dove would
turn the ship and come back for her. He would!

Dry-eyed, her brain glazed with shock, she kept watch all
afternoon. Pax curled beside her. Daisy and Goody came
clumping out onto the wharf, coaxing her.

"Jericho, it's cold. It's fixin' to rain. Come home now.
Come'a. Mrs. Phipps says come home. Mrs. Phipps is
worried." They plucked at her sleeve. She slapped them
away.

Samuels came with her cloak. Only then, as warmth returned, did she notice she was frozen, shaking, the cutting
March wind and icy raindrops lashing her face. Samuels
coaxed too, his West-Indies voice soft and singy. "Come'a,
Jer'cho. Come'a, girl. Come home, come home."

He took her hand. She tore it away. He tried over and over
and over. At last he sighed, looked up at the coming storm
and left, too. The sky darkened. Lightning flashed. Cold rain
fell like sleet. Pax whimpered, pawing at her.

Still she sat, dry-eyed, swatting the icy raindrops off her face, waiting. Finally Black Bartimaeus came, standing over her like a tall black tower. Black Bartimaeus didn't say anything. He didn't speak. He just picked her up in his enormous arms, ignoring her kicks and screams, ignoring it when she beat on his chest with her fists and then burst into sobs that wouldn't stop.

Calmly, the elderly black giant carried her home.

They told her later that she had grieved herself into illness. She didn't remember. She only knew that when Dove left, the month had been March and patches of dirty snow had still lain in the yard. By the time she was well enough to go back to school, June had come and baby robins had hatched in a nest in the wolf skull that was nailed to the wall above the cow-shed door.

It would always remain a wonder to her that so much time had passed without her knowing. For she remembered so little: the smell of the posset Mrs. Phipps made her drink whenever she opened her eyes; the smell of pine whenever Black Bartimaeus sat at her bedside whittling; the smooth, piney texture of the wooden chick or carved owl she would find in her hand when she awakened; the monotonous sound of her own blood dripping into a basin, drop by slow drop, whenever the fort surgeon came and bled her.

The first day she left her bed, she felt so dizzy she had to cling to the wall as the room looped and spun around her. Though weak and wobbly, she was determined; and, hanging onto walls, she made her way to Dove's room and went in. Too exhausted to seek a chair, she sank to the white pine floor and sat. Her eyes moved listlessly around the room, taking it in.

Everything was the same. Everything was still there. Yet everything was not the same. Though the room had Dove's things in it, it was no more Dove's room than a dead body is the place where a person lives after he dies.

She gazed listlessly at the familiar bed, the blue silk bedcurtains she'd mended for Dove when he'd stuck a fencing foil through them. She watched motes of dust float lazily in the window's sunshine. She let her gaze fall upon the mahogany wardrobe.

With effort, dizzy, she struggled to her feet, went to his wardrobe and pulled the doors open. Only one shirt remained, an old linen one, hanging on a peg. She took it, and, because she was too weak to walk to a chair, sat on the floor, holding it, smelling it, trying to remember Dove's scent. It was Mrs. Phipps who found her.

"Jericho, you're up and about, child! This is wonderful."

"He's not c-coming back, is he."

"Jericho. Child . . ."

Mrs. Phipps hesitated, then came to her. Mrs. Phipps's gown brushed against her. A cool motherly hand felt her forehead, feeling for fever.

"Child, let's have Black Bartimaeus carry you down to the kitchen. Goody and Cook can make you a posset drink."

"He's not c-coming back, is he."

Mrs. Phipps hesitated, then tried cheerfully, "We've new-hatched chicks. Would you like to see them? I'll have Daisy bring two or three into the kitchen."

"He's not, is he!"

There was a long moment of silence. Mrs. Phipps gently patted her cheek.

"No, child," she said softly. "He is not. Master Dove is not coming back."

PART TWO

JERICHO

1666

Chapter Nine

On a warm sultry day in May, in the year 1666, an unlikely trio debarked from a ship into the confusion and clamor of St. Katherine's Docks in London.

An elderly black giant came down the gangplank first, his step unsteady, his kinky gray hair shining like silver in the bright sunlight. As he came, he led an old one-eyed mongrel on a leash and sent solicitous looks over his shoulder. Two women followed. The first was an old war-horse, short and stout of body, garbed in severe black. Unsteady on her sea legs, she clung to the arm of a young woman who was . . . a beauty!

Lolling in the shade of a chestnut tree, avoiding work on the hot day, a group of porters sat up in attention.

"Looky."

"Oh, mother, me balls are turnin' blue."

Desultory laughter peppered the warm air. Pungent remarks flew, and a variety of colorful cures were suggested. The porters sprawled on the cool grass to gawk.

She was a beauty, all right. She had witch's hair—a thick, curly, flaming red mane of it. She had fair skin, fetchingly dusted with freckles, and midnight-blue eyes.

But no one sprang up to offer service. Glancing at her cheap gown, they stayed put. She was servant class, like themselves. There was no fat gratuity to be earned *there*. And the day was too hot to labor for coppers.

Spotting the chestnut tree and men sprawled under it, Jericho came marching in a beeline straight to the porter who sat frontmost.

"Will you give me some information?"

"Mebbe. Mebbe not." The others snickered.

Jericho could take the hint. She gave the drawstring of her purse an exasperated yank and drew out a coin. She squeezed it in her palm for a moment, loath to part with it. She'd earned that coin—and every other in her purse!—teaching dame school. She'd saved, determined to have her own dame school someday.

But this was no time to be stingy. Mrs. Phipps was feeling the heat. Even Black Bartimaeus looked unwell. His heart again? Swiftly, she gave the coin to the lazy porter. "Can you tell me where I can hire a runner? To take word we've arrived?"

He made a show of staring at it. "My, my. A whole copper. Sure you can spare it, missus?"

"Yes!" Jericho said tartly. "But see to it that you earn it."

The others laughed. But this time the porter was the goat of their laughter and knew it. He got to his feet with a grin. But lazily. It was only a copper. Jericho wanted to smack him.

"Now then, missus. What d'ye want t' know?"

"I-I-I—" She stopped, drew a breath and started again. If she let these dock sluggards addle her, she'd soon be stuttering like a magpie. "I want to send a message to Number Nine, Seething Lane. I want to send word to Mr. John Phipps that his mother has arrived."

"Mr. John Phipps, missus? Mr. John Phipps, the rich merchant?" He whipped off his cap and bunched it respectfully.

Jericho's eyes widened. Rich? She'd known John was prospering. His letters had come regularly. But rich? Good heavens. She smiled her pleasure at John's good fortune.

"Yes," she said emphatically. "*That* Mr. John Phipps."

To her amazement, John's name worked magic. Suddenly, the porters could not do enough. Offers of service innundated her like a flood, and a pushing and shoving match broke out. The oafs cuffed each other with their caps. A full-fledged fight threatened. She drew a vexed breath. She was hot and tired. Now this.

"Stop this at once!" she demanded in her firmest dame-school voice. To her surprise, they did. Then, she dealt with them as she would bickering children, fairly dividing the tasks, dispatching one to John's house and the others to the ship to get the trunks. If John was rich, he could pay. *She* certainly couldn't.

When they'd trotted off in all directions, a latecomer hung on her heels, grinning maliciously. "Ye needn't ha'sent 'em at all, missus."

She threw him a suspicious look. "Why?"

"Ye know that Mr. John Phipps? Why, he comes down t'the docks twice a day in his fine coach, he does. Ever'body knows that. On the lookout fer his mother, he is. Has been two weeks."

If that belated scrap of news hadn't been so wonderful, she'd have been tempted to grab his dirty cap and whack him with it. But she gazed about happily. On the far side of the unloading area, safely out of the chaos, Mrs. Phipps and Black Bartimaeus rested on a shady bench under a tree. Tethered to the bench, Pax was already snoozing, asleep at their feet. Satisfied they were resting, she let her gaze sweep over the immense stone fortress that dominated the river, dwarfing everything else. A thrill shot up her spine.

The Tower of London. She'd heard of it. But she hadn't expected it to be so—huge. Good heavens, it must cover forty acres. She stared up at it, awed.

Behind the Tower, rising in a haze, the chimney smoke of London feathered into the sky like ten thousand gray ostrich plumes as the vast city cooked, baked, brewed, forged, and went about its daily work. Strong smells wafted in the air: cooksmoke, soot, fish, breweries, tar, turpentine, pitch. Out on the Thames, the river was so thick with ships under sail that she couldn't see the south bank.

London. Dove's London. Dove . . .

Was Dove in the city? Her heart flip-flopped unevenly. Instantly, she took herself to task for it. No! She wasn't going to feel those childish feelings. She wasn't a child anymore. She was a grown woman. Almost twenty. Dove de Mont was nothing to her. Besides! What had she been to him all these years? Only a postscript, hastily scribbled to the bottom of his annual letter to Mrs. Phipps: *My regards to the grubworm.*

The grubworm, indeed! She pushed Dove from her mind and put her attention where it belonged. Mrs. Phipps, Black Bartimaeus. She threw them a loving glance. Exhausted, they'd followed Pax's example. They'd nodded off. They're old, she realized with a sudden pang. Someday I won't have them anymore. It was a horrid thought. She swung back to the porter who'd been chattering at her.

"Is there an inn nearby? Somewhere Mr. John Phipps's mother can lie down and rest while we wait?"

"Oh, ye don't want t'do that, missus."

"Why?"

Grinning, he gestured with his cap. "Plague, missus."

She stirred uneasily. "But the plague is over! Mr. John Phipps wrote. There was a plague last year, yes. A horrid death toll, more than one hundred thousand. But it's over."

"Oh, nay, missus. There's still a dab o' plague in London."

Despite the sweltering heat of the day, Jericho felt a cold prickle. Had she traveled all this way to get the plague? To die? She glanced worriedly at Mrs. Phipps and Black Bartimaeus, glad they were resting, glad they weren't hearing this.

"Some mulled ale, then," she directed. "If you wish to be useful to Mr. John Phipps's mother, fetch us some ale." Opening her purse again, she fished out a shilling and directed him to go to the nearest ale house.

"Gimme three shilling more, missus, and I'll fetch ye each a bunch o' posies for yer pockets."

This was too much. "Posies!"

He grinned an unlovely grin. "Certain, missus. T' charm off the plague. Ain't ye heard the chil'run sing? *Ring around the rosy, pocket full o' posy, ashes, ashes, ye all fall down.* Oh, ay, missus, first sign you got plague is a rosy spot risin' on yer skin. And if a ring forms around it? Plague, missus. Then it's fall down, ye will, and ashes to ashes, dust to dust.''

It was ridiculous. But what if it wasn't?

Wiping her brow, she fished out three more shillings and gave them to him. When he'd trotted off, she looked into her purse and sighed. She'd been in London less than an hour, and already it had cost her four shillings and a halfpenny. At this rate, she'd never get her dame school.

She waited a long time. The knave did not come back. She clenched her jaw in disgust. Another lesson learned. Giving up on the ale, she was about to rejoin Mrs. Phipps and Black Bartimaeus when a horse-drawn coach came clattering down the steep street to the docks. Even before the horses halted, the door was flung open and someone sprang out. He was a well-dressed, brawny man, a fine-looking man in his prime. Hatless and in a hurry, he strode into the chaos of St. Katherine's Docks, his sandy brown hair full of sunlight.

John! Jericho felt her smile begin all the way down in her toes. She started forward, then stopped herself, unwilling to intrude. This was a mother-son reunion. She moved only close enough to enjoy it with her ears as well as her eyes.

Taking several swift, abortive steps in one direction, then in a second direction, John spotted his dozing mother. He stopped dead. He threaded his way through hogsheads of tobacco that were being unloaded, went to her, squatted, and gently touched her sleeve. ''Mother?''

She awoke with a start, blinking. ''John! Black Bartimaeus, look! It's John. It's my son John. John!''

''Mother.'' Jericho smiled with delight as John gathered his mother into his arms. They hugged, kissed, even wept a little.

''Seven years, son! It's been too long. Much too long.''

''And who's fault is that, m'girl? Didn't I write you a hundred times to leave New York, didn't I? Come live with your son John in London, I says. Come let him treat you like a queen, I says. Didn't I, didn't I, eh?''

"And how could I leave?" she chided, her plump chin flattening happily. "With your two brothers giving me grand-babies to dandle on my knee every year? And such darling babies! If only you could see them—" She broke off, aghast. "Oh, son. I am so sorry about your wife. To marry and bury in the same year? It is too cruel to be borne. And to lose your firstborn in the childbirth, too. Oh, son!" She burst into tears. Jericho's heart surged protectively. She started forward, then stopped herself and let John do the comforting.

"There, there, Mother. There, there. 'Tis all in the past. 'Tis past and done. I'm fine now."

Jericho watched in silent sympathy, her eyes drinking John in. He was handsomer than she'd remembered. During the reunion, Black Bartimaeus had risen and stood shyly apart, watching in silent manner, but grinning from ear to ear. When John spotted him, he whooped.

"Black Bartimaeus! Great day, it's *you*. Man, it's good to see you!" Black Bartimaeus tried to offer a handshake, but John would have nothing so formal. He threw his arms around the elderly giant and hugged him. Positive that John was harming the people he loved, Pax lunged into a frenzy of barking. John swung the dog an idle glance, then blinked.

"My God. I would know that scruffy one-eyed pirate any-where. Great heaven. I cannot b'lieve my eyes. It's—it's—what was his name? What did little Jericho call him?"

"Pax," Mrs. Phipps supplied happily, drying her tears.

"If that's Pax," John said, "then where—where's Jeri-cho?"

It was her turn. Eager, and at the same time suddenly shy—Would he remember her? More to the point, would he still like her? He'd liked her in New Amsterdam.—she stepped forward.

"John?" she said uncertainly. "Hello, John."

He whirled and stood thunderstruck. His mouth went slack.

"Great heaven. Jericho?"

She nodded eagerly. "Hello, John."

"Jericho. You're beautiful. Good lord. Is it really you? You've gone and grown up on me. I cannot believe my eyes."

He held out his arms and she went into them eagerly.

"It's you who's the beautiful sight, John. You look so prosperous and handsome." She'd hoped for a bear hug, like he'd given Black Bartimaeus. But he hugged her gingerly, diffidently, shyly.

"Me? Nay. I'm the same big, clumsy brute I always was. But you! Jericho, you take my breath away and that's a fact. Let me look at you. Let me feast my eyes." Though she protested, he made her turn around and around. His eyes swept her from head to toe. Polite, he didn't linger on her feminine parts. But he didn't miss them, either. She'd been looked at before. But this was different. This was John. She flushed in delight. A wild thought took wing and soared. Maybe Dove would think she was pretty, too. Instantly, she scolded herself. Did her every thought have to be of Dove?

When he'd finished looking, he swung Mrs. Phipps a teasing grin. "Why didn't you tell me, Mother? Keeping this a deep, dark secret, was you?"

Mrs. Phipps beamed. "I *did* tell you. Don't you read my letters? I wrote you that our Jericho had grown up into a very pretty young woman. I wrote you that she was quite old enough to be *married*."

"But reading it ain't seeing it, now, is it."

"Married." What a peculiar thing for Mrs. Phipps to say. Flustered, Jericho promptly changed the subject and asked about the plague.

John sobered and grew grave. With a few quiet words, he informed them of the city's status. The plague was officially over. To show good faith in the city, King Charles and his court had returned to Whitehall Palace. But summer was a chancy time. Therefore he had decided *not* to let them spend the summer in the city. They would sup and sleep at his house tonight, but tomorrow they would go to Arleigh Castle, at Lady de Mont's invitation. Mrs. Phipps was pleased. Jericho wasn't. Her heart beat unevenly. She wasn't sure she was prepared to see Dove.

John's house on Seething Lane proved to be much like the man, staunch and sturdy, with a look of permanence to it. The handsome, four-story, plank and plaster dwelling stood shoulder-to-shoulder with its neighbors, side walls touching

in what Jericho was beginning to recognize as London's mode
of building. Set upon the high ground of Tower Hill, the
house afforded a lovely view of the Thames River.

Later that evening, after the four of them had dined and
talked to their heart's content, Jericho helped Mrs. Phipps to
bed and saw to Black Bartimaeus's heart tonic, then came
downstairs and rejoined John in his dining chamber.

The dishes had been cleared away. So had the linen table
carpet. A decanter of wine and two pewter cups stood on the
polished table. The candles in the wall sconces burned softly.
Outside, crickets chirped and a breeze blew in the window.
The air smelled totally different here. A moment passed before she could identify the difference. Then it came to her.
America was a continent of pine forest and smelled of it.
England was not and did not. A wave of homesickness washed
over her.

But she took her seat opposite a smiling John and returned
his smile. America was no longer her home. England was.
She would have to get used to it. But suddenly she missed
her loved ones almost more than she could bear. Maritje,
Daisy, Samuels, Goody, Cook.

"A tad more wine, Jericho?"

"I oughtn't. I've had plenty. Supper was so merry."

"Feathers. What's a reunion for, if not to take joy in it?"
He poured. She was already aglow with wine. It was dangerous. The more she glowed, the more her thoughts dwelt
on Dove.

She sipped her wine and John sipped his, an easy com-
panionship flowing between them. During supper, John had
teased her gently, vowing he missed her stutter. He'd made
her laugh. Conversation at supper had been merry. Even
Black Bartimaeus had said a few words, and John had mentioned Dove several times during the meal, but in a general
way. Loosened with wine, she ached to ask specifics. Did
Dove remember her? Did he ever mention her, speak of her?

"That was a wonderful supper John."

"No more'n you deserve."

"I fear we ate like starved gluttons. Especially the salad
greens and the strawberries."

He chuckled softly. " 'Tis a long voyage without greens, with only salted meat and hard biscuit." He leaned back in his chair, comfortably hooked an elbow over the chairback and gazed at her. "I like the way you are with Mother, Jericho. You're as good to her as a daughter would be."

"I love her. She's been a mother to me."

"I can see that."

Jericho smiled at him. With a sudden surge of sympathy, she said, "John? I have been wanting to tell you. I was very sorry to hear of your wife's death."

"I'm obliged, Jericho. Thank you."

"All of us were. Daisy, Samuels, Goody, Cook. Black Bartimaeus, too. Mrs. Phipps cried when she got your letter. The very next day, she began making plans to return to England."

"Thank you, Jericho. That's most kind to say." He drew a breath and picked up his wine cup. He didn't drink. He merely swirled it. The pewter caught the candlelight and threw dots of light upon the polished table top. He stared at the dots, musing.

"Ay," he mused softly. "Emily was sixteen when I married her, seventeen when I buried her. Ay, Jericho. It gives a man pause to know that the seed he plants in a woman can kill 'er."

Jericho gently watched him. "But she wanted the baby, didn't she? I would, if I were married."

"Oh, ay. She wanted it. We both did. We was silly as two children when we learned she'd quickened." He shook his head helplessly.

"It's a risk women take, John."

"Ay. But should they? I dunno."

Jericho's heart beat softly for him. He swirled the wine in his cup, still not drinking. "Oh, ay. We was fond, Jericho. 'Twas a love match. Emily, she made things . . . cozy for me. You know?"

Her eyes threatened to fill. "Cozy." The word painted a picture of John's loving marriage. She could almost see it— the young wife bustling about her house, making everything ready for her husband. The young husband heading home from work, an eager spring in his step as he neared his front door.

She reached out and put a comforting hand on John's. "You'll marry again some day, John. You will. The day will come when you will want to."

Instantly, his warm hand covered hers. "I believe I will, Jericho. For a long time, I thought not. But now . . ." He gazed at her. "Now I'm believin' I will want to."

She wasn't used to having her hand held. It bothered her. She wanted to pull away. But she couldn't. This was *John*. Besides, he seemed unaware of holding her hand as he sat musing, lost in thought, staring at the candlelight. In an absent-minded way, he rubbed his thumb over the crocheted wristband she wore to hide her birthmark. She stiffened and abruptly jerked her hand away.

John looked up, startled. He looked at her wristband. "I'm sorry, Jericho. I'm a thoughtless fool. I didn't think. It must remind you of that horrid night you was abducted."

A bit shaken, she managed a smile. "It's nothing." But she tucked her hands in her lap.

John leaned forward, concerned. "You don't still have them nightmares? About foxes?"

She shook her head. "I outgrew them. The same way I outgrew the stutter. But . . ."

"But what? Surely you never had no more trouble like that? Surely nobody bothered you?"

She hesitated, then decided to confide in John. "No. No one bothered me. But as I grew up, Mrs. Phipps used to receive a letter from London every year, asking to buy me, to buy my indenture."

"Who from, for heaven's sake?"

"We don't know. The letters came from an agent who did not name the person he represented. Mrs. Phipps just tore the letters up and tossed them into the fire. But the letters worried me, John."

John frowned deeply. Then the frown faded, replaced by a teasing smile. "Of course, someone wanted to buy you. Likely some man who'd visited New Amsterdam and had seen you. You're a beautiful girl, Jericho. What man *wouldn't* try to buy you?"

She didn't believe that was it. It was more. A sensitive man, John saw her distress and promptly changed the subject. Topping her wine cup, he leaned forward in a sprightly, vigorous manner and launched conversation in a happier direction.

"So Jericho. Tell me about your life!"

She smiled. There wasn't much to tell, but she told him what there was. After dame school, she'd attended Latin grammar school at the fort. After that, she'd taught dame school herself. She loved children, she loved teaching. She intended to have her own dame school someday.

"Now, I *am* impressed," John said when she finished, his warm brown eyes smiling. It was pleasant being praised by John, and she flushed. He toyed with his wine cup. "What about suitors? Surely there were suitors in New Amsterdam."

She laughed. "I'm a bondslave. Bondslaves cannot marry."

"But suitors did try?"

"Mrs. Phipps sent them packing."

"Did you mind?"

"No." She took a sip of wine and felt the glow of it. Suitors. After knowing Dove, what suitor could measure up? He would be the standard she measured against for the rest of her life.

"Then there's no one you're sweet on? Back there?"

"No. Not really. No one."

"I'm glad to hear it!" he said with enthusiasm.

She looked up in surprise, but he immediately took the conversation in a different direction. For the next hour they talked happily. She told John all about New Amsterdam. New Amsterdam was New York now, but she couldn't get used to calling it that. Nor could he. At one point in their talk, John's eyes lit with a spark of interest. She'd mentioned Lizzie, his old sweetheart at Ten Boom's tap house.

But as the candles burned lower and the evening slipped away, she knew her chance to ask about Dove was fast vanishing. Aglow with wine, she boldly seized the moment.

"John. Tell me about Dove."

"Tell you what about Dove?"

She turned her pewter cup round and round in her hand, careful not to spill the wine, careful not to spill what was in her heart. Outside, in the balmy darkness, the crickets chirped loudly, and in the quiet of the night she could hear sounds drifting up from the river. The tide was in. Ships' winches cranked, cranking up anchor chains as ships prepared to sail.

"What is he like these days? Is he the same?"

John leaned on his elbows and smiled. "He's the same. A wild man, an arrogant jackass. And the best and truest friend a man ever had."

"Then he's the same."

"He's the same."

"Oh," she breathed in relief. "I don't know why that pleases me so. But it does. I didn't want him to be changed."

John gave her a puzzled smile.

"John?" Her wine cup shook a little. She set it down. "Does-does he e-ever—w-well—talk about me? Mention me? Talk to you about me?"

His puzzled face went blank. He stared at her. Then, in a voice that was suddenly too hearty, he said, "Why of course he does! Great heaven. He mentions you all the time. Why, the last time I was at Arleigh Castle, he said t' me, 'John, I wonder how our Jericho is doing? I wonder how she is?' "

She had her answer.

Dove never spoke of her at all. He never even gave her a thought. She wasn't even a jot or tittle in his busy lordly life. The pain and anger were blinding. He'd promised a little girl he would keep her! But he'd gone off and forgotten her as if she'd been no more than a mildly annoying gnat that had buzzed round his head. True, he'd sent money for her upkeep. But that didn't count. The little girl who'd grown up waiting year after year for her master to send for her, hadn't wanted money. She'd wanted Dove.

She managed to hold her head high and smile at John. "He's well and happy, then."

"Dove's more'n well and happy, Jericho," John said, warming to his subject. "He's on top o' the world. Nay, he's the happiest fellow *in* the world. I'll tell you a secret. Dove is going to be married."

Why did that hurt so? He was nothing to her and she was

nothing to him! Yet, several moments passed before she could speak.

"Well," she said. "That's wonderful, John."

"I'm truly glad you think so. It's more'n wonderful. You'll rejoice for Dove when you hear. Can you guess who Dove's going to marry?"

She shook her head. She didn't want to know, either.

"Remember the lady whose letters you was always swiping and hiding when you was a little girl and head-over-heels for Dove? Her. Lady Marguerite."

Jericho was dismayed. "But she's married, isn't she?"

He took a swallow of wine. "Was. *Was* married. Marguerite's husband passed away in France last winter. She will sail from France any day now. She and Dove will be married this summer. At Arleigh Castle."

Her heart absorbed it. Took the full assault of it.

"Well," she said shakily, "I'm glad Dove is getting what he wants." Then, unable to bear more, she rose unsteadily. "John, I drank too much wine. I want to go to bed."

"Of course!" His chair scraped and he was around the table in a bound. Taking a candlestick, he lighted it at the wall sconce, then took her by the hand and led her upstairs to the room she was sharing with Mrs. Phipps. At the door, he gave her the candle and smiled gently.

"Dove was right."

"What?"

"Years ago. In New Amsterdam. What he used to call you. He was right. You *do* have pansy eyes."

He leaned forward to salute her. Expecting a salute on the cheek, she was startled to get one on the lips. It was a real kiss, and definitely not a mistake. Bidding her good night, he swung off down the hall.

She watched him go. Dear life! Was John courting her?

Chapter Ten

" 'Od's blood!"

It wasn't like John to curse, but he cursed now as the coach lurched into a spine-jarring pothole and emerged listing, leaning to one side, causing all of them to slide a little on the leather cushions. Immediately, the driver shouted "Whoa" and pulled up the horses. When they got out on the country road, the driver was standing there in the settling dust, hat in hand.

"I'm sorry, sir. I didn't see the pothole until I were on top o' 'er. The axle, sir. I fear she's cracked."

John sighed. "No use cryin' over spilt milk. We'll rig it as best we can. When we get to Arleigh Castle, you can fix it proper. Let's get to work."

The men peeled off their coats and rolled their sleeves. Jericho led Mrs. Phipps and Pax to shade. They watched the men work. It was laborious toil. The coach had to be unloaded, the trunks unstrapped and lifted down. Among the trunks was one that made Jericho squirm. A trunk of John's wife's gowns. John had insisted she have them. She'd tried to refuse. They represented too intimate a gift. But Mrs. Phipps had sided with John. She'd given Jericho's cheek a fond pinch. "Take them, silly goose!"

The men put their shoulders and backs into the work, sweating and slaving for an hour before the coach stopped listing and stood upright again. Finished at last, they were about to board and be on their way when horse hooves sounded and three of the most enormous dogs Jericho'd ever seen came streaking down the road. She grabbed Pax and held onto him. At first she'd thought them wolves. Covered with wolf shag, they had huge heads and long, skinny bodies. She was relieved when a whistle shrilled and the beasts whirled and streaked back to the approaching hunting party.

Six horsemen came trotting, a spare horse carrying the draped, gutted carcass of a deer, its pink tongue protruding, its soulful eyes glazed in death.

"Curtsy, Jericho," Mrs. Phipps whispered, tugging at Jericho's skirt. " 'Tis His Grace, the duke of Blackpool."

They both curtsied. Jericho didn't need to wonder which one was the duke. Haughty and erect, he rode up to them on a high-spirited stallion, the enormous dogs flanking his horse, docile now. John respectfully introduced his party, but Jericho sensed John disliked both the duke and the duke's steward, a weasel of a man he addressed as Fox Hazlitt. Fox. It wasn't a name she liked. Long ago, she'd figured out that the men who'd abducted her that Christmas Day hadn't been talking about a fox; they'd meant a man named Fox. But this was England, not New Amsterdam. Fox was a common nickname. She'd heard it often. Still, she felt uneasy.

A haughty man, the duke took no interest in the introductions until John presented her. Then his dark eyes turned to frost. For an instant, he gazed at her so coldly she almost jumped.

"The duke disliked me. I felt it," she said to Mrs. Phipps when the hunting party had trotted on, leaving a trail of dust swirls and dripping deer blood in its wake.

"Nonsense. 'Tis merely his way. He likes no one. I remember him as a boy. Butter wouldn't melt in his mouth. I have always felt sorry for his duchess, Lady Angelina. She was to have married Master Dove's uncle, Lord Aubrey, you know. They'd been in love since childhood. But Blackpool prevailed. She was forced to marry him. And what could Lord Aubrey do? He was only a boy of fifteen or sixteen himself."

Jericho had to hide a smile. Always scolding Daisy for gossiping, Mrs. Phipps was quite a gossip herself. But her smile faded as she glanced down and saw her wristband had slipped. She hoped the duke hadn't seen her birthmark. She didn't like anyone to see it.

"What sort of dogs were those?" she asked John, as he helped her into the coach. "They look as if they could snap a sturgeon in two."

"Wolfhounds," John answered with a smile. "And they could. Blackpool breeds 'em for hunting." Pax leaped into the coach, and John leaned down and scratched his ears. "As for you, old pirate, you'd best stay clear of them. They'd chomp you down in two gulps."

"Don't say that." Jericho wasn't afraid of dogs. But these hadn't been dogs, they'd been queer beasts.

John shot her a puzzled look. "I was only teasin'."

"Well, don't!"

John cooled his heels for an hour after they'd arrived at Arleigh Castle, then, losing patience, tapped on the door of Jericho's sleeping closet. When she didn't answer, he opened the door and poked his head in. Just as he'd suspected. She was sitting on her cot looking as if Doomsday had come. He'd guessed she would feel that way once she got a gander of Arleigh Castle. The social chasm between bondslave and lord was all too apparent.

"Come'a, Jericho. I'll give you a tour."

"No."

He knew why. She was scared to see Dove.

"Come'a," he coaxed. "I was born here. Come'a. Let me show you everything. 'Twould be my pleasure . . ."

Stubborn, she shook her head. He rubbed his broad palm on the edge of the door. He understood her now. Last night he hadn't. He'd lain awake half the night, trying to puzzle her out, trying to think why she was so skittish whenever the subject was Dove. It had evaded him. He'd tossed and turned in his empty, lonely, womanless bed. Finally the answer had hit him like a brick. She was still head-over-heels! She'd grown up, but she hadn't grown *out* of that.

Great heaven. He'd spent the rest of the night wondering what to do about it. For he was fast losing his heart. Oh no, he didn't need Mother's clumsy hints. The idea had sprung

into his head the moment he'd set eyes on her at St. Katherine's Docks. He wanted her for his wife.

"You can't hide in here forever."

She gave him an irritated look. "I'm not hiding."

"No? Then come."

She wasn't one to duck a challenge. That's what he liked
best about her. Goaded, she rose, and, with a glance in the
small looking glass to check for tidiness, came with him. But
not happily, he noted. He sighed. This courtship would take
some doing.

Jericho found herself trembling as she went with John. She
scolded herself. You're a grown woman, not a child! Behave
with sense. When you see Dove, behave like a proper bondservant. Curtsy, address him as 'Lord' Dove and speak only
when spoken to. Her plans formulated, she felt better. But
why wouldn't her stupid hands stop shaking?

"Is . . . Lord Dove in?" she asked cautiously.

John cocked an eyebrow at her as he led her through the
maze of busy kitchens. "So it's 'Lord' Dove now, is it? I
feared it might be, once you got a glimpse of the castle. 'Tis
a bit overwhelming, ain't it."

"It's not overwhelming," she answered tartly. "It's ob-
scene."

Stifling heat rolled through the meat kitchen. Little bow-
legged turnspit dogs trotted gallantly in their cylinder cages,
turning the spits. She glanced at them with sympathy, glad
Pax didn't have to labor like that.

John chuckled. "Come now. You're not going to hold it
against the de Monts that they have wealth, are you? As to
Dove's whereabouts?" He gave her a searching look. "Nay,
he's not in. He's out somewheres. With his brother, Lark.
But don't fret. If you don't see Dove today, you'll see him
tomorrow."

"I don't care if I ever see him."

"Do tell!"

She looked at him askance. Had John guessed? He couldn't.
She hadn't said a word. Wary of him—John was smarter
than she'd remembered—she stepped out into the sunny
castleyard as he held the door for her. Her spirits lifted.

A breeze blew from the river. She could smell sweet meadow grass.

"I've decided, John. I'm going to ask Dove to release me from my indenture. Now. Before I'm twenty-one. I want to get on with my life. I don't want to belong to a master forever."

He eyed her skeptically. And cows can fly, he thought.

The tour proved more than awesome. It proved thrilling. John took her to the windy battlements where they sat upon iron cannons and feasted their eyes on the sweeping view of meadow and fields and woods and river. He took her to the rich gilded state apartment that was kept in readiness for the king's visits. As the afternoon wore on, she saw more gilded leather, more gilded woodwork, more marble and brocade and paintings than she'd dreamed existed in the whole world.

The result? She felt ridiculous. What a goose she'd been, a bondslave child in love with a lord, boasting to Maritje Ten Boom that when she grew up Dove was going to marry her! It was a wonder he hadn't pinned her ears to the privy wall along with the wolfheads. Her heart softened toward him. Dove had been kinder to her than she'd guessed.

Brooding on that, crossing the stone-paved castleyard with John, she glanced up and suddenly saw a figure that made her heart jump. "John! That man heading for the stables. Isn't it Mr. d'Orias? What is *he* doing here?" D'Orias's dark distinctive figure was unmistakeable. His long, black, knife-straight hair swung against his wide shoulders as he walked.

"Ay, it's d'Orias. As to what he's doin' here . . ." John gave her a teasing smile but said no more. With a wave, d'Orias changed direction and came toward them. D'Orias greeted John and nodded to her pleasantly, but didn't recognize her until John prodded. Then he clapped his hand to his forehead.

"Ah! *Si, Si.* Dove's little skater from New Amsterdam."

"You saved my life in New Amsterdam, sir. I have kept you in my prayers all these years."

A gallant man, he denied it, but said, "*Grazie.* I thank you for keeping me in your prayers." His warm eyes twinkled. "I trust you have kept Dove there as well?" She flushed.

Had she worn her heart on her sleeve as a child? Probably so. He swung his dark head to John. "Has Dove seen her yet?"

"No."

"Well, well," he said, smiling. "This should prove an interesting summer."

John disliked the remark. His grip on her hand tightened, and d'Orias didn't miss it. It was an awkward moment, but it dissipated when a lady stepped out of the castle into the bright sunshine. Their attention flew there. Jericho didn't need to ask who the lady was. She had Dove's bright golden hair and his jaunty walk. She was holding the hand of an adorable little girl who had black, knife-straight hair. Spotting d'Orias, the child broke free and came running.

"Papa! Mama says I may go riding with you and her." Jericho looked at John in astonishment. He winked.

"Did she, my precious?" D'Orias squatted, scooped up the child and kissed her. "Then you may. I am to have a double treat today, am I? I am to go riding with not *one* beautiful woman, but two? *Si?*"

The child giggled and smacked her lips to his. *"Si."*

Lady de Mont arrived on the heels of her daughter. Jericho could see that Dove's mother and d'Orias were deeply in love. The did nothing overt to display it, but whenever their eyes met, it was with staunch pride. Lady de Mont greeted John warmly, and when John presented her, Jericho curtsied, all but tongue-tied before the great lady. Lady de Mont, however, was most civil to her.

"We must find you a pleasant occupation here at Arleigh Castle, Jericho." The golden head swung in Dove's lightning quick way. "What do you think, Leonardo? Perhaps the girl would enjoy being chamber maid to Dove's Marguerite when she arrives."

Jericho was stricken. Watch Dove with his Marguerite, the way she'd watched him with Mrs. Verplanck? Her eyes flew to d'Orias. He gazed at her thoughtfully.

"My lady, I think not," d'Orias interceded smoothly. "I daresay the girl can better serve in some other capacity."

"Oh?" Indifferent, Lady de Mont shrugged elegantly and pounced on a new topic, the London plague. The three talked solemnly for a bit, and then, with their little daughter Ginevra tugging impatiently at d'Orias's hair, demanding her ride, he and Lady de Mont strode on to the stables.

Crossing the castleyard with John, Jericho fell silent, full of distress and unhappy thoughts. Misreading her silence, John squeezed her hand. "You mustn't think ill of them. 'Tis rumored they are secretly married."

She glanced up. "What? Oh. I could never think ill of Mr. d'Orias. As for Lady de Mont, she is so like Dove that I . . . I could not dislike her, even if I tried."

John's jaw tightened. Had she said something wrong? With a rare display of testiness, he lectured her. "Even if it turns out they ain't married, Jericho, you'd best remember one thing. The nobility's different from you and me. They live by their own standards and answer to no one. They do as they please. God knows, *Dove* certainly has."

Their footfalls echoed off the castleyard's paving stones.

"You mean like Mrs. Verplanck. In New Amsterdam."

John's big hand shifted to hold hers more securely. "That's exactly what I mean. When Dove sailed out of New Amsterdam, he forgot Hildegarde Verplanck as easy as—as easy as a man'd forget a used handkerchief."

A solemn warning. Jericho took it to heart. She didn't want to be a Mrs. Verplanck. Not even for Dove. Giving John a smile, she said, "Is there any more of this obscenely rich castle to see, John?"

He flashed her an approving smile. "Tons!"

Comfortable with one another, enjoying each other's company, they stopped for cider in the kitchen, then roamed on. They were in a corridor, admiring the new parquet flooring that had come from France, when, at the distant end of the gilded corridor, masculine laughter rang out. Two magnificent goldenhaired men swung into view. They wore riding boots, snug breeches, and loose white shirts. Deeply tanned, they were laughing, talking, and striding along like healthy young panthers.

She clutched John's hand. "Who are they?"

"I think you know, Jericho. And the man with him is his brother, Lord Lark."

"Stay with me!"

He gave her hand a pleased squeeze. "Count on it. Wild horses couldn't budge me." Even as John murmured, the men's voices grew louder and more jovial, and then the men parted, Lord Lark swinging off into another corridor, Dove striding toward them alone, his long golden hair brighter than the gilded woodwork that arched around him.

"John!" he called out, his voice echoing down the long corridor. "This is wonderful. Any news yet of Mrs. Phipps? When will her ship arrive?"

"It's come," John called. "She's here."

"Splendid! I want to see her."

Jericho's rapid breathing matched the quick pace of his stride. Oh dear God. He was everything she remembered and more. Eighteen was twenty-seven. He was taller, broader of shoulder, handsomer. But he was still Dove. She saw it in the way he cocked his head in curiosity as he came toward her. She saw it in the undimmed brightness of his eyes. For an instant, the years vanished and she was eleven years old, standing barefoot in the lane outside Dieter Ten Boom's tap house, clutching her bundle, scared and tired and hungry, yearning for someone to take her home and keep her. She took a step. John gripped her hand.

"Jericho, don't. You'll regret it."

Without thought, she wrenched free.

"Dove!" she croaked, picked up her skirts and flew.

Dove halted in mid-step, startled. Who in hell was she? He stared in amazement as the most beautiful girl he'd ever seen came hurtling toward him, croaking his name. *Deja vu* slammed him in the pit of his stomach. That hair, those eyes . . .

Floundering, he glanced at John, desperate for a clue. Shoulders angrily hunched, John pumped his way up the corridor, but not fast enough. The girl reached him first—sweet, happy, eager, trembling. Dear God, those eyes . . .

"Dove!"

"Yes, well . . ."

"Dove, don't you remember me?"

He grasped at straws. He'd slept with a red haired girl one

drunken night in London. She'd been pretty. But not this pretty. And what would she be doing here? He'd been very drunk. Maybe he'd made some idiotic promise. Her vivid eyes begged to be remembered.

"Of course I remember," he said quickly. "The George and Vulture. The room on the third floor. In the morning, when the oystermonger's cart came rattling down the lane, we let down a bucket on a rope and broke our fast with oysters." He smiled at her. "We ate them in bed. I remember perfectly. The innkeeper had a fit. His sheets."

The brilliant, deep blue eyes widened in shock. He was astonished to see a flash of outrage. She backed away. Backed away as if he had a roaring case of the pox. Picking up her skirts, she whirled and fled. John tried to catch her as she barreled past, but she swatted his hand away and flew down the corridor. An instant later, a door slammed somewhere in the castle, loud and angry. He was astonished.

"Who *was* that?" he demanded. "That exquisite girl?"

"It's Jericho, you damned fool."

"Jericho! Jericho who?"

"How many Jerichoes do you know?"

"But—it—can't be. Jericho's no bigger than—no taller than—" Stunned, Dove sketched a short skinny eleven-year-old with his hands. "And she's in New Amsterdam."

"Thickhead! Mother arrived yesterday. She brought Jericho with her on the voyage. Black Bartimaeus, too. She's grown up, Dove. That was Jericho. Damn it, it's been eight, nine *years* since we left New Amsterdam."

"Has it?" Dove's mouth fell open. He stared down the empty corridor. "Oh, my God. It's Jericho, and I've insulted her. I took her for a girl I slept with, John, and she knows it. Hell, I'd best go after her!"

John caught his arm. "I want to talk to you."

Dove shucked him off. "Later! Hell, John, that was *Jericho*."

"*Now*."

Dove paused. It wasn't like John to insist. Surprised, Dove swept John's face with a glance and saw anxiety, worry. He'd not seen that look since the awful days when Emily . . .

"All right."

"In private."

"Yes." They went rapidly to Dove's apartment, strode in through the salon, through the bedchamber and into Dove's work closet. It was a commodious room with man-size chairs and a long writing table. A locked mahogany cabinet for private papers dominated one whole wall. They helped themselves to rum. Dove slung himself onto the cushioned window seat and impatiently waited for John to speak. It was no use trying to hurry him. He'd have better luck trying to light a fire under a walrus.

Waiting, he gazed out at the familiar view—meadow, fields, copses, green rolling countryside. In the meadow, a girl with red hair was running like thunder. He smiled softly. So that was Jericho, was it? Dear God, she was pretty. She looked angry enough to run all the way to Timbuktu. Dove watched, enchanted.

Strolling to the window, John watched too, then slugged down his rum in a single gulp. Dove lifted an eyebrow. John was a temperate drinker, rarely drinking rum, let alone swilling it. Dove waited with growing interest as John chose a chair, sat, and crossed one leg upon the other.

"How many maidenheads have you had over the years, Dove? How many cherries have you picked?"

Dove looked at him, startled. "Say what you mean."

"Indulge me. How many?"

Dove gave him a long piercing look. "Not as many as people think."

"But enough."

"Enough."

"Then you do not need Jericho's."

There was a long moment of silence. "Again, I make the same request. Say what you mean."

"I b'lieve I'm falling in love with her, Dove. I b'lieve I want to make her my wife."

Dove set his rum cup down. Out in the meadow, Jericho had stopped running. Now she stomped along, angrily putting distance between herself and the castle. Her flaming red hair was a lovely contrast to the green meadow. His lips parted softly as she cast an angry glance at the castle. John wanted to marry her. He felt a queer, possessive sting. And why should he? He'd scarcely thought of the grubworm in years. Yet the thought of John marrying her . . .

"And Pansy Eyes. She wants to marry you?" *Pansy Eyes*. It startled him. Where had that pet name come from? Out of some dusty closet in his mind? He hadn't thought of it in years.

"I have not yet asked her. There are two problems, Dove. The first is Jericho's indenture. You own it. Legally, she is yours until she is twenty-one."

Dove absently gouged the cushion with his heel. The round-bottomed rum cup keeled over and rum flowed onto the green silk. He scarcely noticed. Jericho, married. The grubworm, married. It didn't feel right. This is John asking, damn it! Your best friend. Dove lunged to his feet, went to his writing table, fished out a key and unlocked his mahogany cabinet, flinging the doors open. The inside was honeycombed with shelves, drawers, pigeon holes—all of the papers neatly arranged.

"Her indenture is likely in here. Dig it out. Or ask my steward to do it. I'll sign it over to you. She is yours."

"I am obliged, Dove. But that wouldn't serve the purpose. You'll oblige me more by giving Jericho her freedom. When she asks for it."

When she asks for it. It was a foreign thought. Somehow, he'd never pictured the grubworm wanting to be free of him. It hurt a little. But he smiled blithely.

"Done. The second problem?"

John took his time answering. "She is in love with you."

It caught him off guard. He waited for the joke. When it didn't come, he prompted. "You jest."

"Nay. She's in love with you. Head over heels. Call it puppy love, if you want, but I b'lieve she never got over her childhood worship of you. You are her hero. She loves you."

Dove glanced out the window. The anger had gone out of the distant figure. Now she trailed along disconsolately, her fine straight shoulders slumped. Somewhere along the way, she'd picked up a stick. Idly, she batted it.

"She's a grand girl, Dove. It's not just how pretty she is. It's more." John rattled on, a man in love. Dove listened to all the good things about Jericho without surprise, but with a lowering of spirits. Unable to take more, he cut John short.

"Why is it I sense a request coming? And one that I will not relish?"

At ease now, John laughed and settled into his chair. Reaching for for the rum decanter, he poured himself a small bit and this time sipped it.

"I want you to let her down easy. Be good to her this summer while she's here in Arleigh Castle. Show her a bit of attention. She may be grown up, but inside she's still the same, sensitive little sweeting she was in New Amsterdam. I want her to have time t'get over her fancy for you, Dove. When she does, when the time's right, I'll ask her to marry me."

Dove folded his arms. "Let me get this straight. What you're really asking me to do is play nursemaid to her maidenhead. Guard it so nobody else gets to her before you do. Is that it?"

John smiled faintly. "That's the general idea."

"That's a hell of thing to ask of a friend."

"You've asked more of *me*."

John was right. Dove *had* asked more. Year after year of their friendship, Dove had asked more, while John asked nothing.

"I'm willing to do more than ask, Dove," John said softly. "If you want, I'll get down on my knees and beg. Don't take Jericho to bed."

Dove looked at him. A warmth had returned to John. There was an expectant happiness in him that Dove hadn't seen since before Emily's death.

"Don't talk nonsense! I told you she was yours and I meant it. I won't tamper with her, and I won't let anyone else tamper. I'll take care of her. I give you my word." To seal the pledge, he stripped off his gold signet ring and slung it to John's lap.

John shook his head. "I don't need your ring, Dove. Your word is gold with me."

"Maybe *I* need you to have it. Maybe *I* need to see the empty space on my finger." He glanced out the window. "Pansy Eyes is as lovely as—as a summer day. And this has been a long, celibate season for me, waiting for Marguerite."

John hesitated, then rammed the ring onto his finger. He got to his feet. "If you cross me in this, Dove . . ."

"I won't cross you. Hell, John, I've reformed! From now on I'm a one-woman man. When Marguerite arrives, I intend to keep her so busy in bed she'll walk bow-legged."

When John eyed him skeptically, Dove retrieved his cup, topped it with a splash of rum and topped John's. He toasted.

"Here's to this summer. To two weddings, eh? Mine and Marguerite's, and yours and Jericho's. Drink to it?"

John hesitated, then clicked his cup to Dove's. A brotherly sound. Then, arms draped around each other's shoulder, they stood at the window, looking out. Jericho was a small, distant figure, trailing forlornly across the meadow.

"Your bride-to-be is heading toward the woods," Dove said. "She might get lost. Hadn't you better go after her?"

John smiled his trusting smile.

"Nay. It's not me she's longing to see."

Jericho ran until she could run no more. Then, breathless, she halted and stared about her. A field full of sheep. How apt, she thought. Sheep were stupid. So was she.

Miserable and heartsore, she tramped on, putting the castle behind her. He hadn't even remembered her. Worse, he'd thought her a tart. Oh, why had she ever left New Amsterdam!

Discouraged, she picked up a stick and idly batted at buttercups. She wandered up a slope and dropped to rest under an ancient oak tree that was surely as old as the castle. She stared at the distant castle. Let him live in it.

She was sitting there, arms wrapped around knees, when she saw Dove coming for her. A distant figure, golden hair blowing in the wind, he came loping over the meadow, his step distinctively Dove, lighthearted and jaunty. She turned her back on him and stared out at the river.

Before long, his step came springing up the slope. He dropped down to sit beside her. Grass rustled as he leisurely stretched out, making himself comfortable. She gave him her back.

"Hello, grubworm."

Her heart contracted. But she stared resolutely out at the river.

"I'm sorry about what happened back there. I'm sorry I mistook you for a wench. Not that you look like a wench," he added quickly. "Hell, you look as much like a wench as a church looks like a tap house."

Tears burned. She refused to shed them.

"Suppose we start anew. Suppose I say, 'Hello, Jericho. I'm glad as hell to see you.' Suppose you say, 'Hello, Dove. So am I.' "

She stared at the river. Dove sighed. Ornery as a porcupine. This was Jericho, all right. What had she used to spout at him in New Amsterdam the few startling times she'd blown her top? *You're mean, Dove.* Only she'd pronounced it "m-m-mean."

He smiled in fascination. Did she still stutter? He hoped so. He'd never said, but he'd liked her stutter. It had been charming.

He let time pass. Impatient with all else in life, he had infinite patience when it came to women. He liked women. So he waited and picked grass. Tossed it blade by blade at her stiff back. Sunshine sprinkled down through the oak leaves. Clouds sailed by. The river rippled. Behind him, back in the meadow, a ewe bleated, calling its wandering lamb.

"We used to be friends, grubworm. What happened? You used to like me well enough to track me all over New Amsterdam. You and that butter-box friend of yours. What was her name? Mary? Martha?"

"Maritje!"

Ornery as a corncrake. Still, he was making progress, wasn't he? At least she'd spoken to him.

"Maritje. That's right, I'd forgot."

"You forget everything!" She almost took his head off. Dove gazed at her back, astounded. What in hell was *that* all about? He hadn't a clue. He let a few more judicious minutes pass. He tossed grass. Then, when he judged the time right, he reached out and gave her skirt a playful tug.

"Hello, grubworm. I'm glad as hell to see you."

Jericho's throat throbbed. She could no more resist Dove, or stay angry with Dove de Mont than she could stay angry with a thoughtless child. Reluctantly, warily, she turned. She tucked her legs under her, shielding them with her petticoats, wishing she had a similar shield for her heart.

He was so handsome. He lounged on his side, handsome as a prince, casually propped on one elbow. Plucking blades of grass, he was flicking them away in boredom. His busy hands stopped as she mustered her dignity and met his eyes.

"Hello, Dove. So am I."

Dove felt a queer stab. For a moment, his head completely emptied. *Lord, what hair, what eyes!* John flew to mind. An unwelcome intrusion. He cleared his throat.

"You've grown up. You're damned pretty, grubworm."

"Y-you l-look well, Dove."

She still stuttered! Fascinated, he stared into those vivid eyes, stared until she grew uncomfortable and withdrew her gaze. She grew very busy, nervously pleating a fold in her cheap green skirt, pleating it over and over, pressing it with slender fingers.

"W-we had a safe crossing," she offered. "Decent weather most of the way. Only one bad storm. Black Bartimaeus and I fared fine, but Mrs. Phipps suffered dreadfully. She was terribly seasick."

"That's good," he said, transfixed. Did gangly brats grow up like this? Grow into beauties overnight?

She looked up, eyes bright with surprise.

He recouped. "I mean it's good you had a safe crossing. It's too bad Mrs. Phipps was seasick."

"Oh. Y-yes." She gave him a wary smile. Her first. Iridescent chips of blue glowed deep in her eyes when she smiled. *So this was Jericho!*

"W-we brought Pax along. I hope you do not mind."

He was mesmerized. Ugly duckling into swan. Caterpillar into butterfly. "Who?"

She gently prompted him. "My dog. Rather, he is Black Bartimaeus's dog now. They've grown old together. They are completely devoted."

"No, hell, I don't mind. Bring anybody you want. The more, the merrier." He couldn't stop staring at her. He wondered if she was a virgin. John thought so. He thought so, too. A girl had a different look in her eyes once she'd strolled down the lane.

"Shall we take a stroll? We've a lot to catch up on."

He was amazed when his simple invitation caused her distress. Didn't she want to be with him? He was as astonished as he was hurt. It stung.

"You don't *have* to stroll with me, Jericho. It's not a command, it's an invitation. Feel free to say no."

She worked the pleat in distress. "I-I w-would like to."

Dove eagerly jumped up and extended a hand, but she pretended not to see it and got up by herself. That stung, too. She didn't want him to touch her. Taking care to respect that, he led her to the river path. In love with him? John had rocks in his head.

They walked along the river and talked. Conversation was stiff at first, but that was to be expected. She was wary of him, and he was damned puzzled by her. They talked in fits, starts, fragments. Her small bursts of loquacity were followed by self-conscious silences and sidelong glances.

He tried to put her at ease. He told her about his own life since leaving New Amsterdam. He asked her about hers. By asking a series of nonchalant questions as they walked, he reached the same conclusion as John. She was a virgin. She'd led a sheltered life. Mrs. Phipps had kept her under her thumb.

A virgin. It pleased him. He was surprised. Hell, a verdict in the negative would've given him *carte blanche*. Not even John would expect him to keep his hands off a beauty who'd already been down the lane. Yet he found himself pleased.

John. He glanced down at his hand. The missing signet ring had left a band of pale, untanned skin. *"Let her down easy."* A hell of a thing to ask a friend. Was she in love with him?

They came to a half-dead willow tree that he and John had

played in as boys. The tree grew almost horizontal, jutting out over the water, its lower, dead, leafless limbs making ideal fishing seats. "Shall we?" he said, leaping up on the limb. It shuddered.

She looked at the limb dubiously, then at him. But she was Jericho. The brat he'd known in New Amsterdam had never backed away from a dare. Taking hold of a hanging branch, she boosted herself up and stepped out on the limb, too. Holding onto branches, they inched their way out, then sat side by side, feet pleasantly dangling above the shallow sunny water. With their combined weight, the limb creaked a time or two. She threw him an alarmed look.

"Dove, is this safe?"

"Perfectly. I have fished here a thousand times."

John. *"Let her down easy."* He bit the bullet.

"Have you heard my good news? About my marriage?"

She looked out at the river. "Yes. John told me."

"Congratulate me, Jericho. Don't be stingy."

"I hope you will be very happy."

"Happy? We'll be delirious. I doubt we'll get out of bed for a month." He studied her for a reaction. There was none. He was mildly disappointed. Hell, she was supposed to be in love with him. Vexed, he probed. "You *do* know about bed, don't you, grubworm?"

"I'm not a child, Dove!" Salty, definitely salty.

"No," he agreed. "Of course not." He thought it best to swallow his smile. "A stroke of luck, Marguerite's fat old shoat of a husband kicking the bucket. He died at table, you know. Choked to death stuffing himself with roasted pig. Appropriate, eh? A pig doing in a pig?"

She shrugged.

Let her down easy. "Marguerite and I have been in love since we were children. Can you feature that?" He watched her again. More vexation. She merely shrugged. He plucked twigs from the limb overhead and tossed them into the river. They landed with soft plinks. Minnows darted up to investigate. "We would have become betrothed, but the war spoiled things. Marguerite's guardian sided with Cromwell. We de Monts naturally remained loyal to the king. Marguerite's guardian forced her to wed. When I returned from New Amsterdam, her marriage was a *fait accompli*. She was already gone, tucked away in France.''

To his surprise, she threw him an angry look.

''If I loved a man, *no one* could make me marry someone else. I would find a way to wait. An army of 'guardians' couldn't drag me to the altar.''

Dove heard this with a good deal of irritation. Though he'd never admitted it, not even to himself, deep in his heart he'd expected Marguerite to behave just like that. He'd expected her to dig in her heels and wait. That Jericho should find his sore spot annoyed him excessively. But he let it pass. They watched the play of sunlight on the water beneath their dangling feet.

''Is she pretty?'' The words came in a leap.

''No, she's beautiful!'' Again she found something to watch out on the river. ''She's beautiful, grubworm. She has dark brown hair, sparkling brown eyes, a small waist and a fantastic pair of—'' He caught himself. ''Never mind. She resembles her older sister, Angelina. The duchess of Blackpool. But Marguerite is much more beautiful.''

A shadow flitted across the picture. It didn't sit well with Dove that his entire family opposed the match. Damn it, Marguerite couldn't help it that she was sister-in-law to that bucket of slime, Blackpool. Besides. The objection was unfair. Hell, Uncle Aubrey and Blackpool were cousins.

''Why isn't she here?''

''She's in France, dunce. Waiting out the London plague. She will come when it's safe. Then we'll be married.''

She looked at him with spirit. ''If *I* loved a man—''

''Say it,'' he warned curtly, ''and so help me I'll tumble you off into the water.'' He gave the limb a warning shake. It creaked.

''Well, I *would*,'' she said, bringing to mind a brat he'd known in New Amsterdam, a brat who'd been forbidden to go skating on Christmas Day and had gone anyway. He couldn't help but smile. This was fascinating. Brat into beauty. Ugly duckling into swan.

''Let's talk about something else,'' he said. ''Tell me about

New Amsterdam. I want to hear about everyone I knew there. Even old Stuyvesant.''

After a moment, her wary smile came into play. "All right.''

Jericho had tried her hardest to resist Dove. But she would've had more success wading into the ocean and forbidding the tide to tug at her. Dove was Dove. He hadn't changed a bit. And, blast it, she still loved him.

So she gave up trying to resist him and let herself enjoy him. It was heaven. Sitting with Dove above sparkling sunny water on a glorious summer day, a river breeze caressing her skin, talking with him, laughing, reminiscing, getting his total attention—it was heaven.

Dove still teased mercilessly of course, and made curt remarks. But that was his way. She didn't want the leopard to change his spots, she only wanted the leopard to like her. And he did. Dove *liked* her. She could see it in his eyes.

They talked playfully of everything under the sun. Dove was so quick. He leaped from topic to topic in lightning fashion, sometimes leaving her a mile behind, her brain racing to catch up.

"Hildegarde Verplanck! Whatever happened to her, grub-worm?''

"She had a baby.''

"When?''

"Approximately nine months after you left.''

He slanted a wary glance at her, golden hair spilling to one shoulder. "And?''

"And what?'' She could tease, too. After all, she'd learned from a master of the art.

"Jericho!''

She kept him in suspense a moment longer, then smiled broadly. "Maritje Ten Boom and I agreed. It was the ugliest baby we'd ever seen. He had enormous ears, a big nose and a squint. Just like Mr. Verplanck.''

Dove chuckled. "Thank God for that.''

"No. You'd best thank Mr. Verplanck for that.''

He threw her an amused look. "Brat,'' he complained.

Her heart fluttered. It was wicked to hope he would kiss her. He belonged to someone else. But she hoped. "Daisy," he demanded, leaping to a new topic. "Tell me about Daisy and Samuels."

"They're doing grand, Dove. They're healthy, happy, prospering. When Dieter Ten Boom died—"

"Ten Boom died?"

"Yes. Moribund throat. Very sad. After, Daisy and Samuels rented the tap house. Samuels cooks and serves up. Daisy rules the tap room. When gamesters get the least bit rambunctious, she raps them on the head with her broom." Dove chuckled appreciatively. "They have six children now," she finished.

"Six? Good lord. They cannot have been married five years."

"They started early."

He threw her another amused look. "So you know about things like that, do you? You know about starting early?

"*Dove*. I've grown up."

"I've noticed. Believe me, grubworm, I've noticed."

Her heart pounded. Whenever he looked at her like that— his hazel eyes bright with admiration—she was in danger of melting. Like a failed pudding. She looked down and fidgeted with her skirt. What if Dove asked her to go to bed with him? Men did that to their bondslaves. Did she have the right to refuse?

But he leaped in a harmless direction.

"All right, grubworm. Earn your keep. Tell me about the day New Amsterdam became New York. I understand not a shot was fired. The colony was only too willing to shuck off Stuyvesant and the Dutch West India Company, eh? I want every detail. Leave out a single detail, and there's gruel in your bowl tonight."

With a smile, she did. She was in the midst of telling how, on a fine spring day in 1664, three English warships bearing the standard of the duke of York had come sailing into the harbor, when—suddenly—the limb they were sitting on creaked ominously.

"Dove—"

It dipped with a lurch. They grabbed for each other.
"Grubworm, we'd best—"
With a loud crack, the limb gave way.

When John strolled down the hill from the castle, wondering where in blazes Dove and Jericho had disappeared to,
he was first relieved, then vexed to see the bedraggled, high-
spirited pair coming across the meadow, striding like young
colts through the late lingering swaths of sunlight, their voices
ringing. They were soaking wet, but as merry as if they'd
come from a party.

John didn't like it a bit. He didn't like the tight way Dove
held her hand, nor the way Dove cocked his head at her in
that goddamned charming manner. Most of all, he didn't like
the way they looked together. They made a dashing couple,
Dove's hair golden bright in the setting sun, Jericho's, a
flaming red. Worse, there was an unnerving harmony between
them. Even their strides matched. Hell, they were suited!
Even a blind man could see it.

He didn't like it a bit. Striding angrily toward the absorbed
couple, he considered his options. In a few days he would
be sending a shipment of gentlemen's hats to France. Suppose
he also sent a letter to Marguerite in Paris? He would hint
that Dove was growing restless waiting for her. Marguerite
was a canny female. If John knew pepper from salt, she would
read between the lines. If Marguerite was as canny as he
remembered, she would sail for England at once. He permitted himself a grim smile. *All's fair in love and war, Dove!*

When he reached the two cheerful chatterboxes, he gave
Dove a look that said plain-out what he thought of the she-
nanigans. But to Jericho, he gave an indulgent smile.

"Let me guess," he said affably. "Dove went and took
you to our fishing tree, now, didn't he. When we was children, he used to dunk Lady Marguerite there about once a
season."

He was almost sorry he'd said it. The bounce went out of
her. Her happy smile softened into unhappy surprise.

"Yes," she admitted, eyes soft with bewilderment. "That's where he took me." Instantly, she withdrew her hand from Dove's. Her hand hadn't belonged there and she knew it.

Dove was irked. "Hell, John, don't make such a big to-do over it. She'll dry out."

"I know," John said pointedly. "Marguerite always did." Then, claiming the slender hand Dove had been holding, he walked along with them, deliberately turning the twosome into a threesome.

Jericho was badly shaken by the afternoon. Sitting at table in the kitchen that evening, eating supper with the young talkative turnspit boys and scullery girls, Jericho brooded, lost in sober thought. She'd almost lost her heart to Dove all over again. She mustn't let that happen. She would end up in bed with Dove. Just like Mrs. Verplanck. And when his stupid Marguerite came, Jericho knew she would be discarded like—like a used handkerchief!

Janie, a ten-year-old scullery girl with big blue eyes and corkscrew curls, leaned over her stew bowl. "Jericho? We was wondering. Are you Lor' Dove's new nightgown lady?"

New nightgown lady? Out of the mouths of babes. Her cheeks heated, and she felt her skin flush pink. Around the table, six pairs of innocent young eyes waited for her answer. Had the children been adults, she would've snapped their heads off.

"No," she said firmly. "Of course not. I would never consider being anyone's nightgown lady. Nor should you when you grow up, Janie. It isn't decent."

"But you like Lor' Dove, don't you, Jericho? We all like Lor' Dove. Ever'body do." Harry. Stick thin, Harry was ten years old, too. He tended the turnspit dogs.

Jericho softened, looking around the table at the worried, waiting faces. The children were as taken with Dove as she had been at eleven.

"I like him," she admitted. "Of course, I like him."

Relieved, the children went diving back to their stew bowls.

But Jericho got up, appetite gone. She took her bowl and scraped it into Pax's. Cheeks still flushed, she strengthened her resolve. From this minute on, she would steer clear of Dove. She would go nowhere near him. She would stay away from him. For she was determined. She was *not* going to be just another Mrs. Verplanck.

Chapter Eleven

John left the next morning. Plague or no plague in London, he had his shops to tend, and he left despite Mrs. Phipps's objections, left with his pockets stuffed full of charms, posset powders, magical incantations—all manner of things friends pressed upon him for good luck, to keep him safe. Worried, remembering the children's rhyme, Jericho gathered a bouquet of "posies" for his pocket. His quiet eyes brightened, and he kissed her cheek.

"I'm obliged, Jericho."

"Stay well, John."

"That's a promise. And here's another." He stuffed the posies into his pocket and swung one booted foot up on the mounting rung of his coach. "I'll be back for Mid-Summer's Eve. 'Tis a country party. 'Tis held in Arleigh Castle meadow every year. The whole parish turns out. Everyone from St. John's Basket. There'll be bonfires and dancing until dawn. I'll escort you."

She felt a prick of dismay. Mid-Summer's Eve? A night traditional to courting couples? "John, I don't think—"

"There's something special I'll be wanting to ask you on Mid-Summer's Eve. With luck, I'll have something special to tell Dove, too. Maybe I'll even be able to *bring* him someone special."

His expression changed. With a glance up at a specific

window in the second story of the castle, he suddenly leaned down and kissed her full on her startled mouth. Then he got into the coach, waved, and rode away.

Up in the second floor of the castle, Dove was dressing in his apartment and watching John's departure as he dressed. When John planted his mouth on Jericho's, Dove gave the shirt ribbons he was tying such a ferocious yank that ribbon parted company from cloth. He glanced, vexed, at the silken scraps, then wrenched the ruined shirt off. Did John *have* to kiss her? Couldn't he make do with a Dutch handshake? Hell's bells, whose bondslave was she, anyhow?

"Uncle Aubrey, halloo up there!"

"Dove, hallooo! I'll be down shortly."

Jericho squinted into the bright May sunshine and made a tent of her hands, letting her gaze climb three stories to the roof of Nordham Hall, trying to match the pleasant, booming voice to any of several men who were scrambling about the rooftop of the enormous old Tudor countryhouse, repairing it. Ropes, pulleys, scaffolding, ladders—all of it spider-webbed the facing of the house, and workmen scampered up and down from ground to roof to ground as surefootedly as sailors in a ship's rigging.

Against her better judgment, Jericho found herself in Dove's company again. Not five minutes after John's coach had rumbled off, Dove had come bounding into the scullery with his beguiling smile, sweet-talking her, trying to coax her into going with him on an errand to his uncle's house. Smarting from the previous afternoon, she'd been prepared to shun him. But when he'd cocked his head at her, looked at her with those bright hazel eyes and called her "beauty," she'd melted, spineless as a wet pudding. So here she was. Vexed with Dove. More vexed with herself. Worse, she'd abandoned duty. Mrs. Phipps's linens needed laundering. Black Barti-maeus' needed a fresh supply of heart tonic mixed. Not least, Pax needed a bath.

"Hallooo, Uncle! Don't bother. We're coming up."

Taking her elbow, he led her to the largest ladder, a solid contraption of oak, braced bottom and top with ropes. He called to two passing workmen to come brace it further. Surely he didn't mean her to climb it? She squinted, looking up three stories to the distant roof.

"Dove, don't be ridiculous. I cannot."

"Why not?"

"I'll fall."*

"Nonsense. How can you fall? I'll be right behind you."

"Dove, women don't climb ladders. My petticoats."

"You're wearing drawers aren't you?"

"Talk decent," she scolded, and the two workmen he'd summoned stood there chuckling. Dove draped his hands on his slim hips and smiled.

"You used to have nerve, grubworm. What happened?"

She had no intention of climbing any ladder. He was teasing her and enjoying it, blast him. She stood there stubbornly resolved until his next comment made anger flash in her like gunpowder in a musket pan.

"Hell, Marguerite used to climb with me all the time— trees, ladders, whatever. The higher the climb, the better Marguerite liked it. Marguerite's fearless."

Marguerite! She had heard that name once too often. Before she could examine the sanity of it, she whirled, grabbed hold of the ladder and began to climb. She turned a deaf ear to Dove's plea, "Jericho, stop! I didn't mean it—I was teasing—hell! You there—you men—hold the ladder!" She climbed as fast as she could climb. Marguerite, she thought, as she slammed the arch of her foot into each ladder rung, Marguerite, Marguerite. The ladder shook and vibrated as Dove came leaping after her.

"Jericho!"

"You told me to climb, Dove. I'm climbing."

"You stubborn witch!"

She was doing fine. She passed the windows of the first story. She passed the windows of the second. Then, midway up the third, she made the mistake of looking down. The men below, holding the ladder, were foreshortened into gnomes. She looked out. The green countryside swooped and rocked. She threw her arms around the ladder and clung.

"Oh, hell," Dove snapped. "I knew this would happen." The ladder shuddered violently as he angrily butted his head into her buttocks. "*Move*, grubworm. *Go*."

"I can't."

"Jericho! This is not funny. *Move*."

The world continued to spin. The blood pounded in her ears. Above, up in a place she dared not peek at, a man called down gently to her. "We're holding the top of the ladder, child. A few more steps, child. Come now. Courage."

"Jericho!" Dove climbed to stand on the rung below hers, straddling her with his hot angry body and arms. "Damn it, this is one hell of a time to turn gutless. *Move*."

She had no breath. "I'm dizzy."

"Jericho!"

"I'm going to fall."

"Fall and I'll wring your neck! Fall and you take me with you. Now close your eyes. What you can't see, you can't fear. Feel your way up with your hands and your feet. *Move*."

"I can't."

"Jericho. If you don't *move*, I'm going to rip off those clumsy petticoats and personally place your foot on each rung."

He wasn't bluffing. He was furious. Drawing a shaky breath, she shut her eyes and blindly hazarded her way up another rung, clutching the ladder so tightly her knuckles ached. "Good girl," Dove said in a kinder but nervous voice. "You're nearly there. One more step." And when she'd hazarded to step up again, successfully boosting herself to the next rung, he smoothly coaxed her up another, then another and another. Finally, strong arms grabbed her from above. She was hoisted up. Blind with fear, she buried her face in a man's warm sweaty chest, clutching handfuls of shirt. She clung, sobbing. Holding her very gently, the man ranted at Dove. "Dove, of all the harebrained stunts!"

"I was only testing her nerve, Uncle."

"Testing her nerve? Someone should test your skull. To find out if there's a brain in it."

Jericho tried to open her eyes. But the roof was swaying like a ship, and the countryside rolled like an ocean. She felt seasick. She shut her eyes and clung.

"Hell, Uncle, where's your sense of humor? I was only teasing her. I didn't intend for her to climb the ladder. I intended to bring her up through the house, by way of the attic stairs. Who could know she'd take my dare?"

"This is reprehensible, Dove! I cannot forgive it."

"Grubworm? You're all right, aren't you? Grubworm?" Genuine worry rang in Dove's voice. She didn't want him to worry and didn't want to cause trouble between Dove and his uncle. Eyes shut, she nodded mutely. She groped toward the sound of his voice with one shaking hand, needing his touch.

"Take her, Dove. For reasons beyond my comprehension, she is willing to have more of you. I'll get her a cup of wine. To soothe her nerves."

"Get one for me too, Uncle."

"For you," his uncle snapped, "I'll get hemlock."

Jericho was transferred into Dove's arms. She clung, clutching his shirt, his hair, and for once he bypassed crude remarks. He didn't remark about her breasts heaving against him. Instead, he stroked her hair.

"Are you all right, grubworm?"

She nodded, swallowing chunks of air.

"I-I-I think I'm afraid of heights."

"I think so, too." There was a smile in his voice.

Still half-blind with terror, she let him lead her over the sloping roof to a tall brick chimney-pot. They sat. He planted her safely between his knees, her back against his warm chest.

"All right, grubworm?"

She nodded. Gradually, her panicky breathing slowed. A vague awareness seeped in. The roof beneath her was solid, the slope of it mild. She opened her eyes. A dozen brick chimney pots marched across the roof like sentries. Slabs of roofing-lead and stacks of lumber were piled everywhere. Workmen hammered and banged and whistled and strolled about as if the roof were on the ground and not halfway to the top of the sky. She felt she might, after all, live. She drew her first normal breath, and Dove nudged her hair away with his face and rested his cheek against hers.

"Tell me. Do you take every dare that comes down the pike?"

How wonderful it felt, cheek to cheek. "No."

"Then why did you?"

"I . . . I don't know."

"You don't know," he murmured. "Then I'd best take care what I dare you to do, hadn't I. For you're likely to do it, aren't you, Pansy Eyes."

She turned her head and looked at him. His bright hazel eyes were shining with admiration. His mouth was only inches from hers. She had difficulty breathing.

"Dove, you should be drawn and quartered!" His uncle came striding back. "The girl is obviously frightened to death of heights. Here, take the wine cup. Help her sip it. My servant will bring you a cup, too. Not that you deserve it."

"Your hospitality overwhelms me, Uncle." Jericho took a grateful sip as Dove held the cup then set it aside. "Grubworm? Say hello to my uncle, His Grace the Duke of Nordham. Uncle Aubrey? This is my bondslave from New Amsterdam."

Shirt sleeves rolled, wearing garb as common as that of his laborers, the duke of Nordham squatted, and Jericho found herself looking into the most vivid blue eyes she'd ever seen. The duke was a lithe, sinewy man like Dove, but older. His shoulders were broader, his chest was thicker, his limbs meatier. He had the look of a soldier. His hair was curly, and except at the temple where it was going gray, his hair was as obnoxiously red as her own. Jericho liked him at once.

"You must call me Lord Aubrey. Pay no attention to that 'His Grace' business. I've not yet broken in my new title." He smiled wryly. "Thus far, it fits about as comfortably as a new pair of shoes. I trust you have a name, child? Aside from the abominable one my uncouth nephew sees fit to use?"

She was late finding her breath. Her panic on the ladder had drained her more than she'd known. "My lord, it's Jericho. Jericho Jones."

"A pretty name for a pretty girl."

"I am obliged, my lord." She flushed with happiness. She'd been prepared to like Dove's uncle, and she did. She'd heard about him all of her life.

"Not at all. I am the one obliged—obliged to make an apology. I apologize for having an idiot for a nephew." He gave Dove an impatient look. "You must bear in mind that not *all* de Monts are demented. Only a few of us."

She stole a glance at Dove. Drinking the wine the servant had brought, he was smiling and unperturbed. Plainly, the love bond between nephew and uncle was a given. Jericho felt a twinge of envy. To have family, to belong to a family who loved you no matter what you did . . . Then, with a start, she remembered her manners. Dear life, a duke. She should curtsy. She started to rise.

"Oh, for God's sake." Dove shoved her down. "Can you feature that, Uncle? Grubworm was going to curtsy. On a rooftop."

Lord Aubrey smiled. "You're from Dutch New Amsterdam, are you? Then a Dutch handshake will do. Welcome to my house, child. And the next time?" He wryly lifted one eyebrow. "Pray use the door?"

She had to smile, the reprimand was so gently given.

"My lord, I will. I promise."

"Good." He extended his hand for the handshake. Jericho took it and received the jolt of her life. Lord Aubrey had a birthmark on his right wrist. In the exact same spot as hers! But his was larger and never could have been hidden under a crocheted wristband. It flowed like a red blight up his forearm. She glanced into his eyes, startled. But he'd already risen.

Taking the wine cup his servant brought him, he again squatted to chat with Dove. Jericho gazed at him with wide-eyed wonder. Red hair. Blue eyes. A birthmark. Lord Aubrey and Dove embarked on a lively conversation. They tried to include her, but she was still too startled, too shy of conversing with a duke. To his polite questions, she responded with a soft, "Yes, my lord. No, my lord." In awe of the duke, she was also content to sit in Dove's arms. She was very nearly in heaven. Now and then, when he leaned forward to make a point, his golden hair brushed her cheek and she felt she could willingly stay on the roof forever.

And the day was wondrously fair. A breeze blew. Sunshine poured down. Fleecy clouds raced overhead. Workmen whistled tunes and hammered and banged and called to each other as they worked. As her fear of heights diminished, she looked out boldly, unafraid. How pretty England was. How tame compared to the wilds of America. The countryside rolled for miles.

Noting her interest, Lord Aubrey broke off conversation with Dove and gallantly pointed out landmarks. A soldier, he did it from a soldier's point of view. Jericho was touched and a little bit amused. If one dared be amused by a duke! Ignoring the beauty of the countryside, he pointed out military sites. An ancient Roman battle had been fought just to the east, he said, gesturing. A medieval battle had been fought not far to the west. Ignoring a pretty gorge with a sparkling rushing stream, he pointed out the dusty road that General Monck had used, riding down from Scotland with his army to force Parliament to restore the throne to King Charles II.

"And that castle in the distance, my lord?" She pointed.

His eyes narrowed. "Blackpool Castle," he said curtly. Finishing his wine in a swallow, he hove to his feet and went back to his work, rejoining his workmen. Jericho was dismayed.

"I said something wrong."

"You certainly did, dunce. You mentioned Blackpool Castle."

"And that's wrong?"

"It is around the de Monts."

She was sorry to lose Lord Aubrey's company. She'd liked him. And his birthmark utterly perplexed her. She sat quietly thinking about him, thinking about Mrs. Phipps's gossip. Lord Aubrey and Lady Angelina, the duchess of Blackpool . . .

When it was time to go down, a workman came to help Jericho down the attic stairs, through the dark attic and down another flight of stairs to the third floor. She waited there in the corridor for Dove.

Dove lingered on the roof. Or, rather, he found himself detained by a curt gesture from his uncle. Tossing hammer aside, Aubrey de Mont wove his way around stacks of lumber and roofing lead. His shirt was sweat streaked. He swiped an elbow over his sweaty forehead. "What in the devil is going on, Dove? Between you and that girl?"

Dove shrugged amiably. "Nothing. I'm just passing the time, Uncle. Until Marguerite arrives."

His uncle's eyes flashed. "Passing the time! Dove, that is despicable." He swiped a shirtsleeve at his forehead again. "If I'm any judge of females—and I believe I *am*—that girl is the decent sort. She's not a wench. Passing the time? Good lord, Dove!"

Dove shuffled his feet irritably. Normally, criticism rolled off him like water off a duck's back. But not when it came from the uncle he loved, the uncle who'd been a father to him. His hackles rose. "Hell, I'm not sleeping with her, if that's what you're so all-fired interested in knowing!"

"Then what *are* you doing? Merely breaking her heart? Open your eyes, Dove. That girl loves you. She's wearing her heart on her sleeve."

"I know."

"You know! Is that all you have to say?"

Drawing an irritated breath, Dove draped his hands on hips, and with a few brief verbal swaths painted Jericho's history. He finished by telling him of John's intent to marry her and of his own promise to John to take care of her this summer.

The duke of Nordham listened with growing astonishment.

"And you call *that* taking care of her? Making her climb three-story ladders? Hovering over her like a fox guarding the hen house?" Aubrey snorted. "Good lord, Dove. Remind me never to ask you to take care of anyone *I* value."

Dove tapped his toe. He winged an impatient glance out at the horizon. "Are you going to feed us or not? If not, we'll saddle up and go."

Aubrey's hackles went down. The fire in his eyes banked, and he gave Dove's shoulder a fatherly pat. "Of course, you're to dine with me. The girl, too. I'm glad to see you, Dove. I'm always glad for your company. You're always welcome here."

"You've got a damned funny way of showing it, Uncle." Turning on his heel, Dove left the roof and angrily barreled down the attic stairs.

Jericho waited in the third floor corridor, worrying for Dove. Finally, she heard his quick light step on the stairs. He came trotting down. "Did he scold you?" she asked anxiously when he emerged in the corridor. "For bringing me up on the roof?" He glared.

"Scold me? What do you think I am, six years old?"

After the sweet, protective way he'd taken care of her on the roof, she'd hoped to see warmth in his eyes, not irritation. "I only mean the fault is more mine than yours. I'm the one who climbed the ladder. He should scold me, not you."

"The hell with it. Come on. We're going to dine with a duke. And a damned ornery one at that." Grabbing her hand, he led her through the corridor, then down a broad handsome staircase that descended in a series of landings through the center of the house. The rooms Jericho glimpsed in passing were impressive, fitted with dark paneling and dark, massive pieces of furniture. But despite its grandeur, the house felt oddly cheerless. This wasn't a home, it was a house. There was no woman's touch to Nordham Hall.

"Dove, *I* cannot dine with a duke. I'm a bondservant. I cannot dine in a duke's dining chamber. I would die."

"*This* duke eats in the kitchen."

And to Jericho's amazement, he did. They took midday meal with Lord Aubrey at an ordinary table set in a corner of his busy, bustling kitchen. They dined with servant noise clattering all around them, and they ate simple hearty fare, the sort a soldier would favor. They drank ale from a communal kitchen tankard. While they ate and drank, Lord Aubrey and Dove conversed with obvious affection. Whatever had angered Dove on the roof had been forgiven and forgotten. While uncle and nephew talked, Jericho ate quietly and listened and watched.

She watched Lord Aubrey. Red hair, blue eyes. A birthmark. She felt a queer prickle. She watched his smile, his every gesture, listened to every word he uttered. He doted on Dove. That was plain. He behaved like a father to him. A nice man, she decided. Dove was lucky. When her thoughts drifted, and she speculated on the duke's odd habit of eating in a noisy kitchen when he had a big grand dining chamber to dine in, her heart suddenly contracted. Why, he was lonely! That's why he did it. She gazed at him with newborn sympathy. How strange, she thought, to feel sorry for a duke.

After midday meal, Lord Aubrey bade them a warm farewell and hurried back to his work. Walking to the stables with Dove, she looked over her shoulder and watched Lord Aubrey scramble up the ladder in his surefooted way. She felt wistful leaving him. Oddly sad.

The stable smelled clean. The pungent scent of horses and fresh droppings filled the air. Dove resaddled their horse, doing so in a quick, slapdash way that told her he was as indifferent to horses as he was to dogs and cats. She wondered, vaguely, if he liked babies.

"Has your uncle never married, Dove?"

"Never." Dove rammed in the bit. The horse could like it or choke.

"Why not?"

"I don't know. According to servant gossip, Uncle Aubrey and the duchess of Blackpool were once in love. The servants say Uncle Aubrey never got over it. But I say it's hogwash."

Jericho thought of Mrs. Phipps and gazed out the stable door. Lord Aubrey's strong figure was visible on the roof. "Maybe it's not hogwash, Dove. Maybe that's why your uncle grew so cool when I asked about Blackpool Castle."

Dove threw her a glance. "He grew cool, dunce, because *all* de Monts hate Blackpool."

"Why?"

"Because he's slime." Dove slapped the reins over the horse's dark mane. "Blackpool's slippery as a slug. During the war, we de Monts immediately declared for the king and never wavered, even though it meant exile, even though Cromwell seized our home and Mother had to take us and flee to France. Blackpool gave his allegiance to Cromwell. The coward!" Dove glanced at her. "Come here, beauty. Mount up."

"Beauty." Just like that. Her heart fluttered. Dove swung himself up into the creaking saddle, then kicked his foot free of the stirrup. Crossing her wrists the way he'd shown her, she gave him her hands, wedged her foot into the stirrup, and he popped her up onto the postilion.

"Why wasn't he executed when King Charles returned from exile and reclaimed the throne?

"Because the king granted amnesty to everyone except the actual regicides, the traitors who'd beheaded his father. Those, he executed. And good riddance."

Midway in the ride back to Arleigh Castle, they stopped beside a creek that sparkled with bright summer sunshine. Dove tramped into a copse of walnut trees, probably to relieve himself, and Jericho knelt by the creek. Taking off her wristband, she bathed her face and arms. She felt slightly sunburned. The sun had brought out a rash of freckles. She looked at her arms in disgust. Lady Marguerite probably didn't have a single freckle on her whole perfect body.

When she'd shaken her hands dry, she rebuttoned the wristband over her birthmark, then knelt quietly, staring at her wavering reflection in the creek's surface. Red hair. Blue eyes. A birthmark. She thought about Lord Aubrey. Red hair. Blue eyes. A birthmark.

Dove came back, squatted beside her and bathed his face and hands. When he finished, he playfully flicked a squirt of water at her. She flicked him back. How handsome he was, squatting there, springy-legged in his snug leather riding breeches, the leather stretched tight over his thighs. Afraid of where her eyes might wander, she glanced back at her own reflection.

"Dove? Your uncle has a birthmark on his wrist. In the exact same spot as mine."

"What of it?"

Idly, she dipped a finger into her reflection, stirred it, and the red hair, the blue eyes rippled away. Indeed, what of it? It was stupid to fantasize. She'd done enough of that as a child, pretending that somewhere in the world she had a mother, a father. "Nothing."

"John tells me you want your freedom. Your indenture."

"No!!" She looked up at him, stricken. It had come out of the blue. "I-I mean yes. I want my freedom. But not until I serve out my indenture. I owe you."

Dove flicked a bit of water at two mating dragonflies. Their pulsing wings were a shimmering iridescent green. "Hell, grubworm, you don't owe me a thing. If you want the truth,

I liked owning you. When you want your indenture, ask. It's yours.''

She nodded mutely. It was kind of Dove. But the prospect of freedom, the prospect of not belonging to him anymore, collected in her throat like a choke.

It was time to go, but neither of them moved. The moment lengthened in a quiet stillness. The only sound was the tethered horse, munching grass. Dove wiped his wet hands on his shirt front. The white linen clung, showing every lean masculine plane. She looked and then quickly averted her eyes. When she glanced back at him, his bright hazel eyes were regarding her with speculation.

"Do you want to kiss?"

She looked down at her hands folded primly in her lap and counted her heart beats. Thump-thump, thump-thump, thump-thump. In the periphery of her vision a ladybug with black spots on its delicate shell wings climbed a blade of grass, and beyond the ladybug, the lovely breeze-stirred stream lay dotted with sunlight.

"Yes."

"So do I." Lounging on his side on the mossy stream bank, he propped himself on one elbow, beckoned and smiled gently. "Come here, beauty . . ." She moved, bunching her skirts, walking awkwardly on her knees until she knelt beside him. But when he didn't sit up to kiss her, she had second thoughts.

"Dove, I don't think we should kiss lying down."

"Certainly, certainly!" he said. "Real kissing is done lying down. Ask anyone."

"Dove—"

"We are only going to kiss, Jericho. And cuddle a bit. I swear. I give you my word." With hands as gentle as kitten paws, he reached up and drew her down into his arms.

"Dove, I don't think we should—"

"You don't mind if I lie partly on top of you, do you? Like this?" With a twist of his handsome shoulders he showed her, and she found herself lying under him, her breasts softly crushed to his warm chest. Her heart pounded.

"Do you mind?" he inquired politely.

"N-n-no."

"Good. Are you ready? Or do you first want to get used to lying together?"

She felt dizzy. "Dove, I think we had best k-kiss only once."

His shoulders slumped and prickles of frustration appeared on his handsome brow. "Only once." Then he grew cheerful again. "If it's to be only once, then let's make it a good one, eh?"

"All-all right." She waited nervously for him to kiss her, but he didn't. Instead he frowned, and, with his fingertips, gently jiggled her chin until her lips parted.

"What-what are you doing?"

"You'll see."

"Dove, I don't think we should—"

Deaf, he brought his mouth down and kissed her, and she *did* see. It was a jolt. For as he kissed, he gently tasted her, as if she were a sweet pudding and he a naughty child stealing a lick. Stealing several licks. She gasped in surprise. She'd never been kissed like this at Maritje's Ten Boom's waffle frolics. Dizzy, she gripped his shoulders.

"What's wrong?"

"Dove, I-I-I don't think you should kiss me like that."

"Why not?" Her heart was pounding so hard she couldn't think of an answer. "Don't you like it?" he asked politely.

"Y-yes, I do, b-but—"

"Then reciprocate, grubworm. Kiss me. Kissing is a reciprocal arrangement. Do it to me."

He brought his mouth down. Trembling, she lifted her mouth and kissed him. When his lips parted, waiting expectantly, she tasted him—shyly at first, and then, when he made soft sounds of pleasure and crushed her closer, more boldly. She found she wanted to give, and she gave. She gave with all her heart, and he returned the compliment with fervor, crushing her in his careful gentle arms.

"Jericho! My God, this is sweet."

"Dove, I'm dizzy . . . like wine."

"Kissing can do that . . . kiss me again."

"Dove, w-we should stop . . ."

"Do you want to?"

"No!"

"Nor do I."

It was glory, kissing and fondling with Dove on a soft summer's day. Time and the world faded away. The summer breeze stirred their hair as they kissed. Birdsong trilled in the trees overhead. The stream gurgled peacefully. They were lost in sensuality, hearts pounding, their breath moist and musky. Dove began something new.

"Dove—"

"Let me. You'll like it. I swear I won't harm you."

Dizzy with love, she grew dizzier still as he swooped her up and rolled her atop him. With panting breath and urgent hands, he fitted her hips to his. Through layers of gown and leather breeches, his bone-stiff need pressed against her feminine need. Holding her hips, he began to move. She gasped.

"Dove—"

"Let it! Let it happen, Jericho. Put your mouth on mine."

When the shocking, spiraling pleasure peaked and she cried out, he crushed her close and bucked urgently, his body hot as flame. When it was over, when her bones drained away like water, she wilted upon him, breathing as hard as he. After several long and drowsy minutes, Dove rolled her off onto the ground beside him. She lay drowsy in the crook of his arm. His face was flushed. He radiated heat. A sheen of moisture covered his brow. He gave her a sheepish grin.

"I spent in my breeches."

She lifted her heavy head. "What, Dove?"

He propped himself part way up on a lazy elbow and smiled.

"You've never done this before, have you?"

"No, of course not." She flushed. Suddenly, she had a very clear idea of what he'd meant. As he watched her color rise, his smile broadened. He tousled her hair.

"You're sweet."

Then he rocked to his feet and strode off downstream. While he was gone, she tidied herself as best she could. But the grass stains on her skirts were in to stay. What if Mrs. Phipps saw? What would she tell Mrs. Phipps?

Dove came striding back, his hot flushed look gone, his eyes bright and clear and smiling. His passion spent, he gathered her in his arms in a sweet friendly way, as a man might gather in his wife. But when she lifted her mouth to be kissed, he gave her a swat on the buttocks.

"Lesson number one. Hell, Jericho, don't be so willing and eager! When a man wants to kiss you, play coy occasionally. Say no once in a while." But he said this with such warmth and smiling light in his eyes, that she smiled, too.

"I fear I could never say no to you, Dove."

He sighed a great sigh. For a long moment, he rested his smooth warm forehead on hers. They rubbed noses in affection.

"In that case, grubworm, you and I are in for a peck of trouble this summer. John had best get his ducks in order."

"John?"

"Never mind. Give me one last kiss and we'll go."

She drew back and smiled playfully. *"No."*

Amusement brightened his eyes. "Jericho!"

"No, no, no, n—" Throughout the kiss, she continued to murmur no until Dove put a stop to it.

"Jericho," he warned coming up for air, "be silent, or so help me, I'll take you to the nearest bondslave market and swap you for a sheep!"

They rode back to Arleigh Castle talking and chatting about a hundred different things. Jericho felt supremely content. Her contentment lasted all the way to the castle. It lasted until Dove lifted her down from the postillion and she turned to see Janie coming pellmell across the castleyard, feet flying, white apron flying.

"Jericho? Oh, Jericho, come quick! Something awful's happened!"

Jericho froze. She knew. Forgetting Dove as if he'd never existed, forgetting the beautiful day as if it had never happened, she picked up her skirts and flew.

Chapter Twelve

Jericho nursed Black Bartimaeus night and day for two weeks.
The doctor came daily from St. John's Basket. Mrs. Phipps
came to his bedside a hundred times a day. Dove came. But
his exuberant visits so tired Black Bartimaeus that she had
to forbid Dove entry. Leonardo d'Orias and Lord Lark looked
in. The servants looked in. Pax wandered in and out, thrusting
a mournful muzzle into a black hand that was now too weak
to pet him. Even Lady de Mont looked in once. But Jericho
never left his side.

She anguished. How selfish she'd been in these opening
days in England, thinking only of herself, of her own foolish
feelings for Dove. Self-absorbed, she'd neglected the dearest,
kindest man of all.

As the anxious days passed, the plain, ordinary tasks she
did for him lent themselves to plain, ordinary thinking. Sensible thinking. She thought long and hard about Dove. He
was a lord, she was a bondslave. Even if she won his love,
she could never hope to marry him. The most she could hope
to be was his mistress. And what was a mistress? In plain
words, a whore. Even the king's famous mistresses—the
countess Lady Castlemayne and the actress Nell Gwynne—
were called whores, their names well known and bandied
about in tap houses as far away as New Amsterdam.

Is that what she wanted? Did she want to be known as
Lord Dove de Mont's whore? Did she want that?

During Black Bartimaeus's waking moments, she sat holding his hand, talking softly to him. He must try to get well,
she urged. For as soon as he was well and strong again, she

would ask Dove for her indenture. Then she would take Black Bartimaeus to London. They would rent two rooms. They would live in one room, set up her dame school in the other. She would take good care of him. They would make a good life together. They would scrimp and save. As soon as they'd saved enough for ship passage, she would take him home. Home to Amsterdam. Home where they both belonged. Home to Daisy and Samuels, Goody and Cook. A faint squeeze of her hand told her how much he longed for just that.

Worn-out and weary, she was in the scullery mixing up a nourishing posset drink for Black Bartimaeus early one morning, when Janie came running with a letter. Deciding it was from John—Mrs. Phipps had written him the sad news—she broke the red wax seal and eagerly unfolded the letter. Her lips parted in bewilderment. It wasn't from John. She raked a hand through her mussed, neglected hair and read.

*Mistress Jericho Jones, the Kitchens, Arleigh Castle
The Ninth of this Instant, The Year of our Lord, 1666*

It has, by Fortuitous Chance, come to Our attention that the Indenture under which you are Bound shall be served out within the Twelvemonth. I hereby Invite you into Employment at Blackpool Castle as Head Housemaid. It is a pretty post, having under it nine underhousemaids and paying, besides the Goodly sum of Twenty Guineas annual, a silk Gown and a sturdy cloth Cloak with silver buttons granted each Twelvemonth. I await your reply.

> *Mr. Fox Hazlitt, Esquire*
> *Chief Steward*
> *Blackpool Castle*

She didn't know what to think. She swallowed uneasily, remembering the day John's coach broke down. It was eerie being singled out by a man who didn't even know her. It stirred up the old anxiety of those odd letters that would come now and then in New Amsterdam, wanting to buy her.

Hazlitt. She strained to picture him. A weasel of a man. Quick, darting eyes. She had no trouble picturing the duke. He had been as cold as granite. She felt a prickle.

Without bothering to write a reply, she tore the letter in bits and tossed it into the scullery slop bucket. Shaking her hair, she shook the peculiar offer out of mind. She went back to doing what she wanted to do. Taking care of Black Bartimaeus.

Dove grew vexed. Enough was enough. He was damned fond of Black Bartimaeus, and he was overjoyed that the old black giant had rallied and was getting well. But Jericho still waited on him hand and foot. Dove couldn't get her attention if he fired a cannon under her tail.

Whose bondslave was she, anyway? What did he have to do, paint his face black and fall down in the middle of the kitchen clutching his heart?

More vexing, the one time he'd managed to corner her in the scullery, hoping for a kiss, she'd pushed him away with a prim request. Please, could she have her indenture release? If he would release her now, she would be forever grateful. She and Black Bartimaeus had made plans. They were going to London. They would hire rooms to live in. She would set herself up teaching dame school. She wanted to leave Arleigh Castle as soon as possible.

The plan had been preposterous. A grubworm and a sick old man fending for themselves in a rough city like London? London would devour them! It had scared him. Angered him. Going deeper, it had hurt him. Hell, she made it plain as the nose on her face that she didn't want to belong to him anymore. Shocked and hurt, he'd lashed back.

"The sooner the better, grubworm! Hell, I'll be tickled pink to be rid of you. It isn't all strawberries-and-cream owning a bondslave, you know. Bondslaves are a damned nuisance, a millstone around the neck. There's *food, clothing, shelter* to provide. Then there's the *ton* of money you spend sending the bondslave to *school*. And when the bondslave doesn't *learn* anything there, when the bondslave's too stupid to prevent itself being abducted in the dead of winter, then you have to slog through waistdeep snow, freezing your balls off, rescuing it. Hell, yes! Certainly you can have your indenture. Take it. It's a load off my shoulders. I'm glad to be rid of you.''

Her eyes had glistened. But she was a stubborn little thing. She didn't shed a tear.

"I'm sorry," she'd said wearily, "I cannot stay here at Arleigh Castle, Dove. I just cannot."

Hands draped on hips, he'd winged a glance out the scullery door. How could she say that to him? How could she kiss him the way she'd kissed him and not want to belong to him anymore?

"Fine, go! You want to go? Go. I'll provide a horse. I'll provide a cart, a wagon, a coach, a sled. Hell, I'll provide someone to take you to wherever you want to go, and if you want to go by water, I'll provide a rowing boat. Feel free to go as soon and as fast and as far as you want. With my compliments, grubworm!''

He had the satisfaction of seeing one crystal tear slide down her pretty cheek before he wheeled and stomped out of the scullery. He went to his apartment in a vicious humor, rammed a key into the lock of his mahogany cabinet, grabbed his iron strongbox and rifled through his properties. He found the tattered dog-earred indenture on the bottom. He picked it up. He hadn't glanced at it in years. He'd never read it. It was written in Dutch; he couldn't read Dutch. Holding the soiled shabby scrap in his hand, he felt a tremor. He remembered a dice game. He remembered a homely ragamuffin with chopped-off red hair, asleep on a tap-house stoop . . .

But, hell! She wanted to be free, didn't she? So be it. He grabbed a quill and viciously rammed it into his silver ink pot. His hand hovered angrily over the document, preparing to sign.

He couldn't. Sighing, he threw the quill down. Ink flew. He sat and propped his chin in his hands. *Pansy Eyes*. He couldn't send her out into the world just like that. She was such an innocent. The world? A briar patch. It would trip her up before she'd taken two steps. And he would worry.

Besides, what would John say? He'd promised John he would take care of her this summer.

He shot to his feet and tapped the indenture on his thigh. Finally, he went to his bedchamber, to his testered, draped bed, yanked up the silk brocade coverlet, yanked up the mattress and stuffed the indenture under. He sent word down to Jericho. Her indenture was missing. He couldn't find it. But as soon as he found it, she could damn well have it and be gone.

Hurt, he stayed away from the kitchen that day, but awoke the next morning fretting. What if she left Arleigh Castle without waiting for her indenture? What if she just took off and left?

He paced his work closet, worrying. She'd probably head for London. He doubted she would go to John. She was too stubborn to ask for help. The grubworm! He fretted. London was a grand city for a man, chock-full of drinking houses, gaming houses, brothels, theaters, cockpits. There was even a bear-baiting pit in Southwark. A man could count on having an exhilarating time in London. There were a dozen rousing good sword fights on the street every day. But, Pansy Eyes there? He didn't like the idea.

He tried to think how to make her stay. If she had some lengthy task to perform for him . . . if he could count on her sense of obligation. She'd been a pest in New Amsterdam, but a damned *loyal* pest. Whenever he'd needed anything, she'd been the first of his servants to jump up and run for it.

Pacing, chewing a knuckle, he glanced at his mahogany cabinet. The double doors stood open. He gazed at the neat, tidy, interior. Not a paper out of place. His accounts' steward, Will Hewett, now gone to Yorkshire to be with his sick father, kept his business affairs in perfect order. An idea flickered. Then glimmered bright and humorous. He smiled broadly.

"You sent for me, Lord Dove?" Jericho asked softly, her expression sweet, contrite as she stood in the doorway of his work closet. "Your servant said you needed my help. He said your papers are in a muddle. He said you wish me to sort them and put everything right again.''

"Yes." He jerked in sudden spasm, waking to the fact that he'd been staring at her. His heart beat queerly. How damned pretty she was! She wore a fresh blue frock and she'd brushed her lustrous hair long and loose and straight—at least as straight as the thick ropey curls would permit. "I thought you might do that for me, yes. Not, of course, if Black Bartimaeus needs you. Tend him, by all means. But in your spare hours. If you will?''

"Yes, of course I will," she said loyally. He felt a prick of guilt. He quashed it. Hell, he was doing this for her own good.

"Come in. I'll let you be the judge of what needs to be done, Jericho.''

Her vivid dark blue eyes took in the room uneasily before she stepped in. He could see she was shy of being in his personal apartment, in his personal rooms, so he took care to put her at ease by being businesslike. It took some effort. For what he wanted to do was kiss her.

Wide-eyed, looking about as if satyrs might come jumping out of the woodwork in a lord's personal chamber, she gingerly followed him to the mahogany cabinet. When he unlocked it and flung open the doors, papers came tumbling in an avalanche. Ledgers thumped to the floor and lay there, covers bent like broken wings. Papers sailed in every direction, skidding on the polished floor, sailing north, south, east, west. She gasped. Speechless with shock, she stared at the mess on the floor, stared at him, then stared with equal disbelief at the mess in the cabinet. Dove stared too, pleased. He'd done a good job of making a shambles.

"Dear life, Dove!" she said, her shyness gone in shock. "Is this the way your accounts' steward keeps your papers?''

"I guess it is." ·

"This is a disgrace! To treat important papers so? To keep your account ledgers in such a slovenly manner? Why the man is a scoundrel. He should be horsewhipped. He should be pilloried.''

"He should, he should," Dove agreed.

She knelt in the mess, whipped up a stained paper, and
sniffed it. "Rum! He drank *rum* while he worked on your
papers. Dove this is unforgiveable." She ranted on like a
fishwife, her blue eyes blazing. Dove thoroughly enjoyed it.
He enjoyed having a woman indignant on his behalf, standing
up for him, taking his part. He'd always liked it. It was a
damned pleasant sensation.

Jericho shot a glance at him.

"How can you smile at a time like this?"

He wiped the smile from his face. "I'm not," he said
staunchly. "I'm angry as hell."

"Well, you should be," she urged, gathering up an orphaned paper, trying in her feminine way to smooth out the
wrinkles. "These poor papers! It will take days to recopy the
stained ones, to sort them out, to determine which paper goes
with which."

"Weeks probably," Dove offered cheerfully. "Maybe the
whole summer. I am thinking of dismissing him. What do
you think?"

She looked at him in utter astonishment.

"Dismiss him? I think you should shoot him."

He bit back a smile. But when she glanced at him again,
this time sharply, warily, possibly on the edge of suspicion,
he knew he'd best not overplay his hand.

"Well, I'll leave and let you work," he said. She didn't
even hear him. She was already on hands and knees, beginning to sort.

"Yes," she muttered, absorbed in the task. "I'll start at
once . . . I'll start right now."

Smiling at her determined, ramrod little back, he left.

Jericho attacked her work with zeal, fueled by indignation.
How dare that steward disrespect Dove so! She wanted to
kill him. At the least, she wanted to box his ears. But now
and then as she worked, a doubt flickered. The kitchen staff
was surprised Will Hewett had left Dove's papers in shambles. She put down her pen and frowned. Would Dove be
likely to . . . She thrust the suspicion away. Dear life, only
an imbecile would! Besides, Dove had shown no sign of
having lured her up to his room to kiss her. For two days,

he'd left her strictly alone. She'd told herself she was relieved. But the truth was, she was disappointed.

On the third day he lingered. Dressing for riding, in leather breeches, boots, and a linen shirt with sleeves rolled, he casually took a chair on the opposite side of the table and chatted with her as she worked. She felt ridiculously glad of it. And a little uneasy. Their afternoon at the creek had opened a new door for her. Now she knew what a man's body was and how it could stir her. She also knew that what they'd done had not been proper. It had not been decent. She brushed at her flushed cheeks as Dove sat talking to her. She, nervous and agitated. Dove, calm as a house cat.

"Shall I bring my chair around? Sit beside you? Show you precisely how I want that ledger copied?"

"If-if-if you like." She brushed her hot cheeks.

He leaped up at once, brought his chair around and sat next to her. She bent to her ledger, aware of his masculine scent, aware of every golden hair on the tanned wrist that rested on the table. Aware, aware. Each time he showed her where to enter a number, his arm brushed hers.

"Excuse me," he would apologize politely.

"Y-yes." She would swallow thickly.

When a half hour had gone by in this unnerving manner, he suddenly leaned toward her and gave her cheek a soft peck. She jumped. She gazed at him uncertainly. When she made no protest, he leaned toward her again and gave her lips a soft sweet peck. Her lashes fluttered, her breathing stopped, her heart ceased to beat. With the gentlest fingers in the world, he lifted her chin and kissed her again. This time, when the kiss ended, their lips clung.

"Pansy Eyes," he whispered.

"D-Dove? I don't think you should k-k-k-kiss me."

"Why not, beauty?" he whispered, drawing her up from her chair and into his arms. As he kissed her, holding her as if she were as fragile as a new hatched chick, he walked her backwards, kiss by kiss, into his bedchamber.

"Dove, we-we can't do what w-we did in the woods."

"Sweeting, you liked it. So did I."

"That-that-that's not the point. It's not-not decent."

He stopped walking her backwards for a moment and lifted his searching mouth from hers, his brow wrinkling in devilish prickles.

"Well, what *can* we do, then?"

"O-o-only kiss."

"Only kiss?"

"O-only kiss," she said firmly. She made him cross his heart and promise.

Jericho found her indenture entirely by accident while Dove and Lord Lark were at Whitehall Palace in London, attending to the business of the king's war loan. The endless on-and-off-again war with the Dutch had escalated. There'd been a terrible battle in the North Sea in early June. England had suffered devastating losses, both in ships and in men's lives.

At work in Dove's work closet, she'd gone into Dove's bedchamber to borrow a handkerchief from the nightbox beside his bed. Kneeling there, she glanced and spotted a scrap of paper under the bed. Irked that a housemaid should sweep Dove's room so carelessly, she ducked under the bed, retrieved it, and sat back on her knees to see what she'd retrieved.

The paper was tattered, dog-eared. The writing was in Dutch, but smudged, the ink so faded she had trouble making it out. She held it up so the light from the window would strike it.

Bound into Service one redhaired English infant—

Her heart banged. She jumped up and flew into Dove's work closet. Wrenching open the drawer of the writing table, she rifled it until she found Dove's magnifying glass. She seized it.

English? English? She'd thought herself Dutch!

The blood throbbed so violently in her temples that it blacked her vision for a moment, blinded her. She drew a deep breath to calm herself.

English. Why hadn't any of her masters bothered to tell her! She'd always assumed Dutch. No one had ever told her different.

Holding the trembling magnifying glass to the faded Dutch script, she read:

> *Bound into Service one redhaired English Infant. It being Female and having dark blue Eyes and bearing upon its spoilt Skin three Birthmarks, one Mark upon its Breast, one upon its right Wrist, one upon the Nape of its Neck. This Infant shall be bound in Service and shall dutifully Serve its Master for Twenty-One Years from This Instant.*
>
> *Set down and so decreed on this twentieth day of August in the Year of our Blessed Lord Jesus Christ, Sixteen Hundred and Forty Six by:*
>
> *Derrick Vanderzee, Ship Master*
> *The Jericho*

The Jericho. A ship. She'd been named for a ship! Why hadn't anyone ever bothered to tell her? Dove couldn't have told her, of course. He didn't read Dutch. But she'd had other masters, Dutch masters. *They* could have told her.

Her heart pounded in excitement. English, not Dutch. She wasn't Dutch, she was English. A hundred questions whirled in her head. Had she been born in England? Or had she been born on the ship? On the ship probably, else why would they name her for it? But her parents had been English. She pressed the backs of her hands to her hot cheeks to cool them.

In excitement, she read the indenture again. Her heart pounded with the possibilities. Perhaps she could trace her parents, find out who they'd been. If she'd been born aboard *The Jericho*, then what had happened to them? Had they died, leaving her in the hands of the captain? Or had her parents not wanted her? Had they been superstitious people, frightened of a baby born with witch's hair and with three birthmarks, three *duivel* marks? She bit her lip, not wanting to think that, rejecting it. Perhaps her mother had been an unmarried girl, caught in forbidden pregnancy. Possibilities darted through her mind like minnows in a creek. Whatever the circumstances, one fact came shining through. She was English. She might even have living relatives in England. She might have family!

Family. The blood in her temples throbbed.

She wished Dove were home! Dove might be able to tell her how to trace her parents. But he wasn't. Taking the indenture, she dashed out of the work closet to find the one person who could be counted on to give her sensible advice.

She found Leonardo d'Orias in the stable, but to her disappointment he was busily engaged with three stable hands, examining a new pony he and Lady de Mont had bought for their little daughter, Ginevra. She couldn't intrude. Curbing her excitement, she waited quietly at the stable door. When several minutes had passed, d'Orias gave the pony's flank an approving slap, turned and came directly to her.

"How can I help you?"

Drawing the indenture out of the deep pocket of her brown work apron, she told him, and with an accommodating gesture, he led the way out of the stable, across the stone-paved castleyard and into the kitchen courtyard. They sat on the sunny stone apron that circled the kitchen well, and there, he gravely gave her his attention, just as if she were a person of importance and not merely a bondslave. Her heart swelled with gratitude.

She read the indenture to him, translating it from Dutch to English as she read. Her tongue thickened and grew clumsy when she came to the part about the birthmarks. But she forced herself to read it. The birthmarks might be significant. They might lead to her parents. Besides, d'Orias already knew of the birthmark on her wrist. And he, himself, had a birthmark on one arm.

"So. *The Jericho*," he said with a kind smile. "You are thinking that you may have been born aboard the ship and named for her, *si*?"

Her excitement surged. "I think so, Mr. d'Orias. Yes."

"Possible, possible. However, the term 'infant' can apply to any babe under the age of one year, yes?"

"I've thought of that, too. But if I'd come aboard at the age of one, I would surely have had a name. To what purpose would I have been brought aboard nameless?"

He gazed at her thoughtfully, his dark eyes glowing with thought, his black knife-straight hair shining in the afternoon sunshine. "To what purpose indeed? It is a puzzle."

Her excitement surged higher. "Mr. d'Orias? Do you know of *The Jericho*? Have you ever heard of her? Is she a Dutch ship? Could she perhaps have put into port here in England, trading for English goods before sailing on to New Amsterdam? If I could find out, I might learn who I am."

He took the indenture from her hands and gazed at it.

"*The Jericho*. The name rings no bell. But then, twenty years ago I was not in England. I was in Italy. In Genoa."

"Is there a way I can find out?"

"No. But *I* can and *I* shall. I have contacts. But it will take time." He rose to his feet, a tall, impressive figure dressed as usual in black. His black leather doublet was lined with scarlet silk. "In the meantime, let us go and ask Lady de Mont if she remembers anything of a Dutch merchant ship called *The Jericho*. Come."

Jericho faltered. "Lady de Mont?"

His sensual lips quivered in amusement. "She does not bite. Truly. She is a nice lady."

"Oh, I know," Jericho said, embarrassed. "Lady de Mont is very kind. It is only that I am a small bit . . ." She didn't know how to put it. But d'Orias did.

"Scared of her," he said, amused. "I tell you a secret, *Si*? So am I. Sometimes I shake in my boots. Come along. Come. I tell you another secret, *si*?" he said as they crossed the kitchen courtyard together, going toward the archway that led to the main apartments in the castle. "Lady de Mont and Dove are cut of the same cloth. They are two peas in a pod. They are very strong people. The secret of dealing with strong people is to stand firm in your convictions. Do not allow them to bully you. For if they detect weakness, they will devour you."

She had to smile. Dove *was* like that. A beloved bully.

D'Orias opened the heavy door and let her pass through.

"I also tell you this," he said softly, their footfalls echoing in the arching corridor. "The strongest people in the world are also the most fragile, the most needy. They need more than our love. They need our total adoration."

Quietly absorbing this bit of wisdom, she knew it to be true. Why else would Dove be drawn to *her*? She adored him and always had, and he knew it. Her heart softened as she thought about her indenture. Where she'd found it. Hidden. Under his bed. He'd obviously hidden it! He didn't want to give her up.

"I don't know what to do, Mr. d'Orias."

Walking beside her, d'Orias chided, "You know perfectly well what to do. Stand firm in your convictions. Remain chaste. If he invites you to become his mistress, refuse. Preserve your self-respect. And? Stop kissing him on the bed."

Startled, she looked at him, stricken. "You know about that?"

"The whole castle knows of it."

She flushed scarlet. What a fool she'd been to assume no one knew what went on in those long afternoons in Dove's work closet. No wonder Mr. Pennington, the head steward, looked at her with such contempt.

"Go to London," d'Orias continued. "Proceed with your plans. Be a dame schoolteacher. Be your own woman. Live your own life. This is the only way to make Dove respect you."

She knew he spoke sense. "I will miss him."

D'Orias smiled. "Not half so much as he will discover *he* misses you."

They found Lady de Mont in her work closet, toiling over papers, her golden hair piled high on her head, a few loose strands of it spilling to the shoulders of her silken chamber robe. Busy, Lady de Mont was crisp but civil.

"As to the year 1646, Leonardo? A Dutch ship called *The Jericho*? I cannot help. I was in France that year. With my young sons. Cromwell had seized Arleigh Castle, sequestered it. However, the girl might ask Aubrey. Run, catch him. He bade me farewell a few minutes ago. He is leaving just now for Nordham Hall."

Jericho felt uneasy as she hurried to the stables with d'Orias. She didn't want to bother a duke. She worried, too, that Lord Aubrey had heard the gossip about her kissing Dove. She'd felt extremely uncomfortable in Lady de Mont's chamber, with Lady de Mont's frank eyes assessing her.

But, Lord Aubrey received them kindly, delaying his departure and swinging down from his mount in the sunny stableyard. To her relief, d'Orias did the talking, putting the case before the duke. Lord Aubrey listened, then rubbed his forehead in thought.

"*The Jericho?* A Dutch merchant ship, was she?"

"*Si*, Aubrey. We think it probable. Yes. A Dutch West India Company ship."

"*The Jericho.*" Lord Aubrey rubbed his jaw. "Hmmm. No, no, I must apologize. I can remember no ship called— ah, wait. Wait. It is coming back. Now I recall. A Dutch merchant ship by that name went down at sea in '56 or '57. Crew and cargo lost. I remember rejoicing. The ship was carrying supplies meant for Cromwell's army."

Jericho's heart sank. If the ship was gone, so was all hope of checking the ship's log. D'Orias, however, gave her an encouraging glance.

"Do not despair. St. Katherine's Docks may have records. And even though we are at war with the Dutch, letters can be sent to Holland. I will, in fact, do so."

Lord Aubrey cocked his head kindly. "What year were you inquiring of?"

"1646, My Lord."

A startling change came over him. Where before he'd been amiable and friendly, now he became abrupt and cool. His facial features hardened—jaw, lips, brow.

"I cannot recall the year," he said curtly. Thrusting foot into stirrup, he swung up into the creaking saddle, saluted d'Orias and rode off in a clatter of horse hooves.

Jericho's heart sank even further. "I said something wrong."

D'Orias gazed after Lord Aubrey. Then he gazed at her.

"No," he murmured thoughtfully. "You said nothing wrong. Something else perhaps upsets him. Something we know nothing about. Nothing to do with you."

Still, she drooped. "I had best go in now, Mr. d'Orias. I have work to do. Papers to copy for Dove. I want to finish as soon as I can. Then, I will ask Dove to sign my indenture and I will—leave for London. Start my life. As I should."

"*Si*. Do that. It is best. Jericho, a life without self-respect is no life at all. Believe this. For I know it to be true."

She nodded unhappily. Thanking him for his help, she went.

D'Orias watched the girl trudge across the castleyard, her

red hair bright as flame as sunshine caught it. Startled, he turned and gazed at Aubrey's distant figure. Cantering away down the road from the stable gate, cantering in the sunshine, Aubrey's red hair was a pinpoint of flame. Blue eyes, birthmarks. Both of them. His scalp prickled.

"Odd," he breathed. "Very odd."

By the time Dove returned from London, Jericho had tucked the indenture back under his mattress where he'd likely hidden it. She didn't mention the indenture to Dove. She wasn't ready to leave him just yet. Mr. d'Orias was right; she should go. But she wasn't ready. She loved him too much. And he loved her a little bit, too, didn't he? He'd hidden her indenture, hadn't he? He didn't want her gone.

Against her better judgment, knowing she was being stupid to disregard Mr. d'Orias's kind warning, she was on the bed with Dove again a week after he'd returned. They were kissing, being playful, laughing and talking, when suddenly, in the bowels of the castle, Lord Lark's loud voice rang out, resonating through the great house.

"Dove," Lord Lark shouted, "Good news. Marguerite's arrived! She's in London, waiting for you to fetch her!"

Dove stopped kissing her in mid-kiss. He jerked up, his eyes bright and blank, focused on something distant, wonderful.

"Hallelujah," he whooped. "I'm on my way!"

Rolling off the bed, he hit the floor running. The door opened and shut with a bang that echoed and he was gone, his eager booted footsteps clattering down the stairs.

Jericho lay there, stunned, her mouth still wet from his kisses. When the fury came and the hot anger engulfed her, she sprang up and paced his rooms, stalking up and down, wanting to smash and spoil every lordly thing in it. She wanted to shriek when she couldn't make herself smash even one single wretched thing. Smashing things wasn't her way, even in fury.

Frustrated, she stalked to his bed, yanked up the mattress

and grabbed her indenture. Stalking into his work closet, she seized a sheet of paper, grabbed a quill pen, stabbed it into the ink pot and scrawled in large, angry letters:

Sign My Indenture

Wrenching the candles out of two tall silver candlesticks, she rammed the indenture onto one candlestick and the demand onto the other, impaling them. Then she strode out, banging the door shut behind her.

Chapter Thirteen

On Mid-Summer's Eve, John and Jericho went for a walk. Leaving the revelry behind in the meadow, leaving the dancers and the drinkers and the wild carousing children, they strolled out into the long, lingering twilight of this June the twenty-first, the longest day of the year. Aimless, they followed a meadow path that meandered toward St. John's Basket. Pax came with them, sometimes bounding ahead with youthful vigor, sometimes plodding behind like the "old man" he truly was.

Jericho said little. John said less. He knew when to hold his tongue. He could guess what she was feeling. Only that morning, a jubilant and triumphant Dove had returned, escorting Lady Marguerite to Arleigh Castle for a prenuptial visit. They'd arrived in a magnificent, gleaming new coach drawn by six white horses—Dove's betrothal gift to Marguerite.

As they strolled, Jericho idly picked up a stick. Now and then, she batted it at some wildflower they passed, whisking its head off, cleanly decapitating it. John's eyebrows rose. To destroy wasn't her way. She was a gentle thing. But he understood. When the one you love is in someone else's arms—oh, ay, he understood far too well. He'd heard the gossip. He wanted to break Dove's neck. He felt angry with Jericho, too.

"Pax is enjoying the walk," she said after a bit, breaking the silence of the past half-hour.

"Yes, he is."

Whack! A yellow buttercup lost its head. John watched the petals flutter to the ground.

"I should take him walking more often."

"He would like that."

"Yes." She said nothing more. The meadow was silent too, silent with the loud peaceful noise of crickets. Here and there, a firefly winked. The air smelled of clover. The sky was full of mauve twilight. The merriment they'd left behind echoed so distantly it might have come from another planet.

As they strolled, Pax nosed up a field mouse and with a brief spurt of returning youth chased it, but quickly gave up, panting, and fell in step, plodding at their heels once again. The moon rose, a pale nothing in a sky full of bright twilight. Day would linger long on this festive night honoring both the sun's solstice and the birth of St. John the Baptizer.

"Have they set the date?" she asked. Whack!

"September the fourth. It's settled, so forget it."

John glanced over his shoulder. A trail of headless flower stalks lay in their wake.

"Why are they not marrying at once, for heaven's sake?" Whack! Cross, definitely cross, he decided.

"Lady Marguerite wishes her wedding clothes made by her Paris dressmaker. The dressmaker cannot come until July."

Whack! "Wait for clothes when Dove wants to marry her? She sounds a fool. They sound like a pair of fools. A perfect pair."

John decided to be wise and say nothing.

"I feel reckless tonight."

He pressed his lips together. Reckless? An understatement. She was so nervy with emotion he could feel the prickle of it under his own skin. But he gave her a mild answer.

"Is that so."

"Yes. Let's do something reckless."

"Such as what."

"I don't know."

"Well. That is a problem then."

She gulped a deep breath, like a swimmer needing air.

"Do you want to sleep with me tonight, John?"

They strolled along. He eyed her, his anger surfacing. "No."

Her color rose. Even the bit of freckled chest that showed at the top of her modest bodice colored in hot embarrassment. Agitated, she gave her fingers mindless work to do. With fierce, nervous little movements, she shredded the bark from her stick and strewed it.

"I'm sorry, John. That was a stupid thing to say."

"Yes, it was."

But to show her he felt no rancor, he plucked the silly stick from her hand, winged it into the field and took her hand as they walked. He gave it a comforting squeeze. Sleep with her? Sweet Mary. He would give his eye-teeth to sleep with her. But not like this. Not just to spite Dove.

He gently swung her hand as they strolled. It was a warm, firm little hand, a hand he'd like to hold for the rest of his life. A covey of quail flew up in the path, whistling their shrill, dainty alarm, and Pax went into a barking frenzy. When his lungs gave out, he straddled the path, wheezing, head hanging, coughing his old-dog cough. Jericho stooped and hugged him. Pax didn't need the hug, but John suspected Jericho did. So when she popped up again, he companionably draped an arm around her waist and walked her on. By and by, she reciprocated, slipping an arm around his waist. There was no romance in her gesture. He wished there were. They strolled into the mauve twilight. He could feel her sadness. He wanted to shoot Dove.

"Do they—are they—sharing one bedchamber?"

"Such a question."

"You would know. Dove tells you everything."

"Only if I ask. But I would not ask, now, would I? 'Tisn't proper. 'Tisn't any of my business. Nor *yours*, Jericho."

But she looked so bereft, he suffered a pang.

"However. If you want my opinion, they are not. Lady Marguerite is a canny woman, and canny women always withhold the bed privilege until marriage, now, don't they? It gives them control. And God knows, Marguerite likes to control.''

Jericho glanced up. ''You don't like her?''

''I didn't say that, now, did I. I merely said she likes to control. She has some sterling qualities. She is intelligent, witty, and when the mood strikes her she can be impulsively generous. Like Dove.''

John gazed at her. As the twilight grew duskier, her vivid coloring intensified. Her eyes glowed a deep purplish blue. Her hair shone like copper. Sleep with her? Sweet heaven. Yet he managed to keep his voice steady.

''She's not so bad, Jericho. She's a nice lady.''

Jericho snorted. But in her heart, she suspected it was true. She'd watched Lady Marguerite arrive and had seen nothing amiss. True, Lady Marguerite had alighted from the coach with the grand air of the highborn, and there'd been a superior lift to her chin. But, dear life. What woman wouldn't feel superior, marrying Dove? Worse, she'd been beautiful. She had an exotic heart-shaped face. Her eyes had an exotic, upward tilt. Her hair wasn't an obnoxious mass of unruly red; it was dark and sleek as a raven's wing. Her skin wasn't freckled, but flawless as cream. Jericho doubted Lady Marguerite could stutter if she tried. She drew a discouraged breath.

''If you want my opinion,'' John went on, ''I b'lieve Marguerite will be the ideal wife for Dove. She will keep him under her thumb. She will make him toe the line. She will make him grow up. She won't put up with his wild, thoughtless ways. Not after they're married.''

Instantly, John saw he'd taken the wrong tack. For he got a scathing glance. He held his tongue. When they came to the end of the path, he helped her jump a shallow ditch, and then they were on the dusty road that led into St. John's Basket. Excited villagers flocked toward them, heading for the festivities in Arleigh Castle meadow, women bustling by in fresh white caps and aprons, baskets of fragrant baked goods on their arms. The men hustled along, too, a wooden staff with a clay lantern pot swinging from each man's shoulder. No one in St. John's Basket could remember the origin of the custom, but after dark on Mid-Summer's Eve, every male in the village participated in a Night March. John thought it a grand and thrilling sight, a hundred or more lighted lanterns marching around the walls of Arleigh Castle.

John greeted each passing man and woman by name, for he knew them all. He felt a surge of pride walking with Jericho. Her vivid coloring, her excellent figure drew the eye of every man who went by. But she didn't seem to notice. She was lost in thought, pondering. When they were alone in the lane again, he thought to finish the subject of Dove and Marguerite once and for all, and then speak of something dearer to his heart. He squeezed her hand.

"There's an old saying, Jericho. In every marriage, one of the two does the kissing and the other offers the cheek. With Dove and Marguerite, it's always been Dove doing the kissing and Marguerite offering the cheek."

She glanced at him in dismay.

"You mean she doesn't love him?"

He sighed. "I didn't say that, now, did I. Of course, she loves him. She's crazy for him. Always has been. I'm only sayin' that the one who offers the cheek controls the marriage. Marguerite doesn't do much kissing. But she collects a lot of kisses."

She drew a breath and sent agitated glances out at the cottages they passed. "She's horrid. Now I truly do hate her, John. I do."

Did he detect a tiny blaze of tears in her eyes? *Damn!* He'd hoped to put Dove-and-Marguerite to rest. He'd hoped to talk about himself tonight, not goddamn Dove. He'd hoped— hell, admit it. He'd hoped to propose marriage.

Marriage. They walked along, their footfalls muted in the dust of the lane. They passed a cottage. The fragrance of mint drifted from a kitchen herb garden. Marriage. He let the word seep into him, work its way down into flesh and bone and marrow, into the center of his being. Face it, John. If you wed Jericho, *you* will be the one doing the kissing, and she will offer the cheek. For her heart belongs to Dove. Can you be content with that? Can you? He knew the answer. Sweet heaven, yes!

He gave her hand a squeeze.

"It's not all bad, you know. Being the one doin' the kiss-ing."

"Dove deserves better than that."

"We all deserve better than that. Everybody in the whole wide world. But most people learn to be content with what they get. For love's a queer thing, now, ain't it. It goes where it will, and that's a fact. Jericho, there's no amount of pushing or shoving or tugging can make it go where we want."

In the deepening twilight, he saw her lips tremble. But she was no baby. By and by, she gave him a staunch look. And even a smile.

"I'm enjoying the walk."

He smiled broadly. "Good. So am I."

Jericho felt better once she was back in the midst of the revelry, sitting on the grass at the edge of the dance field with John, companionably sharing a tankard of ale. She blanched when Dove appeared suddenly up on the castle hill, standing in a large group of nobles and ladies, his golden hair distinctive and shining in the moonlight. Her heart beat unevenly. What a sight they made, the silk-clad nobility lei-surely strolling down the hill, their fine clothes shimmering in the moonlight, the rich silk leaping into bright color as they drew nearer the roaring bonfires.

She drank deeper from John's tankard. She already felt tiddly with drink. But perhaps tiddly was the best way to feel tonight. Tiddly, she wouldn't think of Dove and Lady Mar-guerite. When she'd drunk, John idly picked up a twig that lay in the grass and tossed it into her lap.

" 'Tis your boon. Your prayer, your wish for the coming year. Make a wish and toss the stick into the fire. Everyone will toss a boon into the fire on Mid-Summer's Eve."

"Did you?"

"Yes."

"What did you wish for?"

"A wife."

A calm statement. Not flirtation. Her gaze flew to his.

Steady brown eyes, a steady, unfurrowed brow, a steady, decent spirit. He was a fine man. He would make a good, kind-hearted husband. But he wasn't Dove.

"John, I am not the wife for you."

"I think you are."

"No. No, I'm not."

"What are you then, Jericho? What is it you plan to be?" He sent a flickering glance at the hill, at the descending lords and ladies. "A mistress for a married lord?"

She looked swiftly away. So he'd heard the gossip about kissing on the bed. She was deeply ashamed. John's regard, John's good opinion of her was something she didn't want to lose.

"It was stupid of me."

"Yes, it was. It didn't hurt Dove's reputation; people expect that of him. It hurt your's."

She flushed and acknowledged it with a nod of misery.

"As to what I am going to do. I'm going to be a dame schoolteacher. In London. And after that, in New York, as soon as I earn passage money for myself and Black Bartimaeus. I don't plan to marry. Not ever."

John sighed in irritation, but he didn't press. Out around the blazing bonfires, dancing began in earnest. These were not the parlor dances Jericho had danced at Maritje Ten Boom's waffle frolics. These were wild romps. When the first few young men came leaping through the bonfires to impress their sweethearts she gasped in shock, but then she got used to it.

A tent pavilion stood at one end of the dance field, for the nobility to use. Few of them used it. Most of them strolled amongst the villagers. Lord Lark ignored the pavilion, and with a pagan whoop, slung off his silk coat. He leaped into the dancing, leaping through bonfires. The villagers whooped and cheered.

Only Lady Marguerite wanted no part of the common people. She headed straight to the pavilion, crooking her finger at Dove, bidding him come. Dove's expression as he watched Lord Lark at his fun was downright disheartened, and Jericho's softer self felt sorry for him. Dove loved a party. He loved nothing better than to get drunk and cheerful. How wonderful he would be, jumping through the bonfires. But her harder self refused to feel sorry for him. Kiss her on the bed for days on end, and then jump up—"Hallelujah!"—to fetch his bride, would he?

"Do you want to join the dancing?" John asked.

"Yes!"

"This dance is pretty wild. Should we wait for a milder?"

"No! The wilder the better."

Drinking wine in the pavilion with Marguerite, Dove impatiently scanned the crowd for Jericho. Where was she? He'd sent for her the minute he'd arrived home and had walked into his room to find her message.

Sign My Indenture

Her demand impaled on a candlestick! It still made him smile. She hadn't come when he'd sent for her, so he'd sent twice more. She hadn't come those times either, and his exhilarated, large-hearted mood had turned to irritation. Grubworm! She had a stubborn streak a mile wide.

Hell, he hadn't sent for her to kiss her. He had Marguerite to kiss now. He'd only wanted to talk. He liked talking to Jericho. He enjoyed being with her. The truth was, he'd missed her during his stay in London. And that had surprised him. A queer business, missing the company of a bondslave. Queer and damned bewildering. Planting one hip on the table edge, he swilled wine from his goblet, then leaned down to kiss Marguerite who sat on a chair beside him, beautiful and sparkling. When she kissed him back, he eagerly rid himself of the goblet, drew her up and into his embrace. He kissed her again with total satisfaction. Well, *almost* total satisfaction.

He frowned. "Damn it, Marguerite, how can you have lived in France and not like French kissing?"

Draping her silk-clad arms around his neck, she smiled. "I don't know, darling. I do not like it, that's all."

"Could you learn to like it?" he asked hopefully.

"No. Sweetheart, don't wrinkle my gown."

He sighed in disappointment, loosened his grip, and kissed her the way she liked.

"Dove, how long must we stay at this peasant revelry?"

He was taken by surprise. He searched her beautiful up-turned face. "Don't you like it? Hell, I'm damned fond of Mid-Summer's Eve. So were you when you were a child. I like rubbing elbows with the villagers."

She lifted one beautifully plucked eyebrow.

"We'll leave whenever you like," he conceded.

"Thank you, darling!" Her ravishing smile brought a deep dimple to each cheek. Her sooty lashes fluttered provocatively. He stroked her silken back and sighed in utter happiness. Hope sprang up.

"Marguerite, tonight. Can't we?"

She shook her head in a positive no.

"I might conceive."

"What of it? It's a natural consequence of love. Now or two months from now, what difference does it make?"

"Dove, we've discussed this endlessly! I will not have people counting to nine after we wed. My *gown*, sweetheart, you're wrinkling my gown."

"We could use something. A shield of sheep gut?"

She drew back in distaste. "I am not a whore, Dove. Condums are for whores. Darling! Don't wrinkle my gown."

"Sorry." He tried to think. "Bits of sponge soaked in vinegar?"

She made a wry face.

"I could come out. At the last moment."

"But you wouldn't. I know you, Dove. I've known you all of my life. You would get carried away."

He tried to find humor in all of this, but it was damned difficult. He loved her so much, wanted her so badly.

"I could dip my pecker in boiling oil. Would that suit you?"

"Dove, don't be crude."

"Crude, hell. I'm in *love* with you."

"And *I* am in love with *you*. But we *must* wait." Her voice grew crisp. "Besides, the marriage contract is still being drawn up for us to sign."

"So? I don't give a damn about money, endowments, dowries, legal claptrap."

"That's because you are a man. A woman has to protect herself. The law being what it is, a widow can end up penniless. Look at what happened to me. Nearly everything went to my husband's despicable children. What did I get? A paltry chateau in Rouen. A few thousand francs in income a year."

Dove stared at her in surprise. Somehow, it came as a rude jolt, Marguerite anticipating his imminent departure from this world. He was damned shocked. And hurt. His face must have shown it, for she twined her silken arms around his neck and gave him her provocative kitten look.

"Silly! I *love* you. I plan to be married to you for at least fifty years, Dove."

"Well, so do I," he said, testy, his belligerance rising. "But maybe I ought to order your shroud and coffin *now*. Just in case."

"Dove, don't be sarcastic. Marriage is a practical arrangement as well as a love arrangement. Practical matters *must* be spelled out."

He managed to remain disgruntled for another couple of minutes, then caved in. Hell, she was so damned beautiful. And he loved her. Sensing his capitulation, she lifted her mouth to be kissed, and he gratefully kissed it. When the kiss ended, he ran his hand up and down her warm silken back. He sighed and reluctantly let her go. He was wrinkling her.

"Let's put a boon on the fire, Marguerite. Together. Make a wish together."

"Don't be silly, sweetheart. Peasant nonsense."

His heart fell a little. He helped himself to more wine. Fiddle music filled the night, gay and lilting. He drank and tapped his toe to the rhythm. Out on the dance field, Lark had his arms around a fairhaired girl from the village and would surely take her to bed tonight if she proved willing. The music and the merriment soared louder, wilder.

He spotted Jericho!

She was dancing a wild country dance around one of the bonfires, her mop of red hair flying as she linked arms with the other women. A soft smile sprang to his lips. *Sign My Indenture*. Skewered, by damn. On a candlestick. She had grit, that grubworm. Smiling, he refilled his goblet and took a gulp. Marguerite tugged at his coat.

"Dove, you will get drunk," she said disapprovingly.

His spirits rising with the wine and the sight of Jericho, he flashed her a cheerful smile. "No. No, I won't. I promise."

But the faster Jericho danced, the faster he drank. Somehow, she filled his senses. He couldn't tear his gaze away, he couldn't stop watching her. Each time her red hair swung in the firelight, he smiled softly.

When a clamor went up from the freely imbibing parish— "Lor' Dove! Come dance, Lor' Dove! Come'a! Come'a! Jump ye the boonfire! Bring yer sweetheart!"—he swung to Marguerite with zest.

"Marguerite! Let's join the dancing."

"On the grass? With peasants? You jest."

"Then I'm going."

"You most certainly will not," she objected. "Dove, your dignity, your rank. I will not have my future husband—"

But, full of wine and high spirits, he shucked dignity and rank as quickly as he shucked his silk coat and whipped it away. He went leaping out onto the dance field. "Hooray!" the parish welcomed him. "Lor' Dove, Lor' Dove!"

Jericho was exhausted but happy. She wiped her brow and shook the damp fabric of her bodice, shaking cool air into it. Damp patches clung under her arms and to the small of her back. But she didn't care. She didn't want to stop. John was right. Nobody could dance and be unhappy at the same time.

Laughing breathlessly with Janie and Birgit, the scullery children, she went with them to the ale barrel, dipped and drank. Then she returned to the dance field. A circle formed for the next dance. Fed fresh wood by overzealous boys, the bonfires blazed and roared, sending sparks whooshing up to the stars. Jericho threw back her head and watched them soar. She felt dizzy, tiddly, happy.

The men and boys formed a circle around the women. The

women marched ten steps to the right, the men ten to the left. To her delight, Jericho found herself partnered next with ten-year-old Harry, the turnspit, who blushed sweetly as she gave him her hands.

The fiddlers rippled into introductory notes. Men joshed their partners or flirted with them, depending upon their luck in the draw. Feet tapped. Everyone drew a breath, ready to go. Then, just as the music plunged into the dance, a roar went up and the fiddlers stopped. Jericho whirled. Surely no one would jump *this* bonfire. This one was too big. Too hot, too blazing.

She watched, gasping, as someone came leaping through the flames, like a golden stag—arms flung overhead. A wonderful leap! The crowd cheered wildly. With springy quick steps, Dove landed right in front of her.

Tiddly with ale, she felt nothing but joy. He stood there, hazel eyes bright and humorous, hands casually draped on hips, as if he'd jumped nothing more dangerous than a mud puddle.

"I got your message, grubworm."

"Were you horribly angry?"

He grinned. "Horribly."

Ignoring the loud cheering, he extended his palms in invitation. Without an instant of hesitation, she partnered him. The fiddlers struck up, and Dove yanked her off her feet, taking off at a gallop. Exhausted minutes earlier, she felt a wild surge of vigor. With his lively, smiling eyes on her's, scarcely ever looking away, she felt she could dance until her feet were stubs. Dance? She could fly!

And soon she saw she might have to! For this dance was rough and downright dangerous. Bounding around the bonfires at a sidestepping gallop, men swung their shoulders into other men's shoulders, knocking them down, and after the first startled minute Jericho saw *that* was the point. Men whooped and butted each other like bulls, trying to knock each other down, and if even a knee brushed the ground, the dance master thumbed the couple off the field.

And Dove didn't spare her. He didn't allow her to be bumped—when a collision seemed certain, he grabbed her by the waist and whirled her out of the way, taking the bump himself—but he danced her into the thick of it, as happy and drunk as a coot. She knew he was drunk, for he shouted odd things to her over the noise of the wild cheering.

"Do I wrinkle your gown?" he shouted.

"What?" she shouted back, deafened by the loud music and the cheering.

"Your gown," he shouted. "When I kiss you, do I wrinkle your gown?"

"Dove, are you drunk?"

"Yes! Answer me! Do I wrinkle your gown when I kiss you?"

"I don't know," she shouted back. "Dear life, I've never noticed."

"That's what I thought," he shouted, and with a grin, grabbed her and wrenched her into a sidestepping gallop that stripped the breath from her. They danced like maniacs. The bonfire spun. The flames bounded upward like huge golden feathers, as if kin to this golden Dove who was cheerfully dancing her into her grave. She grew so dizzy, she could scarcely keep her feet. Her breath flew from her lungs.

"Dove!" she gasped.

"Do you want to stop?" he shouted.

Stop? Of course she should want to. Only a mad woman wouldn't. Yet something wild and wayward flared in her.

"No!" she shouted.

"That's the spirit, Pansy Eyes!"

"This is like Collect Pond," she shouted. "The day you skated me into a snowbank."

"It's better than Collect Pond," he shouted back. "You were an ugly duckling then. Now you're a swan!" She grinned. He liked her. He did!

The dance field was quickly decimated. Laughing and whooping, crashing and banging, dancers dropped right and left and were thumbed off the field. The cheers of bystanders roared. Dear life, she thought. And she had presumed England was a civilized country.

Soon only one other pair remained in the boisterous contest, young Harry who'd partnered Janie. They made so sweet a couple—Harry's earnest, galumphing prance and Janie's bouncing curls—that no one'd had the heart to give them a finishing bump. Dove's eyes gleamed.

"Let's go get 'em, grubworm."

"Dove, for heaven's sake—"

But he took a fresh grip on her wrists and charged, yanking her along, yanking her feet out from under. Then, she saw his intent. For though he went charging at Harry like a bull and swung his shoulder with a bloodcurdling whoop, his shoulder merely grazed Harry, and it was Dove himself who staggered as if gored, and it was Dove who fell down in the grass, taking her with him, pulling her down on top of him, a tangle of petticoats and breeches.

The crowd rushed in to cheer Harry and to slap his proud little shoulders. As petticoats and feet shot by, Dove crushed her close and kissed her. It was a drunken kiss, wet and ardent. She pushed him.

"Dove, behave!"

He kissed her again, hot, sweaty. "Jericho," he whispered, his wine breath feathering her lips. "Oh, Jericho, I need you. Come to my bedchamber tonight? Come to my bed? Become my mistress?"

Her chest pounded. "Dove, dear life! Let go. Let me up."

"No. Not ever."

He tried to kiss her again, but she wrenched free and scrambled to her feet. Grabbing his elbow, pulling and tugging, she hoisted her drunken lord to his unsteady feet. For she'd spotted a silken gown promenading across the field, coming toward them.

Her breast fluttered with trepidation as she tugged Dove and sent darting glances across the field toward Lady Marguerite and John, who strolled toward them.

"Dove, behave! Look. Lady Marguerite is coming. Stand up. Dove, you're strangling me."

"Where?" he demanded.

As best she could, while being strangled in his heavy, drunken arms, she nodded, indicating Lady Marguerite's approach. His eyes found her and lighted with love. He was so plainly besotted with his Marguerite that she wanted to kick him.

"Isn't she beautiful, grubworm? Isn't she?"

"Yes, yes, she's beautiful. Dove! Stand up alone. Don't lean on me. Let me go!"

He drunkenly smooched her temple. "Never. Hell, I'm a happy man. I've the bride I love and a grubworm who loves me. Who could be happier?"

"Who indeed," she said darkly and gave him a shove. He listed for a moment, then found his balance just as John and Lady Marguerite approached.

"Darling, such a dance!" Marguerite sailed into his arms, all silken grace. Jericho looked at her jealously. "Such vigor! I fear you tramped upon your partner's toes."

"Marguerite! Sweetheart, I'm so happy. You've come down onto the dance field."

"But, of course, darling. I love you."

Dove wrapped sweaty arms around her and they kissed. Jericho looked away and glared into space. When she glanced back, John was looking at her with vexation. She glared at him, too, then turned to go.

"Grubworm, wait!" Dove said. "Come here." He grabbed her arm. It angered her to look at him. He was so obviously a fool in love.

"Dove, I want to go."

Nestled silkenly in the crook of Dove's arm, Lady Marguerite lifted one perfectly plucked brow. "She calls you 'Dove'? Your bondslave calls you 'Dove' and not 'Lord Dove'? You permit it?"

Jericho flushed. She'd not meant to call him that in public. But Marguerite's sleek perfection had addled her. That, and the ale she'd drunk.

"Of course," Dove boomed with drunken cheer. "She has called me Dove ever since she was knee-high and stuttering like a chittering squirrel on 'Lord'."

Jericho felt the blood rush into her cheeks. To be humiliated like this . . . She didn't know where to look.

"Darling! Surely she can say 'Lord' now, at this age? I think it only proper my future husband be addressed by his title and not by his given name."

"If you insist," Dove agreed cheerfully. "Grubworm? From now on, you call me Lord Dove."

John snapped, "Dove, don't be mean."

Her cheeks burning with shame, Jericho groped for her last remaining shreds of dignity. "May I go now, 'Lord' Dove?" she asked.

He grinned playfully. "After you have curtsied to your new mistress."

Something flashed inside. Something hot and rebellious. She threw a stormy look at Lady Marguerite and stubbornly stood her ground. John touched her gently. "Jericho," he warned in a whisper. She shook him off.

"Curtsy," Dove requested again.

Her spine filled with steel.

"She is not very obedient, is she," Marguerite said with amusement. It was meant to rile Dove, and it did. The smiling good-humor went out of his eyes.

"Grubworm," Dove warned, his voice losing its drunken affability, temper rising in his eyes. She lifted her chin, defying him. She ought not to have done so. She was embarrassing him in front of his bride-to-be, and she knew it. Furious, he swore at the top of his voice.

"Damn you, Jericho, this is not New Amsterdam. Curtsy!"

It was a humiliating insult. His loud bellow drew glances from all over the dance field, sounding like precisely what it was—a scolding for a disobedient servant. Tears of shock sprang to her eyes and burned there.

"Dove, for God's sake!" John said.

Eyes brimming, Jericho lowered a knee in the curtsy she should have offered in the first place. A curtsy was Lady Marguerite's due. She knew that. She'd known it all along. Then, unable to stop the tears a moment longer, she whirled and ran.

Dove felt like dung, watching Jericho rush from the dance field crying, and John rubbed his nose in it.

"You've done some thoughtless things in your time, Dove," he snarled before taking off after her. "But this takes the cake!"

Dove watched her run from him, her heart plainly broken. Why in hell had he done that? He'd stabbed her to the quick, insulting her in public like that.

"Darling! Give me one more small betrothal gift?"

Staring after Jericho, stunned, he responded by rote.

"Anything." Suddenly, he was cold sober. God, how could he make it up to her? Those big, dark blue eyes, huge with shock and betrayal. He'd never insulted her in public before. Not even in New Amsterdam, when she'd been an eleven-year-old pest, driving him out of his skull.

"Will you give me whatever I ask?"

"Yes, yes, anything," he said absently. He felt sick. She was on the hill now, going up the path to the castle, her cheap white bodice reflecting moonlight. He watched John catch up, put a comforting arm around her, slow her down and walk her on.

"You promise?"

"Yes, yes, anything you want. Anything." He would sign her indenture tomorrow. Hell, he would sign it tonight and take it to her. She deserved her freedom, didn't she? She'd been damned loyal. Yet, the thought of releasing her, letting her go, gave him a sting.

"Swear on your father's grave."

"Yes, yes, I swear," he agreed absently. "Anything, Marguerite, anything you want."

Wrenching his gaze from Jericho's distant figure, he turned. He'd scarcely been listening. Buoyed up somewhat by his honorable intentions, his determination to make it up to the grubworm, he took Marguerite into his arms and gave her the attention a beautiful bride-to-be deserved.

"What is it you want, sweetheart? Name it. It is yours."

"Swear on your father's grave that you will give your Marguerite whatever she asks?"

"So be it. I swear on my father's grave. Ask what you will."

She twined her silken arms around his neck. "Darling! I want that bondslave. I want her indenture. I want to own her."

Chapter Fourteen

Dove awoke at noon the next day with a sinking feeling. Had he done what he suspected he'd done? Oh, God. His throbbing head bore testimony to it. For after pledging his word to Marguerite, he'd felt so low he'd gone tearing into the midst of the revelry and had got himself rip-roaring drunk. He vaguely recalled being carried up to the castle by a jovial group of pig farmers.

"Joseph," he croaked, unable to open his eyes for the pain of it. His own voice boomed in his skull like a cannon.

"On the nightstand, milord," his manservant called cheerily. "At your elbow, milord."

Dove groped blindly. His fingers closed around a goblet. The noxious libation he unsteadily brought to his lips smelled like fish oil that had stood in hot sun for three months. But Joseph's remedies worked. Girding himself to swallow it, he shuddered, then swilled it down in one gulp. Falling back on the pillow, he grabbed a second pillow and pressed it to his eyes.

"Joseph? Get Jericho."

"Ay, milord."

Maybe it wasn't true. Maybe he'd only dreamed it. Hell, what had the grubworm ever asked of him? Money, jewels, silk gowns, privileges? No. Only to have one measly year knocked off her indenture. Only freedom. Guilt washed in like dead fish in the tide.

By and by, Joseph returned. "Mr. Pennington will not allow Jericho to come up, milord. Jericho is assigned to new duties, milord. In Lady Marguerite's apartment."

"Oh, hell." It was true. Rolling over, he buried his face in the pillow and breathed feathers. "Get John Phipps," he mumbled.

"Mr. John Phipps was here earlier, milord. You do not recall, milord? He stood over your bed, shouting at you, milord. Quite loudly."

Vaguely, Dove remembered it. "Ask him to come in again."

"Mr. John Phipps had his business to tend in London, milord. He left two hours ago, milord. And if I do say so— left in a vile temper."

"Oh, hell." Dove breathed goosefeathers.

"Will there be anything else, milord?"

"Yes," Dove muttered. "Shoot me."

Sleeping fitfully that night on a pallet bed in the servant's hall amidst two-dozen snoring servants, Jericho awoke to the sounds of a disturbance.

"Sorry—sorry—hell, did I step on you too, Harry? Sorry. Percy, old boy—stepped on your hand, did I? Hell, I'm sorry. Go back to sleep, go back to sleep."

She rose on one elbow and blinked. Dove was groping his way through the large dark hall, bumping into cots. Flouncing onto her stomach, she punched her pillow and settled into it like a stone. Talk to him? Never.

"Jericho?" he whispered loudly, trying to find her, "Jericho?" She ignored him. But he found her anyway, after several minutes of popping about in the dark like a ridiculous rooster. Finding her, he squatted.

"Jericho?" he whispered. "What in hell are you doing here? Why aren't you in your room? You gave me a scare. I thought you'd run away."

She remained mute as stone, then changed her mind and threw him an angry hiss.

"Ask Mr. Pennington. Go ask! Ask!"

"He withdrew your room privilege?"

"Yes!"

"But why?" he said in astonishment. "Why would he do

a thing like that?'' With a lithe movement, he commandeered the small space between her cot and Janie's, lowering himself to the floor to sit Indian style. He looked so handsome in the darkness with his golden hair, his white shirt glowing, that she wanted to weep.

"Why, why, why!" she snapped. "How should I know? Go ask him. Go—" She started to fire more at him, but her throat closed. She'd loved her little sleeping closet. It was the first room she'd ever had all to herself. In New Amsterdam she'd shared with Daisy and later with Cook. She'd enjoyed keeping the room scrubbed and polished, keeping it Dutch clean. She swallowed hard.

Waking on her pallet, bright as a bird, Janie raised up on one elbow and put in her penny's worth. "Lor' Dove?" Janie whispered. "Maybe Mr. Pennington took away Jericho's room priv'lege because he saw you sneak down to visit Jericho sometimes in the middle of the night."

Dove glared at the child. "I do not *sneak*. God's soup, Janie, this is my house, and if I want to visit my bondslave in the middle of the night, I do not have to *sneak*."

"Well, you tiptoe then."

"Tiptoeing is not *sneaking*, damn it. I tiptoe because—well, out of consideration to other servants who are sleeping."

"Oh."

Now the tears truly threatened. For she'd loved Dove's middle-of-the-night visits. They'd been such innocent visits, with him chattery and full of wine and high spirits, or perhaps, on other nights, sober and feeling low, touched by his peculiar midnight melancholy and wanting to talk of half-remembered tragedies—of snarling dogs and spurting blood and of seeing a beloved father's throat torn out before his very eyes. And she! Hunched on one end of the cot, arms wrapped around her knees, sympathetically listening in the darkness, talking with him, gladly sharing the high or the low. And if they'd parted with a sweet kiss at the end of it? Well, why not! She swallowed hard.

"Janie, stay out of this," she whispered.

"Yes, brat, stay out of this," Dove demanded in a whisper.

"Roll over and go to sleep. Jericho, I'm guilty as hell. I feel—"

"I canna Lor' Dove."

"Why not!"

"You be sittin' on the hem of my petticoat."

"Oh, for God's sake." He wrenched the petticoat free, and obediently Janie rolled over. But Jericho knew she was all ears. Janie and everyone else.

"Dove, go away," she whispered. "Just go away. Haven't you done enough? You've betrayed me, and you've betrayed Black Bartimaeus. Just go away. You're waking everyone."

Sleepers stirred throughout the room. On the pallet to her left, Birgit mumbled, her dreams disturbed.

"Jericho, damn it, we can't talk here."

"Good! Go away."

"Jericho, come into the corridor. I want to talk to you."

He stroked her hair, a loving stroke, but she yanked her head away. "No. I'm not required to talk to you anymore, Dove. I don't belong to you anymore. I belong to someone else now. My indenture belongs to someone else."

"Oh, hell! Sweeting, I feel so bad about your indenture."

On the men's side of the room, a burly form reared up in the darkness. "Pipe down over there!"

"Pipe down yourself," Dove snapped back. "This is Lord Dove, and *I* will pipe down when I'm damn good and ready."

The rough voice sweetened to a whisper. "Yessir, yessir, milord. 'Twon't bother nobody a tad. Make all the noise ye want, Lor' Dove."

"I intend to!" Dove said, then turned and resumed his whispering. "Jericho? Beauty? Come out in the hall with me."

"No."

"Jericho, I've come to apologize."

"Fine. Then you've done it. Now you can go before you wake every single person in this whole stupid castle. An apology is fair exchange for a year of a person's life."

"Jericho, I'm sorry."

"Sorry! Go tell that to Black Bartimaeus," she hissed. "*He* was more than sorry. He was heartsick. We had wonderful plans, Dove. Plans for my dame school. Go tell *him* you're sorry. Tell Black Bartimaeus.''

She punched her pillow and settled into it like a rock.

"Jericho, listen to me."

"No."

"Jericho, I've asked Marguerite to set you free. She is considering it."

If he'd thought to make her jump for joy, he'd missed by a mile. She reared up off her pillow and hissed like a snake poked by a sharp stick. "You *asked* her? You *asked* her? Why don't you put a ring through your nose, the better she can lead you about with!"

His clothes rustled and he sprang up like a shot. She saw with dismay that she'd wounded him in a way no woman should wound a man. For a moment, his face looked as hurt and vulnerable as a little boy's. Instantly, she sat up.

"Dove? I'm sorry. I didn't mean—"

"Hellcat," he snapped aloud, forgetful of the sleeping, snoring lumps around him. "Rot in bondage or take your indenture and leave tomorrow. I care not."

With that, he left, leaving a trail of startled sleepers behind him, sleepers who rose up on their elbows, confused, gawking, blinking. As the grumbling hall settled down once more, Jericho lay wide-eyed on her pillow and absorbed the pain of it. She ached. She ought not to have spoken so to Dove. She'd hurt him. But neither should *he* have wounded her, giving her indenture to Marguerite. They'd hurt each other. She dabbed at moisture in her eyes.

There was a slight, birdlike rustling, and Janie reached over and put a small comforting arm around her.

"Jericho? Does this mean you and Lor' Dove don't like each other no more?"

She wiped her eyes. "No," she whispered when her clotted throat allowed her to speak again. "We like each other, Janie." God help us, she thought, we like each other too much.

* * *

"The king is coming, the king is coming!" Chattering a mile a minute, Janie dashed into the scullery like a whirlwind and danced on her toes, too excited to stand still. "Jericho! You can see the king coming plain as day from the castle wall. He's not riding in the royal coach with his mistresses —he's astride his own mount. Oh, Jericho, he's galloping, racing all the court gen'lmen!"

Jericho could muster up little enthusiasm. In the two heart-sore weeks that Dove had ignored her, cutting her dead whenever their paths crossed, she'd felt no enthusiasm for anything. But she couldn't daunt a child. She gave Janie a smile and a hug.

"Run up to the castle wall, then. Watch the king arrive. I'll cover your post. You too, Harry," she added, turning to the young turnspit. "But only for a minute," she warned. "Lest Mr. Pennington come in and find you gone."

It was nasty work, tending a turnspit. Puffs of smoke flew up, hitting the eye like fine sand. Dripping fat popped in the fire, making sparks fly like red-hot grapeshot. At other fire-places in the kitchen, turnspit dogs trotted in their cylinder cages. Patient little souls. But as nasty as the turnspit could be on a sweltering hot July day, Jericho preferred it to serving Marguerite, who had made her life a misery. Jericho had jumped at the chance to volunteer for kitchen work during the king's visit.

When the venison was pronounced done and the cooks had removed it to the warming oven, Jericho went up to the castle wall to see the king's arrival for herself. She joined the claque of servants who'd gathered on the wall above the gatehouse. Slipping an arm around Mrs. Phipps, she stood with the excited, trembling woman, watching.

Down below, the castleyard boiled with activity, and off in the distance, on the road from London, a dozen coaches trundled toward Arleigh Castle, followed by a vanguard of mounted Swiss mercenaries who wore the House of Stuart scarlet. Their pole-ax pikes sparkled in the sun, scarlet flags fluttering. Janie and Harry were right, Jericho admitted to herself. It *was* exciting.

Overwhelmed, growing excited, she scarcely knew where

to look first. Her gaze swept the castleyard and found Dove at once. But that was only natural. She could find Dove in a dark closet. Her soul was tuned to him the way a homing pigeon is tuned to the pigeon cot.

How wonderful he looked in a suit of rich black silk, the sleeves puffed and banded tightly with black velvet bands. She chose not to notice the woman on his arm. She didn't care to notice that Marguerite had never looked lovelier, a vision in diamonds and pearls and royal blue silk. She looked down at her own grease-spattered skirt.

Having raced and arrived ahead of his entourage, King Charles II stood in the courtyard conversing with the de Monts. He was easy to spot. Except for Black Bartimaeus, the king was easily the tallest man in all England, topping six feet by six inches. Truly a "black prince," he lacked the Stuart fairness. He was swarthy, his complexion dark.

His manner, however, was charming. Famous for winning the love of his subjects—highborn or low—he now proved it. Glancing up at the gatehouse and seeing the large throng of servants, he lifted his lacy wrist and waved. Mrs. Phipps nearly swooned. A sensual man, the king's gaze roved languidly from servant girl to servant girl. When his eyes stopped on Jericho, he doffed his plumed hat and smiled. She was utterly stunned.

"My stars, child, curtsy!" Mrs. Phipps whispered, all agog. "You've gained the king's notice."

Quickly, Jericho curtsied, but she couldn't help but respond to the king's charming smile with a grin of utter delight. Dear life, to be noticed by the king of England!

Mrs. Phipps tugged at her skirt. "Child, take care. The king has an appetite for pretty women."

Rising from her curtsy, Jericho knew a moment of uneasiness. But the king's attention was fleeting, and he'd already turned to converse with Lady de Mont, Lord Aubrey, Lord Lark, and with Lord Raven, who'd come to Arleigh Castle for this special event. Only Dove continued to scowl up at the gatehouse until Lady Marguerite tugged his arm, drawing him into the conversation.

With a clatter as loud as thunder, coaches rumbled into the courtyard, and the castleyard became a beehive of activity.

When the first splendid coach came to a swaying halt and a footman jumped down to unfold the step and open the door, the king himself strode forward to help two passengers debark.

"That's Castlemayne," Mrs. Phipps murmured excitedly as the king took the gloved hand of a tall, aloof lady who wore pearls and silk, and who stepped down onto the red carpet as if it were her due. "Lady Castlemayne is the king's favorite."

"I can see that," Jericho said with an impish smile. "She is carrying."

"A mark of the king's favor," Mrs. Phipps quipped tartly, then softened. "Ah, well. The queen is barren, poor man. Every man of tender sensibilities desires children. What's to be done?"

Jericho's gaze flew to Dove. Dove would want children. What if Marguerite proved barren? Would he turn to someone else? To *her*? What would she say? Would she be willing to bear Dove's children? She breathed unsteadily.

With charming manners, the king helped a second lady to alight, and the servants murmured excitedly. Unlike the aloof Castlemayne, this royal mistress was petite, an elfin creature with a playful smile. Jericho liked her at once, but Mrs. Phipps pursed her lips in disapproval.

"Nell Gwynne, the actress. What is the world coming to, I ask you, when women boldly take to the stage, donning men's breeches and stockings, displaying themselves as bold as any man? You may be certain His Majesty's father would not have allowed it in *his* London."

Jericho watched Lady de Mont greet Castlemayne and Nell Gwynne coolly but politely. A king's mistresses had to be tolerated, evidently.

"Anyhow, here comes a bitter pill for my Lady de Mont to swallow." Mrs. Phipps pointed as a black-lacquered coach came rumbling under the gatehouse wall, drawn by four sleek black horses that wore ostrich plumes on their head harness. The coach halted, swaying, and a footman jumped down from his post at the rear, unfolded the brass stepping rung, wiped it clean of road dust, and respectfully opened the door.

The duke of Blackpool descended—slim, haughty, folding

his travel gloves, glancing about with a condescending air. He was followed by his steward, Fox Hazlitt. Jericho drew an uneasy breath. The past weeks had been so busy, so full of constant, unhappy thoughts about Dove, that she'd all but forgotten the offer of employment.

Glancing about, the duke extended a lacy wrist for a lady to use as she debarked from his coach. She was a beautiful lady, pale and gentle looking. As different from the duke as day from night. When her gloved hand faltered, fumbling to find the duke's wrist, he sent her an irritated glance. The meanness of it pricked Jericho's heart.

"Is that the duchess of Blackpool? Is that Lady Angelina, Lady Marguerite's sister?"

"Yes."

"She's lovely."

"Too many have thought that over the years," Mrs. Phipps said tartly. "Including Lord Aubrey." Leaning closer, Mrs. Phipps whispered furtively, "Do not breathe a word of this. But many years ago, it was rumored Lady Angelina gave birth to a stillborn child while her husband was in France. Some thought it Lord Aubrey's child."

Jericho cared nothing about the rumor, but her gaze flew sympathetically to Lord Aubrey. She liked him. She watched him with a tender heart, feeling for him. If Lady Angelina was his love, he must be feeling incredible turmoil at this moment. But he was a military man, and when it was his turn to greet the duchess he comported himself with military bearing, stepping forward, kissing her hand without a flicker of emotion. Lady Angelina, however, was made of frailer stuff. Her lovely face went white. Jericho saw her tremble.

Returning to her kitchen duties, Jericho could think of nothing else. Poor, lonely Lord Aubrey. Poor, unhappy lady. Then, throwing herself into the frenzy of work that came of feeding a king and his enormous entourage, she promptly forgot them.

For the next five days Jericho worked to exhaustion. Everyone did. But no one complained. Devoted to Dove's mother, every servant in Arleigh Castle toiled hard to make the royal visit a success. Lady de Mont herself worked harder than any servant. She was in the kitchen before dawn, consulting with Mr. Pennington. She came again long after midnight, dispensing appreciative words and smiles to everyone, even to the turnspit boys and scullery girls. Had she asked, her staff gladly would've lain down and died for her.

Jericho toiled and sweated in the July heat. In a single day, she gutted and cleaned a mountain of trout, then plucked and gutted a hundred quail, threading their dainty carcases on spits and tending them over the hot cookfires. She kneaded bread dough until her arms nearly fell off, then worked some more, serving in the cheese house, cranking the cheese basket, packing the curds into the cheese press and winching it tight, then rubbing and turning the hundred cheeses that were already aging on the shelves. Each midnight, she dropped onto her pallet, slept like a rock, then leaped up at dawn to do it all over again.

By the fifth night, she was exhausted. She'd been asleep on her pallet cot only minutes when she awoke to find Dove shaking her shoulder.

"Jericho, wake up. I need your help."

She lunged up on one elbow, rubbing sleep from her eyes. "What is it, Dove? What's wrong?"

"Nothing. I need your help, that's all. Come into the hall."

Putting resentment aside, she grabbed her shawl, slung it around her nightrail and jumped up at once. This was no time to sulk about her indenture. If Dove needed her help, he needed her help. Barefoot, she followed him through the maze of exhausted snoring servants and into the hallway. A fat tallow candle burned in an iron wall sconce, shedding light.

"What is it, Dove?"

Hands draped on waist, he stood on one hip in disgust. "Hell! Lady Castlemayne is patron to an imbecile of a playwright. She's brought the dolt's latest play with her. It struck her fancy to hear the play read aloud, with all of us reading parts. And what strikes Castlemayne's fancy, strikes the king's fancy." Dove gave her an irritated look. "I've never seen a man so ruled by a petticoat!"

She tugged at her shawl, pressed her lips together and held

her tongue. This was no time to comment on the iron "petticoat" who ruled *Dove*—Marguerite, the shrew.

"Yes? What do you want of me?"

"We are short one female reader. I need you to read a part."

She stared at him, incredulous. "You what?"

He gestured, impatient, cranky. "I need you, Jericho. Now! Get dressed. I need you to read a part."

A moment passed before she could believe her ears, before she could get her breath. "Dove, *I* cannot a read in a play."

He swung his golden head angrily. "If you can't do a simple thing like read, then I've wasted a hell of lot of money schooling you, haven't I! Certainly you can read. I thought of you at once. The idiotic goddamn play is titled *The Dutchman's Daughters*. It's written to satirize the Dutch in this goddamn war. You'll read the first daughter's part. It's only a few pages, Jericho. You can read it and be back in bed in an hour. Many of your lines are in Dutch. Duck soup for you."

She listened to all of this in utter astonishment. When he'd finished, she gasped, "Dove, I cannot read before the king. I cannot! I would stutter."

"All the better," he said grouchily. "The stupid play portrays the Dutch as thick-headed butter-boxes. A stutter is perfect."

"Dove, I cannot! I would die of fright."

He raked an impatient hand through his hair. "Jericho! This royal visit is important to my family. It's vital. It has to go right."

"I know, but—"

"Then get dressed. And hurry, damn it. Hell, even my Uncle Aubrey is under the gun, forced to read. And you know damn well he'd sooner be shot than stand on a platform and read in a play. But he's doing it. If you have any regard for Arleigh Castle, any regard for my family, you'll do it, too."

She hesitated only an instant. "I'll get dressed."

When he gave her a weary smile, she realized how worried he was about this royal visit. For normally, parties never wearied Dove. He exulted in them. She remembered from New Amsterdam.

She whirled to fly, then turned back. "Dove? I—" She looked at him gently. "I'm sorry for what I said on the night you came to apologize."

He shifted his feet and winged a glance down the corridor. "Did you say something that night?" he said with curt impatience. "I don't recall it."

"But, I—" She fell silent. If he chose to ignore it, she knew her remark still festered. "Anyway," she finished softly, "I'm sorry. I didn't mean it."

"Hell, Jericho, I don't know what you're talking about. Now stop yapping. Hurry!"

She threw on her clothes by candlelight in the scullery alcove, pulling one of John's wife's gowns from the box on the scullery shelf and shaking the wrinkles out of it as best she could. She dressed, raked a comb through her hair and flew into the hall. Dove rapidly laced her up and they rushed through the dimly lit corridors. It was not until they'd reached the door of the magnificent state apartment where Swiss guards in scarlet tunics stood on duty, that she glanced down and saw her naked wrist.

"My wristband! Dove, I forgot to cover my birthmark. I have to go back."

"Forget it."

"Dove, I can't. I feel naked. I need it. I—"

But he threw the tall carved door open and pushed her into the room. For a moment, she stood dumbstruck, as awed as a country mouse. She had never witnessed the nobility at play before, and it was an eye-opening experience. Aristocratic chatter and merry laughter filled the high-ceilinged, gilded room. Wine flowed like water. Gold coins glittered in impossibly high stacks on gaming tables where nobles sat playing cards, flinging out their wagers as carelessly as if the coins were chicken feed. Some of the lords who'd brought mistresses along openly toyed with them, kissing them, fondling their breasts. Even the king lounged sensually on a gilded, red brocade daybed, one arm draped around Castlemayne's bare shoulders, the other draped around Nell Gwynne.

She was shocked. But she hadn't an instant to remain so. For Dove took her arm and yanked her through the gilded room to a platform stage that was being hastily erected by footmen. Grabbing a chapbook from a pile of chapbooks on the floor, he slapped it into her trembling hands.

"Page four. Don't fail me, grubworm."

"I w-won't."

He smiled. "That's the spirit, Pansy Eyes!"

Dove hurried off to his duties as host. Retreating into a corner with the chapbook, she sat on a foot stool and nervously found her part and read it. As she read, she sent darting glances around the room. The play was foolish, but the king's party was intimidating. She counted twenty-five lords and half that many ladies.

Dressed in black silk, the duke of Blackpool lounged in a gilded chair, attentively near the king. The duke wore the latest in fashion, petticoat breeches with a rich cascade of lace at the knee. His duchess, the Lady Angelina, sat in a gilded chair beside him, pale as a lily, gowned in black silk. The duke kept one silken arm casually draped on the back of her chair, his slender fingers now and then toying with her lovely white shoulders. She didn't like it. Her stiff posture and the flush on her high, delicate cheekbones said so.

Lord Aubrey stood on the far side of the lavish, tall-windowed room, as far away from the duke and duchess as it was possible to be. Jericho's glance swept on. Marguerite sat giggling with Lord Lark, chapbook in hand, practicing their parts, and Lady de Mont was everywhere at once, as serene as a queen, seeing to her guests' every whim. Jericho wished Leonardo d'Orias were here. She would not be half so scared if, now and then, she could look into his calm, encouraging eyes. But he was absent. Jericho could guess the situation. Unwilling to put his beloved Lady de Mont in an awkward stance during the king's visit, he'd simply left the castle. Jericho wondered if he'd gone to London. If so, he might be taking the time to look into the sailings of *The Jericho*.

Nervous, Jericho studied the play and did not look up again until Lord Aubrey ambled her way and discovered her in the corner. She quickly rose and curtsied, but he gallantly waved her back to her seat.

"A foolish business, eh, child? I would rather put my head in a noose than make a fool of myself on a stage."

Despite her jitters, she had to smile. "I, too, my lord."

"Yes, yes. But I daresay it can be endured. I daresay anything can be endured. Anything."

Was he speaking of the play? Not entirely. For in an absentminded way, he let his glance drift across the room to the duchess of Blackpool. Jericho felt a rush of tenderness for him.

"Your service to Lady Marguerite is going well, I trust?"

"Yes, my lord. Thank you." It wasn't. But she would sooner cut out her tongue than complain to Dove's uncle. She liked this big, soldierly man.

"So. We shall sink or swim together then, eh? The Dutchman and his daughters? I am to read the Dutchman's part, God bless me. You are to read the first daughter?"

"Yes, my lord."

"Well, well, so be it. You must not be addled." He smiled down at Jericho and gave her a gallant word. "Were I truly a father, I could not want for a prettier daughter."

Her heart lifted. Oh, she liked him! She truly did!

"Thank you, my lord. I am obliged."

He drifted back to the party. An hour passed before the noisy, carousing lords were ready to settle down to the play-reading, and as segment after segment of the hour ticked away, Jericho grew more and more nervous. Finally, it began.

Angelina felt faint as she sat watching the play. Was her fever playing tricks on her? Was she seeing things? Or did that girl bear an uncanny resemblance to Aubrey? The same red hair, the same blue eyes. Even a birthmark on her wrist! Or had fever painted it there? She fanned herself. The room was overheated. Her silk gown was heavy as a blanket. She felt hot, dizzy.

Her head swam. Attempting to rise, to leave the masque, she couldn't. Her knees would not. Weakly, she sat back down in her chair, gown rustling.

"Another spell, my dear?" the duke purred in his soft, exquisite voice as the foolish play went on.

She sent him a wary look. "No. 'Tis only the warm July night. The candles steal the air. I cannot get breath."

"Ah. I thought it might be something else. A shock of some sort. You shivered as if . . . someone had walked across your grave, my love . . ."

"It's nothing."

"We shall have you bled again."

"No! I don't want to be bled. It isn't good for me. It makes me weak."

"I shall be the judge of that." Leaning toward her, he languidly kissed her neck, a proprietary gesture meant to remind her she was his property. Dear God, she needed no reminder. She'd been painfully aware of it from the day she'd become his unwilling bride at fifteen. He touched his lips to the throbbing pulse point in her throat. She tried not to flinch. But his touch was as repulsive to her as it had been on their wedding night.

He patted her hand and smiled maliciously.

"Watch the play, my angel."

Trapped, feverish, she returned her eyes to the stage.

"That girl bears a remarkable resemblance to Aubrey," the duke purred in a whisper a few minutes later. "Do you not think so, my love?"

Angelina dabbed a lace handkerchief at her hot brow. Had he arranged for her to be tortured like this, to see Aubrey's love-child? For the girl was surely Aubrey's daughter. It would be like Blackpool to do so. He was like a cat. He enjoyed tormenting. He'd insisted she accompany him on this state visit even though she'd been ill, in a sickbed. He'd commanded it.

"I had not noticed."

"Ah. Then doubtless it is only my imagination," he purred. "Yet, some twenty years ago, there were rumors Aubrey had sired a child somewhere in the parish of St. John's Basket . . ."

She felt faint. He had never mentioned the rumor before, never in all the years of their marriage. And she had guarded her secret well. Thank God he did not know the truth.

"As to that, I do not know."

"Ah. I thought you might. I thought Aubrey might have confided in you, told you about his *amours*. You and he were such firm . . . friends . . . during childhood."

"That was a long time ago."

"Ah." To her relief, he spoke no more, pawed her no more. Frightened of him, careful to please him, she sat watching the play. She grew hotter, more feverish. When she could take no more, she risked his displeasure. Rising, she curtsied to the king and left the room in a rustle of black silk.

Standing onstage, reading, Jericho was in absolute misery. How could Dove have asked such a favor of her? Her heart was banging so loudly she could scarcely hear her own voice, and when she nervously began to stutter, the king threw back his dark head and laughed wholeheartedly, presuming she'd stuttered on purpose. She wanted to die. Her face flushed hot as a cookfire. Standing beside her, holding the chapbook because her hands were shaking too badly, Lord Aubrey was equally uncomfortable, but he staunchly rode it out. He delivered his lines in a flat, loud monotone, as a soldier might. And such wicked, bawdy lines—written to slur the Dutch. She blushed to say them.

Jericho was greatly relieved when her part was finished. She quietly left the bright candlelit stage and slipped out of the room, leaving the ongoing play in progress. Out in the quiet corridor, she took a moment to breathe deeply and to cool her burning cheeks with the backs of her hands. Then she hurried off. She was halfway down the corridor when a door open and shut, and Dove's soft call stopped her. She turned and waited under a candle sconce in the dim light while he came loping.

"You did well, grubworm! I'm proud of you."

"Dove, don't ever ask me to do anything like that again. Don't ask me. I nearly died."

"But you did well. Thank you."

"I stuttered."

Folding his arms, he smiled his warm affectionate smile. No one had eyes like Dove. No one in the world. Bright hazel, full of warmth, shining like jewels. He was so handsome in his snowy white linen shirt and silk breeches.

"Hell, I liked it! I liked your stutter. While you were reading, I kept thinking about the day I won you. At Dieter Ten Boom's tap house, remember? You stuttered like a chittering little squirrel that day."

"I was scared that day," she said firmly. "And I was scared tonight."

"I cheated. In that dice game. Did I ever tell you?"

Startled, she looked at him. For a moment she couldn't take it in. He'd cheated. He'd deliberately set out to win her. Oh, dear God. He'd been kinder to her than she'd ever guessed, a boy of eighteen bothering with a ragged little bondchild.

"No. No, you didn't tell me Dove," she said in awed wonder.

He refolded his arms, and then, to her bewilderment, folded them back the way they'd been. As if he were nervous. Nervous talking to *her*? Dear life. Her eyes widened.

"Jericho." Again, he refolded his arms. "About Mid-Summer's Eve. I want you to know you'll soon be free. I've insisted Marguerite free you."

She gazed at him in soft surprise. "Why, thank you, Dove."

"Not at all. You deserve your freedom. Hell, grubworm, you've earned it. I've not been the easiest master in the world. Nor, I suspect, has Marguerite been an easy mistress."

She let that pass. She couldn't bring herself to hurt him by agreeing about Marguerite. They stood there, uncertain, gazing into one another's eyes. The candle flame flickered as a draft caught it.

"Hell, Jericho. You needn't go to London to start a dame school. You could start one right here. Here in Arleigh Castle. Teach the servant children." He shrugged enthusiastically. "I'd pay for it. I'd gladly pay for it."

Her heart grew soft and warm towards him. He didn't want her to go. He wanted her to stay. And she wanted to. But if she stayed, what was there for her? Only the misery of watching him marry Marguerite. And if she stayed, she would become his mistress. She knew it, and she knew Dove knew it. There was too much fondness between them for it to end any other way.

"I think I'd best go to London," she said gently.

He looked down in disappointment, understanding that she was refusing more than the dame school. At the distant end of the corridor, the guard changed. Ten Swiss guards in scarlet tunics tramped into place, replacing the others who tramped off. The floor of the corridor vibrated with the matched cadence of their step. She and Dove glanced at them.

"I have to go to sleep now, Dove," she said lovingly. "Morning comes early in the kitchen."

He swung his golden head and glanced at the window at the end of the corridor. Night was already lifting. The sky was gray. "Hell, yes. It's late. Go. Sleep tight. You did well tonight, Jericho. Thank you."

"Good night, Dove."

"Good night, grubworm."

They moved off in opposite directions, Dove's lithe step taking him back to the silly play, hers taking her back toward the kitchens and the sleeping hall. At the end of the corridor, she glanced back over her shoulder to treat herself to just one more glimpse of him. To her surprise, he was glancing over his shoulder at her.

When Angelina left the play and the king's presence, she sought fresh air for her nerves. Hurrying along the corridor, she passed the Swiss guards, then went down the staircase to the ground floor and out into the castleyard. She crossed the dark silent castleyard, then went up the stone steps to the castle wall. Atop the wall, the walkway lay bathed in moonlight. With no difficulty, she found the favorite battlement where she and Aubrey had played as children. Their first kiss had come on this battlement. How old had they been? Twelve, thirteen?

Aubrey. She hadn't felt the warmth of his kiss, the warmth of his arms around her in twenty long, endless years. Shivering, she wrapped herself in her own arms. Aubrey. The girl on the stage. It bewildered her. Was the girl his daughter? By some other love? She ached.

As he was reading on the platform, participating in Castlemayne's nonsense, Aubrey saw Angelina leave. How could he not? He was attuned to her every movement, painfully aware of every breath she took. When his part came to a finish, he stepped back out of the bright candlelight, left the

makeshift stage and the ongoing play, and quietly slipped out
a side door. Satisfied that Blackpool would remain glued to
the king's side—his cousin had always been an ass-kissing
sycophant—he stepped into the corridor.

Pausing in the dimly lighted corridor, he brushed his hand
over his mouth, considering where she might have gone.
Midway down the hall, under the flaring light of a candle,
Dove hovered over his pretty bondslave, the two young people so absorbed in each other they did not even see him. With
quick, quiet steps, he set off in the opposite direction.

"Aubrey!" He'd come up the stone stairs silently and had
found her dreaming in the moonlight, standing on "their"
battlement, looking as pale and lovely as a painting. She
turned, visibly trembling as he slowly went forward.

He was trembling himself. He was not a man who'd trembled in battle, but he trembled now. He didn't know what to
do, what to say. Sweet God, he'd not been alone with her
in twenty years.

"Angelina, my precious darling . . ."

Her eyes grew large and lustrous with tears. The moon
glowed upon her white shoulders, her black silk gown, her
pearls, her gold locket.

"Aubrey, please do not call me that unless you mean it.
Please, please. Else I cannot bear it."

He breathed unevenly. He ached to touch her, hold her.

"Not mean it? I mean it with all my heart. Angelina, you
are my soul mate. I think of you as my wife—the only wife
I have ever wanted or shall ever want."

"No! There was someone else. Someone you loved and
had a child by."

"Someone else? Never." Stepping forward, he longed to
put his trembling hands around her waist and draw her near.
She was so thin his hands would span her waist. It shocked
him. Was she unwell? She had always been delicate, frail.
She gazed up at him, bewildered, distraught, overwrought.
A tear spilled off her dark lashes and rolled down her cheek.

"That girl. She's your daughter."

"What girl? Who?"

"The girl reading with you. In Castlemayne's play."

A soldier, a simple man accustomed to simple, straightforward thinking, he found this beyond comprehension. For a moment, he could not even recall who he'd read with in the wretched play. He frowned.

"You don't mean Dove's redhaired bondslave?"

"Yes."

His jaw dropped. He was utterly astonished. For a moment he couldn't even get his breath. "Angelina. She is not my daughter. Good lord, sweetheart, why should you think such a thing? She's a bondslave. From the New World, from the colony of New York."

Her lovely eyes flooded with uncertainty. "But look in the mirror, Aubrey. She is your image. She has your hair, your eyes, even your birthmark on her wrist. Had our own daughter lived, she might have looked exactly like that girl."

He breathed more calmly, certain of himself. "Red hair is not uncommon. Nor blue eyes. As to the birthmark, I have never noticed, nor am I interested. Birthmark or no, she is *not* my daughter, Angelina."

She looked up at him with eyes swimming. How else could he convince her? He drew her to his breast and crushed her gently. They both trembled and clung. They hadn't touched like this in two decades. It was so wonderful he was afraid to breathe. Out on the meadow, a restless meadow lark trilled. He let it sing its song, then buried his mouth in her soft hair.

"Angelina. Beloved. I have had wenches during these empty years, yes. That I will not deny. I am a man, and a man has his needs. But I have not sired a child. Judge me. If I had sired a child, would I not acknowledge her, provide for her, shelter her, protect her? Am I a man who would turn his back on his responsibilities? Oh, my beloved . . . trust me."

She lifted her face to him, tears sparkling in her eyes like crystal, reflecting the moonlight.

"I trust you, Aubrey. I always have and I always shall."

With a throaty groan, he crushed her close, crushed his mouth to hers. His kiss was rough, for he was so needy, as a beggar, so starved. But she was needy too. Her feverish lips clung, her hands clung. They kissed passionately, desperately, the years falling away like gossamer veils. Only

when a lantern winked, carried across the castleyard by a
sleepy lackey, did they draw apart, breathless.

"I must go, Aubrey. The duke . . ."

He crushed her delicate shoulders in his hands.

"Angelina, leave him! Separate from him. Let me take
you to Nordham Hall, and damn the world's opinion. We are
yet young. We can have years of happiness together."

"No," she cried out. "Do not tempt me. I beg you."

"Angelina, you must. Come to me. Come."

"No! He would kill me. And you, also. You don't know
him. He's like a cat. He stalks, he plans. He is a cruel
vindictive man. I love you, Aubrey. I will not put you in
danger."

"Danger be damned! I'll kill him."

"And the two of us to live with his blood on our hands?
No."

She tore out of his embrace, leaving his arms heartbreak-
ingly empty, and fled along the walkway, her footfalls as
weightless as a bird's. He leaped after her, caught her on the
shadowy stairs and crushed her to him.

"Angelina. Does he hurt you? I demand to know. If he
hurts you—by God, he'll not live to see another sunrise."
He could see the pulse beating in the hollow of her throat.

"No. He doesn't hurt me. He frightens me, but he doesn't
hurt me. Please believe me, Aubrey."

"In bed? Does he hurt you in bed?" He tensed, fearing
to know, needing to know.

She shook her head and one crystal tear spilled. She wiped
it away. "No. I am his property," she said bitterly. "He
never harms his own property."

His throat filled with emotion. Longing to croon love words,
longing to lead her gently to his bed, he crushed her close.
But lantern light flashed again in the castleyard. With quick
trembling hands, Angelina swiftly stripped off the locket she
wore and pressed the hard gold into his palm.

"Keep this. A keepsake. Keep it in memory of me and in
memory of our baby. Before the midwife buried our baby,
she cut off a curl of our baby's hair. She gave it to me. I put
it in this locket, and I have worn it over my heart for twenty

years. It is yours now. Take it. Cherish it, as I have. Stay away from me, Aubrey. For my sake and for yours. Stay away!'' In a rustle of black silk, she rushed down the stone stairs and left him.

Later, alone in his bedchamber, he opened the locket and touched a rough soldier's finger to the delicate snippet of hair.

It was red.

Chapter Fifteen

The next day was the oddest, most bewildering day of Jericho's life. Dawn had no sooner come and Jericho was no sooner at work in the scullery, when a maidservant she did not know entered the scullery and came straight to her.

''Come at once,'' she whispered. ''Her Grace, the duchess of Blackpool wishes to speak to you.''

Certain the woman was addressing someone else, Jericho glanced over her shoulder. But no one else was near. Everyone was busy with tasks.

Jericho whipped off her apron, raked her fingers through her hair, and swiftly followed the maid. She was alarmed. Hurrying through the silent corridors, her footfalls echoing in counterpoint with the maid's, she tried to think of one single reason a duchess would send for a bondservant. She couldn't. She grew frightened.

It was the stupid theatrical, she decided. The masque. The duchess had taken offense at it. And at me! Why did I let Dove talk me into doing it? Anxiety rising, she followed the maid through rich, opulently carved double doors, through a rich gilded receiving room that lay in dawn shadows, and into a blue and gold bedchamber.

The duchess of Blackpool stood waiting, looking wan and

pale. Her black silk dressing gown scarcely concealed the
thinness of her body. Her brown hair, undressed and brushed
loose, fell to her shoulders in waves. Her skin was as pale
as the fragrant white roses on her dressing table.

Jericho curtsied anxiously.

The duchess waited until the maid had left, until the door
had closed with a firm click. Then she glanced out the window
at the haze that was stealing across the meadow. She looked
weary enough to drop.

"Do not be afraid, child. I only wanted to see you, to talk
to you for a bit. Who are you, child?"

Jericho stared at the lovely strained face, bewildered.

"I—I am a bondservant, Your Grace. My name is Jericho,
Your Grace, Jericho Jones."

"But *who* are you? *Who?* Where do you come from?"

Jericho scarcely knew what to say. "I—I am from New
Amsterdam, Your Grace," she answered in growing wonder.
"From New York, that is. I was Lord Dove's bondservant
there. I arrived in England this May."

"You lived there all your life? In New Amsterdam?"

"Yes, my lady."

"And your parents?"

Jericho gazed at the lovely, distraught face in utter and
complete bewilderment. Why should a duchess care who her
parents were?

"I—I have no parents, my lady. I was orphaned as a
babe."

"I see. But you were born Dutch? In Dutch New Amsterdam?"

Such strange questions.

"I believe I was born of English parents aboard a Dutch
ship that was heading for New Amsterdam, Your Grace. A
ship called *The Jericho*. I believe I was named for her."

"And your parents' name was Jones."

Jericho felt a flush steal up her throat. The old shame of
having no family to claim, no identity, no place in the world
where she truly belonged . . .

"No, Your Grace. Lord Dove gave me the surname 'Jones.'
He chose it at random. As for m-my parents, there is no

record of them. I do not know their names. I feel certain my mother died aboard *The Jericho*. I think perhaps she died giving birth to me, God rest her soul.''

''I see.''

Abandoning her post at the window, the duchess slowly paced her rich silken chamber. Jericho watched her with ever-growing wonder. The duchess was plainly distressed. Now and then she would absently wring her lovely hands, as if immersed in a sea of worries. Smudges under her eyes told of a sleepless night. Jericho's heart softened with sympathy. Poor lady. She is sick. Perhaps sick in the mind, as well. Else she would not summon a bondservant at dawn and behave so oddly.

''Are you acquainted with the duke of Nordham?''

A question in an utterly different direction. Taken by surprise, Jericho answered as best she could. ''I know that the duke of Nordham is Lord Dove's uncle. He has been kind enough to speak to me on a few occasions.''

''Yes, yes.'' The duchess gestured gently. ''But do you know of him in any other way? Did you perhaps know of him in New Amsterdam?''

''Lord Dove spoke of his uncle, my lady.''

''But more than that, child. Did Lord Aubrey perhaps send money for your upkeep whilst you were growing up?''

Jericho stared in confusion. ''But why would he, my lady?''

Lady Angelina flushed, and the first spots of color rushed into her lovely strained face. ''Of course, he would not. I ask a foolish question.'' She gave Jericho a scared look. ''Child? Have we met before? Have we? I feel so . . . drawn to you.''

''No, my lady.''

Thoroughly confused, Jericho watched the lady pace.

''How did you come to be Lord Dove's bondslave?''

''My lady, he won me. In a dice game. In a tap house in New Amsterdam. I was eleven years old.''

''Eleven?'' The duchess turned, startled. ''Eleven? You were born when? In what year?''

Such strange questions. The poor lady was surely ill.

''I believe it was 1646, my lady,'' she volunteered gently.

"I know I was an infant in that year. My indenture states it."

"1646?" Pale before, Lady Angelina grew paler still. Lost in thought, she paced, black silk dressing gown rustling. She said nothing for so long a time that Jericho wondered if she was dismissed, if she should curtsy and quietly go. Suddenly, the duchess paused in her pacing and turned.

"You have a birthmark on your right wrist. I saw it last night. As you read on stage."

Jericho was wearing her wristband, but the comment stirred up the old anxiety, the memory of Collect Pond. Her heart began a slow, fearful pounding, "Yes, Your Grace."

"Have you any other birthmarks on your person?"

Her skin prickled. The old anxiety churned. Collect Pond. Ice skating. The men. She drew a frightened breath and lied.

"No, my lady."

The duchess of Blackpool had waited tensely for her answer, her eyes dark and cavernous, but once she had her answer the thin taut shoulders relaxed under the silk gown.

"Of course, you do not. It was a ridiculous question. Forgive me for asking it. But for an instant I had the oddest feeling . . . the most compelling feeling . . . never mind." Quickly, the duchess went to her velvet covered nightbox, lifted the lid, reached in and came back carrying a tiny brown velvet pouch.

Jericho shook her head. "No, my lady. I've done nothing deserving of payment."

"Take it."

"I beg not, my lady. Please. I have not earned it."

"Take it. Please." Lady Angelina reached for her hand with a joltingly cold one, tucked the pouch into Jericho's palm and gently closed Jericho's fingers around it. "Take it, child. You will not be a bondslave forever. One day you will be free. My coins will help you start your new life. Life is hard, child. Take it. Take whatever is given you."

Jericho didn't know how to refuse. "My lady—"

The duchess nervously tossed her hair. It drifted upon her shoulders like limp silk. Jericho saw one or two gray hairs, shining like silver.

"Go now. Go, and take great care that no one sees you leave my rooms. Tell no one that we have had this little talk, you and I. *No one*, do you understand? Please. You must not tell even one person. Not Lord Dove, not even my sister, Lady Marguerite." The duchess flushed then and looked away. "Especially you must not tell His Grace, the duke of Blackpool. Even if the duke should question you, you must not tell him I have talked with you. Promise me, child."

Jericho gazed at her in wonder. How strange. She nodded quickly. "Yes, my lady. I promise."

"Now go, pretty child. Quickly. Be discreet. Take care going out, take care that no one sees you."

Again, that queer heart tug. She was loath to go and leave the duchess here alone, sick. But she'd been dismissed. She couldn't disobey.

"Yes, my lady."

Jericho curtsied and let herself out. She closed the bedchamber door with a quiet click, then hurried through the salon and out the double doors, shutting them quietly, too. Recalling the duchess's odd request, she stood in the silence and scanned the corridor before moving. It lay empty and quiet, steeped in dawn's shadows. She stole away.

It was not until she turned a corner that a door unexpectedly opened and a figure came out, suddenly rearing up in her path. Fox Hazlitt. She'd nearly collided with him. He was as startled as she. He glanced at her with quick eyes, then cast an appraising glance in the direction she'd come from. Heart pounding, she gave him a wide berth and passed by on the other side.

Absorbed with the near mishap, she forgot about the tiny pouch in her hand until she reached the kitchens. Suddenly curious, she opened the pouch and shook the jingling contents into her palm. Gold glittered up at her. Not shillings, not silver, but gold. She gasped. Great heaven. Five gold coins. It was a fortune. It was almost enough for passage money for herself and Black Bartimaeus.

Later, when she found a moment to be alone, she went to the scullery closet where she kept her box of belongings. Lifting the box down from the shelf, she rammed the pouch into the bottom of it, safely hiding it in an old mended stocking, under petticoats and books.

The day grew odder still. Two hours later, she was summoned upstairs again. This time she was frightened. For the duke of Blackpool now demanded her attendance. Startled out of her wits, she had no choice but to comply. With a pounding heart, she followed the duke's livery clad footman through the corridors, her thoughts in turmoil. Fox Hazlitt, she thought. He saw me coming from the duchess's rooms. But, no. He didn't see me at the duchess's door. I was merely in the corridor. It's the letter, she thought. The offer of employment. I never answered it. The letter? Or the duchess?

Entering a rich receiving room, she followed the footman into an even richer bedchamber. There, the footman abandoned her, retreating with a bow. When the door shut behind her with a click, her pulse stepped up its beat.

The duke of Blackpool sat at the table in front of a sunny window. He was leisurely breaking his fast. The lace of his shirt cuff drifted over the table, hovering, as he idly picked and chose tidbits for his breakfast plate. Sunshine glinted off silver salvers, silver bowls. When his plate was prepared to his liking, he turned in his chair and crossed one slender, silk-clad leg upon the other.

Jericho curtsied deeply.

He beckoned, lace drifting. "Nearer. Nearer, my dear." He smiled, but the smile didn't rise to his eyes. His eyes remained peculiarly untouched by it. There was a chill to the duke, and she grasped at once why the duchess was afraid of him. Ice water ran in his veins.

Knees unsteady, she obeyed and went forward. When she stood before him—standing in the spot he indicated by delicately pointing with his gold eating-dagger—he leaned back in his chair and smiled again. It was unnerving the way he gestured with the dagger.

"So. You are a bondservant, are you?"

Her mouth was dry. She pressed the tip of her tongue to her lip to moisten it. "Yes, Your Grace." In his cat-soft voice, he began to question her. His questions were remarkably like Lady Angelina's. It made gooseflesh rise on her arms.

"Do I make you uncomfortable?"

She started. Great heaven. Those frosty eyes could see all the way to her soul. Afraid to lie, she told the truth.

"Yes, Your Grace. A little. I beg you to excuse it. And I beg you to excuse it that I did not write to answer your steward's kind offer of employment. I was—busy," she finished lamely.

He smiled and gestured in an amiable way, wrist lace floating with each gesture. Observing her uneasy eyes following the dagger, he set it down. "Of course, I excuse it. But, come, come. You must not be uncomfortable with me, my dear. I mean you no harm. On the contrary, I mean you a great deal of good."

She found it hard to believe, but groped deep within herself for tact. "Yes, Your Grace. Thank you."

"I observed you in the masque last night. The masque was a foolish piece of business, but you did well."

"I-I am obliged, Your Grace." I want to leave, she thought. Please let me leave and go back to my work.

"So well, in fact, that I want you to come and serve at Blackpool Castle when your indenture ends." She stared, wordless. "You would serve Her Grace, the duchess, if you will. The duchess has not been well, you must understand. I have long had in mind to hire a personable and intelligent young woman to companion her. I would pay extremely high wages."

Jericho felt a pang. Serve that kind, sick lady? Take care of her? She was drawn to it. But Blackpool Castle? Never. The de Monts despised Blackpool. Dove would never forgive her if she took employment there. Besides, her heart was set on her dame school, on Black Bartimaeus, on New York.

Curtsying, she refused as politely as she could. "Your Grace, I most humbly thank you. I am sensible of the great honor you do me. But I cannot, Your Grace. I have made other plans."

The irrational flash of anger in those frosty eyes startled

her. It was almost hate. But the look passed so quickly she wondered if she'd imagined it. For he smiled pleasantly.

"Consider it, my dear. Take your time and consider it. I shall make it worth your while. As for now, you may go. Thank you for coming to me."

Rattled—why should a total stranger flash such a look of hatred at her?—she curtsied again. Go? She couldn't go fast enough. But when she reached the door, his soft, cat-voice pounced again.

"One trifling question." Gripping the ornate door latch, she dutifully turned. "Did you, by any chance . . . visit the duchess of Blackpool's chambers this morning, my dear?"

Her heart began to pound. The duchess had specifically bade her not to tell the duke. The breath fluttered in her throat.

"N-no, Your Grace."

He smiled. "Ah. My man, Fox Hazlitt, thought you might have done so. Doubtless he was mistaken."

"I *w-was* in the corridor this morning, Your Grace. Dishes are often put outside the chambers late at night, to-to-to be collected by kitchen servants in the morning." That much was true. "I was collecting." Her heart pounded.

"Ah," he said pleasantly. "That is so, of course. Thank you, my dear. You may go."

With a final quick curtsy, she let herself out. Drawing an enormous breath of relief, she put the perplexing incident behind her and hurried back to her work.

Within the bedchamber, the duke of Blackpool seethed— his thoughts dark, turgid, violent. He shook with rage. Collecting dishes? How dare she stand there and lie to him! He'd trembled with the urge to strangle her on the spot.

The blood in his temples pulsed thickly. Oh, he would kill her all right, this adulterous spawn of Angelina's and Aubrey's. He would have his revenge. Just as he'd had his revenge on Royce de Mont a quarter-century earlier. He would use dogs.

His temples throbbed as he visualized it. The wolfhounds leaping, snarling. The screams. The blood. He could smell the blood! Suddenly, pain pierced him. He looked down at the dagger in his hands and winced.

His own blood dripped from the slashes in his palm, thick rich droplets, the color of scarlet.

A third frightening thing happened to Jericho. Exhausted, caught up in the kitchen frenzy of this final day of the king's visit, Jericho had all but forgotten her strange morning encounters when, at midnight, the chief steward, Mr. Pennington, bore down upon her with the news that the king wished to see her.

Frightened out of her wits, she swiftly washed and threw on a fresh gown. Tense, she followed the king's footman through the quiet, dimly lit corridors. What did the king want? She was afraid to guess. At the rear door of the king's apartment, a Swiss guard stepped aside with an amused knowing look that scared her, the footman opened the door, and she was in the king's bedchamber. Alone. Her chest thudded.

Bathed in candlelight, gilded wood glowed everywhere. An intimate midnight supper for two lay spread upon a small, lion-footed table. Two gilded swan's-neck chairs were drawn up to the table, and beyond the table, she saw a magnificent bedstead. Panicking, she swiftly looked away from the bed.

She nearly jumped when someone moved on the far side of the room, rising from a chair in the midst of the glittering luxury. The king came strolling toward her, smiling. It was a cynical smile, but not ungentle.

"How good of you to come, my pretty."

"Y-your M-majesty." Frightened, she dropped to a low curtsy and stayed there until he gestured for her to rise. He was a tall, towering man. At leisure, he wore no kingly clothes. He wore a linen shirt, breeches, wool stockings, chamber slippers. He'd discarded his elaborate black wig and wore his own hair, which was thinning and going gray.

He smiled. "Shall we sup first?"

First. First. Her heart pounded. He led her to the supper table and seated her. Her spine was so stiff with fright that for a moment she could not unbend and sit. Seated, she clenched her shaking hands in her lap.

Although His Majesty had seated her with her back to the enormous, glittering, gilded bed, she remained excruciatingly aware of it. She was also aware of his sensual gaze. Could a bondslave refuse a king? Was it done? Did she have the right? Her breath filled her throat like a hurricane.

When she did not—could not—eat, His Majesty now and then fed her a tidbit from his own spoon. It clung to her tongue like char and went down like grit. When he asked idle, leisurely questions that were meant to put her at ease, her answers were so trembly and faint she could scarcely hear them herself.

His dark, sensual gaze lazily roamed over her. Though she kept her eyes on her untouched plate, she was agonizingly aware that he looked at her breasts, her lips, her hair. Her heart thrashed like a bird caught in a snare. Could she refuse? Did she have the right? Dare she? Delicately wiping crumbs from his sensual black mustache, the king crumpled his linen napkin, set it aside and rose. She felt faint. Leisurely, he strolled around the table and smiled down at her.

"Shall we take a wee nap? To digest our repast?"

Her breath came in frantic heaves. His Majesty took her icy hand in his warm one and helped her rise. Standing, she grew dizzy. She couldn't breathe, couldn't see, couldn't think. She threw him a frightened look.

"Your Majesty, I cannot!" She dropped to her knees, beseeching. "Forgive me, Y-Your Majesty, but I cannot, I cannot."

Frightened she squeezed her eyes shut, expecting royal wrath. But it didn't come. Instead, she heard a small, rueful chuckle. Gently, he touched her chin, lifting her gaze to his.

" 'Oddsfish, small wonder. I am a great ugly fellow, am I not? A swarthy black devil. The 'black prince' they call me. They say I am so ugly that babes bawl at their mother's teat when they see me riding through the streets of London."

She was breathing so hard, she had to gasp to find air enough to speak. She gazed at him with desperate eyes.

"Your Majesty is not ugly—no one so kind could be thought ugly—it is only that I—I love someone."

He patted her chin, his gaze sensual.

"Ah. You wish to save your virginity for your sweetheart? Your love gift to him?" She had never thought of her virginity in that way, but she did now, and thoughts of Dove filled her, flooded her.

"Oh, yes, Your Majesty," she implored. "Yes, Sire, yes."

"Then you shall." Taking her hand, he lifted her to her feet. He smiled cynically. "If your sweetheart should prove unworthy of your gift, come to Whitehall Palace in London. Ask for my private steward. Remind him that you are the pretty girl from Arleigh Castle, and he will bring you to me."

And be your whore? Like Lady Castlemayne? Like Nell Gwynne? Never. But she answered him with all respect.

"I am obliged, Your Majesty. Thank you, Your Majesty."

Alone and out in the quiet corridor again, her knees suddenly went so weak that she had to reach out to brace herself against the wall. Relief flooded her in torrents. When her heartbeat finally grew steady, when her legs would work again, she picked up her skirts and rushed through the silent corridors and staircases to Dove's apartment. She had to tell Dove. If he heard it from others—heard the king sent for her—he would assume the worst and despise her for it.

The clocks in the castle were striking the hour of three, striking randomly, some early and some late, when she slipped into his work closet and groped her way through the darkness to his bedchamber. Outside, clouds obscured the moon. A little light spilled in. But not much. Most of his bedchamber lay in shadow.

"Dove?" she whispered from a safe distance. In New Amsterdam she'd learned to keep her distance if she had to wake him. Startled out of sleep, he was apt to grab the dagger he kept on his nightstand. Asleep and vulnerable, Dove was the small boy who'd watched his father's murder.

He awoke that way now, out of bed in a shot. Stark naked.

"Who is it!"

"Dove, it's Jericho."

"Jericho?" he said after a startled instant. She'd seen naked men before, soldiers being cruelly punished on the wooden horse at the fort in Dutch New Amsterdam. She'd seen Negro slaves stripped naked so buyers could inspect them. But their bodies could not compare with Dove's. He was so perfect, so handsomely made that she felt no shame at all looking at him.

Grabbing a pair of drawers that lay on the floor, he whipped them on and came forward, hastily tying the waist ribbons.

"Jericho! What is it? What's wrong? You gave me a start."

"Dove? The king sent for me tonight."

He blinked. "What?"

"His Majesty sent for me. After midnight."

His chest lifted in a leap. In the moonlight, his bright eyes filled with so much sudden expression that she couldn't be sure what he'd heard. He made no response at first. None at all. Then he grabbed her and crushed her close.

"Oh, Jericho, I'm so sorry. Oh, sweeting, Pansy Eyes. The bastard! He brought two whores with him. Aren't two enough? Did he have to spoil you?"

"Dove, he didn't—"

"This is my fault," he berated himself, pressing a hot kiss to her temple. "If I'd given you your indenture when you asked for it, if I'd let you go . . ."

"Dove! Dove, he didn't. The king didn't touch me. He only supped with me. I—I refused him, Dove. I only came to tell you, to wake you, because I knew you would hear servant gossip tomorrow and I didn't want you to believe it of me. I didn't want you to think the worst and despise me."

He gazed at her, stunned. Then a slow, dazed smile broke on his lips and lighted to incandescence in his eyes.

"You refused the king?" he said incredulously. "You did?"

"I did."

"You've got balls, grubworm. A bondslave refusing a king! I've never heard of such a brave thing. Hell, how did you manage it?"

"I told him I cared for someone else."

His glowing eyes ranged over her. Even in the darkness she could see the gold flecks in them, the spinning of his thoughts. The corners of his mouth lifted in a tender smile.

"Would that 'someone' be me?"

"You know it is."

He hugged her hard. She wrapped her arms around him.

How good it felt just to hug, as if they belonged to each other. They hadn't hugged since Marguerite's arrival. Content to be hugged, she nestled her cheek into the crook of his neck. For a long time, they just hugged, Dove rocking her in his arms, his chest bare and warm, the warm pungent fur of his underarms brushing her bare shoulders.

"Oh, beauty. What a kettle of fish, eh?"

"Yes. It's a kettle of fish."

His warm breath feathered over her forehead. "Grubworm, if I could, you know I would ask you to be my mistress."

"You already asked me. On Mid-Summer's Eve."

He rested his smile on her temple, tasting her skin with the tip of his tongue. "I was drunk that night. Tonight I'm sober. Sober, I can't ask you."

"You mean because of Lady Marguerite?"

"No. Hell." His voice fell in disappointment. "I get the feeling Marguerite wouldn't care if I kept a dozen mistresses. It's not Marguerite. It's *you*, Pansy Eyes. You're not the sort of girl a man makes into his mistress. You're too . . . special. I would feel I had soiled you, making you into a mistress, a whore. Secondly, there's the matter of John."

"John?"

"He loves you. He wants to marry you, beauty."

"I know. Dove?" She gazed into his eyes. "Sometimes I don't know what to do with my life. Sometimes I don't know."

His chest rose sharply. He drew a tight breath.

"Marry him, Jericho! Marry John. Then I won't have to spend my life worrying about you, wondering where you are, how you are. Hell, there's not a better man in all England. He'll be good to you. He'll take care of you."

She shook her head and buried her face in his golden hair, savoring the clean smell of it, determined to remember the smell of his hair, his skin, for the rest of her life.

"I don't love John. I love you." She trembled. It was the first time she'd dared tell Dove she loved him. It had cost her dearly to say it, and it hurt when he glossed over it.

"What does it matter? He loves you. He wants you for his wife. He'll take care of you."

She shook her head with pride. "I'll take care of myself."

"Oh, sweeting. You make this so goddamn hard."

"I'll have my dame school in London, Dove, and later, in New York. I'll earn my own living. You won't have to worry about me. I'll take care of myself and I'll take good care of Black Bartimaeus, too."

He gave her a ferocious hug. "I hate your brave plans. They scare the hell out of me. Jericho, London is not New Amsterdam. London is a big rough city. It's full of beggars, thieves, pickpockets. You'll be a sitting duck for every coney catcher who comes down the street."

"I'll learn," she insisted.

"Oh, sweeting." He sighed and rested his forehead on hers. Closing their eyes, they savored the intimacy, hearts beating in warm, wonderful unison. It was a special moment. She knew she would remember it all her life. The darkness was as soft as velvet. A little silvery moonlight fell across the floor in soft stripes. The night was quiet and gentle and lovely.

"Dove? Do you love me a little? Just a little?" She had to know. She had to have something to take with her.

"What do you think?"

"I think you do."

"I think so, too."

They clung, making the moment last. He loves me. Not as much as he loves Marguerite. But he loves me a little. He does! And oh, I love him so . . .

"Do you want to kiss on the bed?"

She hesitated. "It's late. I should go."

"Ten minutes."

"Ten minutes."

She overstayed. It was the shank of day when she awoke. The sun was shining, Dove was snoring and the castle clocks were striking ten.

She jumped up, alarmed. If someone caught her here! Kissing Dove's unshaven jaw, she swatted at her mussed, wrinkled petticoats and ran. Had she been paying less attention to wrinkled petticoats and more attention to the corridor as she popped out of Dove's apartment, she might have avoided trouble.

For Lady Marguerite's French maid sailed past, carrying Marguerite's silver breakfast tray in her arms. Jericho instantly averted her face. But it was too late. The maid's shrewd eyes had seen her. Heart drumming, worried, Jericho hurried to her work in the kitchens.

Chapter Sixteen

The king's party left at noon, loud and merry. Mounted on horseback, the de Mont men and Lady de Mont rode out with the king, courteously escorting him to the next great house on the royal itinerary. When the last coach had rumbled away, Arleigh Castle sighed in relief. Servants kicked off their shoes and gathered around the kitchen ale barrel for well-deserved rest and some merrymaking of their own.

Jericho didn't join them. For she'd been the target of sidelong, "knowing" glances all morning. And how could she answer them—I did not sleep with the king, I was asleep with Lord Dove?

Impossible. Dove would strangle her. So she and Black Bartimaeus took Pax and went for a walk. Not ten minutes away from the castle, she was summoned back. She was wanted in Lady Marguerite's apartment immediately. She went with apprehension. How much had the French maid seen? Had Marguerite guessed she'd spent the night in Dove's chamber? It had been so innocent. They'd kissed, yes. But nothing else.

Lady Marguerite lay lounging on a silk-cushioned daybed in her lavish withdrawing chamber. Wearing a chamber robe of forest green silk, she was reading. When Jericho entered, Marguerite glanced up and slammed her book shut. Jericho's chest tightened. She knows. Marguerite drew an ill-tempered breath.

"So. The king's latest whore."

Jericho's lips trembled in anger. "I am *not* a whore, my lady."

"You contradict me?"

"If you call me whore, yes. I contradict you."

They looked at each other with mutual dislike. Temper tics, two short vertical lines, appeared between Marguerite's perfectly plucked brows.

"Such cheek. I could have you flogged."

"Then flog me. But I am not a whore, and I will not be called so. Not by you, nor by anyone."

Marguerite's exotic eyes flashed with anger, and anxiety washed through Jericho. She'd not meant to enrage Marguerite, only to defend herself. Dove would be furious if she angered his betrothed.

"Bah!" In a small burst of temper, Marguerite distractedly picked up her discarded book, then banged it down again. "I care not if you are whore to every king in Europe. I did not summon you here to find out if the king gave you the pox last night. I called you here for a different purpose."

"Yes, my lady." Jericho took care to curb her own temper for Dove's sake.

"Lord Dove has asked me to free you."

"Yes." She already knew that.

"Because I love Lord Dove," Marguerite underscored the words sharply, "and more to the point, because *Lord Dove* loves *me*, I have seen fit to honor his request. Therefore you are free. I have freed you. Your indenture, your disgusting, dirty document, is over there. I have signed it, releasing you from service as of today. Take it and be gone." Marguerite wagged an irritable, jeweled finger at her writing table.

Jericho drew a stunned breath, then quickly collected her wits and went to Marguerite's lovely rosewood writing table. Her indenture lay upon it, face up. She picked it up with trembling hands. It was true! Marguerite's bold signature lay slashed across the document. She was no longer bound, but free. She was free! She'd wanted freedom all of her life, ever since she'd grown old enough to discern the difference between bondslave and freewoman.

"You will leave Arleigh Castle at once."

Still stunned, she could scarcely find her voice.

"Yes, my lady. I-I will leave within the week."

"You misheard me," Marguerite corrected sharply. "I said you will leave at once. Not within the week, not tomorrow, not even tonight, but *now*. This very hour."

Jericho's eyes flew from the indenture to Marguerite in shock. She felt a surge of panic. Leave immediately? Not say goodbye to Dove? Leave without talking to him, without hugging him, without thanking him for his many years of goodness to her? Leave, perhaps never to see him again? Panic filled her.

"My lady! I would bid Lord Dove farewell. He was my master for half my life. I was but a child when he took me in. He was good to me, h-he was kind to me. I would thank him."

"*That*, particularly, you will not do. You will leave Arleigh Castle at once and you will take care never to set foot here again. For if you do, I will see you punished as a trespasser." Marguerite rose to her feet, her silk rustling angrily. "There is a horse and cart leaving for London this very hour. The bondslave wages due you are in it. Now, begone. Do not keep the carter waiting. You are boring me."

Jericho was stunned. Not say farewell to Dove? Not even farewell? "My lady, I beg!"

"Go."

"My lady—"

"Go! If you are not gone within the hour, I shall have you put in chains and hauled to Newgate jail for the thief you are! It is only because I love Lord Dove that I do not press charges. He would be upset to discover his precious bondslave is a thief. He is too tenderhearted by far."

"Thief?" The fantastic accusation cut through her dazed mind.

"I am missing a ring."

Jericho's thoughts whirled. "I-I-I know. You have been missing the ring for weeks. We—all of us—every servant in the castle has been searching for it. *I* do not have your ring."

"Oh, of *that* I am quite sure," Marguerite agreed caustically. "You do not have it because you have already sold it."

"S-sold it!" Jericho could scarcely get breath. Her mind reeled. "I am no thief."

"No?" Silk hissing, lacquered heels ringing, Marguerite went to the fireplace, seized something from the mantle and whirled. "Then what is this?" She dangled a tiny brown velvet pouch by its drawstring, as she might dangle a disgusting dead rat by its tail. It was the money pouch the countess of Blackpool had given her.

"You searched my things!"

"Indeed, I did. I sent my steward to search your belongings this morning." Marguerite tossed her glossy head and uttered a harsh laugh. "God love me, you don't think I am so obtuse as to dismiss a servant without having her box searched for pilfered goods, do you?"

Jericho couldn't get air. "It's mine! I am *not* a thief."

"Indeed. Then where would a bondslave get five gold coins? Whoring for the king?"

"No!"

"Payment from Lord Dove? For bed service?"

"No! No!" Her breast surged. "The coins were a gift. I was given them by the duch—" She choked the words back and painfully swallowed them. She'd promised not to tell. "I-I am not at liberty to say," she finished lamely.

Marguerite's lip curled in scorn.

"As I thought. You stole my ring and sold it."

"No. My lady—"

Marguerite tossed her head in disgust. "Get out of here. Go. Leave Arleigh Castle at once. If you are not gone within the hour, I shall tell everyone that you are a thief. Everyone! Then try to get your precious dame-school license."

Shocked at the jealousy in Marguerite, Jericho backed away. She would do it. She meant it. Labeled thief, Jericho would never again teach dame school. With a scared, pounding heart, she turned and hurried out of the apartment.

One hour! She sprang into action. She ran for Black Bartimaeus, told him to pack their things. Then she ran to Mrs. Phipps's rooms, awakened the befuddled woman out of an afternoon nap and kissed her, not lingering to explain. She ran back down to the kitchens, swiftly hugged Janie and Harry and others she'd grown fond of. While the children wept and tearfully helped Black Bartimaeus carry their belongings to the cart, Jericho rushed up the rear staircase, down the corridor and into Dove's apartment.

She flew into his work closet, sat in his chair, and grabbed paper, quill, ink pot. The clock ticked. One hour, one hour. She stabbed quill into ink pot and prepared to write. But the words would not come. Tears of frustration rolled down her cheeks. She batted them away, glanced at the racing clock and wrote.

My dear beloved Dove,

Pray, forgive this jumbled letter. My heart is so full at this moment, I cannot think straight. Lady Marguerite has freed me, and I leave at once for London. I am taking Black Bartimaeus with me. Please do not worry, we will be fine.

Dove, you may hear I am a thief. I beg you not to believe it. As for the gold coins your lady will surely show you, I beg you to believe I did nothing dishonest or dishonorable to get them. The coins were given to me. I am not at liberty to say by whom.

Dove? Take good care of Mrs. Phipps. She is not so well as she pretends. Take care of Janie and Harry too. They are, after all, only children. Give Mr. d'Orias my love. If your uncle, the duke of Nordham, should ever ask after me, please tell him I shall always remember him with the utmost respect and admiration.

Lastly, Dove, what can I say to you? Only that you have been the kindest, most wonderful master a bondslave ever had. Only that my heart breaks to leave you. Only that I shall miss you to the end of my days, to my last breath on earth.

I am no longer bound in indenture, but be assured that in my heart I am and shall forever be,

Your Devoted Bondslave
Jericho Jones

The castle clocks began to bong, striking the hour. Alarmed, Jericho jumped up, shook blotting sand on the ink to dry it, and with quick, trembling hands, folded it. Distrusting Marguerite, she didn't leave the letter on Dove's writing table. Instead, she went into his bedchamber and hurriedly tucked the letter under his pillow, where he would surely find it when he returned. For one aching moment, she rested her cheek on his pillow, remembering the sweet kisses they'd shared there. Then, as the clocks of Arleigh Castle chimed and bonged, she ran.

Marguerite stood in her apartment window and gazed down at the castleyard, watching the cart as it rattled away, carrying the girl, the tall elderly Negro and an ugly one-eyed dog.

Good riddance.

When the cart was out of sight, she hurried briskly to Dove's apartment. She searched all of the logical places a lover might leave a letter and found it in the most telling place of all—bed.

She read it, then tore it into a hundred minute pieces. Going to the open window, she leaned out and tossed them to the wind. She watched with satisfaction as they drifted down into the castleyard like snow, lost forever.

Chapter Seventeen

Jericho's first month in London was nearly the disaster Dove had predicted. Country bumpkins? She and Black Bartimaeus were worse than bumpkins. They were dunces. She hated London. It was crowded and noisy and rude and thieving; it stank of privies, and there was dirt everywhere—soot that belched from its ten thousand ugly chimneys. They'd not been in the rude, bustling city ten minutes when Black Bartimaeus had his pocket cleanly picked.

Resisting the impulse to run to John, she comforted Black Bartimaeus as best she could, then set her jaw in determination. This wicked city would *not* best her.

They slept the first night in a poulterer's kitchen on Poultry Lane and struck out on foot the next morning to find lodging. After a discouraging day's hunt, they finally found two rooms they could afford, above a cookshop on Wattling Street.

Wattling Street was little more than a crowded alley, the second stories of the houses and shops overhanging the street, almost meeting, shutting out sunlight, leaving the street in perpetual shadow. But it had redeeming features. St. Paul's Cathedral stood at the top of Wattling Street, on Ludgate Hill. They'd thought the street respectable and themselves lucky to find cheap lodging there, for richly dressed ladies and gentlemen promenaded on Wattling Street all day long, going up and down to St. Paul's.

They quickly discovered their mistake. The "ladies" were countesses-of-the-trade. The "gentlemen"? Coney catchers and highwaymen. As for St. Paul's, it was a great disappointment. Prostitutes used the nave for trysts, and the enormous cathedral lay in disrepair and neglect, its outer facing covered with wooden scaffolding. Only its five acres of solid lead roof were awesome.

Despite the setbacks, the two rooms above the cookshop gradually became home. Jericho and Black Bartimaeus worked hard to make them so. They scrubbed the grimy walls. They scoured the few sparse pieces of furniture. They attacked the blackened floor on hands and knees, scouring until years of grime lifted and the silky, lovely English oak reappeared. A week after they'd moved in, Jericho patted the sweat from her brow, looked about her little home, and smiled. It was Dutch clean. Better yet, it was all hers. Hers and Black Bartimaeus's.

The next week, she went to the city hall to prove her competence and to purchase her dame-school license. It was the proudest moment of her life when Black Bartimaeus nailed the license to a painted board and displayed it in their second story window.

She got her first pupil that day, the cookshop owner's

daughter, a little girl who had a harelip and impaired speech. Remembering the agony of her own childhood stutter, Jericho gladly accepted the child. She made a vow to herself. She would *never* reject a defective child.

Other children followed. Within a week she had a full dame school, twelve little children from Wattling Street.

While Jericho taught upstairs, Black Bartimaeus sat downstairs in their street door, guarding her school. Wattling Street was wary of him at first. He was so tall, and black as ebony. But soon Wattling Street warmed to his presence. Their children were safe. Wattling Street was safe. No street ruffian dared try his tricks with this black giant on guard.

As she'd guessed he might, John found them before two weeks had elapsed. Mrs. Phipps had written him, and he'd traced them through the city hall, through her license. He came stomping up to their rooms in a temper, enraged that they had not come to him at once and angry about the trouble Marguerite had caused. But mostly he was furious to find them living on Wattling Street.

In heated anger, he tried to talk her into leaving, moving into his house. He chronicled all of the perils that could befall a girl and an elderly sick man living alone in London. Jericho heard him out and then firmly told him they were staying. John was vexed but she didn't budge. He didn't give in gracefully, but at least he gave in.

A worrywart, he dropped in to check on them daily, his expression half-amused, half-vexed. Often, when she'd finished teaching for the day, he treated them to watercoach rides and lobster dinners across the river in Southwark.

Proud of his hat shops, John took them there often. They loved it. It was fascinating to watch the process by which a beaver pelt that had been trapped by a Mohawk in the wilds of New Amsterdam became a fine felt hat, handsome enough to grace a lord's head.

On one such visit, John insisted they choose a hat, any hat in the shop. His gift. Shyly, Black Bartimaeus chose a tall-crowned hat of bright scarlet. When it was her turn to choose, Jericho selected a less flamboyant hat. Low-crowned, it was a lovely, wide-brimmed felt hat of periwinkle blue.

"It matches your eyes," John said softly as she turned from the looking glass in excitement. She had never owned a hat before. Not a real hat. Bondslaves wore coifs.

Her heart fluttered. She gazed into his warm brown eyes for a moment. If it weren't for loving Dove, it would be perfectly possible to fall in love with this warm, kind man. Addled by the thought, she turned away in uncertain confusion.

John felt his heart beat a little faster. What he'd seen in Jericho's eyes—that flash of surprise—had given him more hope than he'd had all summer. He had a chance with her. Despite Dove, he had a chance!

Teaching one afternoon, sitting on a stool amidst her pupils, she heard a step on the stair and glanced at the door with a smile, thinking it John.

It wasn't John. Fox Hazlitt, steward to the duke of Blackpool, stepped into her schoolroom. Her smile fled in bewilderment. Lying at her feet, Pax lifted his head and growled. She shushed him. Giving the children sums to do on their slates, she rose and hurried to the door, uneasy, disturbed.

"What do you want?" She didn't like him. There was no point in pretending she did.

"I bring a message from His Grace, the duke of Blackpool. Suppose you get rid of them brats—" He gave the children an uninterested, contemptuous glance. "—and we go to a lobster house and dine and drink a bit, and then I'll deliver His Grace's message." His oily smile suggested more.

Dine and drink with him? She'd sooner dine and drink with a weasel.

"No. Tell me here and now. Then go. I'm busy."

He didn't like that. His eyes narrowed to slits. He delivered his message by rote. "His Grace would be kindly disposed if you would reconsider his offer of employment. Her Grace, Lady Angelina, has fallen gravely ill, and His Grace believes that if you were to companion her, you would restore Her Grace to good health."

Jericho felt a pang. Lady Angelina, desperately ill? She'd liked the lovely duchess. More than that, she'd felt drawn to her. Picturing the duchess suffering on her sickbed, Jericho winced. She felt a tug. Go to the lady? Serve her until she grew well again? Take care of her?

She glanced at her restless pupils. Jemimah with her harelip. Blind Elizabeth, petting and fondling Pax. Caleb with his club foot. These children needed her, too.

She shook her head. "I'm sorry," she said firmly. "I am very, very sorry the duchess is ill, but I cannot help. I have my work here."

"His Grace will be deeply disappointed." Jericho's temper flashed, for he'd delivered these words like a threat, as if she were still a bondslave, subject to other people's orders.

"I gave you my answer. Now go."

His eyes narrowed even more. He looked angry, as if she'd upset his applecart, upset some well-planned scheme. But the look passed, and he smiled smoothly.

"The offer stands open. Any time you desire it."

"No."

"Very well. Then I bid you good day, Mistress Jones. Until we . . . meet again." An amenity? Or a threat? He smilingly doffed his hat and left.

When he'd gone down the stairs and into the street, she glanced down at her arms. Goose bumps. She rubbed them away. It bewildered her that the duke of Blackpool had kept track of her. It disturbed her that he'd known where to find her in London.

Shivering despite the sweltering July heat, she pushed Fox Hazlitt and the duke out of mind and hurried back to the children. But the thought of the duchess lingered. She was very sorry about the duchess. Very sorry indeed.

Each Lord's Day, John came to fetch them by coach, walking down from Cheapside Street because Wattling Street was too narrow to accommodate a coach. He would take them to church. After church, he would feed them an excellent dinner in his home. Then, if the day was a fair one, they would climb into his coach again and ride to the Tower of London to join the merry throngs of Sabbath Day strollers.

Black Bartimaeus especially loved the Tower. From the Tower wall, one could see all over London, all the way to St. Paul's on Ludgate Hill. Best of all, he loved the exotic wild animals that were kept in cages there for London's amusement. Eyes shining, he would plant himself in front of the cages for hours on end, watching the lions and apes and crocodiles that had been familiar to him in his childhood, before Dutch slave-ships had raided his coastal village and carried him off. Neither John nor Jericho had ever seen him so happy as when he sat watching the animals, and they vowed to each other they would bring him to the Tower every chance they got.

Though London days could be pleasant, London nights were more frightening than Jericho had bargained for. At night, the unlighted city lay pitch dark, and footpads and robbers roamed bold as brass. Sword fights broke out in the dark alleys, and the unnerving clash of steel swords could be heard nightly, coming from St. Paul's pitch black churchyard.

Gradually, however, life settled into a rhythm, and except for missing Mrs. Phipps—and missing Dove with all her heart—Jericho was tolerably happy. She'd been born to teach. And she was doing just that. She was taking good care of Black Bartimaeus, too.

On the last day of July, another visitor surprised her. Answering the knock on her street door one evening, she gasped in delight.

"Mr. d'Orias! How did you find us?"

"Mrs. Phipps." He smiled warmly. Filling the stairwell with his imposing presence, he followed her up the stairs to their rooms. Quick to grant her privacy, Black Bartimaeus took Pax for his evening walk.

Dressed in his usual rich black, with a shirt of snowy white linen, d'Orias took off his fine, black-plumed hat, set it on the table, looked about with an approving nod, then seated himself in the chair she pulled to the cool of the window for him. She pulled up her own chair, smiling. For a while, they talked of her dame school and other pleasantries. When a moment of silence came, she drew a shaky breath.

"How is Dove?"

D'Orias smiled gently. "Unpleasant. Cross as a bear. Nothing pleases him of late. He dislikes everything, objects to everything. He quarrels with everyone, even Lady Marguerite."

Her chest pounded. Maybe Dove missed her. But he hadn't responded to the letter she'd left under his pillow. If he'd wanted get in touch with her, he could have. Mrs. Phipps knew where she was. Jericho had written her. Probably, he'd believed Marguerite's ugly tale—lock, stock, and barrel. Believed she'd stolen Marguerite's ring and sold it. Her fingers restless with agitation, she put them to work pleating a fold in her skirt.

Allowing her to choose the subject, d'Orias sat silent, his black eyes gentle, waiting, permitting her to speak of anything she wished. She drew a deep breath.

"I did not steal Lady Marguerite's ring, Mr. d'Orias."

"I know you did not. I never believed it for a moment. As to the gold coins found in your box, I do not believe you gained them by selling Marguerite's ring."

She looked quickly away. Out beyond the rooftops, dusk was gathering. The sun's final bright rays of the day bathed St. Paul's enormous, five acre lead roof. Down below, in Wattling Street, night had already fallen, and the alley lay in darkness.

"Thank you for believing in me. I cannot reveal who gave the coins to me. I am not at liberty to say. I promised."

"Nor need you say." Hesitantly, gingerly, he added, "I trust you did not . . . get them from the king?"

"No, of course not." A thought struck. She looked at him with shocked eyes. "Is that what Dove thinks? That I earned the coins in bed with the king?"

"I fear so, yes."

"But it's not true!"

With the dusky twilight settling upon the rooftops of London, pigeons fluttered in cooing flocks to their roosts, filling the air with the sound of their soft warbling.

"If you say it is not true, I believe you. Your word is trustworthy. If Dove chooses to believe otherwise, he is a thick-headed young fool. Now. A new topic, yes? If I may? For I must leave soon."

She nodded. D'Orias leaned forward, elbows resting on knees and broached his subject gently.

"I have come mainly to tell you news of . . . your parents. I have not forgotten my promise to look into the matter."

Instantly alert, she put Dove out of mind. She tensed. "Yes?"

"*The Jericho* sank years ago, as you know, as Lord Aubrey told us." She nodded expectantly. "However. The harbormaster's widow at St. Katherine's Docks remembered the Dutch ship, *The Jericho*, in particular a sailing in 1646. Two passengers, a young married couple whose own suckling infant had tragically just died, came aboard *The Jericho* with a newborn infant they'd purchased on the docks to replace their own dear child. The widow had remembered, because her husband, the harbormaster, had to intervene when *The Jericho*'s captain balked at taking the infant aboard, thinking the infant bad luck. You see, the infant had 'witch's' hair and . . . three red birthmarks, 'duivel' marks."

Jericho absorbed it in shock. For a moment she found it difficult to get her breath. She pressed her fingers to her temples, trying to assimilate what he was telling her, trying to make sense of it.

"Who did they buy me from, the people who bought me?"

"No one knows."

"Where are they, the people who bought me?"

"Dead. They died on the voyage. Moribund throat swept the ship."

"The harbormaster's wife. Can I see her, talk to her?"

D'Orias's rich Italian voice grew very soft, compassionate.

"Alas, no. I am sorry. She is dead also. She died of the plague last summer. I have the story secondhand, from her son."

Emotions surging, Jericho couldn't sit any longer. She lunged up and stood at the window. She spread her trembling fingers on the sill. Though the sun still lingered on St. Paul's lead roof, Wattling Street was already dark as midnight. She could hear Black Bartimaeus below, entering the stairwell, turning the iron key in their street door, safely locking them in.

"I almost wish you had not told me. I would prefer to believe my mother died giving birth to me aboard ship. It's hard knowing I was born in England. Knowing my mother birthed me and didn't want me. Knowing my own mother sold me."

D'Orias hesitated. "There is one thing more I fear you must know. The harbormaster's son recalls his mother's story because eight or nine years ago, his mother received a visitor, a man who made similar inquiries about *The Jericho* and about an infant girl with three birthmarks."

She turned abruptly. She drew a short breath.

"Who was the man?"

"The son did not see him. He does not know. He had the story from his mother."

"Eight or nine years ago? Nine years ago? That's when the men abducted me at Collect Pond, Mr. d'Orias."

"Yes."

"Someone means me harm!"

D'Orias leaned back in his chair and calmly crossed one leg upon the other. "Someone *meant* you harm. *Meant*. In the past. Then, for some reason, whoever meant you harm changed his mind. Or perhaps he himself died. Else you would be dead by now," he pointed out gently.

Though her lips trembled, she saw the sense of it. If someone still wanted her dead, she would be dead by now. She'd been a young, defenseless child. Children are easy to kill. Yet, no one had tried to harm her in all the years since Collect Pond. Still, she felt a sense of dread, of foreboding.

"W-why w-would anyone seek out a babe who'd been sold at auction? And so many years after its birth?"

"Why indeed? That is the question, isn't it." D'Orias rose, plucked his fine hat from the table and put it on. "I shall persevere and attempt to find out. In the meantime, you must not worry. Whatever happened in the past is long over. I am certain you are safe."

"Yes," she agreed anxiously, wanting to believe it. Her uneasiness lessened as Pax and Black Bartimaeus came up the stairs. Her two beloved guards. She was safe. Dear life, she shouldn't tremble like a ninny about something that had happened a decade ago. Was she a child or a grown woman!

D'Orias shook hands with Black Bartimaeus, and then Jericho escorted him down the stairwell, turned the iron key in the lock and let him out. Wattling Street lay dark as a cave.

"Goodbye, Mr. d'Orias. Thank you for coming. Tell Mrs. Phipps that I miss her, that I love her. Tell her Black Bartimaeus and I are well and happy. Tell her we have twelve pupils! And tell her that John comes to see us every day. Tell—tell her I intend to visit her each and every day when she comes to London to live with John at the end of summer."

"I will tell her," he agreed gently. "For now, farewell."

"Farewell."

When he'd gone, she shut the door, locked it, and hung the key on its peg. In his staunch, dependable way, Black Bartimaeus came down the stairs to check the lock and to lower the thick stout door bar. At the door at the top of the stairs, they repeated the process, locking, barring.

She was perfectly safe. Yet, when she thought of all d'Orias had told her and thought about what had happened so many years ago at Collect Pond, a shiver curled up her spine. Someone wanted her dead. But who? And *why*?

Chapter Eighteen

August had come bearing down upon London in a heat wave and the heat showed no signs of letting up. The city baked. Cooling rains failed to come, despite fervent Lord's Day prayers offered up in all of London's churches, and the hot, crowded, close-packed city grew dry as tinder. Jericho feared for fire. She and Black Bartimaeus kept their fire buckets ready, filled to the brim.

On the fifteenth day of that blistering hot month, she was standing in her street door in the afternoon, dismissing her pupils, when she glanced across the alley, and her heart jumped. There, lounging in the doorway of the grog shop, a tankard of ale in hand—stood Dove. Seeing him again was like a physical blow. For a minute she couldn't breathe, couldn't think. Her hands began to tremble. He was watching her with those bright eyes. Wearing a sweat-stained shirt with his hat pushed back, he looked as hot and uncomfortable as the day.

Her heart pounded. Stooping, she quickly hugged and dismissed her pupils with a word of praise for each. When the children had scampered off, she made her way across the alley, which was crowded and noisy with people coming and going.

"Dove. W-what are you doing here?"

Pushing himself off his leaning post, he tossed his drained tankard to the serving girl in the grog shop. "I'm just passing through."

She gazed into those bright, intense eyes. Passing through? Arleigh Castle lay twenty miles to the west. Passing through on a day so hot even the watercoaches had deserted the Thames? She didn't believe it for a moment.

"How-how did you find me?"

"I didn't," he said irritably. "I told you, I was passing through. I stopped for ale and happened to glance out . . . and, well, there you were, standing there with those little children."

It was so flagrant a lie, that her heart beat even louder. He'd been worried about her. Worry had brought him to London. He'd come to make sure she was all right.

He flicked a glance at her windows. "Is that where you live?"

"Yes. W-will you come upstairs?" She nodded at her rooms. "Sit for a bit and talk?"

He rebuffed her with a headshake. "No. Hell, I'm busy.

My tailor . . . my wedding clothes. I don't have time. No time at all.''

She swallowed her disappointment. He might be worried about her, but he was also angry. She knew why. Marguerite's stupid ring. And more, the gold coins found in her box.

A pushcart came trundling, rattling, noisy, filling the narrow alley with its din. She waited until it rumbled past, and its noise died away. Blocked by the cart, annoyed pedestrians now surged by.

"Dove, I didn't steal Lady Marguerite's ring."

"I know that," he said in a surly voice, glaring at a man who'd jostled her in passing. "Hell, Marguerite found the damned ring. That is, her maid found it. It had been caught in the fold of Marguerite's bedcurtains.''

"I see." Jericho felt a ripple of anger. Stupid woman. Blaming her for something she'd done herself. She'd lost her own ring in her own bed.

Restless, angry, Dove took his hat off and reamed it through his fingers. "Marguerite felt bad that she'd called you a thief. She said so. At dinner. In front of my mother, Uncle Aubrey, everyone. She also said she intends to send your coins to you and put in one of her own. To repay you for the wrong.''

"Did she?''

"Hell, yes. I thought it generous of her, considering . . .''

Generous? It wasn't generous, it was clever. Marguerite had won Dove's admiration with that ''generous'' gesture. She looked away, irritated. Marguerite manipulated him as easily as—as easily as a street puppeteer worked his puppets! Why couldn't Dove see it? Was love that blind? She threw him a resentful look.

Slop water splattered into the street, tossed out of an upper window. They jumped out of the way, barely avoiding the spray. A passing pedestrian, however, got a hatful, and a strident quarrel broke out. The man cursed the woman in the upper window and shook his fist. The woman cursed back. The quarrel escalated as the woman's husband came lunging out of the street door in his shirt tails, brandishing a sword. The pedestrian drew his sword. With excited cries, people surged around them, watching the entertainment, egging them on. But the day was too hot for a sword fight, and the quarrel lost steam.

Dove winged an irritable glance at the noise.

"Well, I'd best be going," he said. "Hell, I can't stand here nattering all day. I'm a busy man."

Going? All resentment fled. Unspoken words throbbed in her throat, aching there, longing to spring out.

"Dove? I know what you're thinking. About the gold coins."

He denied it with a vehement headshake. "I'm not thinking anything at all! Hell, sleep with anyone you want. You're a freewoman now, not a bondslave. Sleep yourself silly. Start at the top floor of Whitehall Palace and sleep your way down to the cellar if you like. Sleep with the whole damned city of London, if you want."

"Dove, I didn't sleep with the king."

"Who cares! *I* don't."

She drew a shaky breath and waited until staring, gawking, eavesdropping pedestrians passed. "The coins are mine, yes. That I admit. Dove, if I could, I would tell you who gave them to me. But I pledged my word not to tell. But it was *not* the king, Dove. Nor any man."

He refused to look at her. He went on reaming his fine hat, absentmindedly destroying it. He'd worked his way around to the ostrich plume. Feathery bits of this expensive ornament flew like chicken fluff.

"Yes, well, the hell with it," he said in curt disbelief. "Enjoy the coins in good health. Marguerite intends to see they are returned to you."

"Dove? Please believe me?"

It was a struggle to stay angry with her. Dove wanted to believe her. He didn't want to picture her lying under the king, her soft pretty limbs spread. He couldn't bear it. She was so damned . . . special! He glanced at her. Those vivid blue eyes. The sweet sprinkling of freckles. That flaming red hair. Hell, in her cheap green gown, standing there in the midst of those little crumb crunchers, dismissing them, hugging them, she'd made the prettiest sight he'd ever seen. For a moment, it had knocked the breath out of him.

The slop-water ruckus died down, and Wattling Street began to flow again with its usual trashy foot-traffic—nightgown ladies, coney catchers, pickpockets. Glaring at Wattling Street, he cursed under his breath. Jericho didn't belong here. What was John thinking of, letting her live here? Damn it, didn't John love her? A dame school, for God's sake. On Wattling Street! He flexed his shoulders in heating anger.

"Yes, well, I'd best be going," he said harshly. He watched her reaction. She wanted to be rid of him, didn't she? She'd made it plain, hightailing it out of Arleigh Castle the instant she'd got her goddamned freedom. No goodbye. Not even a note. Angered afresh, he looked away from the hurt that rose in those pansy-soft eyes.

"C-could you stay a little longer, Dove? Black Bartimaeus will be disappointed if he doesn't see you. He's at the Tower. He likes to spend afternoons watching the caged animals, whittling figures of them for the neighborhood children. He took Pax along. They'll be home by sundown."

He slanted a glance up at the narrow band of sky, the only strip of daylight in this shadowy, fetid, stinking alley. Stay? If he stayed one more minute, he would grab her and take her to bed. He wanted her so badly his groin ached.

"No. Damn it," he said crossly, "I don't have time to stop and chat with every bondslave and slave I've ever owned."

"W-will you come again?"

"I don't know, Jericho."

"Black Bartimaeus will be disappointed."

"I don't *know*, Jericho," he burst with growing exasperation. "Hell!"

His explosion made her eyes fill. Damn it, what was he doing? He hadn't ridden all the way to London in this damnable heat to make her cry. He'd come to make sure she was safe, happy. And here he was, doing her more harm than could the whole goddamned city of London and every pervert in it. Angry with himself, he lashed out at her.

"Don't nag! If I decide to visit, I'll visit. If I don't, I won't. Goodbye, Jericho," he finished curtly, clamping hat on head. Without a backward look, he swung off down the crowded street. His horse was stabled at Cornhill. He'd avoided Cheapside Street and John's shops. He didn't want John to know he couldn't stay away from her.

Jericho watched him go, her throat tightening, bands of

misery tightening around her chest. He strode away so fast, he went so fast, he was leaving so fast. Tall and goldenhaired, he was pushing his way down the crowded street so fast. So fast he was melting into the anonymous flow. He was leaving so fast. Leaving . . . leaving . . . He was leaving!

Her throat convulsed. Then burst.

"Dove!"

At the bottom of Wattling Street, he whirled even before the shriek was fully out of her mouth, as if he'd been listening for it, willing it, wanting it.

"Dove!" she shrieked again. Seizing her skirts, she went flying. Dove didn't hesitate an instant. Eyes bright and fierce, he came bounding through the crowd, knocking people aside left and right. For frantic moments, it seemed she would never get to him, and her hysteria rose. A sea of people separated them. People blocked her way—people in front, people to every side, people blocking her, people in the way, Marguerite, Lady de Mont, people, people.

"Dove," she shrieked in anguish. "Dove, Dove don't leave me!"

And then, suddenly he was there, grabbing her, crushing her in his arms. "I won't, I won't. Jericho, I won't."

He crushed a feverish kiss to her mouth, then swept her through the gawking crowd to her door, pushed her inside, stepped in, slammed the door shut and banged the door bar down. There, at the bottom of the hot airless stairwell, there in the cavelike darkness, they sprang into each other's arms and kissed wildly.

"Dove—"

"Sweeting—beauty—Jericho."

They couldn't stop kissing. Hot, overheated, on fire with need, they couldn't stop kissing, they couldn't stop touching. Inches away, on the other side of the door—on the other side of the world!—Wattling Street ebbed and flowed with its familiar strident foot-traffic, but here in the cavelike stairwell, there was only the sound of their wild panting, their needy kissing. His hands were all over her—on her breasts, her neck, her face, gripping her buttocks, plunging between her legs.

When they couldn't get close enough, Dove tore off his shirt, and Jericho wrenched her bodice down, wriggling her arms free of it. They moaned, flesh touching flesh, their love whispers as wild and shaky as their kisses.

"Dove, I missed you so—"

"Oh, beauty—when I found you gone I went insane—"

"I left you a letter—"

"Did you, did you? I didn't find it—"

Wild and ardent, he scorched her neck with hot kisses, then passionately lapped at her skin, his tongue hot and quick. When her lips greedily sought his, he eased her against the wall and held her there, kissing her, his knee gently wedged between her legs. His mouth went everywhere. His kissed the birthmark on her breast, the birthmark on the nape of her neck, the one on her wrist. He was so excited that he was almost rough.

She grew drunk on his kisses. Drunk on the smell of his sweat. Intoxicated by it, she inhaled it until she grew dizzy. When he tore his hot mouth away and gave her an instant to breathe, she pressed her scorched cheek into his hot, musky chest and clung. He radiated heat like the sun.

"Dove? It's going to happen, isn't it?"

"Yes. God help us, grubworm, it's going to happen."

He swept her up the stairs. Then, while Jericho hid her breasts with her crossed arms, Dove sprang to the schoolroom windows and yanked the curtains closed so violently a curtain ring flew. He sprang into her sleeping closet and did the same. Then, they hastily shed their clothes, their eyes upon each other, bright and scared.

A few shaky moments later, lying naked upon the bed, waiting for him to shed the last of his garments, she spread her legs for him, supposing that was what she should do. A tender expression sprang into his flushed, excited face, and, she knew she'd done something naive. Bars of hot fire striped her cheeks. But when she clamped her limbs shut, Dove leaned down and stopped her with a passionate kiss.

"It's beautiful! You're beautiful, Jericho. You have done exactly right for me, exactly right."

"Dove, I never slept with the king—"

"I know, I know. I never really believed it. Not really."

Then, he lowered himself onto the bed, between her legs. The straw mattress crinkled, and he was there——male, naked, hot, eyes bright with excitement, his fine shoulders and his spill of golden hair shutting out the world. She felt shaky. Hot and cold at the same time. As if she were coming down with the ague. She ought not to be doing this. It was wicked. She didn't care. She wanted . . . wanted . . .

"Tell me what to do. I w-want to do it right."

"Do you remember when you learned how to skate? In New Amsterdam? On Collect Pond?" He pressed a scorching kiss to her cheek. She moved her mouth so her lips could find his. She was so hot, so hot.

"Yes."

"You were such a little girl. All freckles and bones. You listened to everyone's instructions. But you didn't really learn how to skate until you stepped out on the ice and tried it, did you?"

"It's like skating, then." Drunk with his sweat smell, she could not stop inhaling. Breath after breath after intoxicating breath. Dove . . .

"It's like skating, beauty. But it's also like spring rain, gentle and wonderful. It can also be like a hurricane. It can blow you off your feet and sweep you into waters so tempestuous——so turbulent and deep and whirling, that you feel you're going to drown——"

"Dove?"

"What, what?"

She felt so hot, so cold, so shaky.

"Bring me the h-hurricane."

"Oh, beauty! I'm going to bring you a hundred hurricanes."

Later, when it was over, when he'd finally gained control of himself, when his own wild heartbeat had slowed and he'd looked down to find her lying limp as a flower beneath him, her maidenhead a smear of blood on the sheets, he felt so shaken he couldn't think. Lord, lord, what had he done?

Easing off her, he grabbed a towel from a peg on the wall, tucked it between her legs, then sat on the edge of the bed and held his head in his hands. He trembled, profoundly shaken. God, what had he done? The one thing he'd vowed not to do. He'd taken Jericho. He'd taken his own bondslave. He'd deflowered her. No man of honor does such a thing! Shame welled up. Then guilt. He felt so guilty, he was overwhelmed by it. Dazed by it.

Numb, he gazed around the shabby hovel she lived in. Wall pegs held her few clothes. A shelf held her few pretties—ribbons, a comb, a cracked mirror, a sprig of wildflowers that she'd picked somewhere to brighten her room. She owned so little. And he had taken the one thing of value she owned, her virginity.

He breathed raggedly, confused, ashamed. Guilt seared him. He'd plotted her seduction this summer. He knew that now. He'd softened her up and when her innocent heart had opened to him, when she'd been ripe for the plucking, he'd ridden into London and taken her. Self-revulsion rose in shimmering, sickening waves.

He thought of John and felt sicker still. Bad enough to harm Jericho. He'd broken a sacred vow. Even if John never learned of today, their friendship would be altered by it. For Dove would always be aware that he'd taken John's woman. His guilt would drive a wedge between them. Dove knew that from this moment on, he would behave differently toward John—warier, alert, tentative in every overture. He would not be able to look John in the eye. He wanted to weep.

"Dove?"

"Jericho, don't talk to me, don't talk. I have to think."

"Is-is something wrong?"

"No. It was wonderful." And it had been. He'd had virgins before. But never anyone as sweet as Jericho. This had not been a coupling. This had been a mating. He knew the difference. A mating. He wiped a shaky hand over the beads of sweat on his upper lip. God. What if she quickened from this? Or what if Marguerite found out?

"Dove? What's wrong?"

"Jericho, be silent, damn it!" He lifted himself off the cheap straw mattress and began to dress, swiftly pulling on his clothes, dressing any which way. He had to think. He had to be alone.

Jericho turned her face to the wall, tears springing up.

Something was wrong. Terribly wrong. How could he turn on her like that? Only minutes ago, they'd lain entwined in the tenderest embrace she'd ever known. Now? Her throat throbbed. Had she done something? What had she done? Or worse, had she *failed* to do something? Had she failed her woman's part? Was he disappointed?

Though she tried to hold them back, tears of chagrin seeped hotly under her lashes. That was it, of course. Dove was disappointed. He wasn't used to bedding ignorant virgins. He was used to being with ladies who knew all about bed. She? She had been naive and ignorant. She'd even yelped in pain when he'd tried to force her maidenhead. Her yelp had frightened him, and he'd had to withdraw and start all over again. She closed her eyes in shame, remembering, fighting back the tears. Naive, ignorant, stupid.

She listened to his ragged breathing, as he dressed. He was so eager to leave her. His quick footfalls sounded. He went out into the schoolroom. She heard him help himself to their mulled ale. The tankard thudded on the table.

She lay there hurting, wounded so deeply she couldn't even cry. By and by, his footsteps returned. "Jericho. Get up. Get dressed. We need to talk."

Only that. No loving words, no reassurance. Somehow, she found the energy to drag herself up off the bed, to wash and dress. When she came into the schoolroom, Dove was standing there, hat in hand, ready to leave. That hurt, too. He couldn't wait to leave her. She gazed at him steadily, but he wouldn't meet her eyes.

"Jericho, what happened in there . . . it . . . was a mistake."

"A mistake?" Her voice shook.

Listlessly, he tapped his hat to his thigh. "A mistake," he repeated unhappily. "Jericho, I never meant for anything like that to happen. I never meant it in a million years. If I could undo it, I would. It was a mistake."

A mistake? Is that what he called it? All the tenderness, the sweetness between them had been nothing but a mistake? Her stomach lurched.

"Jericho, it was a mistake."

"If you say that again, I will be sick in the slop pail."

Desperately, she threw her gaze out the window, keeping her eyes on St. Paul's Cathedral, on the acres of lead roof as it caught the last rays of the setting sun.

He sighed wearily. "Grubworm, please don't take it so hard. Please. I beg of you. You'll break my heart."

She *was* going to be sick. She swallowed.

"How do your women usually take it, Dove? With smiles, laughter? With witty repartee?"

"Grubworm."

There was a long silence. Even with the first sounds of evening—women hurrying to the public pump at the bottom of Wattling Street, wooden buckets clunking—she could hear his weary discouraged breathing. A "mistake." It hadn't been love, it had been a "mistake."

"Jericho, I didn't come here today to make you unhappy."

She threw him a resentful look. "Then why did you come! Did you need someone to sleep with this afternoon? And so you decided on me?"

"Jericho, listen to me. Please. Don't tell John. Whatever you do, don't tell John."

Her cheeks heated like fire.

"Do you think I would tell him! Or tell anyone? This was private. Private between you and me, Dove."

"Jericho, listen to me. Please. I want you to marry John. And the sooner the better. What we did today, what happened in that bed . . . could have consequences. The mistake had best be covered. For your sake. And for mine and Marguerite's. I may have quickened you, sweeting."

If he'd hurt her a moment before, it had been a mere sting compared to this. He didn't want her, and if he'd put his baby into her, he didn't want that, either. He was passing her on to John. Like a used shirt.

"You'd best go, Dove," she warned shakily, the hurt slowly finding its defense in anger. "Go now. Go."

"Jericho . . ."

"Go!"

He gazed into her anger, then drew a coin pouch out of his shirt. It jingled heavily as he set it on the table. She stared at it, incredulous, disbelieving.

"Are you paying me, Dove?"

"Grubworm, don't say such a thing." He came forward to take her in his arms, but she recoiled from him, as if from a snake.

"Are you paying me for this afternoon? Like a tart? Like a whore?"

"Grubworm, don't. Don't be like this!"

Her voice shook. "Get out of here, Dove. Get out! This is my house. I want you out of it. Leave. Go. *Go.*"

"Sweeting? I care for you. I do."

"Go!"

His bright hazel eyes burned with misery. Nevertheless, he obeyed. He set his jaw, wheeled around, and trotted down the stairs with quick, light steps. Wounded to the very depths of her soul, Jericho grabbed the offensive coin purse and ran to the landing. Shaking the coins into her palm, she flung them as hard as she could. Coins smote his back, the back of his golden head. When the last coin had rung in the stairwell, spinning on its metallic edge before toppling, he turned unhappily.

"I'm sorry, sweeting," he said softly. "I'm sorry as hell."

"Get out!"

He left. Jericho buried her face in her hands and sobbed.

It was Black Bartimaeus, patiently waiting outside, who later gathered up the coins and squirreled them away for a rainy day. But he never mentioned the coins to her, and for that, she was grateful.

She tossed and turned and wept bitter tears into her pillow all that night, but when she rose in the morning, she lifted her head high and went on with her life on Wattling Street. She put Lord Dove de Mont out of her mind. He didn't exist. She had never heard of him.

She didn't shed another tear. That is, she didn't until her monthly flow came, and then she cried in sheer relief. But one or two of those tears fell for quite the opposite reason. Now she had nothing left of Dove at all. Not him. Not his baby. Not anything.

Chapter Nineteen

An eerie, pulsing glow woke Jericho before dawn on Sunday, September the second, a light so faint as to be no light at all, the silent glow waxing and waning in her bedchamber window. Throwing off her bedsheet, she went to the window on bare feet and looked out. She could see nothing amiss. London still slept. The familiar jumble of close-packed rooftops presented itself, the steep angles rising every which way in the darkness.

Moving silently, so as not to wake Black Bartimaeus where he slept in the schoolroom on his pallet, she went to the schoolroom windows and looked out. There, she saw it. To the east, perhaps a mile away, a rosy, ever-changing glow pulsed on the horizon. An unnatural sunrise? No. Not sunrise. Fire.

She breathed uneasily. Her first impulse was to wake Black Bartimaeus and make him look too. But she couldn't. He needed his rest. His heart was troubling him again. Though he tried to hide it, she knew the signs—his shortness of breath, his long pause at the bottom of the stairs before climbing up to their rooms.

In spite of Black Bartimaeus's objections, she'd paid five shillings to bring a doctor from Poultry Lane to bleed him and prescribe new medicine. She'd had his horoscope cast to encourage him, and she'd gotten him a fresh rabbit's foot for good luck. She didn't know what else to do, and she was scared. John had been dear, casually bringing this heart tonic or that, taking care not to alarm Black Bartimaeus with over-concern, but just behaving in his kind, ordinary, decent way.

John. Gazing anxiously at the pulsing glow, she wished
John were in the city. But he wasn't. He'd gone to Arleigh
Castle for Dove's wedding and would not be back for a week.
Dove . . . Dove's wedding. Misery welled up. Today was
Sunday, September second. On Tuesday, September fourth,
Dove would marry.

Heavy-hearted about that, uneasy about the fire—London's
house-timbers were coated with pitch to preserve them, and
pitch could burn like a torch—she didn't go back to sleep.
Quietly, she dressed, then read by candlelight until daybreak.
Pax joined her, padding into her chamber, his rough old nails
clicking lazily over the floor.

Uneasy, she didn't go to Lord's Day services that morning.
But, a multitude of Londoners did. Sabbath Day church bells
rang cheerfully all over the city, and Londoners strolled about,
indifferent to the cloud of black smoke rising in the east.
Dear life, she thought. A fire is nothing to a Londoner.

At ten of the clock, when the wicked black cloud grew
larger, she and Black Bartimaeus put on their hats and walked
down to the Thames, where watermen clustered in their rowing boats, touting for customers. She buttonholed a sweaty
young waterman who seemed glad to rest on his oars for a
minute and talk with a pretty woman.

"The fire isn't near Seething Lane, is it?" She was worried
about John's house.

"Nay, missus. Nowheres near Seething. The fire, she started
on Pudding Lane, missus, about midnight," he shared, his
bold eyes raking her over. "Started in the king's baker's
house. Prob'ly, the sorry fool didn't damp his oven proper
b'fore going t'bed. Though he's denyin' it to Peter's tune,
y'may be sure. The sorry fool."

"Is it as bad as it looks?" Worried, she glanced upriver,
but couldn't see far. The Thames meandered through London
in twists and turns. The smoke rose blacker now, the fire
undoubtedly lapping up the pitch-coated house timbers.

"Three hunnert houses gone already, missus."

"Three hundred!"

"Ay. The fire, she's spreadin' faster'n the plague last summer. The fire, she jumped up on London Bridge no more'n
a tad ago. 'Tis the wind, missus, the damned Belgium wind."

She nodded. Londoners hated an east wind. Besides being hot and dry, a Belgium wind was thought to be unlucky.

"Can you row us to London Bridge?" She glanced worriedly upriver. If she could see the fire, she could better assess the danger. Pudding Lane and London Bridge were nowhere near Wattling Street. Still . . .

" 'Twill cost ye three shillings."

"Three!" She swung her head, eyes blazing. "Why, that's highway robbery. The distance is but slight. Worth a few pence at most."

"Then walk," the young man said cheekily. "If all London goes up in the blaze, my hire'll be six shillings by nightfall, prob'ly a whole guinea tomorry." The selfish oaf looked pleased at the prospect of his city burning down, making him a rich man. Jericho wanted to slap him.

"We'll walk," she snapped. "And glad to. Your company would likely make us sick!"

She and Black Bartimaeus hurriedly backtracked to Thames Street and struck a fast pace toward London Bridge. Jericho's anxiety grew with every block they walked. Thames Street was crowded with warehouses that were packed to the rafters with flammable goods: tallow, oil, spirits, wine, tar, pitch, turpentine, hemp, hay, lumber. If Thames Street caught . . .

Pushing through the jostling, growing crowds, they made their way down a foul-smelling alley to the river steps at the Old Swan drinking house. Smoke mingled with the fetid alley smells, and distant shouts rang out upon the river. They could hear the crackling roar of a great fire. They went down the river steps in the growing crush of spectators and looked out, aghast.

A blazing inferno engulfed the north end of London Bridge. The tight-packed mass of four-storied houses that had been built on the stone bridge over the centuries now blazed like logs on a hearth. In the fierce roaring heat, the ancient, seasoned house-timbers exploded with earsplitting cracks while chimney stones exploded like musket shot. It sounded as if the city were under seige.

Hearts in throats, they watched the wall of fire slowly engulf the bridge, steadily advancing across it toward the south shore. Scared witless, residents on the bridge scampered to save their belongings. Bent double, some people carried their goods on their backs. Others tied ropes to their furniture and lowered the awkward pieces into barges and lighters that hovered under the bridge, waiting in the rippling water. Some residents simply hove axes into their second and third story walls and shoved their furniture out of the gaping holes, letting it splash into the Thames, in hopes of salvaging it. Stunned, Jericho watched pieces of people's lives drift by: a carved oaken bedstead, a baby cage, a beautiful pianoforte, a sugar chest, a livery cabinet, a cricket stool, a chair.

Up on the burning rooftops, hapless pigeons huddled on their cot, loath to leave familiar roosts. And most of them left too late. They flew straight up into the flames and plummeted down into the river, wings burnings. Jericho put her hand to her throbbing throat.

"Ah, no, please God," breathed an old gentleman who stood watching beside her.

"What is it?" she demanded.

He gestured just as a corresponding groan rose from the crowd. "The water wheel on London Bridge, lass. She's caught fire. 'Twill mean the city's pumps stop working. There'll be no water to fight the fire. None but what a man can dip up from the river."

She swallowed. "W-what will happen?"

"The lord mayor will order houses pulled down, I 'spect. To block the path of the fire. *If* he finds courage enough to give the order. London's a merchant's city, and merchants won't take kindly to pulling down their houses and shops and warehouses. But 'tis the only way to stop a fire as bad as this one."

As they watched, the inferno advanced to the middle of the bridge, roaring so loudly that the sound of it filled their ears and they had to shout to converse. She could feel the heat, even at this distance. Then, suddenly, the fire halted in its path, stymied by a large open space on the bridge that had no buildings on it.

"Huzzah!" The crowd cheered so lustily that the river stairs vibrated underfoot. Jericho cheered, too. But their cheers proved premature. For a gust of wind picked up a shower of fire drops and whipped them to the south shore. The crowd groaned as a haystack burst into flames in Southwark. Carried by the wicked wind, wisps of burning hay flew to surrounding roofs. Frantic cottagers scampered about with buckets, fighting the fire, but she and Black Bartimaeus could see their efforts would prove fruitless.

Saddened by all they'd seen—and apprehensive—they made their way home through the agitated milling throngs.

"We must pack up our belongings. Just in case."

Black Bartimaeus nodded somberly.

"What we can't hope to carry with us—" She tried to think. "—we'll bury in the backyard. In a trench."

He nodded. "I dig the trench."

"No! I'll dig it," she said too sharply, thinking of his heart. But then her own heart softened. What am I doing, what am I doing, depriving this proud old man of his manhood.

"We'll dig it together," she said in a gentler voice. "You're right, Black Bartimaeus. I will need your help."

Pleased, proud to be needed, he nodded, his treasured red beaver felt hat bobbing on his head.

"But we won't leave our home unless it's absolutely necessary. I won't leave my dame school." Her throat constricted with sudden emotion. "It's *mine*. Mine and yours. I won't leave it. Not unless the fire comes to our very door."

He nodded, his dark old eyes aglow with understanding.

"I won't never leave it. Not never."

She gave him a startled look as they walked along, wondering what he meant. It was hopeless to ask. Black Bartimaeus was a man of so few words that people often mistook him for mute. In the last few seconds, he'd already spoken more than he usually did in a whole month. So, reluctantly, she let it pass. They arrived home to find Pax baying. Another omen that something was dreadfully amiss in the city.

The afternoon proved frantic. Hastily, they separated their few belongings into two piles, that which could be carried with them and that which must stay behind. Borrowing shovels, they dug a trench in the backyard, leaving it uncovered, ready.

As Jericho rammed her shovel into the hard bone-dry soil, tears rose to her eyes and mingled with the perspiration trickling from her brow. Her books? The little dame school stools where the children sat so sweetly? She swiped at her eyes with a gritty palm.

The afternoon escalated, flying at a dizzying pace. With black smoke wafting over the city, tainting the air with its scary smell, Wattling Street became alarmed. She and Black Bartimaeus ran on countless errands for neighbors too infirm or too elderly to help themselves. They lugged countless buckets of water from the river.

By midafternoon the thing she'd dreaded, happened. Thames Street caught fire. Now, all London sat up and took notice. Feeding on naval stores and on hay and coal and spirits and lumber, the inferno roared into a holocaust. Belatedly, the hand-wringing lord mayor organized fire posts throughout the city, each volunteer to receive a shilling a day plus bread and cheese and beer. Black Bartimaeus chafed to volunteer, but Jericho forebade him. She feared for his heart. Childlike, he accepted her authority, but he was provoked with her and showed it by sulking.

With Thames Street blazing and roaring like the fire pits of hell, the king rode into the city to take command. It was soon shouted in the streets that the king himself was manning spade and bucket, working shoulder to shoulder with volunteers, his clothes as ruined as any beggar's, his smoke-blackened face as dark as any African.

Despite her anxiety, Jericho had to smile a little. His Majesty *would* behave like that. At Arleigh Castle, he'd impressed her as a man of mettle, a man's man. She breathed easier knowing he was in charge and not the timid hand-wringing lord mayor.

Sleep was impossible that night. Exhausted but scared, she and Black Bartimaeus took turns keeping watch. The air they breathed grew smokier, and all night long the city clamored with noise. Horsecarts carrying tottering loads rumbled up Wattling Street, one after the other, heading for the city gates. Londoners who'd already been burned out surged by with their goods on their backs, heading for St. Paul's Cathedral, intent on taking refuge there. Jericho feared that was a mistake. Under repair, St. Paul's was covered with wooden scaffolding. If St. Paul's caught fire . . .

People shouted that the city gates were jammed, cart traffic at a standstill and carters were making money hand over fist, gouging customers. The cost of hiring even a dog cart had risen to an outrageous fee, half the value of the load carried. Out on the Thames, watermen gouged their customers even more mercilessly.

Morning came, but daylight did not. Enshrouded in smoke, the city remained dark, as if it were midnight. Whenever the sun managed to poke through, its color was red, like blood. The air grew gritty, unpleasant to breathe.

Jericho fretted. Was she being foolish, staying? Should she take Black Bartimaeus and Pax and leave? But where would she go? John's house was no safer than hers. And she couldn't go to Arleigh Castle. Twenty miles was too far for Black Bartimaeus to walk. Besides, Marguerite would scratch her eyes out.

The prospect of being outside the city was more frightening than remaining in it. Multitudes of the burned-out were camping out in the open, in fields, prey to unsavory riffraff who would cut a throat to gain a penny. Black Bartimaeus was too old for such dangers. So was Pax. Jericho felt easier when the wind suddenly shifted, blowing hard away from the city, blowing the fire toward the Thames, containing it at the waterfront.

But that afternoon the unpredictable wind shifted again. It reversed directions and suddenly blew hard as a gale. Unfettered, unleashed, the roaring inferno leaped north with the noise of a whirlwind in it. Londoners who'd thought themselves safe had to grab their children and run, fleeing through burning alleyways, flames licking at their ankles, fire crackling overhead.

Evil, capricious, the holocaust selected parishes of the city at random, leaping over some and sparing them, mercilessly

devouring others. Advancing to a crossroads, the wall of fire
would hover there, gaining strength, roaring. Then it would
select a lane and roar down it. Raging on Cornhill, the fire
incinerated the financial heart of the city, and, devouring the
great spice vaults in the Royal Exchange, sent choking clouds
of incense through London.

Worried for John's shops, Jericho and Black Bartimaeus
threw dampened shawls over their heads and ran through the
pitch dark alleys to Cheapside street. The going was precarious. With London burning, the Londoners' mood had turned
ugly. Vicious rumors swept the city. People shouted that the
Catholics had fired the city, so ordered by the pope of Rome.
Others shouted that the Dutch had fired the city and that the
Dutch army waited outside the city gates, swords drawn,
ready to slay anyone who survived the inferno. Cadres of
angry housewives marched the streets with cudgels, attacking
and beating anyone suspected of being Catholic or Dutch or
even foreign.

Jericho fervently prayed her own slight, Dutch New Amsterdam accent would not be detected, and, despite her anger
with Dove, she was grateful he was not in the city. Dove
was Catholic. Militantly so.

She and Black Bartimaeus found Cheapside in chaos. Carts,
wagons, and coaches choked every inch of this broad avenue.
Harried merchants dashed in and out of their fine shops,
emptying them, removing merchandise, taking it to safety.
Jericho was relieved to find John's sensible shop steward
doing the same. Busy, harried, the steward nevertheless took
a moment to talk to them.

"Cheapside burn? Nay, missus, it cannot. 'Tis only a pre-
caution we're taking. The fire'll never get to Cheapside. Even
were that bloody, malicious, demon fire to change course
and come west, it cannot jump Cheapside Street. Cheapside's too grand and wide."

"Cheapside Street won't burn," she said uneasily to Black
Bartimaeus as they hurried home in the unnatural darkness,
eyes stinging, streaming from the smoke, ash crunching underfoot.

But it did. On Tuesday morning, the third day of the great

London fire, the wind shifted again, picked up force and blew hard as a hurricane. Changing direction, the inferno roared into Cheapside and leaped that broad thoroughfare as easily as a child leaps a puddle.

When the news reached Wattling Street, Jericho's heart grew faint. "We'd best bury our things," she said to Black Bartimaeus in a shaky voice. He nodded gravely.

She was truly scared. But she got a much greater scare as they shoveled in the backyard by lantern light. Working beside her, Black Bartimaeus suddenly slumped, his sweaty black face ashen. With a stunned expression, he slowly folded himself to the ground and sat, clutching his chest.

"Black Bartimaeus!" Flinging her shovel aside, she leaped and knelt before him. "What is it? Your heart?"

Her own heart pounded in dread. Breathless, but smiling for her sake, he denied it with emphatic headshakes, and the spell passed in a moment. Getting to his feet, he reached for his shovel to continue working, but Jericho grabbed it and threw it aside. Grasping his elbow, guiding him, she coaxed him up to their rooms to rest.

She was terrified. She didn't know what to do. When she'd given him his medicine and had coaxed him to sleep, she took their savings, their nest egg, from its hiding place behind the chimney brick, grabbed her shawl and ran out into the midnight-dark streets to fetch a doctor. As she ran, grit burned her eyes, smoke stabbed her lungs. Fire drops fell from above like rain.

The errand proved fruitless and dangerous. The doctor had left his house, leaving it locked and shuttered, and, running home, she spied riffraff lurking in every alley, unsavory fellows waiting like jackals to loot abandoned houses. She felt lucky to reach home without having had her throat slit or worse.

Worried, anxious, she ministered to Black Bartimaeus all that day, a prayer on her lips, fear in her breast. There was nothing she could do but wait, wait with the rest of Wattling Street to see where the fire would go next. Then, at nine of the clock that night, the wind died and a shout went up.

"The fire! She's behind us!"

Jericho ran to her bedchamber window. For excruciatingly long moments, she could see nothing in the smoky blackness. Then, suddenly, she saw it coming. Small tongues of blood red fire lapped at rooftops several streets away, coming, growing steadily larger. Even as she watched, the glowing murky tongues began to lap their way up Ludgate Hill. A rooftop below St. Paul's churchyard burst into flame.

Her heart stopped. The fire would surround them if they didn't leave at once. She swung around to Black Bartimaeus, who'd come to look. "It's time to leave." He nodded.

Grabbing Pax, she whipped a leading rope to his collar, then grabbed the heavy bundle she'd prepared. Black Bartimaeus weakly shouldered his bundle, and they hurried down the stairs. She shut the street door and locked it, a meaningless, empty gesture. It was going to burn. Her beloved dame school was going to burn. She gave Black Bartimaeus the key. He pocketed it. His breathing was so labored. She took his elbow to steady him.

Shouldering their loads, they hurried up the street, eyes streaming from the smoke, throats choky with it. All of Wattling Street poured forth to join them. Men shouted commands, women scolded and clucked at their children as they shepherded them. Babies wailed. Dogs barked. The elderly tapped along on their canes, calmer than all the rest. At the top of Wattling Street, Jericho set down her load and turned for one last look at her dame school. She gazed at it in the smoky darkness, heavyhearted, until the last straggling neighbor had passed by and the street lay empty, desolate, like an empty dream. Above the rooftops she could see the flaming red glow, the fire approaching. She wanted to weep.

"My hat," Black Bartimaeus said softly.

She glanced at the rooftops in alarm. A tongue of orange fire jumped into view. Then she glanced at him. He treasured that hat. Adored it.

"Give me the key. I'll run back for it."

"Nay. I go."

"No, Black Bartimaeus! Give me—"

But he loved his hat, and he was halfway down Wattling Street before she could forbid him, sprinting as if he were eighteen and not eighty. For a bewildering moment, she saw him as he'd surely been in his prime—a magnificent young African chief, majestically sprinting through his jungle kingdom, conquering it.

"Black Bartimaeus, hurry!" she shouted, coughing, eyes streaming. The smoke thickened.

He vanished into the dame school. Another tongue of fire appeared on the roof. She waited, batting at her stinging streaming eyes, her nervous glance going back and forth between her street door and the flames.

He didn't come. Pax began to bark in a frenzy, coughing, hacking. At the bottom of Wattling Street, in the crossroads, at the public pump, an immense wall of fire suddenly appeared, hovering, roaring. It was a malicious sight, and she shuddered.

Still, he didn't come. She was frantic. Dropping Pax's rope, Jericho sprinted down the dark smoky street, running as fast as she could run in the thick blinding smoke. With the fire approching, the air grew hot as an oven. Pax galloped at her heels, barking his head off. Frantic, she threw herself into the doorway and groped her way up the dark stairs. Black Bartimaeus sat midway up the stairs, slumped, clutching his chest, struggling for breath. Terror chilled her.

"Black Bartimaeus!" She threw her arms around him, then jumped up and clattered down the stairs to the street. She shouted in the direction her neighbors had gone. "Help! Come back, somebody! Help us! Help us!"

With smoky air in her lungs, her shouts amounted to croaking hacks. Pax barked wildly. She ran halfway up the dark street and shouted again. But the roar of the approaching inferno swallowed up her cries. Down at the crossroads, at the pump, the hovering wall of fire began to move up Wattling Street. It cast intense heat, heat that made her feel faint, heat that sucked up all the air. Smoke swirled so thickly, she could barely see through her streaming eyes. She ran back to the dame school and clattered up the stairs. Frantic, she tugged at him, trying to lift him, trying to pull him to his feet.

"Black Bartimaeus, we have to run, we have to!"

"Go," he gasped weakly.

"No! Not without you!"

Reflections from the approaching fire spread like smeared red paint on the stairwell walls. Terrified, she seized his limp arms and tugged them over her shoulders. Then, she put her back into the effort, trying to lift him to his feet. Her back nearly broke. With wild, frustrated sobs, she tried again and again. The smoky air was getting hot. The fire crackled and roared. Pax barked frantically, hoarsely. At last, she got him up. His crushing weight nearly toppled her. Her legs buckled. She strained to keep him upright. Ramming her shoulder under his armpit, using every ounce of her strength, she inched him down the stairwell and into the burning street. The smoke was so thick, she couldn't see more than an arm's length ahead. Her eyes streamed. She had no breath left. She had to gasp encouragement.

"That's right—walk—try—walk—we'll make it—to the top of the hill—one more step—one more—"

With the fire roaring behind them, they staggered through the murky darkness. But Black Bartimaeus collapsed a few feet past the grog shop, clutching his chest as his heart attacked again. Pax howled and ran in frantic circles.

"Jer'cho," he gasped. "Run."

"No!"

Frantic, she raked her wits. Lifting the bottoms of her skirts, she ran back to the dame school, stumbling up the stairs in the darkness, coughing, eyes streaming. The ceilings had already sprouted with tiny tongues of fire. It was so hot she felt faint. Grabbing Black Bartimaeus's pallet mattress, she wrenched it through the doorway, pulling it down the stairs with fierce, desperate sobs. Smoke singed her lungs, her throat, her eyes. Wrenching it along she had a moment of sheer panic when she couldn't find Black Bartimaeus in the darkness. But then she did. She positioned the mattress and strained to roll him onto it. He was so heavy.

Eyes streaming, she grabbed hold of the mattress, took a great heaving breath and pulled. Her back and shoulders screamed with pain, but the heavy load inched ahead. She wrenched it again and moved it a few inches farther. She wrenched again, and then again and again and again until she lost count, until she grew dizzy with the effort, her lungs burning, her eyes streaming. The heat, the heat!

Her dame school was swallowed by fire now. She heard the windows shatter, exploding in the heat. Flames raced along the rooftops on both sides of the street now, murky as red blood. Fire drops and flaming debris showered down. She cried out as a cinder struck her cheek. She swatted it away, then swatted sparks off Black Bartimaeus. Pax barked wildly. The heat, the heat! She was going to faint.

"Jer'cho. Go," Black Bartimaeus gasped, his face ashen.

"No!" She tugged at the pallet, her fingernails splitting, bleeding. "If I—can pull you—to the top—of Wattling Street—to St. Paul's—we'll be—safe there—"

To assure herself, she glanced over her shoulder into the murky, soupy darkness, toward the great cathedral. She froze. For even as she watched, huge flames leaped onto the wooden scaffolding that covered the cathedral and spread like a spider web bursting into fire. Within moments, St. Paul's blazed like an enormous torch.

She jumped to her feet, stunned. They were cut off, ringed by fire. They were lost.

"Help us!" she shrieked, choking, hacking, coughing, screaming out to the burning heavens. "Precious God, help us!"

Chapter Twenty

Dove awoke on his wedding day feeling cranky, out of sorts. He couldn't account for it. Hell, this was the happiest day of his life! He was getting Marguerite today, wasn't he?

Still, the nagging feeling persisted. To squash it, to stamp it out, he went early to the bath chamber. Bath servants massaged him, bathed him, washed his hair and brushed it dry. Then he returned to his rooms and put on his wedding finery: silk drawers, silk stockings, a shirt of linen and lace, petticoat breeches of royal blue brocade, a matching coat with silver piping, black leather shoes. He grabbed a handful of rings from his jewel chest and rammed them on, three to each hand. Then he took the engraved gold wedding band he would give Marguerite in the ceremony and tenderly slipped it on his smallest finger.

Dressed, he gazed in his looking glass and knew he should feel as good as he looked. But he didn't. He felt out of kilter with the day, out of kilter with the wedding merriment, out of kilter with his whole damned life.

When word came from John, inviting him to break his fast in John's room, Dove ducked the invitation. The old, easy friendship he'd had with John was gone, shot to hell. Lately, he was as uncomfortable in John's company as a fish in a frying pan. Each time he looked into John's decent face, he remembered that afternoon on Wattling Street and felt like a Judas.

So, avoiding John, he took a stab at cheering himself up by going to Marguerite's apartment. Futile. In a wedding tizzy, surrounded by maids and hairdressers, she gave him short shrift. The perfunctory kiss she gave him said, "Go away." He went. But not without thinking of Jericho. Jericho and her warm, willing mouth. He felt . . . hell, he felt lonesome! A queer way to feel on your wedding day.

At odds with himself, at odds with the whole world, he wandered to his mother's chambers and found her and d'Orias companionably breaking their fast together, sitting at a low table in her private withdrawing room. They chatted for a while, but when his mother's glances grew too piercing, too inquiring, he left.

As the door shut behind her son, Glynden de Mont looked at d'Orias. "For a young man who is getting the woman he has always wanted, Dove looks remarkably unhappy."

"Unhappy?" Leonardo helped himself to more bread and cheese. "An understatement, my sweet. I've seen happier men going to the gallows."

She made a steeple of her graceful fingers, lowering her

lips to them in thought. "I wonder. Do you think it can have anything to do with that pretty bondslave who was here this summer? The redhaired girl?"

"It has *everything* to do with that pretty bondslave."

She looked up in surprise. D'Orias never tired of looking at her, watching her, gazing at her beautiful facile face, her bright expressive eyes. She was so like Dove. Her manner of thinking was like Dove, too. Quick, pouncing, intelligent, every nuance of thought surfacing in those bright hazel eyes.

"He loves her?"

"He *loves* her."

"Dove told you that?"

Leonardo smiled wryly. "How could he tell me, when he does not know it himself?"

She gazed at him for a full minute, then, vexed, gave him her aristocratic shrug. "Nonsense. Dove is in love with Marguerite. Madly so. And if he'd loved that redhaired bondslave, he would have made her his mistress."

"No. He loves her, Glynden. When a man truly loves a woman, he does not make her his mistress. He makes her his *wife*."

Now he had her full attention. It was a statement that trespassed perilously close to their own problem. In her imperious way, she chose to ignore it. So like Dove, he thought with irritation, so like Dove.

"Dove is marrying Marguerite, Leonardo, and *that* is *that*. I do not wish to discuss it further."

D'Orias calmly spread butter on a piece of bread and took a bite. He chewed it, swallowed it, eyeing her steadily.

"Which brings us to another subject you do not like to discuss, yes? The subject of our own marriage?" It had been a sore point between them for years, d'Orias dearly wanting to make her his wife, and Glynden resisting, shackled with stubborn loyalty to her long-dead husband, to her rank, to her duty as preserver and protector of Arleigh Castle.

"We have settled that long ago."

"To your satisfaction, not to mine. I want to marry you, Glynden," he said calmly. "I want to make you my wife. I

want to provide for you and shelter you. I want you to bear
my name. And I want Ginevra to be legitimate. A child of
wedlock.''

"I want that, too. But it is impossible!''

He gazed at her steadily. "In that case, perhaps the time
has come when our paths must . . . part, *si*?''

Her beautiful eyes widened in shock. Vulnerable, she looked
as young and defenseless as a girl. He adored her. He loved
her more than life itself. But there comes a time . . .

"You would leave me?''

He wished he could say more. He wished with all his heart
he could reveal the secret he had been guarding for years.
But that would be a mistake. He needed to be sure of her
love before he confided such a secret.

"Not willingly. I would more willingly cut off my right
arm. But there comes a time when a man must weigh self-
respect in the balance with love. For me, that time has come.
Consider your answer, Glynden.''

Rising, he went out of the room to his chamber, to dress
for Dove's wedding. He left behind him a beloved and profoundly upset woman. For she knew he would do it. He would
leave her.

After seeing his mother and d'Orias, Dove headed for the
bedchamber his Uncle Aubrey used when visiting. He was
about to enter when a maidservant came flying down the
corridor, slippers flapping, serge petticoats swirling.

"Lor' Dove? Have ye seen the sky?''

"What do you mean, have I seen the sky?''

"The sky toward London, sir. Pray, go look, sir. I hope
it's not a bad omen for yer wedding day, sir.'' She crossed
herself.

Dove felt a catch in his breast. The sky toward London
had looked sickish all yesterday. Hazy, faintly yellow. Dog
days, everyone had thought, dismissing it. But now he wasn't
so sure. He rushed down the stairs and out of the castle. He
loped across the castleyard and up the stone steps to the wall,

running along the walkway to the gatehouse. John was already there, dressed for the wedding. Uncle Aubrey was there, too. They turned as he came running.

"What *is* it, Uncle?" To the east, on the horizon, a dirty yellow curtain hung in the sky like an unwashed bedsheet. Rising behind it, the sun was a pallid red disk.

"We don't know, Dove."

"Is it locusts?" Dove had never seen a locust plague, but he'd heard of them, those horrendous swarms from Africa that could, in off-weather years, ride on the winds and turn farmlands into a habitation of famine.

"No. Locusts come in a black cloud, not yellow. And you hear them long before you see them. I've seen locusts in Tangier," Aubrey answered. "But I've never seen anything like this."

They stood watching, thoroughly puzzled. Now and then, a grayish feather drifted down. Leaning out over the wall, Dove caught one. The feather disintegrated on his palm. He caught another and sniffed it.

"Burnt ash."

"Can it be woodland on fire, Your Grace?" John asked.

Worried, Aubrey examined the horizon. "It's possible," he admitted. "I've never known a hotter, dryer summer for England in all my forty-two years. Anything could burn. Anything."

They stood watching for a while longer, joined by others. Unable to solve the mystery, the whole group left the wall worried, murmuring. Going down the stone steps, John invited him to his room to toast his nuptials. Dove couldn't squirm out of it. So he went. But he made short work of it, and when John presented him with a wedding gift—a magnificent silver urn, exquisitely engraved with a scene depicting Dove and his brothers riding in King Charles's coronation procession in 1663—Dove felt so guilty he could hardly lift his head to thank John. Death was preferable to this agonizing sense of having betrayed a friend who'd been closer to him than a brother.

Thanking him with terse words, Dove left in a hurry, leaving behind a disappointed and puzzled friend. But what could he say? I've taken your woman, and I'm sick as hell about it? Forgive me? Shit.

The peculiar sky remained the topic of conversation all morning, and Dove was glad of it. It took the attention away from him. He'd had enough of idiots asking him if he was happy. Of course, he was happy! To reassure himself, to stamp out his doubt, he visited Marguerite again.

This time she didn't send him away. This time she made him happy. She let him sweep her into her private withdrawing chamber and kiss the life out of her. She didn't complain about a wrinkled gown. His happiness soared. Eager to prove his love, he drew his wedding gift from his pocket and presented it to her. A lavish diamond necklace, fifty teardrop diamonds set in gold. Marguerite seized it with a joyful cry.

"It is beautiful, Dove. Thank you!"

"We're going to happy together, sweetheart," he promised.

"Immensely happy, Dove." But he felt a childish stab of disappointment. For as she said those words, she didn't look at him. She looked at the sparkling diamonds.

Despite the unease about the sky, despite servant prattle about omens—which his mother harshly nipped in the bud —wedding guests assembled in Arleigh Castle's ancient ceremonial hall, a hall that had witnessed four hundred years of de Mont marriages.

Standing at the altar, flanked by John, Raven, and Lark, waiting for his bride to come down the aisle, Dove suffered momentary misgivings. His face must have shown it, for Raven winked at him, Lark whispered a ribald wedding-night joke that made him smile, and John murmured, "God bless you, Dove. May you truly be happy."

He smiled his thanks at each, but couldn't meet John's eyes. He wondered if he would be able to speak so generously at John and Jericho's wedding, and decided not. He came face-to-face with the truth. He didn't want *anyone* marrying Jericho. He wanted to keep her for himself. Tucked away like a spare handkerchief. Ashamed of himself, he flushed.

His thoughts flew to Marguerite. Did she really love him?

Or did she love his money? The Marguerite he'd grown up with had loved him. Hell, that Marguerite had adored him! But this Marguerite? Misgivings chewed at him.

There was a faint, expectant rustle. The assembly stirred. Every one turned as Marguerite stepped into the hall, beautiful and radiant in a gown of mauve satin, his diamond necklace sparkling on her breast. She was so beautiful he lost his breath. She sent him a dazzling smile. The same way she had smiled at him in their childhood. All doubt flew. *This* was his Marguerite! This was the woman he wanted!

Midway through the sacrament, as he knelt with Marguerite before the priest, Dove faintly heard whispering in the great hall, urgent whispering. "London . . . 'tis true . . . London . . ."

He glanced over his shoulder. In the front row of chairs, a servant squatted before his mother, whispering earnestly. D'Orias and Aubrey and Esme, Raven's pregnant wife, were leaning toward the servant, straining to catch what he was saying.

London? Dove's spine prickled. Had it something to do with the sky? Dropping Marguerite's hand, he sprang to his feet.

"What is it?" he demanded in a loud voice, breaking the ceremony, bringing it to a wrenching halt.

"Dove," Marguerite gasped.

His mother rose to speak, but she was plainly too upset to do so. Rising, Aubrey spoke for her.

"A servant has just brought word," Aubrey said tightly, addressing the startled assembly. "London is on fire. She has been on fire since Sunday. The entire city is in flames. Lady de Mont wishes you to know you are free to leave at once, if you so desire. Many of you own properties in London and will wish to see to them."

For an instant Dove couldn't take it in. Nor could anyone. A stunned silence swept the hall. Marguerite clutched his hand, her face pale. The priest began to pray softly in Latin, and somewhere among the assembled guests, a woman began to weep. Then, the hall exploded like a hornet's nest. Every-one talked at once.

"My shops." John's eyes were glazed with shock. "My house."

The fear that had been rising in Dove exploded. He turned on John in fury. "The hell with your shops, your house. Jericho!"

Spinning around, he grabbed Marguerite by her satin shoulders.

"I have to go, sweetheart. Immediately. Someone may be in danger."

"Go? Go! What do you mean?" The shock on her face turned to dismay. "Dove, our wedding. Our *wedding*."

"We'll be married the instant I get back." He hit the aisle running.

"Dove, our wedding!" she cried after him. "Dove! Where are you going?"

"To London," he shouted over the rising tumult. "To Wattling Street. I'll be back, sweetheart." Sprinting out of the hall, he hit the castleyard running, Marguerite's complaint ringing in his wake.

"Dove? Dove, this is my wedding day!"

He hit the stables still running, shouting for stable boys to saddle his fastest mount. Two lads sprang up to do his bidding. Waiting, he grabbed a short sword and buckler off a wall peg and rammed it into the saddle sheath.

"Hurry!" The lads *were* hurrying.

"Ay, Lor' Dove, ay."

He paced back and forth in the rustling straw, his heart ticking like a clock. Jericho. Black Bartimaeus. The two of them, coping with a burning city.

The cinch was still being tightened when footsteps came across the castleyard. John burst in, his face flushed red.

"Wattling Street. You've been to Wattling Street, you bastard, haven't you!"

"What if I have," Dove snapped, wrenching the stirrup, steadying the skittish horse. "For God's sake, John, this is no time to argue. London's burning! Saddle up. Jericho, Black Bartimaeus—they're alone."

John's color flushed deeper. "You son-of-a-bitch. You broke your promise, didn't you? You went to Wattling Street

and you took her, didn't you! You took her! That explains
it all—why she's been so downhearted of late. You rode into
London and took her.''

"We'll talk of this later," Dove tried. He grabbed hold of
the saddle and started to mount, but John wrenched his arm,
eyes blazing.

"You son-of-a-bitch, we'll talk of it *now*. You bedded her.
Admit it!''

"Yes!'' Dove said, heating, swatting John's hand off his
sleeve. "All right, I'll not lie. I *was* with her. I admit it.''
In growing anger he added, "I also admit I'll regret it to the
end of my days. I didn't mean for it to happen. Nor did she.
It just happened. You know how it is with Jericho and me
—the fondness there is between us. For God's sake, John!
Have a little pity.''

"Pity? You bastard, I'll show you pity.''

Dove was unprepared. John's fist smashed into his jaw,
knocking him ass-over-kettle into a heap of straw, knocking
the breath out of him. Dove hadn't braced for it, hadn't
expected it. John and he had never fought. Ever. Not even
as children. Taken by surprise, he shook his ringing head to
clear it, then staggered to his feet. Alarmed, the horse had
whinnied and skittered sideways. Regaining his balance, Dove
tried to remount. He wasn't about to fight John. He loved
him. Besides, John was in the right and he was in the wrong.

"Fight, damn you!'' John thundered. "Hit back!''

"No.''

With a bellow of fury, John grabbed his arm, swung him
around, and bashed him again. This time, he flew into the
stable wall, banging his ribs. He dropped painfully to his
knees panting. When he could breathe again, he climbed to
his feet, furious. He lowered his head and took a fighter's
stance.

"You want to fight, John? All right, let's get it over with.
Let's *fight*.''

"With pleasure.''

The gawking stable boys scampered out of the way, and
Dove sprang. It was a furious fight, a dirty fight, with no
holds barred, no rules observed. Cursing, panting, they went

at each other like maniacs, punching, battering, knocking each other from pillar to post. They slammed into walls, knocking down horse harnesses. They tackled each other and wrestled on the stable floor, rolling from one end of the stable to the other, rolling under the sharp, pawing hooves of startled whinnying horses. They cursed and grunted and strained. They rolled through horse dung. The strong pungent smell mixed with the salty smell of Dove's own blood, which spurted from his bashed nostril.

Alerted by the uproar, stable hands came running. Panting, struggling with John, Dove cursed them. "Get out of here!"

They hastily left. It was an even fight. John outweighed him by thirty pounds, but Dove was quicker, agile. Fired with hot anger, they gave each other a battering each would remember. When the fight finally ended, it ended abruptly, by unspoken mutual consent, as if each had lost the heart for battering.

On his knees, panting, breathing hoarsely, Dove swatted dung from his torn wedding coat, grabbed a handful of straw and staunched his bleeding nose. A few feet away, breathing like a winded bull, John grabbed straw and staunched the cut on his forehead.

When breath found its way back into his lungs, Dove spoke, panting. "John, the fire—Jericho—Black Bartimaeus—"

"Ay—I'll saddle up—"

Still panting, John stripped Dove's signet ring from his finger, the ring Dove had given in pledge. John looked at it cynically and hurled it into a dung heap. Then he staggered to his feet and saddled a mount.

They rode hard, galloping their mounts where the road allowed, urging their mounts along at a trot where the road puckered into holes that could snap a horse's hock. Physically, they rode side by side. Mentally, they rode on separate planets. They kept their distance. When it was necessary to look at each other, they did so with the cold wary eyes of strangers.

Our friendship is over, Dove thought, and felt the loss.

Judas! Betrayer! John thought. Even if I win Jericho, what kind of marriage will it be? I will always be aware that he had her first. Worse, so will Jericho. Jericho. My shops. My house. Oh, God, my shops.

The road to London was clogged with carts and people fleeing the city. At times, they had to force their way through. Ash fell in a continual shower, spooking the horses, making them hard to control. As they rode, they questioned refugees. Had Wattling Street burned? Cheapside? Seething Lane? John experienced both the best and the worst moments of his life when he learned Wattling and Seething Streets were safe, but Cheapside Street had burned. His shops gone! Hearing the news, Dove reached out and touched his shoulder in sympathy. John angrily cast his hand off. He didn't need sympathy from a Judas.

Mindful that they would not make London at all if they killed their horses with hard riding, they stopped to rest them. While the horses drank from a stream, John watched Dove fret and pace, his bridegroom clothes ruined, torn by their fight, stained by the sweat of their fast ride. As he watched, a thought struck him. Dove loves her! This is his wedding day, yet there is nothing in his head but Jericho. It was a bitter revelation.

They pressed on, galloping, trotting. Carts and coaches and people on foot clogged the road. Ash fell thicker, like a macabre gray snowfall. Some of the ash was still hot, and the horses shied and bucked, spooked by it. Daylight—such as it was—ended. Night burgeoned up all around them, thick and smoky. Reflecting the flames of London, the sky loomed overhead like an overturned bowl of murky yellow porridge.

Pressing on, cantering the winded horses up the last low hill before London, they topped the rise and yanked the horses to a halt in fright, staggered by what they saw below.

"Christ God." Dove crossed himself. "It's the end of the world. The whole world is on fire."

"God have mercy."

A conflagration of orange and blood red flames raged vividly against the dark night sky for miles. Fire raged everywhere, as far as the eye could see. There was nowhere that fire was not. The scene was like a macabre painting of hell. Wicked, malicious, bloody, evil flames lapped at the sky.

Bound on three sides by its ancient wall and on the fourth

side by the dark, snaking Thames River, London proper burned
like an enormous cauldron of flames. At Ludgate, the gate
they'd been heading for, the fire had jumped the wall. Flames
rampaged in the outskirts of London, devouring Fleet Street,
traveling along Fleet Canal, spreading in all directions, like
a sunburst. Untouched as yet, even Whitehall Palace lay in
its path.

Dove raised a shaky hand to his head. The sight made him
dizzy.

Across the river, linked to the city by London Bridge,
Southwark burned against the dark night sky—its taverns,
its theaters, its lobster houses, its brothels, its bear-baiting
pits, cockpits, dog pits. But London proper was the true
horror. Within the walled city only Ludgate Hill stood untouched, the great tower of St. Paul's Cathedral standing there
atop the hill like a martyr tied to the stake, awaiting the
flames.

John felt his courage fail him. He stared at Dove in utter
disbelief when Dove said, "Let's get going. Let's get into
the city."

"Dove, good God! Jericho cannot be in there. She's a
sensible girl. She will have taken Black Bartimaeus and left
long before now."

Emotionally pent up, Dove turned on him in fury. "Oh,
will she! You don't know her, damn you. You think you do,
but you don't. She's not sensible. She's a mule, she's a
bullhead, she's stubborn as rock. *I* know her. She loves that
goddamned dame school! She won't leave it until she has to.
Not until the last goddamned minute."

John waited until Dove's fury subsided, as shaken by it as
he was by the fire and all he was losing to its flaming maws.
His shops, maybe his house.

"Granted. But use common sense, Dove. The 'last minute'
surely came hours ago. Dove, she's gone, she's out, she's
safe."

"I *know* that. God damn you, don't you think I know that!
But I have to make sure. I have to check. I won't rest until
I know."

"Dove. Be sensible."

"*You* be sensible. Stay here and be sensible, if you wish. *I'm* going in. I'll go by water."

Kicking his spooked horse in the ribs, Dove cantered off into the smoke and hot falling ash. After a moment, John cantered after him. "We'll never get a watercoach," John shouted.

"We'll get one," Dove shouted, "if I have to kill for it."

It almost came to that. They rode hard for Westminster, abandoned their spent horses in the Abbey yard and ran for the river stairs. A waterman was discharging three male passengers, unloading their goods, furniture they'd saved from the fire. Waiting for the boat and frantic, Dove paced the wet mossy stone stairs. Reaching the end of patience, he leaped into the boat, put a foot to an upright virginal, shoved viciously and toppled it into the river. It hit with a splash, rocking the boat, piano keys tinkling. The three men howled in outrage, dropped their loads on the river stairs, and came charging, but when Dove drew his sword they backed off, scared by the crazed look in his eyes. He pointed his sword at the addled waterman.

"Get in! Row."

"Ay, sir."

They took off at full rowing speed, lurching through the river traffic, pulling hard against the tide. Dove crouched in the bow, eyes stinging, streaming. He tried not to breathe the engulfing smoke. Dipping his handkerchief in the river, he tied it over his nose. John and the waterman did the same.

The heat. It was like being roasted alive! And the sound of it. The fire deafened, roaring as if it had the four winds and all the furies in it. As buildings burned, chimney stones and bricks exploded like grenades. Buildings collapsed with loud crashes. Fiery airborne debris showered down, hissing as it hit the water. The only sound Dove welcomed was the distant thundering boom, as somewhere in the doomed city intelligent men used casks of gunpowder to blow up houses and create a fire barrier.

"Faster!"

"Dove. He's rowing as fast as he can."

They spurted past Whitehall Palace, where the Thames

flowed into its forty-five degree turn, heading for London proper. Dove glanced ahead and blanched. His heart nearly failed him. Deep in the city, the medieval Guildhall had not burned. But its ancient, seasoned timbers were so hot the Guildhall shimmered like molten gold. Ahead, the black river flowed into a tunnel of flame. Looming in the tunnel, lighted by the murky, fiery sky and the shimmering Guildhall, London Bridge stood stark as dead bones, a smoking ruin.

"Sweet God," John swore. "It's Judgment Day."

When the waterman let up on the oars, panting, resting, Dove sprang up, shoved him out of the way and seized the oars.

"Guide me, John. Find me somewhere to land that's not burning."

"God Almighty. And where'd that be?"

"Find it!"

This section of the river boiled with boats, with lighters and barges. Working frantically, the king's navy hauled waiting Londoners off river stairs, off wharfs that had not yet burned. Dove pulled down his handkerchief and shouted at a lighter that went plowing by.

"Wattling Street! Is it afire?"

An old granny who was guarding a bird cage on her lap called back, "Not yet, laddie. 'Twill be. Soon. I lived on Wattling Street, I did."

His heart jumped. "A redhaired girl! Her name is Jericho Jones. She lives with a tall old black giant above a cookshop. Is she out?"

"Ay, laddie," the old granny shouted back to him. "She's surely out. Ever'body's out."

"She's out," John said in the bow. But something nagged at Dove. Insecure, troubled, Dove swung around in fury.

"Damn you, find me a place to land! I'm going to make sure."

They put in at Baynard's Castle, an old Norman ruin. Tossing his sword to John and his shoes up on the crumbling stone heap that had once been the fortification's wall, he jumped into the river to wet his clothes, then clambered up over the rocks to his shoes and whipped them on. The smoke was impossibly thick here. His eyes streamed. His lungs burned.

"Keep a sword on him," he shouted down to John, pointing at the waterman. "He'll take his boat and bolt if he gets the chance."

"Not dead, he won't," John vowed.

Just then, the hazy, sooty sky flared with blinding white light, like a long, sustained flash of lightning. Dove swung around. For an instant he stood stunned. It was a sight beyond belief. Covered with a web of repair scaffolding, St. Paul's —that great impregnable cathedral—had caught fire. It went up with the flare of a million lighted candles.

"Mother of God! Dove, you cannot—"

Dove swallowed clots of fear. "Wait for me!"

Yanking his wet handkerchief up around his nose, he took off like a wild man. He ran like a maniac. The smoky deserted alleys and streets twisted and turned like snakes. Smoke swirled everywhere. Smoke and heat. Eyes blinded, streaming, he ran by instinct. He knew every nook and cranny in the walled city. He and Lark had run from Cromwell's troops in this maze, eluding them as easily as a fox eludes a stupid hound. But each lungful of smoke was a separate, distinct agony. Surely, surely he was on a fool's errand. Surely John was right. But what if John was wrong? Pansy Eyes. He had to make sure.

Two or three times he dashed up an alley only to run straight into a wall of roaring fire, and then he had to prolong his agony, breathing smoke, retracing wasted steps, feet flying in panic, his wet clothes already drying in the heat.

Fool's chase, fool's chase.

Now and then, a gust of blessedly fresh wind cleared the air for an instant and he took advantage of it, breathing deep, cleaning his lungs. But mostly he ran and breathed smoke. You could die, you fool. People die of smoke. And for what? John's right. She's out, safe.

Yet he couldn't make himself turn back. Just one look, he promised himself. Just one glimpse of Wattling Street. To make sure. He ran on, smoke-filled lungs on fire, eyes painful and streaming. Finally he plunged out of an alley and into the bottom of Wattling Street. The public pump and troughs were on fire, crackling like kindling. The houses on both sides of the street were on fire. Smoke swirled, black and blinding. Roaring red flames raced along the rooftops, crackling. He couldn't see, he couldn't see. At the top of the street, on Ludgate Hill, St. Paul's was a hair-raising sight, burning with brilliant white incandescent light.

After taking a glimpse through the gritty, blinding smoke, he'd whirled to retrace his steps and run back to the boat when, suddenly, he heard barking. Barking? Somewhere in the murky darkness, in the smoke and flames, a dog barked hoarsely. Pax? His heart quailed.

"Jericho!" he shouted, his voice too hoarse with smoke to make itself heard. "Pax!" But the dog heard, and barked frantically. Dove tore forward, leaping over a burning pump-trough.

Sobbing, coughing, tugging Black Bartimaeus with all her might, Jericho was at the end of herself. She'd reversed directions the instant St. Paul's caught fire. Now she wrenched the pallet downhill toward the bottom of Wattling Street. She had to get away from St. Paul's. They would be roasted alive.

Smoke swirled dark and thick. She couldn't breathe, she couldn't see. She was so scared she sobbed. Smoke billowed in her face, singeing her eyes, her lungs. Fire drops showered down like burning rain. With a ferocious sob, she swatted a blazing ember off Black Bartimaeus, then grabbed his pallet again and dragged him along, her back nearly broken. Pax galloped circles around them, barking. She couldn't find breath. Dizzy, she fell to one knee, then forced herself up and on. Digging her broken nails into the pallet, she wrenched.

I'm going to die, she thought. But, worse, the dizziness made her imagine things. In the terrifying roar of the fire, she imagined she heard Dove. With a sob, she wrenched the pallet onward. It was a cruel trick of her mind.

Suddenly Pax went wild. Barking frantically, he bolted stiff-legged into the billowing smoke and disappeared.

"Pax," she croaked, her voice nearly gone, hoarse. She swiped wildly at her streaming eyes. Her heart jumped sky high as a figure came leaping through the smoke, Pax barking at his side. Her lungs turned inside out.

"Dove," she coughed, staggering to meet him. "Help. It's Black Bartimaeus—his heart!"

Begrimed with smoke, he pounced on Black Bartimaeus and shouted instructions. "Grab fire buckets! Water. Douse us."

With renewed energy, she flew through the thick smoke to the cookshop and came reeling back with the fire buckets, water sloshing. Dove had already thrust his arms under Black Bartimaeus's shoulders. Locking his grip, he dragged the giant drunkenly down the street. Her arm muscles screaming with pain, Jericho threw a bucketful on Dove and Black Bartimaeus, a bucketful on herself and Pax. The water was hot, but it was wet. Their clothes steamed. Then, she grabbed Black Bartimaeus's heavy feet and helped Dove.

"Good girl," Dove gasped, dragging him down the street.

Black Bartimaeus weakly flapped a hand. "Nay. Take— Jer'cho—go—"

"Not without you, old man," Dove snapped.

Even in his pain, Black Bartimaeus's old face lit with a loving smile. He gazed up at Dove, the master he'd loved.

Suddenly, from the direction of St. Paul's, came a tremendous booming crash, a crash so mighty it shook the ground. They swung around, startled. St. Paul's lead roof was gone. It had collapsed into the nave. Fire shot out of the nave, the flames a hundred feet high. In the sudden flare of light, Jericho swung to Black Bartimaeus. At peace, his sightless eyes were fixed, unblinking on Dove.

"Dove, he's dead."

"No!"

Lowering him to the hot ground, they frantically felt for a heartbeat. Another shower of embers fell. One burning chunk landed on Black Bartimaeus's unblinking eyes.

"Black Bartimaeus!" she screamed, swatted it away and lay her own cheek against the burn.

"Let's get out of here." Dove wrenched her to her feet.

At the top of Wattling Street, the ground began to glow and shimmer, bubbling. Through streaming eyes, they watched for an instant, stunned as a silvery, black-crusted, molten river began to flow downhill toward them.

"Dove!"

"Christ, God. It's hot lead. St. Paul's roof has melted. Five acres of it. It's coming in a flood!"

Grabbing her arm, he wrenched her into a flying run. Pax galloped with them, then veered suddenly and bravely trotted back to his beloved black friend, loath to leave him.

"Pax!" Jericho wrenched free of Dove.

With a ferocious shove, Dove pushed her ahead. "Run!" Wheeling, he flew back for Pax, scooped up the heavy dog and came running. Jericho's last glimpse of Wattling Street was one that would be seared into her brain forever.

As the molten silvery lead reached Black Bartimaeus, it jostled him gently, flowing under and around him and over him, rocking him as gently as if he were a babe in a cradle. His clothing leaped into flames first. Then his hair. For an instant, in the light of his own burning hair, his ebony face glowed peacefully. Then, like a pyre, fire enveloped him.

Chapter Twenty-One

John waited under the fiery sky, heart in mouth. What was keeping Dove? He'd been gone too long. John's chest began to pound. He was enraged with Dove. But he didn't want him to die. Not like this. Not overcome by smoke in some foul alley.

Unable to wait, he barked a threat at the waterman, vowing to hunt him down and kill him if he so much as moved the boat an inch. Eyes streaming, he clambered up the stone ruins. He'd almost reached the top when suddenly a grime-covered figure came bolting out of the thick swirling smoke, staggering drunkenly under the load he carried. A begrimed woman ran at his side. It was a moment before he recognized them. Then he bellowed.

"Dove! This way. Over here."

Disoriented by the thick billowing smoke, they veered and came running.

"Hurry, John—St. Paul's roof—it's melted—hot lead coming—a river of it—"

"Mother of God!"

Dove dropped Pax into his arms. John passed the heavy wheezing dog to the waterman. Then he grabbed for Jericho as Dove handed her down. He shot a glance at the smoky alley. Flames licked there now.

"Black Bartimaeus?"

"Dead," Dove said tersely.

John didn't ask more. Taking Jericho, he helped her into the boat. Despite the heat, her smoke blackened skin was cold to the touch, clammy. She was so badly shocked her teeth chattered. John tore off his coat, covered her and pulled her into his lap.

Moving fast as lightning, Dove whipped his shoes into the boat, jumped into the river to douse himself, then grabbed hold of the stern and boosted himself in. The vessel pitched under his violent movements.

"Go!" John barked at the waterman. The waterman dug in his oars. The boat spurted out into the river, leaving the worst of the heat and the smoke and the fearful roaring noise behind. To John's sorrow, with Dove in the boat, Jericho wanted no more of him. She wrenched free and, like a wounded pitiful animal, crawled on hands and knees into Dove's wet dripping arms. Coughing, hacking, she clung to to him. John turned away, unwilling to watch, unwilling to hear the tender endearments Dove poured in her ear.

Holding on to the sides of the boat, stepping over the wheezing dog, he pushed past the oarsman, gave him a gruff order, and sat in the bow. As they spurted away from the city, he watched London burn and he despaired. His city, his shops, likely his house. And now Jericho. *I should've been the one to save her, not Dove,* he despaired.

They landed at a hostler's inn on the south shore, a mile from the city, debarking in the bright white light cast by St. Paul's. The cathedral burned brighter than ten suns, and, viewed from the south shore, the sight of London made the stoutest heart grow faint. In the distance, the city burned like a witch's cauldron, steam boiling up from the Thames wherever St. Paul's molten roof cascaded into it.

Landing, they had no money to pay the waterman, and without a second's thought, Dove stripped off a priceless ring and gave it to the astounded waterman, then stripped off another ring to hire the hostler's bedchamber for Jericho. Somehow, these generous acts filled John with rage, and for a moment he could not think why. Then it came to him. Dove didn't value his possessions. He had been born with a silver spoon in his mouth and had never valued a single goddamn thing he'd owned. And that included a sweet redhaired bondslave from New Amsterdam!

He gritted his teeth, so furious with Dove he wanted to kill him. He made himself a promise. When the fire ended, he would help rebuild his city. He would rebuild his shops twice as large, and rebuild his house, if necessary. And then, Dove or no Dove, he would win Jericho's love and wed her!

When the hostler's wife had bathed Jericho, tended to her burns and put her to bed, John and Dove went in to see her. Determined, John shouldered past Dove and knelt first at her bedside. He blanched at what he found. A wet cloth covered her painful eyes. Her skin was gray. An ugly red scorch mark marred her cheek, and the balm on it and the balm on her lips glistened like paste in the flickering candlelight. Her breathing was painful, labored. He took her limp hand and gently enfolded it in his. Eyes covered, she moved her head.

"John?" She knew his touch. That much he could rejoice in.

"Don't talk, Jericho. You inhaled a lot of smoke. I just want you to know I'm here." Her breathing scared him.

A tear rolled out from beneath the wet cloth and moved down her cheek. "Where—is Dove?"

"I'm here, beauty."

Reluctantly, John kissed her hand and gave way to Dove. He left the room. Worried for Jericho, he was worried about his shop workers too and his servants on Seething Lane. If he could borrow a rowing boat from the hostler, he could row under London Bridge, get out at the Tower and walk to Seething Lane. But first, he thought grimly, he had a few things to thrash out with Dove, God damn him.

Dove squatted beside the bed. A peasant bed, it was of rope construction, but Jericho was comfortable with a goosedown featherbed under her. He'd insisted she be made comfortable. He searched out a spot on her cheek and kissed her cold, ashen skin. He ached, seeing her like this.

"How are you feeling?"

"Better."

He fought rising fear. The worst was yet to come. When the shock wore off she would begin to know she had singed lungs. He'd heard there was no pain more excruciating.

"Bring brandy," he said quietly to the hostler and his wife, who hovered in the doorway, overjoyed by the diamond ring he'd given them.

"Yes sir, at once. Brandy for yer wife, sir."

"She's not my—" He let it pass and didn't finish. The two hopped off like a pair of addled turkeys to do his bidding. He stroked her cold hand. Her fingers clutched his, clinging to them.

"Perhaps it's as well to let them think you're my wife, beauty. They'll treat you even better. I have to leave you for a bit. I want to go back to London. To help fight the fire. You can hear the casks of gunpowder exploding. The king's navy is fighting the fire, blowing up houses to make a firebreak."

She nodded. He looked down at his hand. He still wore the gold wedding band meant for Marguerite. He pulled it off and slipped it on Jericho's finger. For good measure, he stripped off a couple of diamond rings, tucked them in her palm and closed her fingers around them. "Keep these for me." Again she nodded. Her breathing scared him.

"You saved—my life—Dove."

"Include John in that." She nodded. Aching for her, he brushed a damp red curl from the wet cloth that covered her eyes.

"It's the—second time—you saved—my life."

The second time? For a moment he couldn't think. He was so tired. Then he remembered. Collect Pond. Wanting to take her mind off the horrors of the fire, he glossed over it.

"They say the third time's the charm," he tried winsomely, trying to raise her spirits. "If I save your life a third time, I'm stuck with you. I have to keep you."

"I would—like that."

She would like that. He looked down, depressed as hell.

"Dove, is—Pax all—right?"

He hesitated. He couldn't tell her. Only a few minutes earlier, he'd come across the stableyard from the privy and had found Pax convulsing. He'd squatted beside the old dog, wondering what to do. Even as he'd squatted there thinking, Pax had breathed his last and died.

"He's fine."

"I want him—in here—beside me."

He stroked her hair. He understood. She'd lost Black Bartimaeus, so she needed Pax.

"He's better off outside. The fresh air. He breathed a lot of smoke too."

"Oh—yes."

She accepted it, thank God. But her mind was focused on the dog. She weakly lunged up.

"I have—to get ointment—rub ointment—on his feet. His paws—are likely—scorched."

Dove took her shoulders and eased her down onto her pillow.

"I'll do it." The cloth had fallen away. He winced. Her lovely pansy eyes were red, more bloodshot than a drunken beggar's. The candlelight made her blink painfully. He took the candlestand off the sugar chest beside her bed and set it on the floor.

"You?" The offer brought her first, faint smile. "You—don't even—like dogs—Dove."

"This one I like. Without his barking, I never would've found you in all that smoke."

Her effort to rise had made her dizzy. She hacked into a coughing fit, a fierce spasm. He held her up, supporting her. His heart pounded. Would she be all right, recover? People sometimes died of inhaling smoke. He was so scared he trembled.

"Ask John—to do it—rub it well—between—his pads."

"I promise."

Breathing heavily, her eyes closed. She was silent for a long time. He thought she'd fallen asleep. But her ravaged eyes fluttered open. "Dove are—those your—wedding clothes?"

He looked down at his torn, begrimed finery in surprise. Wedding? Had it been only this morning? It seemed a hundred years ago.

"Yes."

"They're—ruined."

"It doesn't matter, sweeting. I can replace clothes. I can't replace my favorite grubworm."

Her eyes fluttered shut. Tears slid quietly down her cheeks. He felt so damned bad. Bad about the fire, bad about Black Bartimaeus, bad that he'd taken her virginity, bad about everything. Dipping the cloth into the basin of water on the sugar chest, he wrung it and laid its wet soothing coolness upon her closed eyes.

"Black—Bartimaeus—"

"Try not to grieve too much, beauty. He had a good life. After he became my slave, he had a good life. Believe that, will you?" He smoothed her damp red hair. Freshly washed, it still smelled of smoke. "I was good to him. At least, I hope I was."

She nodded, tears trickling from under the cloth. "You're—good—to all—of your servants. Black Bartimaeus—loved you. All—of your servants—love you. I—love—you."

Love. His spirits crashed. Hit bottom. He despaired. Suddenly, without warning, she began to thrash back and forth on the pillow. Her lungs pumped.

"Dove! I *hurt*."

"Brandy," he bellowed at the empty doorway, gently pulling her up, holding her. "For God's sake, man, hurry!"

His knees were weak by the time he left her—left her asleep and quiet, the hostler's wife hovering over her—and made his way to the stableyard and down the path to the river where John was borrowing the hostler's row boat. John waited, tense, grim, his face a pale wash in the bright light of St. Paul's.

"Asleep?"

"Asleep."

"Thank God."

"I forced enough brandy down her to fell a horse." Dove riffled a shaky hand through his sooty hair. "She's a tough little thing."

John blazed in anger. "She wouldn't have to be, but for you. But for you, she wouldn't be lying there coughing her lungs out and Black Bartimaeus wouldn't be dead! But no. You had to go and toy with her this summer. You had to amuse yourself, didn't you. You had to make Marguerite so goddamn jealous she sent Jericho packing. And then you had to come riding into Wattling Street—"

"Enough!" Dove flared, glaring at him. "You already plowed that field. How many times are you going to plow it?"

"Plow it? I'd like to ram it down your throat."

They breathed hotly, eyeing each other.

"Do you love her?" John demanded.

Dove didn't hesitate. "No! I'm fond of her, I'm fond as hell. But it's Marguerite I love, Marguerite I'm going to marry." But the words choked him, and he wasn't so sure.

"Then what do you plan to do with Jericho!"

"Do?"

"Do, *do*." John snapped his fingers in Dove's face. "Do you plan to make her your mistress? Your whore! Dress her in silk and parade 'er at court the way King Charles parades Castlemayne, Nell Gwynne and all his other sluts?"

Dove flared. "Don't talk so vile. You know I wouldn't do that to the grubworm."

"Then what *will* you do?"

"I don't know."

John's lip curled in scorn. "Then I serve you notice, 'mil-ord'. I'm going to court Jericho and win her and make her *my* wife. Now get out of my way. I've a house to check on, servants and workers to be tended to.''

John clambered into the boat. It rocked and pitched under his angry movements. Dove grabbed the bow.

"I'll go with you. I'll help.''

John laughed hollowly. "Nay. I don't want your help. I had enough of your 'help' this summer. I don't need your help, Dove. Not today, not tomorrow, not ever.''

John grabbed the oars, dug in and plowed out into the river with powerful strokes. Dove's throat tightened. He called, "Hell, John, I'm sorry. About Jericho. About Black Bartimaeus. About your shops. About everything!''

Rowing powerfully, John tossed a cynical glance to the sky.

"Tell it to the wind! *I'm* not interested.''

Jericho awoke in pain. Breathing was agony. It even hurt to move. Dragging herself out of bed, she used the chamber pot, then got back into bed, weak, spent. Gray daylight glowed in the one small window. Rain pattered against the glass. Rain? She raised up painfully. If it rained, the fire would go out.

"What day is it?" she asked in a painful scratchy voice when the hostler's wife bustled in, carrying a steaming tankard of mulled ale and a plate of fried bread. Her throat felt like gravel.

"Friday, luv.''

Friday! Where had Wednesday and Thursday gone? She'd lost them. Vaguely, she remembered Dove and John coming and going, leaning over her, murmuring encouragement to her. Had she dreamed it, or had Leonardo d'Orias and Lord Aubrey looked in too, all of them sooty and dirty, as if they'd been fighting the fire. She seemed to remember Lord Lark gently touseling her hair. "Get well, pretty. My brother is worried sick about you.''

"Is the fire out?" Her throat. It felt rough as kindling.

"Ay, luv. Thanks be to God. The rain put it out.''

The woman bustled about, clunking tankard and trencher to the sugar chest, shoving the chest nearer with a grunt, plumping Jericho's pillow. Worried for Dove's rings, Jericho fingered the pouch she wore under the nightrail. Safe.

"Praise God, the fire's out, luv. All but Thames Street. Them cellars full o' coal and tar and spirits and oil? Them'll burn months, they say. London, she's a sad sight. A smoking ruin, she is. Your clothes is been washed and put to the fluting iron and mended as best I could. But I fear they still reek o' smoke."

"Thank you."

The woman bustled about. "Lor! Don't thank *me*. Your handsome young husband paid me famous. A diamond ring he give me t'take good care o' you. And another diamond ring to m'husband, for room 'n board. Nigh dazzling, 'tis. We 'spect t'sell the rings and get a pile o' money for 'em."

"Where is Dove?"

"Who?"

Jericho fingered the thick gold wedding band she wore. She drew it off. Turning it, she read the delicate engraving inside the band.

To Marguerite on our Wedding Day—My Love Eternally —Dove

She batted at the moisture that rose to her eyes.

"Dove. My—my husband. Where is he?"

"Over by Whitehall Palace, luv. With his uncle and brothers. Strivin' w'the navy to get bread for the homeless. There's thousands camped outside the wall in the rain, wi' nary a tent over head nor a crust o'bread in their bellies."

She rushed out to empty the chamber pot and rushed back in.

"Where is my dog?"

"Buried proper, luv. Your handsome young husband buried 'im the night he brought you to us."

The woman chattered on, but Jericho covered her eyes with her arm and absorbed the blow. Black Bartimaeus. Now Pax, too. Her beloved two. She forced back the tears. Pax. Black Bartimaeus. Pax.

"You been wed long, luv?"

"No."

"Quickened yet, has ye? A babe on the way?"

Her chin trembled with the effort to hold back tears. It was a sin to cry for a dog when so many human beings were suffering. But she couldn't help it. Pax. Black Bartimaeus.

"No."

"Well, you will, luv. Don't fret. That handsome husband o' yours'll give you plenty of babes. I seen the way he looks at you, luv. He's right fond of you."

Jericho brushed at her tears.

"That's a grand weddin' band ye're wearin', luv. Right rich it is. A lady's ring."

Jericho curled her fingers over the ring.

"It's engraved," she said softly without opening her eyes. "It says . . . *To Jericho on our Wedding Day—My Love Eternally—Dove*"

It was one thing to pretend to the hostler's wife. But to pretend to herself? Folly. Yet she did so as the days went by.

She guessed that maybe Dove was pretending too. For he was as kind to her as a husband. Attentive to her needs. He liked her near. When they supped each night, they supped like husband and wife, eating from the same trencher, sharing the same spoon

Folly. It was folly.

Lord Aubrey's disapproving glances told her so. Leonardo d'Orias's glances carried sharp worry, warning. Lord Raven and Lord Lark did not know what to think. Their looks were curious, puzzled. But John's glances didn't bear describing.

Folly. She knew it.

When she was better, Dove walked her down to the river on a misty rainy day. They wore cloaks and clothing John had brought from his house on Seething Lane. Dove took her to the willow tree where he had buried Pax. She gazed down at the grave, aching. She'd owned Pax since she was nine years old. Memories came back so vividly that she was filled with pain. Pax. Black Bartimaeus. New York. Then they walked along the river, looking across the water at the smoking ruins of London.

She wiped at her eyes. She could see all the way to the Tower of London. The Tower. Were Black Bartimaeus's beloved lions dead of smoke? It didn't matter now. Beyond the Tower of London, ship masts rocked in the pool at St. Katherine's docks. Ship masts. Ocean-going ships. Ships that crossed oceans. A fierce longing surged through her.

"Dove, I want to go home!"

"Of course. I'll take you home. Home to Arleigh Castle."

"*Home*. Dove, *home*. To New Amsterdam. New York."

His eyes brightened with alarm. He turned her to look at him, his hands gripping her shoulders, her wet misty cloak.

"New York? But *why*?"

"I want Daisy and Samuels. I need them, Dove. I need Maritje Ten Boom. She's like a sister to me. And I need Goody and Cook. I need New York, Dove. I need to go home."

His lips parted, then closed, parted again.

"I thought . . . you would stay somewhere near me."

"I can't."

"But I thought you would. I want you to."

"As what? Your bondslave? Your mistress?"

He had no answer, and she really hadn't expected one. Those intense, bright eyes swung away unhappily. The reality she'd thinly been avoiding poked through to her. She gazed at the gold wedding band on her finger. "A lady's ring," the hostler's wife had called it. Slowly, reluctantly, she drew it off.

"This isn't mine. I was pretending it was. But it isn't. It's a lady's ring and it belongs to a lady. To Marguerite."

"Beauty . . ." He accepted the ring as reluctantly as she gave it. Gathering her courage, she gave him a staunch look.

"I fear I've been pretending about you all my life, Dove. When I was young, I used to brag to Maritje Ten Boom that you and I were betrothed, that you were going to marry me when I grew up. I fear I'm an awfully big pretender."

"I fear you are," he agreed reluctantly.

The mist increased, gathering on their skin, on their eye-lashes as they gazed at each other. Dipping into her cloak, into her bodice, she drew out the pouch she wore on a thong around her neck. She dug out the rings Dove had entrusted to her. Dove instantly shook his head, refusing them.

"Dove, I don't want money from you. Or diamond rings."

"Sweeting, if you're bound and determined to go to New Amsterdam, you'll need money. Sell them for your passage."

"No. I'll get to New Amsterdam, to New York—on my own."

His head came up, his eyes bright, worried. "And how will you do that! Jericho, London is burned. There's no call for dame schools or dame schoolteachers."

"I'll figure out a way. Please, Dove. I don't want to be beholden to you. Or to any of the de Monts. Take the rings." Self-respect surging back, she looked at him calmly. She didn't want charity from the de Monts. She didn't need it. She had her resources. If she couldn't teach, she could do servant work. She wasn't afraid of work.

Dove hestitated, then in a childish fit of pique, grabbed the rings and winged them out into the river. They arched against the misting sky, dropped into the water and vanished.

"That was foolish, Dove!"

"Yes? Well not half so foolish as what you're doing. New York. It's on the other side of the world. Damn it, Jericho, I'll worry about you!"

She curled her hand into his, and they walked on, crunching through ash and debris. The wind had deposited half of London on the south shore.

"I'll worry, too," she confessed. "I'll think about you and worry about you every day of my life."

His hand tightened around hers. "Stay in England! Marry John. We couldn't be together. But at least we'd be in the same country. We'd see one another now and then. Talk to one another now and then."

She shook her head. A trickle of collecting mist ran down the inside of her hood. "It wouldn't be fair to John. I've slept with you. John knows it. He hasn't said so, but I know he knows. I see it in his eyes. Maybe it wouldn't matter to him now. But later, after we'd settled into the marriage and grown used to each other, it would matter. He would know I loved you first and best. And it would matter. It wouldn't be fair.''

"So you'll not marry?" he demanded, tense as a wire.

She looked out across the river. The Guildhall was the only building left standing in the walled city. A sad forlorn sight, it reflected what was in her heart.

"I'll marry someday," she admitted softly. "I want children, Dove."

Dove was taken aback. A pleasing image flashed in his mind. Jericho, surrounded by a passel of moppets, each of them with obnoxious red hair, freckles and pansy blue eyes . . .

Jericho watched him tensely, hoping he could see things her way. After a tense moment, his eyes softened and a smile flickered there.

"Little grubworms, little pansy eyes. I suppose you'll want about a dozen, eh?"

Relieved that the tension between them was broken, relieved that they were going to remain friends, she smiled, too.

"A dozen to start," she admitted. "More if I can have them."

He put his arm around her shoulder and they walked on, easy and affectionate with each other, the tension gone. They talked now in a calmer vein about her going to New York. Dove urged her to scotch the idea. When she would not, he urged her to accept financial help from him. Or from John if she didn't want it from him. She refused. She didn't want charity. Finally, in exasperation, he turned on her.

"Jericho! New York's on the other side of the world! How in hell do you expect to get there without help? Skate over on your own spit?"

"I'll figure out a way." She had a plan. But she knew Dove wouldn't like it.

* * *

That night she supped with Dove for the last time. He didn't know it was the last time. But she knew, and when they parted to go to bed, she felt the parting as keenly as a child of eleven—a bondchild in agony, standing in the March wind on a rainy New Amsterdam wharf, watching the master she loved sail out of her life forever. The pain was identical. Immense, bewildering.

In the darkness of her chamber, she grieved like a child. When she was done, she put her childhood behind her once and for all. Determined, she made her preparations for the coming morning. Then she sat on her bed and waited for the inn to fall asleep. When it did, when men's snores buzzed like woodcutters' saws in the common sleeping room, she slipped out of her room and out of the inn.

She hurried across the misty stableyard, as if heading for the privy. When the privy loomed up in the mist, she darted into a stand of trees. Keeping to the trees, she made her way along the perimeter, then dashed across the remaining bit of yard to the stable. Dove slept there. In the hayloft. Aristocrat to the core, he'd objected to the common sleeping room. He'd opted for the privacy of the hayloft.

She lifted the latch carefully and let herself in. The stable was dark and smelled of hay and warm animals. She paused to get her bearings. Horses filled every stall. Most of them asleep, one hock flexed. One or two munched hay. She found the loft ladder, shucked shawl and shoes, and climbed. At the top of the ladder, she crawled into the springy, whispering hay.

Dove slept sprawled on his cloak, lying under a misty window in gray rainy light. She gazed at his familiar beloved sprawl of golden hair, and her heart thrashed against her ribs. Was it so wicked to want one beautiful memory? Was it so terrible to want one night of love to remember?

On Wattling Street, she'd been a virgin, awkward and unsure. She wasn't a virgin now. Now she knew what passion was and what it was like to have the man you love in you, filling you with his own hot passion. She crawled through the whispering hay, stopped at a safe distance and raked her trembling hands through her hair.

"Dove?"

He sat up like a shot, grabbing for his sword. "Who's there!"

"Dove? It's Jericho."

Bleary with sleep, still his eyes brightened to the luster of jewels. He threw his sword away and crawled through the springy hay to her, grabbed her and crushed her close.

"My mate, my mate," he said hoarsely. She didn't know what he meant, but she exulted in the way he'd said it. Crushing a kiss to her mouth, he lowered her into the hay, his sensual, sleep-warm body atop hers. He wrapped his legs around hers. He moved in sexual rhythm, his hot groin seeking hers. The crushed hay sent up a sensual, heady fragrance.

He kissed her, then plunged his tongue into her eager mouth, and with that there began a night so ardent, so passionate, she soared. Sensing her willingness, Dove became a man on fire with love. He did things to her that she had never imagined in her wildest sexual imaginings. Wild and ardent, he kissed her entire body—her breasts, her toes, her fingers, the delicate soft skin of her inner thighs. He worshipped the birthmark on her breast with his mouth. He worshipped her nipples. He sucked the soft velvet hair of her intimate place and gave her such wild pleasure with his serpentine tongue that her head thrashed back and forth in the whispering hay like a madwoman's.

He entered her again and again, as if he could not get enough of her. He was tireless, his hazel eyes bright as jewels. He was like a young stallion mating, spending his seed in her in wet passionate spurts.

It was wonderful. It was heartbreaking. It made her a crazed woman. She grew crazed, knowing this was the last time, knowing this was the end. Each time he kissed her, she kissed him frantically, fearing this was the last kiss. Each time he entered her, she locked her legs around him and held him with all her strength, fearing this was their last embrace. Each time he spent in her, she arched to receive it, fearing this was the last.

Driven by her need, they made love until Dove collapsed of it, gathered her close and clamped her to his heaving breast.

"My mate—my mate—" he whispered into her hair as he drifted to sleep. "Oh, Jericho—you are truly my mate."

Panting toward sleep, clutching him close, she whispered, "Dove, I love you . . . Dove, I love you . . . Dove, I love you . . ."

Just before daybreak, as Dove lay sated and sprawled in dead sleep, Jericho quietly arose and dressed. Crawling through the whispering hay, she stole down the ladder. She slipped on her shoes, took her shawl, let herself out of the stable and ran back to the inn through the rainy drizzle.

In her room, she washed, then quickly dressed again. She threw on her cloak, buttoned it against the rain. Her heart ached. She didn't want to leave him like this, without a goodbye, without explanation. But she had to. For if she didn't leave him this minute, she never would. She would become his mistress.

Cloak buttoned, she seized the bundle she'd prepared and stole out of her room and out of the inn. She hurried through the drizzle to the river. At first light, she hailed a passing waterman and haggled with him until he agreed to row her to Westminster for a few pence.

Alighting at Westminster, she paid the man and hurried on through the awakening city until she found the great road from London. Then she slowed down. Nibbling the bread and cheese she'd brought with her, she determinedly set her face to the west and began to walk.

Chapter Twenty-Two

"Come in, my dear. I am delighted to see you. Come to the fire, come. Warm yourself, my dear. The night is chill, rainy. Come, come, do not be chary of my puppies."

"Yes, Your Grace."

Jericho curtsied, did as she was bade. But warily. "Puppies"? She would not call them that. She moved to the fire. The wolfhounds watched. Not with Pax's friendly gaze, but with huge bulging eyes that protruded from under a fringe of wolf shag. Their jowls looked powerful enough to snap her in two.

Still, the fire's warmth was welcome, penetrating her cold wet cloak, her damp petticoats, her sodden shoes and stockings. For a moment she felt lightheaded. She was so tired. Walking all the way to Blackpool Castle.

But now that she was here, she had the unnerving feeling that she shouldn't have come. She felt a sense of things out of kilter here. Spooked by the feeling, she sent a swift scared glance over the great hall. Ancient armor glowed in firelight. Dogs milled. The man she did not like, Fox Hazlitt, hovered behind his master's chair, as slavish and attentive as any dog. Only two items in the rich hall gave her peace. Two portraits. One of the duchess—beautiful and sad-eyed, painted in her prime—and one of Lord Aubrey, a mended portrait. How handsome and merry-eyed he'd been in his youth. She glanced at his likeness with affection, then carefully brought her eyes back to the duke.

The duke of Blackpool lounged in a Russia-leather chair, one slim leg elegantly crossed upon the other. He was smiling pleasantly, but the smile did not reach his eyes. His eyes remained curiously untouched by it, remote, cold.

"My dear, Fox tells me you have come to accept my offer of hire. To serve and companion my duchess. I am delighted. The salary suits you?"

"It is more than generous, Your Grace."

"You will find my duchess in ill health."

Jericho's thoughts jumped from her own uneasiness. Poor lady.

"I am sorry, Your Grace."

"Yes. Her constitution has ever been . . . frail." He said this not with pity, but with annoyance. She glanced at Lady Angelina's portrait. Such a cold husband. "In her ill health, I fear Her Grace's mind also has become ill. You must grant no credence to any strange things which she may say. She tends toward . . . hysteria."

"Yes, Your Grace." Jericho already knew that, remembering the conversation she'd had with the duchess in Arleigh Castle.

"Fine . . . good . . . excellent." The duke gestured in dismissal, his wrist lace billowing. "Then I charge you to take good care of my duchess, my dear. I want you to be her constant companion. Stay at her side day and night. In short—" Amused at some inner thought, he smiled. "—behave to her as lovingly as a daughter might."

Amusement flickered on Fox Hazlitt's weasel face, too. Jericho saw nothing funny. What was funny about a kind, gentle lady who was sick? She answered earnestly.

"I will, Your Grace."

"Excellent, my dear. I am quite sure everything will work out exactly as I have planned. You may go to her now. A footman will show you to her chambers."

Dismissed, she hurried to the door, glad to go. She disliked Fox Hazlitt. She disliked the huge dogs. As for the duke? He was such a strange cold man that he gave her chills. Following the footman through the corridors, she made herself a firm promise. The moment she'd earned enough money for ship passage to New York, she would leave Blackpool Castle and put all of it—including Dove—behind her forever.

As the door closed behind the redhaired bitch, the duke of Blackpool smiled thinly at Fox. Fox smiled back. Rising, strolling to the largest of his wolfhounds, the one who'd followed the girl halfway to the door, the duke affectionately scratched the hound's ear.

"You picked up her scent, Hunter, did you? Did you? Remember it. Soon . . . very soon . . . you shall have her."

"What are you doing here!"

Jericho had knocked softly on the duchess's door, then entered. She'd found the sickroom in melancholy darkness, the fire dying on the hearth and the duchess standing at the rain spattered window in the cold room, listless and pale as a lily.

"I am here to take care of you, Your Grace," Jericho answered gently. Shedding her damp cloak, she rolled it and set it on the brick hearth. Kneeling quickly, she put kindling wood and logs into the dying fire, took the hand bellows and energetically pumped the coals into flames. The room was much too cold for a frail sick lady.

"Who sent you! Did Aubrey?"

What a strange hysterical thing to say. But the duke had warned her. Jericho rose from her knees and gently approached. She took care to speak softly, as she might to a sick or troubled child.

"Your husband hired me, Your Grace."

"Why? Is it a trick? A new way for him to torment me?"

Jericho's lips parted in astonishment. She didn't know what to say. In the light of the fresh fire, the duchess's lovely face shone pale as death. And she'd lost weight. She was thinner than ever. Firelight played upon her burgundy silk chamber robe and illuminated the few threads of silver in her brown hair.

"There is no trick, Your Grace," she said gently, retrieving the wool shawl that had slipped to the floor and putting it around Lady Angelina's thin shoulders. "His Grace has hired me to serve you, to companion you. His Grace cares for you."

"He cares for no one," she said bitterly. "Least of all, me. I am nothing more than a possession he once decided to acquire." The duchess listlessly let her gaze return to the falling rain, to the raindrops spattering the window. "Were you wise, child, you would leave Blackpool Castle at once. Now. Tonight. He is a wicked man. He plans something wicked for me, I know he does, I feel it."

It was such a feverish, disjointed thing to say, that Jericho discreetly scanned the room for the cause of it. Had the duchess been drinking? She saw no evidence of it, no wine cup or bottle. Tenderly, she glanced back at the duchess, and suddenly she spotted the cause. The duchess's right arm hung limp as a bird's broken wing. A bandage of blood-spotted linen bound the limp wrist. She'd been bled. Jericho's heart opened in sympathy.

"My lady, you've been bled. Please let me help you to bed. You should rest."

The duchess swayed dizzily, hand to brow.

"Yes. Please."

Jericho caught her just as she crumpled. Supporting the duchess's limp weight—she weighed nothing!—Jericho helped her to the silk curtained bedstead, helped her up the velvet covered bed step and into bed.

When she'd settled the duchess in, piling goosedown quilts on her cold shivering body, she ran into the adjoining garde-robe room, found the long-handled brass warming pan in a cupboard, filled it with hot coals, and tucked it into the bottom of the bed, near the duchess's icy feet. Waiting for her to warm, Jericho knelt on the bed step and gently stroked her brow.

"My lady? I want to go down to the kitchen and make you a hot nourishing posset drink. It will build up your blood, strengthen you, my lady."

The weak lovely head moved on the linen covered, goose-down pillow, eyes closed in weariness. "Why bother?" she said listlessly. "In a month he will order me bled again. And the surgeon will do it. The surgeon always obeys the duke."

Jericho was aghast. The duchess was too thin to be bled.

"I won't let him," she said softly. "I won't let him." She hoped she would have a say in it. As companion to the duchess, she might have a say in it.

The duchess smiled weakly, her lovely eyes fluttering open, then closing again.

"You are so pretty. I have thought of you constantly since Arleigh Castle. She . . . would've been your age . . . had she lived."

She? What was the duchess talking about?

"Yes, my lady. Rest, rest." Best to agree with anything that was said, no matter how hysterical.

"But you are not my daughter, are you . . . my daughter is dead . . . dead . . . dead."

The hair on the back of Jericho's neck prickled and rose.

Lady Angelina *was* ill in the mind. Such addled, disturbing talk.

"Rest, my lady." She smoothed the lovely brow. "Rest. Do not tire yourself with talk. We will talk tomorrow. For now, my lady, rest. Rest. Rest."

"Yes . . . I must . . . rest . . ."

When the duchess dozed off, Jericho went to find the kitchens, keeping a wary eye out for the huge ugly dogs. As maid to the duchess she had free use of the kitchen. When she'd fed the posset drink to the duchess and had put her back to sleep, she removed the duchess's stained wrist bandage, gently cleansed the surgeon's incision and rebound it with clean linen. Then, bone-weary, hungry, she ate, drank. She stripped off her own damp clothes, hung them to dry, washed herself and donned a warm nightrail she'd found in a maid's cubbyhole in Lady Angelina's garde-robe room.

There was a trundle bed under the duchess's grand bedstead. Quietly, she pulled it out and got in, utterly exhausted. Overtired, too tired for sleep, she let her thoughts drift wearily. Dove. Had he been upset, waking to find her gone? She hadn't done it to worry him. She'd had to make a sharp clean break for her own sanity. A tender farewell and she wouldn't have been able to leave him at all.

Her thoughts drifted wearily to the duchess and to the duke and to the gloomy, shadow-filled castle and to the unnerving dogs. She would leave Blackpool Castle as soon as she could. She would leave as soon as she'd earned enough money. She would leave . . . she drifted into dreamless sleep.

"I adore your stories of Dutch New Amsterdam, Jericho. They raise my spirits. They make me laugh. Tell me again how Dove won you at dice. Did he *really* throw your drunken master into the canal?"

"Exactly so, my lady." With a fond smile, Jericho glanced up from the petticoat lace she was mending. They were sitting in the garden, taking an airing on a mild autumn day. She had been at Blackpool Castle a month and it was October.

Autumn leaves drifted down. Every day she grew fonder of the duchess. It would be difficult to leave her.

Prompted, Jericho lightly retold the familiar story and was rewarded by Lady Angelina's soft laughter. Jericho smiled happily. She was doing her work well. The duchess improved in health daily. The only sadness Jericho felt was the memory of Dove. And of course she would never get over missing Black Bartimaeus . . . Pax . . .

"I believe I will write letters. I shall write them out here. The day is so fresh and sunny. Run to my chamber, Jericho. Fetch my letter box? Oh——and bring me a handkerchief, please."

Jericho put the mending aside. "Gladly, my lady." She jumped to her feet, then instantly regretted her quick move. She reached out and steadied herself, hand on chair. There it was again. That queasy dizziness. That odd feeling of nausea.

But it was gone in a moment, and she hurried toward the castle, giving the duke's dog kennels a wide berth. Still, the ugly beasts spotted her. Snarling and growling, the wolfhounds threw themselves against the wooden slats of their pens. She walked at a steady pace, her eyes straight ahead, pretending not to see them, determined to show them no fear. But she watched them out of the corner of her eye. In one of the pens, the dogs fought ferociously over a scrap of yellow cloth. She glanced at it, startled.

The duchess had given her a yellow bodice that Jericho had particularly liked and had worn a lot. That bodice had vanished from her closet in the garde-robe room. Her scalp prickled. Instantly, she scolded herself for it. Ninny! Don't be stupid. No one steals a bodice to throw to dogs. It's just a yellow cloth.

Angelina watched the willing girl hurry toward the castle. She's so pretty, she thought. So in love with young Dove de Mont. It shows in the way her voice quavers whenever she says his name. It shows in the way her eyes shine. I wonder if they were lovers. It would not be the first time a lord seduced a pretty bondslave. Is that why Marguerite sent her away? I wonder. There are curious gaps in Jericho's story of her experiences in the London fire. Did she sleep with Dove during those days after the fire?

I should disapprove. Marguerite is my sister. I love Marguerite. But I love the girl, too. I feel drawn to her. I find myself growing fonder of her every day. And how can I disapprove? She reminds me of myself at her age, so desperately in love with Aubrey.

Angelina gazed at her hands wistfully.

I am still desperately in love with Aubrey.

In a hurry, Jericho didn't detour into the garde-robe room for the handkerchief. Instead, she scooped up letter box, quills and inkpot, then foraged for the requested handkerchief in the duchess's night box, which stood on a chair beside her bed. Slipping a hand down under the slippers and nightrobe, she found a stack of handkerchiefs. The prettiest was on the bottom, thickly worked with lace. When she snatched it up, a piece of parchment fluttered to the floor. She retrieved it. A letter. An old one, judging from the faded ink. Unwilling to tresspass, she started to put it back in its hiding place. But as she did, the signature caught her eye.

Your devoted and loving—Aubrey

She stared. Fully aware that she was doing something wicked and wrong, she glanced at the letter. It was dated *Second of September, 1651*. Fifteen years ago!

My darling Angelina,

Tomorrow we go into battle. Cromwell's troops outnumber us thirty to one, and I do not know what tomorrow may bring—victory or death. Therefore, I must write you, precious love, even though you have forbidden me to do so.

When last we saw one another five long years ago —you hidden away in childbed, grieving for our stillborn babe—

Jericho didn't read another word. Aware that she'd been wicked, she whipped the letter back into its hiding place, arranged the handkerchiefs over it and closed the night box.

She hurried back to the garden, ashamed of herself. Still, the glimpse of the letter explained so much. The rumors of

Lady Angelina and Lord Aubrey? Not rumors, but true. They'd loved each other so much they'd risked adultery. There'd been a baby. A poor little baby. Born dead.

A second revelation jolted her. That's why the duchess looks at me so oddly sometimes! That's why she said strange things, the night I came, the night she was so sick. My red hair, my blue eyes. I remind her of the stillborn baby she had with Lord Aubrey!

The poignancy of it touched her. But it stirred anxiety, too. Suppose the duke learned of that stillborn baby? Or did he already know? She shivered, feeling an ominous sense of foreboding. She wanted to leave Blackpool Castle. Leave it and its troubles behind. But how could she leave Lady Angelina ill and frail! She couldn't. I love the lady. I'll stay just a little longer. Just until her strength comes back.

When she rejoined the duchess in the sunny garden, she knelt at her feet and, thinking of the dead baby, gave her a tender smile.

"Here is your letter box and your handkerchief, my lady. What else may I do for you, my lady?"

"You humiliated me, Dove! You made me a laughing-stock. You left me standing at the altar like—like a jilted wench."

Tired, stinking, and dirty, upset with all he'd seen in the past month, Dove dismounted in Arleigh Castle's stableyard and gazed dispiritedly into Marguerite's angry, swimming eyes. He'd just ridden in after a two week absence, and the castleyard bustled with activity, as everyone dashed out, eager for the latest news of London. Fully as tired and dirty as he, Lark, Raven, Uncle Aubrey and Leonardo d'Orias were dismounting. Their horses whinnied, excited to be home, eager for familiar stables, familiar stalls and handlers.

"Marguerite, listen to me!"

"No. You listen to *me*. I will not have it, Dove. I will not be treated like this. You ruined our wedding, Dove, you purposely ruined it."

He was tired and depressed and angry. "In the past month

I've seen a lot more devastation than a ruined wedding! London is burnt, Marguerite. *Burnt*. Don't you know what that means? Can you even imagine it? People are dead. People are homeless, hungry.''

Huge with child, looking as if she were about to pop any minute, his sister-in-law Esme came running into Raven's arms. They kissed tenderly. Dove had hoped for that sort of reception from Marguerite.

"I know why you went! We had the report." Marguerite shot him a bitter look, her voice rising. "You went running after those fool bondslaves, that redhaired girl and that old blackamoor—bondslaves who could well save themselves."

"Marguerite, Black Bartimaeus died! He's dead."

"What of it? Is a servant more important than your own bride? Than your own wedding?"

Marguerite's voice had risen in hysteria. Hurrying out of the castle, alert, anxious, Dove's mother swept it in with a look and came striding regally. She wore a brown velvet riding habit.

"Marguerite, that's enough," she snapped, fire in her eyes. "Dove did exactly right. A privileged class takes care of those who have served it, and if you do not know that, then you had best learn it before you become one of us. If Dove had done any less, I would've been ashamed of him!"

Rebuked by her future mother-in-law, Marguerite dissolved in tears. Picking up her silk skirts, she whirled and rushed into the castle. She looked so beautiful and so genuinely unhappy that Dove felt even lower.

"She will get over it," his mother said to him briskly. "In time, she may even make you a good wife. *If* you learn to handle her, Dove."

"Perhaps." He wasn't sure *how* he felt about Marguerite anymore. His mother embraced him in welcome.

"Was it terrible?" she asked.

He nodded, his throat closing. "Black Bartimaeus died in my arms."

"Oh, Dove." Reaching up, she brushed back a dusty strand of his hair. Her hands were loving and gentle. He'd hoped for a touch like that from Marguerite.

"The redhaired girl?"

"Safe."

"With John?"

He shook his head, his throat closing again. "I don't know where she is right now. I daresay she's disgusted. I daresay she's had a bellyful of John and me, a bellyful of Arleigh Castle and de Monts. I searched for her, but . . ."

Glynden gazed into her son's bright hazel eyes and saw it all—the despair, the worry. Oh dear, she thought. So in love. Kissing his cheek, she told him the bathing room was ready, the bath water hot and steaming. Servants had prepared it the instant their party had been spotted.

When Dove had gone into the castle, she greeted each of her family with hugs and inquiries—Raven, Lark, Aubrey. She left the best for last. Leonardo. She crossed the castleyard to where he stood unsaddling his mount. His fine black clothes were ruined, torn, dirtied. But to her he had never looked more wonderful.

"Leonardo?"

He turned and smiled. "Glynden."

They did not touch. It was something they did not do in front of others. She was countess of Arleigh. She was the widow of Lord Royce de Mont. He? An Italian peasant. Her breath came quickly.

"Before you left, you asked me a question."

His handsome face grew taut, his body tightened.

"*Si.*"

"The answer is yes, *si.*"

He stared at her for a moment. Then, he let his saddle drop and swept her into his arms. "Glynden." Heedless of propriety, he crushed a passionate kiss, a husband's kiss to her eager mouth.

Bathed, barbered, and clean for the first time in a month, Dove, richly dressed, supped with his family privately, in his mother's private withdrawing room, a small gilded chamber that expressed her tastes.

Marguerite did not come to supper. Angry, she sulked in her bed chamber. Esme stayed in her chamber too, feeling under the weather. So supper was a rare and intimate event, a circle of de Monts. The only outsider was d'Orias, and he felt it. It showed in the quiet, speculative looks he sent around the table. It showed in how little he ate.

Dove noticed, because he ate little himself. Long before servants carried away the food, Dove had pushed back his plate. While the others ate and talked, he idly swirled the red wine in his goblet and watched it. Red wine. Red hair. Red wine. Red hair. Jericho. It had stabbed him to the quick, her leaving without a word. Where in hell was she!

Conversation throughout supper dwelled on family business, and Dove paid it little heed. His mind was on Jericho. And Marguerite. He didn't care how much de Mont money should be given to help feed London during the coming winter. He didn't care how much de Mont capital should be invested in the rebuilding of London.

An outsider, d'Orias contributed no opinion. Dove admired that. He admired a man who knew his place. When the meal ended, they rose and took their wine goblets and chairs to the fire. The month was October, the weather, chill. A sensitive man, d'Orias excluded himself from the family gathering and left the room.

Intangibly the family circle drew closer. Dove basked in the fierce strong feeling. De Monts, he thought with pride. We are de Monts. He glanced at each one—his beautiful golden haired mother, Aubrey with his strong ruddy face and red hair, Raven thick-shouldered and dark like their father. Lark, lithe and slim and tawny-haired.

"I wish to say something."

Dove glanced at his mother with mild amusement. When did she not?

She swept them all in with a pregnant look, and Dove set his goblet down, instantly alert. Something was about to happen.

"I do not need your permission to do what I intend to do," she said briskly. "Nor do I need your approval. But because I love you—all of you—I ask for it. I want your permission. I want your approval."

The family gazed at her in curiosity. Lifting her head high, she swept them all in with another look. The fire crackled. The gilded ceiling and woodwork sparkled, reflecting firelight.

"I intend to wed Leonardo."

If she had told them the moon had dropped from the sky, they couldn't have been more startled. There was an astonished silence, then everyone spoke at once. A flurry of objections flew. The widow of a peer of the realm was expected to remain a widow. For the sake of the succession. To safeguard her children's inheritance. Propriety demanded it. Convention expected it. It honored the departed peer.

"And he's Italian," Raven burst out foolishly, leaping upon the inanest objection of all.

"Raven, for God's sake!" Dove lunged to his feet, grabbed the wine pitcher and refilled his goblet. He was in a quandary. In principle, he could not approve of the marriage. None of them could. But he loved his mother. He wanted her happy. As for d'Orias? Dove was damned fond of him.

The only one to speak calmly to the subject was Aubrey. Setting down his goblet, Aubrey leaned forward, elbows resting on knees, eyes worried, the gilded room sparkling all around him.

"Glynden, you know we bear no personal objection to this. All of us have the deepest regard for Leonardo. We admire and trust him. We are fond of him. There is not a better man. Were I in the thick of battle, surrounded by the enemy, Leonardo is the man I would want fighting at my back. However . . . the king must give his consent for the widow of a peer of the realm to wed. This, the king is unlikely to do. D'Orias is a commoner, a foreigner. If you marry without His Majesty's consent, Glynden, you forfeit your position at court. The king cannot receive you. You will no longer be lady-in-waiting to the queen."

Intent, intense, Dove and the others waited for her answer.

"You are duke of Nordham, Aubrey," she said calmly. "At court you are the king's Gentleman of the Horse. Would you value those titles above the love of a spouse?"

He looked away hastily. "No. No, of course not. You know I would not, Glynden. A good marriage is the richest

treasure to be found on this earth." Dove wondered. Were
the old rumors true? Had Aubrey once been in love with the
duchess of Blackpool?

The fire gently crackled on the hearth. The gilding sparkled. For a time there was only contemplative silence. Raven
burst it.

"Mother, do not be hasty. Take time to reconsider."

She smiled and glanced at the diamond and pearl encrusted
time piece she wore, hanging on a shirred black velvet ribbon
on her small waist.

"Raven, my darling son, I estimate I have but one hour
to reconsider. Leonardo and I have sent for the priest. We
will be wed tonight, in the chapel upstairs, in the company
—I hope—of you and all of our loved ones."

Her strong, confident gaze went to each of them in turn.

"Now I ask you. Does Leonardo have your permission to
join this family? Aubrey? Raven? Lark? Dove?"

Dove downed his wine. What the hell. "Yes!"

But the others hesitated. In the hesitant silence, a low voice
broke from the doorway, the cadence softly Italian. Absorbed,
none of them had heard the door open.

"I need no permission to join this family. I am already a
member of it." D'Orias strolled into the room, darkly handsome in his black silk suit of clothes.

"In spirit, yes, certainly," Aubrey conceded. "We consider you family."

"No. By blood tie."

It was a queer thing to say. Dove stared at him, as did the
others.

"Leonardo? Darling, I don't understand . . ." D'Orias
strolled to her, squatted on his long legs and took her waist
in his hands. He gazed lovingly into her eyes.

"I tell you a story, *si, cara*? All of you." His glance swept
them in. "Forty-five years ago in the hills of Genoa, Italy,
there lived a little shepherdess. She was twelve years old.
She was sweet and virtuous, and villagers considered her the
most beautiful girl in the village.

"That summer, English lords came traveling through Genoa,
on a grand tour of the continent. One of those lords saw the
girl and became smitten with her. Although he had a wife in

England, he set out to seduce her. She? She fell in love with the lord. By the end of summer, she realized she was with child. When she told the lord, he merely gave her money and a ring. He swiftly left Genoa and never came back.

"When the girl's condition became apparent, her family cast her out. The village shunned her. Eking out a living tending goats, she lived in a hut in the hills and there—young and frightened and alone—gave birth to a son.

"Born a bastard, the son also was shunned and scorned. The only love he received was from his young mother. As he grew up and saw the slights, the hurtful isolation imposed upon his beloved mother, the son vowed revenge upon the English lord who had sired him and callously abandoned his mother.

"When his beloved mother died, the son was twelve years old. A lone creature, he took to the hills. He became one of the *banditi*. Here in England, you call such—highwaymen."

D'Orias' obsidian dark eyes swept them all in, one by one, his eyes glittering with challenge.

"I was that son. The girl was my mother."

The silence in the room grew thick. The fire crackled. Somewhere in the room a French clock ticked. Dove looked at his stunned mother. She had never heard this before. Her lovely face was dazed. Lark and Raven stared at d'Orias, their eyes intense, lips parted.

"Who was the English lord?" Aubrey asked quietly.

"I think you can guess. It was your father. You and I, we are . . . half brothers, Aubrey."

Dove stared, stunned. "For God's sake!"

But d'Orias paid him no attention. D'Orias's attention, his concern rested solely on Glynden. As she sat ramrod straight, shocked to the core, d'Orias gazed tenderly into her eyes.

"*Cara.* Now you know my secret."

"Why didn't you tell me. Why?" she said in a stunned whisper. "All these years. You were Royce's half brother, Aubrey's half brother, and you didn't tell me."

His dark, compassionate eyes swept her face. "How could I tell you, *cara*, how? You were so fiercely loyal to Royce's memory. Your sense of honor would never have permitted you to fall in love with his half brother. Never. To you, it would have seemed like incest. You would have viewed that love as a travesty to Royce's memory.''

He shook his head. His black, knife-straight hair swept his shoulders, shining as blue-black as a crow's wing.

"And I loved you so much, *cara*. I was not brave enough to risk losing you." He smiled in tender whimsy. "I loved you from the first foolish moment—in the flower market in Paris, when you mistook me for a *banditi* and put your dagger into me."

"But you should have told me," she whispered, dazed.

"When? How could I? No, *cara*, no. You would have thought I intended to claim a portion of the de Mont fortune. You would have thought I intended to take what belongs to your sons. And I did not want that, I did not. I wanted only you."

"Leonardo . . ." Breathless from the shock, she leaned forward and cupped his strong, blunt-featured face in her hands, his black hair a contrast to her fair skin. "Leonardo . . ."

"I had come to take revenge on my father, my father's family. But my father was dead, my half brother Royce was dead. In vengeance, I sought out Royce's widow. When I found her, I did not find the shallow titled countess I had expected. Instead, I found a fiercely brave woman, a woman I knew I wanted for my own wife. Then I sought out Aubrey—my half brother. I found, not the pampered self-indulgent aristocrat I had expected, but a bold soldier, a decent and good man. I made it my business to seek out your sons—my nephews, if you will—one by one, and I found them worthy young men."

Dove stared, mesmerized. That was why d'Orias had come to New Amsterdam! To size him up. He was dumbfounded.

"In short, *cara*, I came seeking revenge. But to my surprise, I found not revenge but my heart's desire—a woman I love, a family I long to be a part of."

Dove glanced at Lark and Raven. Their mouths were open. They were stupified. He glanced at Aubrey. Aubrey's face was flushed, but when he spoke, he spoke calmly.

"You have proof? Proof you are who you say you are?"

D'Orias stood. "I have this." Wrenching up his sleeve,

he bared his birthmark. They had all seen it before, the strawberry red blemish that sprawled over his right wrist. It was like Aubrey's. And like Jericho's, Dove thought with a start. Hell's bells, how odd. He'd never thought of it before.

"And I have this." Reaching into a breast pocket, d'Orias drew out a ring and put it on the low table before the fire. Gold, it caught the firelight and gleamed. It was old. A signet ring. The de Mont family crest was plainly stamped in it. "The ring my father gave to my mother."

"There is more," Glynden said, bewildered, rising. She gazed at d'Orias as if seeing him for the first time. "You are so like Royce. You never met him, so you do not know. But you are so like him. Your bold manner. Your gentleness. Even your walk, your voice, your laugh. It is all Royce. I should have seen it from the first."

He gently drew her into his arms.

"Is it all right, *cara*? Will you still marry me?"

She gazed up at him in bewilderment.

"Yes," she whispered. "Oh yes, yes!"

Suddenly a door opened. Startled, Dove glanced as Esme's maidservant slipped into the room, scurried to Raven and whispered excitedly in his ear.

"She is?" Raven demanded. "Right now? It's started?"

Raven stood so abruptly, his chair crashed. He was out of the room in three strides, his footsteps pounding in the corridor.

Aubrey slowly stood, the corners of his mouth tugging into a smile. "It seems this is to be an auspicious night. Tonight we welcome not *one* de Mont into the family, but *two*." With a soldier's bearing, he moved toward d'Orias, his broad steady hand extended for a handshake.

"Leonardo. My brother. Welcome."

Chapter Twenty-Three

Click-pad-click . . . A soft padding click roused Jericho out of sound sleep. She sat up in the darkness and stared at the locked door. Out in the corridor, something breathed heavily, snuffling at the edges of the door. Then, the click-pad-click resumed and faded down the long hallway.

Jericho held hand to heart until her heartbeat returned to normal. Then, irritated at her own fearfulness, she flicked back her sleep-mussed hair.

Why were those dreadful beasts given free run of the castle every night? She didn't believe for one moment that the duke feared intruders. Who would intrude? Blackpool Castle was remote. The only road leading to the castle was the St. John's Basket road, a rutted coach path now awash with marsh water. The rainy season had come with a vengeance. Rain had been pouring down for a week.

No. The duke loosed his dogs for only one reason. To terrify. Taking care not to wake the duchess, Jericho rose from her trundle bed and tiptoed through the darkness to the livery cabinet, to get a drink of water.

"Jericho? Was that the dogs?"

"Yes, my lady. Don't fret. They've gone. I'll bring you a cup of water." They spoke in soft whispers.

"I do wish my husband would kennel them. They frighten me."

"Don't be afraid, my lady. The door is locked, and I am with you." Groping in the darkness for the water jug, Jericho's hand first found the fruit bowl. Autumn apples spiced the air. Her fingers brushed the hilt of the fruit knife. She gripped it for a moment, for reassurance. A fruit knife was no defense against a wolfhound. But it was better than nothing.

When she'd given Lady Angelina a drink, she knelt on the velvet-covered bed stair and stroked her brow, hoping to soothe her back to sleep. In the shadows of the curtained bed, she gave the duchess a worried smile.

"Are you feeling better, my lady?" It had been a cruelty of the worst sort, the surgeon letting blood again today. What was the duke trying to do, kill her?

The duchess groped for Jericho's hand and squeezed it.

"Jericho, you must never again behave as you did today."

"No, my lady." Jericho flushed in shame. Outraged to find the surgeon at the duchess's bedchamber door, his curette case in hand, Jericho had lost her head. She'd done something rash and stupid. She'd slammed the door in the surgeon's face and locked it, locking him out.

"It is not wise to anger my husband, child. You must never again countermand the duke's orders."

"No, my lady."

"But, I love you for what you tried to do for me."

Jericho drew a quick breath. "I love you, too, my lady!" It was true. The fondness she'd felt for the duchess was rapidly deepening into true affection.

For the offense of locking the surgeon out, she'd been called before the duke, and she'd gone to the great hall scared out of her wits, expecting to be whipped. At the very least, she'd expected dismissal.

But, the duke had merely glanced up from his reading with a cool smile. "You are fond of the duchess?"

"Y-yes, Your Grace. Very fond."

"And the duchess? She is fond of you?"

"I-I-I hope so, Your Grace."

"Good . . . excellent. Then all is progressing as I wish. You may go back to your duties, my dear."

This last had been uttered with such a catlike purr, it had given her a chill. She didn't understand the duke. She didn't understand him at all. Thinking of him, she shivered and gazed at the duchess in the darkness. An impulsive thought sprang up.

"My lady, couldn't you go to Arleigh Castle for a short stay? Arleigh Castle is a cheerful place. There are no swamps and bogs and damp air to strain your lungs. You would get well there, my lady. I know you would." And away from the duke, she would not be bled. Jericho couldn't bear to see her bled again.

"I am not wanted at Arleigh Castle. I am only tolerated there. For my sister's sake. For Lady Marguerite's sake."

"My lady, surely not."

"Glynden de Mont dislikes me."

Jericho stared at her in the darkness, astounded.

"But *why*? You are so good and kind. So generous to everyone. Who could dislike you? No one could, no one—" Jericho bit her tongue. She'd overstepped her bounds. She was a servant. She had no right to speak so intimately.

A barrage of rain hit the window. The window glass rattled, and a gust of cold wind soughed in the chimney. Jericho tucked the goosedown quilt more warmly around Lady Angelina's frail shoulders. If Dove's mother disliked Lady Angelina, it must have something to do with Lord Aubrey.

It was wicked to wish Lady Angelina and Lord Aubrey could be together. The duchess was married. Marriage was a sacred bond. It was sin to break that bond. Still, she wished. Maybe I'm wicked, she thought in bewilderment. Maybe I am altogether wicked. I have given myself to a man outside of marriage. I have been intimate with Dove, and I don't regret one minute of it. I don't regret one kiss or one touch.

"Nevertheless, I am glad for Glynden, glad she wed her Mr. d'Orias," the duchess whispered.

"Oh! So am I, my lady. Very glad." The duchess and Marguerite exchanged letters weekly, and the duchess generously shared Arleigh Castle news. Jericho knew about Lady de Mont and Leonardo d'Orias. She also knew Lady Esme and Lord Raven had a fine new son. Her heart sagged. She also knew Dove's wedding had been reset for next month. This news the duchess had shared gently, as if somehow she'd guessed Jericho loved Dove. But, dear life, how could she guess? Jericho had never said a word and never would.

Her thoughts drifted as she stroked the duchess's temples,

stroked her into sleep. Leonardo d'Orias, Dove's uncle. She smiled at the wonder of it. It was wonderful.

Her smile quickly died as a *click-pad-click* returned in the corridor. There was a snuffling around the edges of the door. For some reason the wretched beasts always sought out the room she was in. It frightened her.

The worst of the storm blew away by morning, but the sky remained gray, turbulent, boiling with heavy clouds. When a gust of wind rattled the windows and awakened her, Jericho suddenly feared the week of cold wet weather had given her the ague. She felt queasy, green around the gills, uncertain of her stomach. But she forced herself to rise and get out of bed. She nibbled dry biscuit, and by and by the queasy sensation passed.

Working quietly, taking care not to wake the duchess, she built up the fire, then went into the garde-robe room to wash and dress. She grew vexed, searching for her brown serge petticoat. Blast! Where was the silly thing? She'd worn it only yesterday.

Its disappearance was not only vexing, it was puzzling. Last week, another of her bodices had disappeared. Why would anyone steal her clothes? If someone wanted to steal, why not steal Lady Angelina's? Her clothes were valuable; Jericho's certainly weren't.

Taking a different petticoat, she finished dressing, then let herself out into the corridor. She hurried down to the kitchens, going quickly, warily, keeping her eyes peeled for dogs. Relieved, she found the corridors clear. The master-of-the-kennels had already whistled them out of the castle, as he did each morning at dawn. Down in the kitchen, she prepared a tray for the duchess, covered it with a linen napkin, hoisted it into her arms and hurried to the stairs.

To her irritation, Fox Hazlitt was on the stairs, coming down. In her six weeks at Blackpool Castle, she had grown to despise him. He was a peacock. Puffed up in his favored position with the duke, he enjoyed making lesser servants grovel. She'd seen him reduce helpless maidservants to tears.

Ignoring him, she took firm hold of her heavy tray and stepped to the right to let him pass. Baiting her, he, too, stepped to her right, effectively blocking her, halting her in her tracks. Thwarted, she stepped to the left. He stepped there, too. The tray grew heavier. The weight of it pulled at her arm muscles.

"This is Her Grace's tray. Get out of my way or I'll go straight to the duke and tell him you interfered with Her Grace's breakfast."

A coward at bottom, as most bullies are, he jumped aside with alacrity. But his weasel face twisted in anger as she hurriedly lugged the heavy tray up the stairs, past him.

"When the time comes," he growled, " 'twill be a pleasure to hunt you. A pure pleasure!"

Her heart was still beating unevenly when she reached the duchess's bedchamber and let herself in. It wasn't until later that his words began to sink in. What did he mean, "hunt her"? What did he mean, "when the time comes"?

November arrived, cold and bleak. Autumn rains had slackened, only to be replaced by something worse. Fog. Standing at any window in Blackpool Castle, Jericho could see nothing but fog in all directions. Fog curled everywhere, drifting like silent, ghostly wraiths through the barren, leafless orchard, drifting in the bogs and fens of Blackpool marsh. She didn't like the weather and she didn't like England. She longed to be home, home in America, home in New York.

"What say you, Jericho? Does this coiffure become me, or am I deluding myself?"

"You're beautiful, my lady," Jericho answered eagerly, truthfully. They were in the garde-robe room, the duchess seated before her dressing table mirror. Jericho hovered near, smiling, watching Lady Angelina's hairdressing maid, Clowie, dress the duchess's hair. A fire crackled cheerfully in the fireplace. Cider simmered in a cider pot.

Lady Angelina chuckled and flashed an affectionate smile in the mirror. "You are the beauty, child, not I."

"I'm all freckles."

"Prettily arranged. Aren't they, Clowie."

"Ay, milady. All the young footmen nigh breaks their necks, vying to fetch 'n carry up here."

The duchess laughed. "And I thought their new dedication to duty was on my behalf."

Jericho smiled. It was good to see the duchess in high spirits. She knew the reason for it. The duke had been absent from the castle for several days, gone on business, and the duchess's spirits had risen accordingly. Let fog enshroud Blackpool marsh. Or let the cold rain fall. Who cared? Here in the garde-robe room, candles burned brightly and cheerful woman-talk flowed.

When the last hair pin was in place, the duchess rose and gestured at her chair. "Sit, Jericho. Clowie shall do your hair also."

Jericho threw her a startled look. "Oh no, my lady. Not at your dressing table. It isn't seemly."

The duchess smiled tolerantly. "If I say it is seemly, then it is *seemly*. Sit, child. I insist."

With a flush of pleasure, Jericho obeyed. Except for when she'd been a girl and she and Maritje had fussed with each other's hair, she had never had anyone dress her hair. Having fun, she laughed in delight as Clowie brushed her hair and drew it this way and that, trying various hairstyles. The duchess stood behind them, smiling, holding ribbons and hair pins, gesturing in the mirror, encouraging. As Clowie stacked her hair high on her head, Jericho felt her excitement growing.

"How do I look, my lady? How?"

There was no answer. Startled, Jericho searched the mirror. The duchess's face had gone pale. Her eyes were huge and dark.

"Leave us, Clowance."

"Ay, milady." The change of mood was so abrupt, so startling that poor Clowie stumbled over the hem of her own petticoat, curtsying, sweeping up combs and comb cases, making haste to rush out.

Worried, Jericho spun around in her chair. "My lady? Are you ill? Is it one of your spells? Shall I help you to bed?"

"There is a birthmark on your neck. On the nape. It is bright red. Shaped like a strawberry."

Jericho's face heated. She'd forgotten about the ugly thing. Had she remembered, she wouldn't have let Clowie pin her hair up.

"Yes, my lady," she admitted reluctantly.

"At Arleigh Castle I asked you about the birthmark on

your wrist.'' Jericho gripped her wrist protectively. She hated this talk of birthmarks. It stirred all the old fears. It brought back the memory of Christmas Day . . . Collect Pond . . . the men . . .

''Yes, my lady.''

''I asked you then if you had other birthmarks on your person. You said no.''

Jericho knew a moment of utter misery. Caught in the lie, she didn't know where to look. She wanted to sink through the floor. Lady Angelina had been so good to her.

''I lied, my lady,'' she admitted, then blurted, ''my lady! I'm frightened when people notice my birthmarks.'' In a rush, in a torrent as headlong as a waterfall, she confided in the duchess, blurting out the story of her Christmas Day abduction in New Amsterdam, of the men stripping her naked, poking at her birthmarks, threatening to cut off her hand.

Listening, the duchess grew even paler. ''You say the men Dove killed said they were going to give your cut-off hand to a fox . . . could it have been a *man* called Fox?''

''I suppose, my lady, yes. But it happened so long ago. It is a muddle in my mind. I was young, upset, scared. All I know is that it had something to do with my birthmarks. Lord Dove never believed that, though. He told me I'd imagined it.''

Angelina swayed. Jericho jumped up and eased her into the chair. ''My lady! You're faint. You've overtaxed yourself today. Let me help you to bed.''

''No. No!'' she said hysterically, covering her eyes for a moment with trembling hands. Jericho knelt close. She'd never seen the duchess so agitated, her eyes so dark and haunted.

''Jericho. This is important. Answer me! Tell me the truth. Have you any other birthmarks on your person?''

Jericho hesitated. This was misery. Agony.

''Y-yes, my lady.''

''On your breast?''

Jericho drew a sharp breath. ''How—how did you know?''

''Let me see it.''

''My lady?''

"Let me see, let me see!" Angelina gestured hysterically. Upset, befuddled, Jericho reached behind and tugged at her bodice until her laces came loose. Flushing with shame, she drew her bodice down. The duchess looked, blanched white as a ghost and rose unsteadily to her feet. She paced the small chamber, wringing her hands.

"Oh, dear God. Oh, dear God! I never dreamed he knew. All these years, he *knew*. He knew! He has been waiting, sly as a cat. Wicked, evil. I never dreamed—"

"Who, my lady? What are you saying?"

Angelina whirled urgently, face white, lips bloodless. "Hush, child, hush. Jericho! At Arleigh Castle I asked you of your parents. You told me you'd been born aboard a ship bound for New Amsterdam. You told me your mother died enroute, birthing you."

Bewildered, very upset, Jericho retied her laces.

"That is what I thought when I told you that, my lady. But since then, I have found further information. It seems I was born in England, before the ship sailed. Mr. d'Orias helped me try to trace my parents. He came to Wattling Street in August and told me he'd discovered but little. I was sold as a babe. At St. Katherine's Docks." Though she tried not to let it, her voice trembled. "I presume my mother didn't want me. She sold me. She didn't want me." It still hurt, and Jericho guessed it always would. Her own mother hadn't wanted her. Her own mother had sold her.

Tears collected in Lady Angelina's wild eyes, glittering there like chips of silver.

"You are wrong, child! Your mother wanted you. She wanted you with all her heart. But you were stolen from her—taken from her the moment you were born—taken before she could even see you or put you to her breast."

"My lady?" Such wild alarming talk. The duchess *was* ill.

"Listen to me!" The duchess swept her to the chair, made her sit, then half-knelt before her, clutching her arm with fingers so cold they felt like dead bones. "When I was a girl I fell in love with Aubrey de Mont. We'd hoped to marry. But when I was fifteen, my guardian wed me to the duke. I had no choice. I was only fifteen.'' She tossed her hair wildly. ''Civil war came. To avoid choosing sides, my husband went to France. He stayed three years. During those three years, Lord Aubrey and I . . . we . . .''

''My lady,'' Jericho broke in, urgently needing to confess. ''My lady, I found the letter. In your night box. The day you sent me from the garden for a handkerchief. Forgive me, my lady, I read some of it.''

''Then you know I quickened. I was terrified. When I began to show, I kept to my rooms. Aubrey visited me in the stealth of night, whenever he could steal through Cromwell's lines to come to me. We made plans for our baby—Aubrey to take our child and raise it, I to visit my child whenever possible. But when my time came, Aubrey was in battle. I sent for the midwife and paid her an enormous sum for her silence. But then—''

''The babe was born dead,'' Jericho supplied. The duchess gazed at her with terrified eyes.

''So I'd thought until now . . . so I'd thought.''

Jericho froze. Her heart stopped. She was afraid to think, afraid to hope. Lord Aubrey. Red hair, blue eyes, a birthmark. Herself. Red hair, blue eyes, birthmarks . . .

''It was a difficult birth, darling. I was unconscious. Or perhaps the midwife drugged me. I cannot know. I only know that when I woke up, my belly was flat and my baby was gone. The midwife told me my baby daughter had been still-born. She said she'd buried it at once, to spare me scandal.

''I was heartbroken. I knew God was punishing me for adultery. When I could stop sobbing, I begged her to tell me what my baby had looked like. She gave me a snippet of hair. It was red. She told me my baby'd had three strawberry birthmarks—one on her tiny wrist, a second on her little breast and a third on . . . the nape of her neck.''

Jericho stopped breathing. For a moment, she couldn't see, couldn't hear. Mist pecked at the windows. She didn't hear it. A candle flared in front of her eyes. She didn't see it. There was only dizziness and the loud roaring of her own blood thundering in her ears. Her lips parted shakily.

''M-mother?''

"Yes! My daughter." Eyes swimming with bright tears, Angelina opened her arms, and Jericho threw herself into them. They knelt on the floor and embraced and wept, wept and embraced. Clutching each other, they murmured incoherently. Angelina swept her to the settee and they embraced again. They kissed, sweet passionate kisses, then clutched each other again. Cheek against cheek, Jericho didn't know which tears were hers, which were Angelina's. But it didn't matter. They were tears of joy.

"Oh, my lady," Jericho gasped. "Oh, my lady."

"Mother, call me Mother!"

"Mother—oh, it feels so good to say that—if you could know how much I've wanted my mother—needed my mother—"

"Jericho—sweet daughter. I knew you were Aubrey's the moment I saw you—but I never dreamed you were mine. I thought Aubrey'd had you by someone else, some other love. My heart broke every time I looked at you—"

"He loves you, my lady, he loves you. I know he does."

"Mother, call me Mother."

"Mother!" They hugged and kissed, words pouring out in a torrent. There was so much to say, so much to ask. Jericho felt her heart would burst. But suddenly, Angelina drew back and looked at her with dawning terror. In a whirl of rustling silk, Angelina leaped up and went to a mahogany wardrobe, wrenched it open and with frantic jerky movements grabbed articles of clothing and thrust them at Jericho.

"Boots, warm stockings. Dress, Jericho. Quickly. You must leave Blackpool Castle at once. You are in danger here."

"Danger?"

Distraught, agitated, Angelina thrust things at her. "Go to Arleigh Castle. Send to Nordham Hall for your father. Tell Aubrey everything. Aubrey will keep you safe."

"Safe? My la—Mother, I don't understand."

Suddenly a wild woman, Angelina shoved her down into a chair, then knelt like a common chambermaid to dress her, thrusting a pair of thick wool stockings over Jericho's mended ones. She was so frenzied, she was almost rough.

"Nor do I. I only understand this is somehow my husband's

doing. It must be. Why else would he lure you here to Black-pool Castle, engage you to serve me? He means you harm. Hurry, darling, hurry!''

Despite the cozy warmth of the fire, a chill as cold as the fog fingered its way up Jericho's spine. She stared at Angelina in dazed disbelief. ''And in New Amsterdam, my lady? Those men who abducted me. Hired by someone called Fox?''

Angelina's frantic hands worked even more swiftly.

''Yes, Fox Hazlitt. I'm sure of it. Hurry, darling.''

Jericho didn't need further urging. She dressed in a frenzy. But when she'd thrown the cloak on and whirled, she found Angelina had not even begun to get ready. She was standing there, watching, her face strained and white.

''Mother! Hurry. Dear life, here, let me help you.''

Angelina stopped Jericho's eager hands.

''No. It is best I stay behind. Until I know you are safe. If he finds both of us gone, he will know. But if he finds me here, as usual, he will not suspect. I shall tell him—tell him I became displeased with your service and dismissed you.''

''But you *can't* stay here. He will *kill* you!''

Again, Angelina shook her head. ''No. If he wished me dead, I would have been dead long before now. I do not yet see all the pieces of this wicked puzzle, but I begin to see he knew about Aubrey and me—knew about *you*—even before your birth.''

''But he does terrible things to you. He will order you bled again!''

Angelina reached out and cupped her face with soft gentle hands. Her smile was tender, motherly. ''You are so pretty. So brave and bold. You are everything a mother could want in a daughter. A bleeding is nothing. If it would keep you safe, I willingly would be bled a hundred times.''

Jericho's chest tightened with fear. Unbuttoning her cloak, she wrenched it off and threw it to a chair. ''If you won't go, I won't, either.''

Angelina seized the cloak and buttoned her into it, as if Jericho were a child of six.

''Mother!''

''Yes, '*Mother*'. That is what I am. I am your mother, and

I ask you to obey me. Go to Arleigh Castle. Send for your father. Tell him all. Aubrey will think what to do.''

"But, I *can't* leave you. I *won't*."

"Twenty years ago, I failed to protect you. I let you be stolen from my womb and sold as a bondslave. I shan't fail you this time. Go at once, daughter. Now. I demand it.''

A thousand anguished protests welled up in Jericho's throat. She swallowed them all. Instead, helpless, she threw her arms around Angelina. They kissed fiercely. Then Angelina seized her arm and hurried her to the door.

"Hurry! Promise me you will run all the way to Arleigh Castle before dark.''

Heart pounding, Jericho managed a smile. "I'll run.''

"Come. I shall see you safely out, in the event the duke has left instructions to stop you. No one will dare countermand my orders.''

They had just stepped into the gloomy corridor when footsteps rang out on the staircase. There was the brisk cadence of expensive boots lightly mounting the stairs. Jericho's pulse quickened. She and Angelina glanced at each other. Angelina paled. The duke's crisp step brought him up the dim staircase, out of the enshrouding shadows. His flunky, Fox Hazlitt, followed. They had been out in the weather and their clothing smelled of mist and fog. Unpeeling his damp glistening cloak, the duke leisurely dropped it into Fox Hazlitt's slavish arms and came forward.

"Angelina, my love. How lovely to see you up and about.'' His voice was silk. Jericho shivered. For now she knew what underlay that silk.

Angelina stiffened. "My lord.''

He came forward and took a kiss from her stiff unwilling mouth, resting a jeweled hand on her frail, delicate ribcage, just under her breasts. A gesture not of love, Jericho knew, but of ownership. His frosty smile swept them.

"What a pretty sight, the two of you. You look as charming as . . . mother and daughter.''

Jericho's chest tightened.

"Think you so, my lord?'' Angelina challenged. "I do not.''

A brave answer. But Jericho wished her mother's voice
hadn't trembled. For the duke's eyes thinned warily, like a
watchful cat's. He gazed at Jericho's cloak, and she tightened.
The cloak was Angelina's. Surely he recognized it.

"Where is the girl going, my love?"

Angelina faltered, and Jericho rushed into the breach.
"To—to St. John's Basket, Your Grace. To buy crimson
silk thread to mend Her Grace's petticoat." She *had* to get
to Lord Aubrey. Lord Aubrey—*Father*, she thought with
shock—would know what to do.

"Tsk, tsk. How uncharitable of you, my angel. Send the
girl out into the cold and fog? With the afternoon spent and
darkness soon upon us? Tsk, tsk. How unlike you to be so
inconsiderate, Angelina."

"I d-don't mind, Your Grace," Jericho said quickly. She
had to get help. For herself, for Angelina.

"I wish the petticoat mended tonight," Angelina said hysterically. "I *will* have it mended *tonight*. I insist."

"This 'petticoat' is of enormous importance?" Did Jericho
imagine it, or did his smile grow chillier? But with a mag-
nanimous gesture, he seemed to concede. "Then by all means,
my angel, you shall have your thread." Just as Jericho drew
a careful breath of relief, he said coldly, "Fox shall go for
the thread. Shan't you, Fox."

"Ay, milord."

Unwisely, Angelina panicked. "I don't wish Fox to go for
me! I wish Jericho to!"

"My lady, my lady," Jericho whispered as Angelina's
hysteria rose. The duchess was not well enough for this
stress. She had not yet recovered from her last bleeding.
But it was useless to try to calm her. Angelina's gentle voice
grew shrill.

"*Go*, Jericho," she shrilled. "Go now. Leave at once."

"Yes, my lady." Afraid for Angelina, still she had to go.
For both their sakes. She could do nothing but curtsy and
obey. She started to move, but three softly uttered words
checked her.

"I . . . think . . . not."

She stopped, afraid to disobey the duke. The glitter in Fox

Hazlitt's malicious eyes told her what he would love to do to her if she took one more step.

"Now, my love. Shall all of us step into your bedchamber and discuss this urgent need for . . . 'thread'?"

Not a question, a command. Jericho threw a panicky glance down the shadowy corridor. She could break and run. Fox Hazlitt might not be able to catch her. But what of Mother? If she ran, the duke might hurt Mother in retaliation. Jericho couldn't bear that.

Pale and shaken, the encounter taking its toll, Angelina weakly entered her bedchamber, followed by the duke. Scared witless, Jericho dutifully followed. Fox Hazlitt brought up the rear, shut the door and leaned against it, a none-too-subtle guard. Jericho's anxiety rose. What was going to happen? Savoring her anxiety, Fox Hazlitt smiled maliciously. Her nerves twisted in knots.

Like the drafty corridor, Angelina's unlighted, unfired bedchamber was ice cold and shrouded in gloom. Fog pressed against the windows, thick as cat fur. The testered bedstead and the livery cabinet loomed dark and shadowy. When Angelina began to tremble, Jericho pulled off her cloak, went to her, wrapped her in it.

The duke watched with cold eyes, then snapped, "Fox! Build a fire. Her Grace is chilled. I will not have her chilled."

The sly weasel jumped to his task, obedient as a dog. The fire crackled to life, illuminating Angelina's strained pale face. As the fire crackled, the duke strolled the room, touching this or that, picking up things and laying them down. It was nerve-wracking. At the livery cabinet, he picked up the fruit knife and slit an apple in two—as a man might slit a throat.

Watching him, Jericho felt the tension rise within her and saw it fully risen in Angelina. Her mother's face was as pale as candle wax, her lips trembling. When the duke took a bite of apple, then abandoned knife and apple and resumed his unnerving stroll, Angelina's delicate frayed nerves snapped.

"Don't hurt her! I beg you, don't hurt her. She has done nothing wrong! Dear God, she did not ask to be born. The sin is *mine*. *Mine* and Aubrey's. Punish *us*. Hurt *us*. Kill us, if you must. But do not hurt my daughter, I beg of you."

"Be silent, you adulterous fornicating whore. You Jezebel. You Bathsheba!"

The epitaph was so cruel that Jericho gasped, and Angelina recoiled as if slapped. The duke's eyes burned. Agitated, he began to pace and rave, frothing at the mouth, bits of spittle clinging to his lips.

"Did you think me ignorant all these years? Did you think you'd fooled me? The two of you? You and my adulterous cousin? You stole from me! The two of you stole from me. You gave *him* the passion that was rightly mine. You gave *him* the child you owed to me. To me, you gave *nothing*. Nothing, do you hear? In our marriage bed, you were as cold to me as dead flesh. And I loved you."

"You never loved me," Angelina cried, wrought up. "*Never*. You loved Glynden de Mont. When Royce left Glynden a widow, you sought her hand in marriage. She spurned you. So you took your revenge. You bought my hand from my guardian because you knew Aubrey wanted me for his wife. You married me for revenge, to break a de Mont's heart."

"At first that was true." Spittle flew from his lips. He paced, as wrought up as Angelina. "Then—unexpectedly! —I grew fond of you. As one grows fond of—of a pathetic helpless kitten."

Her strength gone, Angelina swayed. Jericho leaped forward, but the duke swung his head and warned her off with a look of burning hatred. The vein in his temple pulsed, standing out like a flag, blue and ugly. She stayed where she was. Her mouth went dry with fear. This was a madman.

"You knew of my baby from the first, didn't you! It was *you* who ordered her stolen from me at birth and sold as a bondslave."

"Don't be ridiculous! I didn't order her stolen—I ordered her killed. It was a decade before I learned the midwife had played me false—padded her purse by selling the wretched babe—at St. Katherine's Docks. Oh, yes—I knew—I knew—I knew all about you and Aubrey!" Spittle flew from his lips.

Terror filled Jericho, engulfing her, washing through her like ice water. Inch by careful inch, she backed toward the garde-robe room, her terrified eyes casting back and forth between the duke and Fox Hazlitt.

Angelina grew white as chalk. "Then it was you who ordered her abducted in New Amsterdam. Abducted and killed. She told me of it today."

"Of course, you fornicating adulterous slut. When that failed—when it failed—I tried to buy her—through agents —agents in London. I knew—oh, yes, I knew about you and Aubrey—I knew—I knew—"

Jericho inched toward the door, heart banging wildly. The letters that had come yearly . . .

"When that also failed, I devised a better plan. I knew Dove de Mont would send for his bondslave one day. How ironic, I thought! How amusing to let the she-bastard grow up—let Angelina discover her—and then—*kill* her."

Jericho spun around. She lunged for the garde-robe room. But Fox Hazlitt was quicker. He was on her in an instant, wrenching her arm behind her back, giving it a vicious twist. She shrieked in pain.

"Let her go!" Angelina threw herself forward, but the duke captured her as easily as he would a butterfly.

Jericho panted in pain. She didn't dare move. Hazlitt would snap her arm, break it. She threw a frightened look at Angelina, and from somewhere found the courage to shout, "Let me go! Let my mother go. Don't hurt her or—or I'll kill you."

It infuriated the duke. The vein in his temple swelled, pulsing with fury. His eyes burned like coals.

"Be silent, you vile de Mont spawn. We shall see how brave you prove. Isn't that so, Fox!"

"Ay, milord." Hazlitt gave her arm a twist. She gasped in pain. His breath curled sourly in her hair.

Trapped in the duke's grip, Angelina grew wild-eyed.

"What are you going to do to her!"

The duke's spittle flew. "The dogs, you adulterous bitch!"

For a moment, Jericho didn't understand. Nor did Angelina. Their eyes met in scared confusion. When comprehension came, so did stark terror.

"No," Angelina cried out. "Dear God, you cannot mean that."

"A fitting punishment for you, is it not, my angel slut? To see the fruit of your sin—torn to pieces before your eyes?"

"You *cannot*! It's madness. I would tell the world. I would shout it from the rooftops."

"And who would believe? You have been ill, whore! In the last several years the duchess of Blackpool has been neither sound of body nor sound of mind. Ask anyone. Ask any of the dozen physicians I have brought to your sickbed —ask your own servants—ask your own friends—ask anyone." He turned to Jericho. "Now, my whore's angel—we are going for a walk. Into Blackpool marsh." Ranting, spittle trailed down his chin.

Jericho's terror grew boundless. He was as insane as any chained madman in Bedlam.

"M-mother?"

"Jericho, run!" Wrenching free, Angelina came flying at Fox Hazlitt, fingernails clawing his eyes. Startled, Hazlitt slackened his grip, and Jericho tore loose.

"Fox!" the duke warned.

But Jericho hit the door running. She wrenched it open. She flew down the corridor and down the stairs. She flew through the castle and wrenched open the first outside door she came to. The fog came billowing at her, cold and wet, heavy as wet wool, blinding her, filling her throat. She plunged into it and ran blindly, wildly, stumbling over fog-shrouded ground she couldn't see, crashing through icy puddles that came up out of nowhere, hearing nothing in the foggy silence but the sound of her own terrified steps and the loud thrashing of her own heart. When she ran blindly into a fence, she panicked, whirled, and ran in the opposite direction.

Where was the road, where was the road?

The fog engulfed her, thick as sheep's wool, a silent glowing white. Run, run. Each labored breath she gulped—run, run—went down her throat like wool, wet and thick. She couldn't see, she couldn't see. When objects loomed up, they loomed up suddenly, like monsters in a nightmare, leaping at her.

Run, run. Help me, God, help me. Please! Please!

When a tree branch swung out of nowhere and slammed her in the chest, knocking her down, knocking her windless, she crawled panting through the icy mud, dragging her wet skirts with her, crawling until she found the trunk of a tree and felt her way up, frantically exploring the ridged, rough bark. A plum tree. She was in the orchard. Dear God, she'd run in the wrong direction. She was nowhere near the road to St. John's Basket!

She whirled to backtrack. But behind, in that direction, male voices shouted in the muffling fog. A dog bayed excitedly. Then a second dog, a third. Her chest constricted. With a panicky sob, laboring for breath, she fled the sounds and plunged on through the orchard, plunging from tree to tree. Breaking out of the orchard, she seized her wet unwieldy skirts and ran headlong down an endless slope, running drunkenly, her boots heavy as lead, so caked with mud.

At the bottom of the slope, she tripped and fell, her hands slapping into icy mud. Panting, gasping, she pushed herself to her feet, seized her sodden skirts and ran on. The fog swirled upward for an instant, clearing for a moment, and she stopped to get her bearings, panting, panicking, swatting mud from her forehead.

Ahead lay Blackpool marsh, dark and frightening, its treetops overgrown with tangled vines, its miles of hunter's paths winding through dangerous bogs and mires. She could smell marsh gas and stagnant water. She could hear the quiet pop of sulphurous gases bubbling to the surface.

As swiftly as the fog had cleared, it closed in again, engulfing her in its thick, white silence. Behind, distant but not so distant as at first, dogs bayed excitedly. She had no choice. Seizing her wet heavy skirts, she plunged into Blackpool marsh.

Chapter Twenty-Four

Dove found himself on the road to Blackpool Castle again. He'd ridden this road a half dozen times in the past two weeks, ever since he'd learned Jericho was in service there.

Not that he hoped to see her. Hell, no! If he saw her again
in a hundred years it would be too soon. The ungrateful
grubworm. She'd broken his heart, disappearing out of his
bed—out of his *life*—without so much as a by-your-leave.

And *then* to pop up in service to a man he loathed! To a
man the de Monts despised. It was treachery. Disloyalty of
the blackest sort. He would never forgive her, not even if
she crawled on her knees and begged.

A finger of fog drifted out of Blackpool marsh and crossed
the road, eerie as a ghost. His mount shied. Dove whacked
it. The horse opted for obedience. Dove drew his cloak closed
against the chill mist.

D'Orias was worried about Jericho. But Dove wasn't worried. Worry about Jericho? He'd sooner worry about a wart
hog. Jericho was as tough as old barrel staves. She'd been a
tough brat at eleven; she was tougher at twenty. The London
fire proved that. Worry? Ha! Someone ought to worry about
Blackpool, with that treacherous disloyal grubworm in his
house.

A thick cloud of fog enveloped him, momentarily erasing
the world, replacing it with weightless, white, glowing silence. His horse shied again. Dove kicked it. The horse settled
down. Dove breathed fog. It was cold and wet and smelled
of marsh gas. His nostrils flared, rejecting it.

However . . . if his horse should stumble and go gimp-
legged in the fog, it would be only common sense to seek
shelter somewhere, wouldn't it? Blackpool Castle was near.
Not that he wanted to check on Jericho. Hell, he'd sooner
check on a crocodile. The ungrateful wench.

He drew his sword. He was sitting there in the saddle,
wondering which of his mount's legs to whack with the sword
hilt, wondering if the stable master would kill him, when he
heard a faint eerie sound. From a distance perhaps a half mile
away, from deep in the marsh came the baying of dogs.

He froze. The sound pierced his brain like an icy knife.
Cold sweat broke on his forehead. His armpits gushed sweat.
Sweat prickled on his upper lip, like a mustache. He swatted
it away. For a moment he felt lightheaded.

He cursed aloud to bring himself out of it. Hell's bells!

Was he going to be like this forever? Scared shitless whenever a dog barked unexpectedly? Would he always react like a three-year-old? It was so damned unmanly.

He cursed again. With a hand that wouldn't stop trembling, he rammed his sword into his sheath and wiped his clammy palm on his leather breeches. It was only a dog pack hunting in the marsh. Hunting rabbits, likely.

But his breathing refused to slow down. Why was he reacting so? Breathing hard, he strained to see through the swirling fog. Had there been fog the day his father was killed? He couldn't remember. He'd been only three. He remembered nothing of that day. Whatever had happened that day had retreated into a locked closet in a three-year-old's brain, emerging occasionally in nightmares that still woke him in terror, nightmares that vanished before he could sit up in bed and examine them.

Trembling, he listened as the baying and howling converged in frenzy at a fixed point deep in the marsh. Whatever the dogs were hunting, they'd found it, cornered it for the kill.

He swatted a prickle of sweat from his lip and stared into the white fog, intent, intense, trying to see. Trying with eyes that burned in his skull as brightly as a hundred candles. Trying, trying, trying to see through the fog and into the past. Twenty-four years ago, twenty-four years . . .

His heart began a slow, upward beating.

It *had* been foggy that day . . . now he remembered . . .

Angelina had never done a brave thing in her life. But she was about to now. And the terror of what she intended to do made her heart hammer.

Preparing, she raked her hands through her wild, disheveled hair and licked her bloody knuckle to staunch the bleeding. During the past quarter hour, she'd gone nearly insane. Locked in her bedchamber, she'd battered at the corridor door, using fists, arms, candlesticks, the fireplace poker, footstools—anything she could lift and use for battering.

She'd shrieked, she'd begged. She'd smashed a window
with the poker and had leaned out over the precarious three-
story drop, shrieking into the unlistening fog, screaming for
someone to come to Jericho's aid. But no one had come, the
servants likely in the kitchen, cowed, frightened, ordered to
stay there by the duke.

Sobbing in frustration, she'd clawed at the corridor door
on hands and knees, pleading with Fox Hazlitt as he stood
guard on the other side. She would give him money. She
would give him her jewels. She would give him everything
she owned. Only save Jericho! Let her *out*!

But to no avail. Hazlitt paced the corridor, unmoved by
her tears.

Now, terror pounding, she quietly crossed the room to the
livery cabinet. Overwhelmed by what she was going to do,
she braced her shaking hands on the cabinet for a moment.
Then, drawing a breath for courage, she made her preparations.

Next, she took a silk scarf from her night box. She got a
footstool and moved it to the shadows. She sat on the stool
and braced her feet on the floor. With trembling hands, she
arranged the gossamer-thin scarf in her lap.

She waited, heart racing. After a few minutes, a light
rapping sounded on the corridor door.

"Your Grace? What's amiss? You're quiet of a sudden.
Be you all right?"

She didn't answer.

The rapping came again, more urgent this time. "Your
Grace?"

She said nothing.

Hazlitt pounded loudly. "Your Grace! Is anything amiss,
Your Grace?"

"Yes. I'm bleeding. I cut my ankle on window glass. I'm
bleeding badly."

The iron key rattled frantically in the lock.

Damnation, Fox Hazlitt thought as he went barreling in.
The duke'll nail my hide to the front gate if anything's happened to her. He wants to deal with her himself.

The first thing Fox noticed as he barreled into the shadowy

darkening room was the cold air and the smell of fog. She'd smashed out the window. Had she jumped? Jumped to her death? Frantic, he swung his head to and fro, looking for her.

"Your Grace?"

For a panicky moment he couldn't find her. He started to sweat. The duke! Then, the glimmer of her silk chamber robe caught his eye. She was sitting on a cushioned stool in the shadows. Torn between relief and new worry, he crossed the room in a rush. Bleeding? Damnation! The duke would—

He drew up short. Bleeding? He couldn't see any blood. The silk slippers that peeped from under her chamber robe bore no trace of blood. He stood there, confused. What the devil?

"Your Grace, what is it?"

"I told you. I'm bleeding."

Sitting with her hands in her lap, her face was as white and drained as if she'd lost every ounce of her blood. It scared him. Not for her sake. For his own. The duke would kill him.

"Where, Your Grace! I don't see no blood."

"My ankle. I bound it. The blood is seeping faster than I can staunch it. I think I cut a vein."

"Judas Priest!" She was more trouble than she was worth. Grabbing a linen napkin from the livery cabinet, he went dashing across the room. He dropped to his knees before her. Waiting for her to stick out her foot, he was struck by a fleeting thought. Odd, the way she was sitting there, stiff as a post, scared, her hands clenched in her lap, a scarf over them. Her posture was odd.

It was his last complete thought.

With terror thundering in her, Angelina braced herself. She waited until he lifted his face to her in impatience, waited until his sinewy throat lay bared and vulnerable. Terror stricken, she forced her eyes to search out the pulse point, the artery.

She found it, and nearly fainted. For an instant, she feared she lacked the courage to do it. Then, through the open window came the bloodthirsty baying of dogs as the duke loosed them. Her breast leaped savagely.

With a cry—"My daughter!"—she lunged up and thrust the knife in.

Dove was still shaking and sweating, captive of remembered horror, when the sound of galloping hooves roused him from his dazed trance. The galloping hooves came hard and fast. Shaking, he swallowed, grabbed the reins, kneed his mount to the roadside, tore his cloak open and warily rested his hand on his sword hilt.

Highwaymen? Not likely. Not coming from the direction of Blackpool Castle. But anything was possible. Since the war, England had become plagued with them.

Two horses broke through the billowing fog. They galloped past. Then, spotting him, the riders frantically reined in, wheeled, and came trotting back. The riders were no more than boys. Stable lads. They were panting so hard they had no breath, and their eyes were large with fright.

"Lor' Dove, is'na?" the oldest asked.

"Yes." Wary, Dove kept his hand on his sword hilt. Highwaymen commonly used ploys, ruses.

The lad went on panting. "Lor' Dove—the duchess—milady Angelina—she sent us—t' Arleigh Castle—wi' a life or death—message."

"What message!"

The boy hacked, gulping breath. "Her Grace—made us repeat it—thrice. T'get it true. She said—t'say—ye and yours—are to come—at once—her daughter Jericho—Lor' Aubrey's daughter, Jericho—"

"Daughter!"

"—is in terrible danger. She's fleeing. She's in Blackpool marsh. The duke—he's loosed his killer dogs after her."

Dove grabbed the boy by the collar, wrenched him up from the saddle. Their horses skittered under them, hooves thrashing in puddles, splattering mud.

"What in hell are you talking about! Jericho Jones? Jericho is a serving maid. She isn't the duchess's daughter. She isn't

Lord Aubrey's daughter. And what do you mean, 'loosed killer dogs after her'?''

The boy's Adam's apple bumped against Dove's knuckles as he swallowed in fright. "I don' know, milord. All's I know is what the duchess tol' us. When the duchess come flyin' through the fog to the stable, she was covered wi' blood, her gown was drenched wi' blood, milord."

Dove stared at him intense, stunned.

"My God, what's going on in that house?"

"I don' know, milord. Evil things maybe."

Dove swung his head toward the marsh. The distant barking had grown even more frenzied. The pitch had risen. Something had been treed. Jericho? His scalp crawled.

Shoving the boy into his saddle, he snapped instructions like musket shot. "Ride for St. John's Basket—stop at the first house you come to—tell them to pass the word—Lord Dove will pay a gold guinea to every man who arms himself and comes at once to Blackpool marsh—then ride to Arleigh Castle—you'll find Lord Aubrey there—tell him what you told me—tell him to bring men." Dove threw a frantic look at the sky, the fog thickening overhead, the darkness descending. "And tell him to bring torches!"

"Ay, milord."

The boy looked so scared that Dove clapped a hand to his shoulder and squeezed it urgently. "Do this well and you've a new post at Arleigh Castle. As my master-of-the-horse."

"Me, milord? Me?"

"You."

For a split second the boy's eyes shone with joy. Then with a shout of, "Ay, milord, I'll ride like the wind," he wheeled his horse and thundered off at breakneck speed, the second boy following.

Deep in the marsh the high-pitched barks had risen to a frenzy. Dove felt faint. He fought back the dizziness that welled up. So much blood. There'd been so much blood. His father's blood. He remembered! He'd been soaked in his father's blood when Aubrey had found him in the forest and tenderly carried him home.

He slid from the saddle, and, weak with dizziness, clung

to it for a moment, pressing his face into the leather. Then, with lurching steps, he rapidly tethered the horse to a bush. A horse was useless in marsh. Tethered, it would serve as a signal for the men to follow.

Then, whispering, "Jericho!" whispering her name over and over, using it as a talisman, using it for strength—"Jericho, Jericho!"—he shed his buckler, grabbed his sword, and lurched toward the marsh. Drawing an agonized breath, he broke into a run, running toward the nightmare he'd feared all of his life.

Jericho was exhausted. She ran wildly, arms pumping. When a low tree branch whipped out of the fog and snagged her hair, wrenching her scalp, she cried out in pain. Breathing hard, gulping in draughts of air, she yanked her hair free and plunged on.

She was at the end of herself. She couldn't run another step, she couldn't. She'd passed her limit of endurance long ago. Her lungs heaved and burned like fire. A swordlike pain stabbed in her side, and her heart was beating so hard, so fast, so painfully, that she knew it would soon cease to beat at all and she would die. Somewhere behind in the thick, billowing fog, the gap steadily closed, the distant baying grew closer. She plunged on, running, running.

When she passed the same tree for the third time—a tall, dead, black walnut tree that had fallen into a cradle of living trees, its massive roots upturned and exposed, its dead trunk slanting upward into swirling fog—she flung herself to a halt and uttered a wild sob. A thousand paths meandered through the marsh, crisscrossing, winding, doubling back upon themselves like coiled snakes.

Where was she? Oh, dear God.

She drew a labored breath and ran on. She'd already lost a boot. Sucked off by mud. Frightened by the ever-closer barking, she hadn't stopped to pull the boot out of the mud. She'd abandoned it. Now she wished she hadn't. Sodden and stretched out of shape, her wet wool stocking made her stumble and trip. In a frenzy, gasping for air, she halted, tore off the stocking, tore off her remaining boot and stocking, abandoned them and ran on.

Not ten steps away, she wheeled in hysteria, ran back and scooped them up. Dear God, she mustn't leave a trail. Clutching boots and stockings to her pounding chest, she ran on. When she heard the bubble of marsh gas rising in water, she flung herself to a stop and wildly pitched the things through the fog in that direction. She heard the boots splash. She trusted the stockings had landed there too. Wet and encumbering, her cloak went next. She balled it up and threw it. It hit with a watery plop.

Lungs heaving, she ran on. Twigs and thistles raked the soles of her feet like razors. Wet leaves slid under foot, slimy and slick, making her slip and fall, and, when she picked herself up, made her fall again. When a pocket of fog lifted on a pond, she plunged through the stiff, rustling reeds and went crashing into the icy water, her loud splashes splitting the foggy silence, her wool petticoats soaking up water, dragging behind like an anchor. She prayed the water would destroy her trail, her scent. Shoulders pumping, she dragged her petticoats with her, fighting for a foothold in the mucky pond bottom, fighting to keep her balance. But her soaked petticoats grew heavier and heavier.

With a frenzied sob, she wrenched at her waist bindings and shed them. Struggling free of them, she left them behind, sinking. She plunged out of the pond and ran on in her drawers and bodice.

The howls came louder now. She could hear snarling. Oh, dear God, oh, dear God.

"Run, you de Mont bastard." The duke's voice came as a thin distant cry, muffled in fog. "You shan't escape me. Royce didn't."

Oh, dear God! Out of breath, out of strength, out of speed, she dipped into herself and somehow found the will to run faster. She sprinted through the fog. By hairs' breadths, she missed lethal dark branches that came swinging out of the fog. Once she ran straight into a bog and panicked as the sandy oozy muck tried to suck her down. With frantic mewling cries, she scrambled and clawed her way out of the bog, clutching at bushes and saplings as the shifting mire sucked at her, wanting to claim her.

Exhausted from the bog, she knelt panting. The sound of her own breathing filled her ears. A rasping sound, like clothes being scrubbed on a washboard. Her hair hung in wet muddy strings. Mire covered her, coating her drawers and her legs with thick brown slime, the stench of it like rotten eggs.

She picked herself up, staggering drunkenly, then found her balance, and lurched on. She ran and ran. She lost all sense of time. She lost track of it. It seemed she'd been running forever, running ever since the world began. And the fog played cruel tricks. Sometimes the baying dogs seemed almost on top of her. The next instant, their barks rang from the distance. And always, always the duke's cry, ringing through the fog.

"You shan't escape me, you de Mont bastard!"

She gained a brief respite when the dogs lost her scent at the pond, and she frantically took a few precious minutes to breathe, to let her laboring, worn-out heart slow down. A mistake. When she lurched into a run again, her leg muscles cramped. She hurt so painfully she could scarcely move. She forced herself on.

Encouraged by the confused barking at the pond, she plunged into another marsh pool that loomed up in the fog. Wading with loud drunken splashes, flailing her arms to keep her balance on the slimey bottom, she beat her way through stinging reeds that scratched her face, then ducked under tree limbs that jutted out over the water and slogged through the pond to its end, then clutched at saplings to pull herself out. She took a moment to catch her breath, then ran on.

But this pond didn't fool the wolfhounds. She heard their loud splashes as they leaped into the water. Too soon, their terrifying baying resumed. The duke's voice rang out, closer now, a madman's voice, garbled, frothing.

" 'Tis only a matter of minutes—You shall pay for Angelina's adultery. You shall pay, just as Royce paid for taking Glynden from me—"

Oh, dear God. She ran blindly. When she went careening out of thick fog into a pocket of visibility and ran into the same dead black walnut tree again, its massive hairy roots exposed, its trunk angled in the cradle of live trees, she went wild. Circles, dear God, she'd run in circles!

She wheeled to run again, but the dogs were coming from that direction. She could hear their lunging barks as they loped along, following her trail. Desperate, she clambered up over the massive roots of the dead walnut tree. If she could keep her balance, if she could hold on and not fall, she could creep up the angled tree trunk. She prayed her slight weight wouldn't cause the trunk to shift, to come crashing down.

Holding her breath, keeping desperate eyes on the path behind her, she began her precarious climbing. Hurry, hurry! The bark was rough and wet and slippery. It scratched her knees, raked her shins. When she grabbed at it, clumps of rotted bark flaked off in her hands and she had to throw her arms around the trunk to hold on. The bark raked her face.

She'd progressed ten feet, when she lost her hold on the slippery bark and slid back five feet. The baying grew ever louder. Oh, dear God! She gouged her bruised toes into the bark and pushed, grunting her way up the trunk, the bark scratching her breasts as she clung. She recovered the footage she'd lost and pushed on.

The ground lay some fifteen feet below as the first wolfhound came loping out of the fog like a ghostly beast, its gray wolf shag wet and stringy, its bulbous eyes shining. She clutched the trunk in terror as it lifted its huge head and howled its victory. Three wolfhounds came bounding. All four beasts padded round and round the massive tree roots, leaping into the air, snarling, snapping, baying, filling the marsh with their fearful frenzy. Her heart nearly failed.

The boldest leaped up on the massive roots. Terrified, Jericho inched her way upward again. Don't fall, don't fall, dear God, don't fall or the dogs will be on you. Below, on the massive roots, the boldest hound sniffed, then cautiously began to climb. Jericho's terror grew boundless.

Surefooted on the ground, the tall, rangy beast was not surefooted in the air. He lost his balance, slid off the log with a yelp and fell ten feet to the ground, hitting with a thump. Jericho prayed he was dead. But he was only stunned. He rose and shook himself, snarled at her and leaped up on the massive roots to try again. All the while, the others leaped and howled, trying to leap up and get her. The hound was

more surefooted on this try and mounted higher before he
fell. Jericho inched up the trunk desperately, hanging on to
branches that dipped down from the other trees.

When the frenzy suddenly died for a moment and silence
rang out in the marsh, Jericho looked down in terror. Below
her stood the duke of Blackpool. He looked like the devil
himself, his eyes burning like coals, the fog curling around
his black cloak. He gazed up at her like a madman. The dogs
paced around him, eager growls breaking from their huge
throats, and when he shouted at her he frothed at the mouth,
spittle flying.

"Come down, whore-daughter! I command you. You cannot escape me, you de Mont bitch. You are dead—dead, do
you hear?"

Jericho didn't answer. She used her strength to continue
to inch upward. To her terror, her stiff numb fingers lost a
handhold. She slid down six inches before she dug her nails
into the bark and caught herself. She wrapped her arms around
the trunk and hung on, heart pounding.

"I've done this before," he shouted madly.

Her mouth dry with terror, Jericho inched her way up.

"Royce did not escape—Nor shall you—My dogs tore
him apart—Oh, he was handsome, yes—But not after my
dogs finished with him—I sent him home to his wife, torn
limb from limb—But I spared his son—I spared him for
Glynden's sake! Do you hear, bitch?"

Jericho climbed desperately, heart banging.

"It was not a planned event," he shouted wildly, the madness in his voice ringing in a ghastly way, echoing in the
fog. "I chanced upon him hunting. My dogs had just brought
down a stag. They were in a blood frenzy, and I thought—
why not? I would gain Glynden. And Arleigh Castle."

He was totally mad. He was insane. With his eyes burning
and his black hair mussed, the silvery streaks standing out
in disarray, he looked like Satan. Jericho's heart beat so hard
she could hear it thumping against the hollow tree trunk.

"Come down, whore-daughter. I command you! You have
no right to live. Nor does Angelina. Nor Aubrey. I'll get
you, all of you. Do you hear?"

The dogs circled below, snarling.

"Come down. I command you!"

Jericho swallowed, her voice croaking with exhaustion. "You will have to come up and get me." Maybe he would fall, break his neck.

He looked up at her in wild fury.

"Then I shall."

He shed his cloak but not his sword. A lithe man, he leaped to the roots with little trouble. Terrified anew, frightened she would lose her grip and slide down into his arms, she began to shinny upward. So did he. Under the additional weight, the tree trunk shook. Jericho gripped it. Dear God! He might shake her off! She would fall into the pack of dogs. Circling the tree, anticipating it, the dogs howled, smelling the kill. They went into a wild frenzy—snarling, growling, leaping, baying.

The duke climbed, his dark eyes mad and glowing. He was stronger than she, more surefooted. Even though his boots slid and slipped on the rotting bark, he closed the gap with terrifying swiftness. Lunging, he grabbed for her ankle. She kicked wildly and he lost his grip, sliding down a little.

"Bitch!"

The dogs grew wilder, anticipating blood.

He lunged again. Branches hung helter-skelter in dead limbs. Risking a fall, Jericho let go of the trunk with one scratched bloody hand and grabbed at a dead branch. Dead wood, it snapped off. Exhausted, using the stick for a club, she gathered every ounce of her dwindling energy and bashed the stick into his upturned face. He lost his hold and slid. She abandoned the stick and inched upward again.

"You bitch, you damnable she-bastard bitch," he howled, clutching his eye. The dogs barked in frenzy, howling, leaping, teeth bared, vicious snouts upturned. She could smell their wet musky fur. They smelled feral, like wolves.

The duke sprang up the tree trunk again, shaking it violently. Jericho cried out 'n fear and hung on. This time, the duke drew his sword. He stabbed at her.

"Whore-daughter!"

Jericho kicked wildly, kicking her legs away from the

flashing steel. But he got her. She shrieked in pain as steel pierced her calf. Hanging on with one arm, she grabbed at the wound, trying to staunch the blood with her fingers as it flowed. But some of it dripped down to the ground. She watched in terror as the dogs sniffed her blood and now went truly wild. Snarling like mad beasts, they threw themselves into the air with grotesque leaps, frenzied, trying to get at her. She grew faint. She clutched her wound, then clawed at the trunk, climbing.

The duke lunged at her again. He missed. But his stabbing movements had shaken the tree trunk loose in its precarious cradle. With a lurch the tree slid down a notch. The dogs went into a frenzy. Jericho clutched the violently rocking tree trunk and held on, but the duke slid all the way down to the roots. With an angry leap, he sprang to the ground.

He stood under her, his eyes burning excitedly, his dogs encircling him, prowling around him, excited, snarling at her, baring their fangs, eager for the kill.

"I've got you now, you de Mont spawn. I've only to shake you out of the tree and let the dogs have you. Are you ready, you whore-daughter? Ready to die?"

She had only a moment to think. Thoughts flew wildly through her head. Die? She couldn't! She had so much to lose. She had a mother now. A father. And Dove. She couldn't die. She couldn't die and leave Dove. Frozen in terror, she looked down at the duke, the dogs. Save yourself!

She tore her fingers from her bloody wound. The blood welled up. She kicked out her leg and let the blood splatter down on the duke. It took him by surprise, dripping on him like a red shower. The wolfhounds stopped circling. They sniffed. Their shaggy snouts quivered. Their hackles rose. They crouched.

"No!" the duke screamed, backing away, throwing up his arms in a shield. The first snarling gray form sprang. "No —no!" he shrieked. The others were upon him instantly, taking him down, a dog pack in frenzy, growling, snarling, tearing, ripping, their shaggy maws bright with blood.

Unable to watch, Jericho clutched her wound and buried her face in the rough bark, sobbing, choking, crying, praying.

"Stop, stop, stop. Oh, dear God, make them stop."

It was horrible, horrible. The sounds. His death scream. The ferocious snarling as the dogs tore him to bits, then turned on one another, maws wet and scarlet, to fight over what they'd killed.

In the midst of the frenzy, there came a faint shout.

"Jerichooo . . ."

Lost in fog, the shout came again.

"Jerichooo . . ."

Dazed, she lifted her head. She tore her hand from her wound. The bleeding had slowed. She raked her muddy stringy hair from her ear with a bloody hand and listened. Dove? She raised up.

"Dove," she shrieked. "Go back. It's dogs. They've killed the duke. Go back!"

But he didn't. His answering shouts came bounding toward her through the fog, growing louder.

"Jericho—answer me—where are you—" he shouted.

"In a tree," she shrieked. "Safe in a tree. I'm safe. Dove, go back. Go away. It's dogs."

"Hang on—don't fall—I'm coming—" His voice rang in the fog, ever louder.

"No, Dove, no," she screamed. "Go back."

But suddenly he burst out of the fog, running. He ran to the base of the tree, to the mountain of tangled roots, his sword drawn, his face whiter than the white shirt he wore. Across the clearing, not twenty feet away, the dogs had dragged the duke's body under a bush and were mauling it, rending it. She saw Dove's terror and cried out again.

"Dove, go back! Save yourself."

He shot her a terrified look. For a moment, his eyes were the eyes of a three-year-old child, watching his beloved father being torn to pieces—naked eyes, overwhelmed, bright with fear. He shot a look at the frenzied dog pack and reeled, as if he might faint. His sword arm dropped limply.

"Dove!" Frantic, she shinnied down the tree limb, slipping, the rough bark scraping her shins raw, reopening her wound. "Dove!"

Maws scarlet with blood, the lead wolfhound whipped

around and saw Dove. He crouched, teeth bared, hackles rising on his powerful neck like spikes. Stiff-legged as a wolf, he stalked toward Dove.

Jericho slid to the ground. She grabbed the only thing that lay there, the stick she'd used on the duke. Panting, sobbing, she flourished the stick like a broom and took her stand in front of Dove, who'd gone limp and ashen. But an instant later, she found herself rolling in the mud behind him. He'd shoved her so hard she rolled ten feet before a tree trunk struck her in the ribs and stopped her.

"For God's sake," Dove complained, "stay out of my way."

She crawled to her knees and pushed her muddy hair out of her eyes just in time to see the beast crouch and leap.

"Dove," she gasped.

But it was all over in seconds. For Dove was a swordsman. As the beast leaped, Dove lunged to one side and hove his sword like an axe. Jericho heard the spine crack with a sickening sound. The beast dropped in midleap, landing on the ground with a thud, writhing there, yelping. Dove whirled and got the second springing beast, decapitating it with a single stroke. Blood sprayed everywhere, like scarlet mist. He didn't wait for the third beast to spring, but lunged toward it, throwing it off-stride. Off balance, the wolfhound writhed in midair, baring its soft underbelly. Dove thrust his sword in to the hilt. The beast hit the ground with a thud. With a fierce slash, Dove severed its throat and whirled to face the fourth beast. But the dog backed off timidly, backed away whimpering, then wheeled and fled like the wind, escaping into the fen. Whirling to deal with the remaining beast that still writhed on the ground, its back broken, Dove plunged his sword into its heart.

Then, gasping for breath, he propped himself against the uprooted tree, eyes closed, face ashen, sword arm limp. Jericho crawled toward him and lurched into his arms, breathing as hard as he. Holding his sword in his right hand, ready, he clamped her in his left arm. As if in unison, their knees buckled and they sank to the ground, clutching each other, patting each other, panting.

The fog was lifting. Night was descending. They could hear shouts in the distance, men's voices. With the fog drifting away, pinpoints of torchlight began to appear, like meandering lightning bugs.

Drained of emotion, at the end of her tether, Jericho began to cry. Dove held her close, sour muddy hair and all.

"It's all right, it's all right now," he panted.

"I kn-know."

"That was—the bravest—and the stupidest—thing I ever saw. Did you really intend—to defend me with—that puny stick?"

"I d-don't know."

She felt his lips smile weakly against her forehead. Then Dove pulled free of her, crawled into the marsh grass and vomited his stomach out. When he crawled back, he was sick, trembling. They clutched each other, held each other.

"Blackpool killed my father. With dogs. I remember the whole thing. I remember."

She nodded, so exhausted, she couldn't lift her head.

"I know. He boasted of it, Dove. He boasted to me."

"But *why*? Why would he do such a thing? My father . . ."

"He wanted your mother. He wanted Arleigh Castle."

"Oh, God, God. He was mad. Mother never would've had him. Never. She despised him."

Weak, spent, smelling of mud and vomit, they held each other for a long time, cheek against cheek, not caring how bad they smelled. Somewhere in the distance, men had cornered the remaining wolfhound. The excitement in their distant shouts said so. Muskets cracked. There was a yelp. Cheers rose. Jericho trembled and buried her face in the hollow of Dove's neck. He stroked her muddy hair with a weak hand.

"His dogs. Why did they turn on him, grubworm?"

She knuckled her eyes, trying to rub out the memory. "I was up in the tree. He was standing beneath the tree. He'd stabbed me with his sword and I was bleeding, so I held out my leg and let the blood drip on him."

"Stabbed you?" Dove straightened. "Where!"

She showed him. Encrusted with mud and dried blood, the wound oozed slightly. Dove sprang up. Wrenching off his leather doublet, he used it as a makeshift basin and hastily brought marsh water. He rinsed the cut gently. Jericho tried not to flinch, but the pain was starting, the shock wearing away. Then he tore off his shirt and ripped it. He used part of the shirt to bind her wound, then bundled her into what remained of it.

"Can you walk?"

"Yes. Of course I can." Taking the first step, she proved herself a liar and went down as if her knees were made of melted butter. Dove caught her. Scooping her up into his arms, he smiled softly into her face.

"Spoken like a true de Mont."

Despite the pain that was shooting through her leg, despite the woosiness and the odd buzzing that had begun in her ears, she smiled woosily back.

"Dove? La-lady Angelina is my mother. Lord Au-Au-Aubrey is my . . . father. That-that makes you and me . . ." She couldn't think. The trees were spinning now, whirling around her like Mid-Summer's Eve dancers. A hornet's nest buzzed loudly in her ears. Dove had two heads now. Both of them were smiling at her.

"Cousins," he supplied. "I won't pretend to understand this. But, welcome into the family, grubworm."

"Th-thank you, Dove."

And then a queer thing happened.

To her surprise, she . . . fainted.

Chapter Twenty-Five

Jericho awoke on her parents' wedding day feeling queasy, green around the gills. When she rose up on one elbow in her curtained bedstead in her second floor bedchamber in

Nordham Hall, her stomach rose with her. Hastily, she lay back. She closed her eyes and let the nausea roll over her in sickening waves.

Again? She swallowed the prickly juices that gathered unpleasantly under her tongue. The same thing had happened the previous morning. And the morning before that. Am I sick? It's not like me to be sick. I'm never sick. Not even in the worst New Amsterdam winter. I'm so healthy I never even catch cold.

Swallowing, resisting, her eyes closed, she heard the quiet sound of the bedchamber door opening. She heard her chambermaid tiptoe to the bed. The bedcurtain rings clicked as the girl quietly drew the bedcurtains to the bottom of the bed.

"Lady Jericho?" she whispered. "D'ye be wantin' yer morning tray now?"

Food. A horrid thought. Jericho opened her eyes a slit. Big eager blue eyes beamed back at her. "Not yet. I'll lie abed for a bit."

"Then I'll build up the fire for you, m'lady. Git the room cozy 'n warm for when you rise, m'lady."

"Don't bother. I'll do it myself later." Jericho wanted only peace and quiet.

The girl blinked in shock. "Oh, ye mustn't do that, m'lady. 'Tis servant's work. 'Tis *my* work," the girl said proudly.

Jericho smiled gently at the child. She was only twelve years old. Keen, eager to please. She reminded Jericho of herself at that age, new to Dove's household, desperate to belong, desperate to please.

"You're an excellent chambermaid, Mary. I've never in my life known a better. Yes, please. Make the fire."

The girl's smile lit up the room. She bobbed in curtsy.

The fire soon blazed and warmth sprang into the room. The sweetish smell of hickory firewood stirred more nausea. Swallowing, she sent her thoughts elsewhere.

My lady. Lady Jericho. Would she ever get used to it? She didn't feel like a lady yet. She felt as if she ought to jump out of bed and go down to the scullery to help cook the food for the duke of Nordham's wedding feast. She smiled at the notion. She wasn't a scullery maid, she was the duke of Nordham's daughter, the duchess of Blackpool's daughter.

She had a father and a mother. She belonged to them and they belonged to her.

The wave of nausea came again. Resting a limp wrist on her closed eyes, she rode it out.

"Can I git ye anything else, Lady Jericho?" The girl hovered, eager, wanting to be of use.

"Yes. I want . . . my mother."

"Yes, m'lady." The girl curtsied and flew from the room, pulling the door shut behind her.

My mother. How good it felt to say that. How beautifully and wonderfully good. Fighting queasiness, she strove to think of something else besides her stomach. She let her mind drift over the events of the past two weeks. For a moment, as the memory of the duke of Blackpool came back, her heart pounded. She thrust the memory away. The duke of Blackpool was dead. He couldn't hurt her. Not ever again. And he couldn't hurt Mother, either.

Nor could Fox Hazlitt. He was dead, too. Not by Mother's hand, thank God; Angelina's nature was too delicate to bear such a thing. Angelina had wounded Hazlitt severely. But she hadn't killed him. It had been Lord Lark and Leonardo d'Orias who'd gone back that night and finished him with a sword thrust.

Her thoughts drifted back. After she'd fainted in Dove's arms in Blackpool marsh, she'd come to in Lord Aubrey's strong arms. Woozy with blood loss, she'd fainted again, but not before she'd glimpsed his worried smile and heard him murmur, "Daughter."

When next she regained consciousness, she'd found herself in bed in Nordham Hall, a worried Lord Aubrey holding her right hand, a fretting Angelina holding her left. She'd smiled and had drifted down into a peaceful sleep that had seemed to last days.

People had flocked to Nordham Hall during her recuperation. Mrs. Phipps had come at once. Lady de Mont, Leonardo d'Orias, Lord Lark and Lord Raven had come. John had come. Marguerite had come—but not to visit Jericho. To visit her sister, Angelina.

Dove had come to Nordham Hall several times, but her father had refused him entry. In a livid temper, Lord Aubrey had sent his beloved nephew packing. He was furious with Dove. He put the blame for everything that had happened to her squarely on Dove. He'd threatened to horsewhip Dove if he ever came near her again.

Jericho had been heartbroken. But she'd also gloried in having a father, a father who told "his daughter" exactly what she could and could not do. Told her? Not "told." Ordered, commanded, exhorted, counseled, preached, advised. Lord Aubrey had crammed twenty years of fathering into the past two weeks, and though Jericho was certain she was being fathered to death and would drop dead any day, she adored him for it.

The door was flung inward. Jericho opened her eyes. Angelina came rushing in, silk nightrobe rustling, her dark lovely hair still disheveled from sleep. "Darling, what is it? The girl says you're ill. What's wrong? Is it your leg? Your cut?"

Jericho shook her head on the pillow. "My leg is fine, Mother. It's only a touch of indigestion."

"Indigestion!" Picking up the skirts of her silk robe, she rushed across the room, stepped up on the bed stair and settled herself on the bed. She put a cool hand on Jericho's brow, testing. How wonderful it was to be mothered.

"There's no fever, darling."

"I know. Please don't worry. The queasiness will pass in an hour or two. I won't miss your wedding."

Two vertical worry lines formed in the center of Angelina's smooth lovely brow. " 'Pass'? What do you mean, darling, 'it will pass in an hour or two'?"

"The queasiness passed yesterday morning. And the morning before. And the morning before that."

The vertical lines vanished. Angelina's lovely dark eyebrows shot upward and her eyes widened. "Has there been anything else? Faintness, perhaps? Dizzy spells? Aversion to certain foods?"

Jericho lifted her head in surprise.

"How—how did you know?"

"Oh, my goodness." Angelina took a deep breath. "Jericho. This is important. When did you last have your woman's flow?"

Startled, Jericho rose up on one elbow. A dim awareness

of what it was began to stir in her, filtering in, stealing in. She felt vaguely scared, alarmed.

"I've lost track of it. So much has happened in the past two months. The London fire. Blackpool Castle. But I *must* have had it last month or the month before—" It hit her like a lightning bolt. She looked at Angelina with scared eyes, then quickly looked away, her face heating in shame.

Just then, a loud demanding knock sounded at the door. Lord Aubrey poked his head in. His hair was disheveled, too, and he was still tying the velvet cord of his robe. "Have you sent for the physician, Angelina?" he demanded. "If my daughter's sick, I want a physician. I want one at once."

Angelina got up and swept to the door in a rustle of silk, placed her small, firm palms on Lord Aubrey's broad chest and backed him out of the room. "She doesn't need a physician, Aubrey." She looked like a slender lily pushing a tree.

When her mother returned and sat on the bed, Jericho couldn't meet her eyes. She was too ashamed, too filled with guilt. But Angelina calmly reached out, took Jericho's hands and held them firmly but gently in her silken lap.

"Jericho," she said sternly. "It is high time you and I had a long—and completely honest—talk about Dove."

Jericho's parents were wed at noon in the tiny Catholic chapel on the third floor of Nordham Hall. Because they wished it so, the ceremony was private. But Jericho couldn't have been more thrilled if it had been a rich splendid ceremony in Westminster Abbey. How wonderful her parents were, as they said their vows before the priest. Kneeling in a handsome silk suit, his broad soldierly back straight and proud, her father spoke his vows in a strong sure voice and his eyes never once left Angelina's.

Angelina? She repeated her vows with happy pride. Garbed in rose silk and Flemish lace, she had never looked lovelier. Watching her mother, Jericho remembered their morning talk. It had been a frank, intimate talk. Jericho had poured out her heart, and Angelina had listened tenderly. They talked of Marguerite. In Angelina's opinion, Marguerite was fond of Dove, but not deeply in love with him. It was also her opinion Dove was not in love with Marguerite. It was willfulness that made him want her.

"Tell him about the baby, darling."

"No." Jericho had shaken her head, stubborn, adamant. She didn't want Dove to wed her out of necessity, because he'd gotten her with child. If he wed her and not Marguerite, she wanted it to be for only one reason—love.

They'd talked for a long time and Angelina had given Jericho stern advice. Its wisdom had pierced her to the core:

"You are *not* a bondslave. You are the daughter of a duke, the daughter of a duchess. And Dove had best learn that. If you ever again permit Dove to treat you like a bondslave, you will be a bondslave in his eyes forever. Even if he marries you."

They'd talked so long and so lovingly that all sense of time had fled until Lord Aubrey, dressed in his wedding clothes and plainly provoked, stuck his head in the door with a querulous complaint.

"Isn't anyone here interested in a wedding?"

As the priest pronounced the benediction, Jericho glanced up from her wool-gathering. Pronounced man and wife, her parents rose from their knees and kissed. Then they turned, radiant with joy, and Jericho flew into their arms. They kissed and hugged. She and Angelina shed a few happy tears, and even Lord Aubrey's eyes grew suspiciously moist.

Then, arms around each other, a staunch family of three, they were heading down the corridor to a private wedding dinner in Angelina's withdrawing chamber when a manservant came hurrying up to Lord Aubrey.

"Your Grace? Lord Dove is downstairs in the entry hall. He requests your permission to speak with Lady Jericho."

Jericho's heart jumped. She threw a scared, hopeful look at Angelina. Lord Aubrey's happy mood died. His temper flared.

"Oh, does he! Well, you may tell my nephew to leave this house at once. Tell him I refuse to allow my daughter—"

Jericho didn't wait to hear more. Giving her father a quick apologetic kiss on the cheek, she broke away and ran, scared to linger a moment longer. If she lingered and heard him forbid her, she would be obliged to obey. She picked up her skirts and flew.

"Jericho," he called after her in annoyance.

Angelina watched her beautiful daughter go, then sighed and turned to cope with Aubrey.

"What is she doing!" he demanded.

"I would guess she is running so that she cannot hear you forbid her. She doesn't want to disobey you, Aubrey. But she wants very much to see the man she loves."

"You mean Dove?"

"Who else?"

His temper flared afresh. "I'll horsewhip him. I warned him to stay away from her. By Judas——" Riled, he took an angry step in that direction, but Angelina caught his silk sleeve.

"Aubrey. Dove can no more stay away from Jericho than—than *you* could stay away from *me* when we were young."

The truth of it arrested him for a moment. He glanced at her in startled chagrin, but flared again. "I won't have Dove toying with my daughter!"

"Nor will I," Angelina agreed firmly. "Nor will Jericho allow it anymore. We had a very long, very serious talk today. About something extremely important."

His curiosity piqued, he lost his angry color and frowned down at her. "About what?"

"Now darling, be calm. She is with child. By Dove."

"With *child*," Aubrey thundered.

"Hush, my love, please. Hush, hush, the servants . . ."

Aubrey took a raw gulp of air, his color growing as red as his hair. "I'll kill him. I won't horsewhip him, Angelina, I'll kill him."

"No, you will not." Angelina took a firm grip on his arm and tugged him along in the opposite direction. "You dote on Dove. You know you do. You love him best of all your nephews."

He jerked around, and Angelina had to recapture his arm.

"That fornicating puppy! If he's quickened my daughter, by God, he's going to marry her. I'll *make* him marry her, or I'll have his head on a platter. The betrothal to Marguerite will have to be broken, Angelina. No matter the cost. By God!" Heated, he swung around again. A soldier, he needed action. Angelina understood that, and clung to his arm like an anchor. She tugged him back in the opposite direction, tugging him along. It was like tugging a granite boulder.

"And what would that accomplish? Think, my love. What would you gain? Would you have our daughter suffer humiliation, knowing Dove was *forced* to marry her?"

Flushing in anger, he had no answer but a soldier's answer.

"By God, he'll have her whether he wants her or not!"

"Aubrey. Listen to me. Listen. Think of our daughter."

"I *am* thinking of her. I won't have my daughter treated like a common wench. I should've kicked his backside all over the Thames after the London fire. No doubt he slept with her then. And with a bride-to-be waiting for him at Arleigh Castle. By Judas, I'll kill him!"

As he wheeled around again, determined to deal with Dove, Angelina leaped in front of him and calmly rested her palms on his hot heaving chest. His vivid blue eyes were so angry they shot sparks. She tugged at his silk lapels.

"Aubrey. Listen to me. Jericho is a woman. A woman needs to know her husband married her out of affection and not simply because he got her with child. Jericho wants Dove to wed her for love. For love, Aubrey, *love*. In the end, love is the only important reason. Love, Aubrey . . ."

Agitated, his soldier's mind set, he ground his jaw. But at least he listened. The outrage in his flushed face lessened.

"Aubrey. Our daughter is a brave intelligent young woman. Let her handle this. Please?" she begged softly. "Please, Aubrey?"

A muscle in his jaw convulsed uncertainly. When the anger in his face softened to uncertain irritation, she knew she'd won and drew a breath of relief. He sent a final, fierce look down the corridor, but made no move to follow it.

Relieved, she slipped her hands under his silk lapels.

"Now, my love. This is our wedding day. On our wedding day, can you not think of anything more interesting to do than scold your beloved daughter and horsewhip the nephew you adore?"

For a moment he said nothing. Then, the corners of his handsome mouth twitched. A faint glimmer of humor twinkled in his eyes.

"I think I can," he murmured. "I think I can . . ."

"And what might that be, my lord?"

"Wench." Scooping her up in his arms, he kissed her soundly and carried her down the corridor, straight to his bedchamber.

Nordham Hall's square center staircase descended to the entry hall in a series of broad landings and short flights of stairs. Jericho flew down the first flight with scared eager steps, her jade green gown brushing the bannister, silk rustling. Descending to the next landing, she reined herself in. Dear life, she wasn't eleven years old!

Descending to still another landing, she remembered Angelina's wise advice, and she slowed down. She wasn't a bondslave. She was the daughter of a duke, the daughter of a duchess. She needn't lay her heart at any man's feet. Not even Dove's.

Scared at the enormity of the thought, but determined to preserve her self-respect, she held her head high and forced herself to descend the final flight of stairs at a slow, leisurely pace.

Waiting downstairs in the oak-paneled entry hall, Dove paced and stewed. He'd been stewing and pacing for the past two weeks. Ever since Blackpool marsh. He'd asked himself questions by the cartload. And all of the answers had come out the same: Jericho.

When he heard steps on the staircase, he eagerly swung around. For one startled instant, he didn't recognize her. For what he glimpsed coming down the stairs was a regal beauty—a young woman so stunning she might've belonged to Queen Catherine's court. He picked his chin up off the floor and gaped some more.

She—Jericho!—came drifting down the stairs with leisurely indifference. As if it didn't matter that he was waiting! Stunned afresh, he gaped at what she wore. Silk and a low cut bodice. Bosom, for God's sake! When he could tear his eyes away from her creamy, freckled breasts, he hastily gave her a once-over. She wore her hair in a new way, combed back and tumbling richly to her bare shoulders. Her rich red hair exquisitely framed all of that—that—that bosom.

Dove felt suddenly unsure of himself. Hell, he'd come to tell her he'd decided to marry her. He'd come to tell her he was going to get down off his high horse and wed her. He'd come to tell her he'd decided to give her what she'd always wanted: himself, legally shackled to her in matrimony.

Suddenly, that approach didn't seem wise. As she stepped down into the entry hall in a rustle of silk, he marshalled what was left of his scattered wits. Bosom, for God's sake!

"Hello, Dove," she said calmly. *Calmly.* Wasn't she excited to see him? The grubworm he used to know in New Amsterdam had come running like a rabid squirrel every time he stepped in his door. He felt flustered. A new feeling. He didn't like it.

"I want to talk to you, Jericho. In private."

"Certainly. The winter parlor?"

He stared at her, stunned, as she went past him in a drift of rippling silk. "Certainly. The winter parlor?" What the hell sort of response was that? She reminded him of Marguerite! Had her hips always twitched that way when she walked? With so damned much confidence?

As he leaped after her, an unwelcome thought jarred. Maybe the rumors were true. Maybe suitors *were* swarming to Nordham Hall like bees to a honey pot. Aubrey was rich, Angelina was rich. Jericho was an *heiress*.

Hell! She hadn't gone and fallen in love with one of those goddamned fortune seekers, had she? For the first time in his life, he felt unsure of himself. He hated the feeling. It made him cranky. The more confidently her high heels clicked in the corridor, the crankier he got.

* * *

Confidence? Jericho wasn't feeling a shred of it. Inside, her heart was pounding like a child's. Why had he come? Did he love her? Why wasn't he at Arleigh Castle with Marguerite?

Scared to hope, she clipped briskly into the winter parlor. Intuition, a sixth sense, told her this would be a crucial visit. It would be, and Angelina was right. If she let Dove treat her like a doormat, she would be a doormat for him the rest of her life.

Briskly, she went to the warm crackling fire, turned and linked her shaking hands behind her back, out of sight. Dove followed her in and banged the door shut. Her heart sank. He was going to be cranky. Well, she thought, rallying, talking to her baby, your father is not the only person in the world who can be cranky. *I* can be cranky too.

In his lightning-quick way, Dove swept the parlor with a glance. Ignoring the changes in the room, he swung toward her. He was in a vile temper, but trying to hide it. She knew Dove, knew every one of his temperamental signs. She waited warily.

"So, Jericho! It seems we are cousins." A cranky pleasantry.

"So it seems, Dove."

"We are of equal rank now."

Equal rank? If she let him get away with this, if she let him take an inch he would grab a mile.

"Not quite. You are the son of an earl and a countess, but I am the daughter of a duke and a duchess. I fear I outrank you, Dove." Had she said that? Dear life!

Dove flushed bright red. Standing balanced on one hip, his bright golden hair sweeping his shoulders, he tapped a toe and winged a tentative look out the tall parlor windows, out at the bleak November countryside.

"I don't need this, Jericho," he snapped. Wheeling, he headed for the door.

Jericho panicked. "But it doesn't matter, Dove," she offered quickly. "Rank doesn't matter. Rank doesn't matter at all. Truly, Dove, it doesn't matter at all. Truly, Dove, truly."

He rested a hand on the doorlatch and sent her a withering look. "You're quite sure I needn't bow? Kiss your hand and call you *Lady* Jericho?"

Flustered, she stumbled all over her tongue, eager to make amends. "Dove? I'm so glad to see you. I'm so happy to see you. Truly, I am. I've thought about you every minute of every day. I wanted to see you so badly. I wanted to thank you for saving me in Blackpool marsh. I wanted to tell you how brave you were, facing those monstrous dogs. I know what it cost you to do that. I know how frightened you must've been, but you came anyway, you came to save me." She ran out of breath. "Dove? How are you? How are you, how have you been?"

"I've been just fine," he snapped.

She didn't want to be his doormat, but she didn't want to be his superior, either. What she wanted was to take her place at his side, as his wife, as his trusted comrade, his best friend.

In his changeable way, his cranky mood lifted a little, and he suddenly looked at her with bright, worried eyes. "What about you? Your leg is healed, isn't it?"

She smiled to assure him. "My leg is fine, Dove. There's a scar. There'll always be a scar. But a scar on the leg doesn't matter. A scar on the leg doesn't show. I suppose if-if-if-if a man wanted to marry me, it-it-it might be a different matter. A hus-husband might mind. About the scar." She gave him a scared look.

"Hell, no," he put in quickly, his eyes bright. "No, a husband wouldn't mind a bit. A scar on a leg wouldn't matter. Not to a husband. Not a bit."

It was such a wonderful thing to say that Jericho's heart began to pound. She waited for him to say more, but he flushed suddenly, which was peculiar for Dove. Oddly tongue-tied, he looked away. Aimless, he prowled the room, looking at things, touching things, picking up this and that, as if Angelina's refurbished parlor were suddenly of intense interest to him.

She felt suddenly tongue-tied, too. It was a strange way

to feel with Dove. One thing she and Dove had always shared easily was talk. The uncomfortable silence lengthened unbearably. Outside, the cold November rain drizzled down. On the hearth, the fire crackled and popped. From the downstairs kitchen came the faint, happy sounds of servant merriment, the servants enjoying their wedding feast.

He glanced at her with bright eyes. "Marguerite is going back to France. She decided this morning."

Jericho's heart stopped. Going back to France? What did it mean? She didn't know whether to rejoice or grieve. Was Dove going, too?

"She . . . broke our betrothal this morning. She said she . . ." Roaming the room in a self-conscious, restless way, he lifted the edge of a gilded leather wall hanging, peered at it, then let it slap back against the wall. "She . . . decided we weren't suited after all."

"She-she-she did?" Jericho's heart began a slow upward pounding.

He threw her an annoyed look. "Is that all you can say about it? Just 'she-she-she did'?"

Jericho touched her flushed cheeks with the backs of her hands to calm herself.

"I mean, Marguerite must be very upset."

He shrugged. "How upset can you be, returning to France with a betrothal settlement of fifty thousand pounds in your purse? Besides . . ." He became very busy examining a figurine. His voice fell. "It seems there's been . . . someone else all along. Someone waiting in the wings. A titled but penniless Frenchman. Well, he won't be penniless now, not with my fifty thousand pounds."

"Dove, I'm sorry."

He squinted at her. "You're *sorry*?"

"Well, no. Marguerite wasn't right for you, Dove. She is a fine lady." A lie. "And-and she loved you with all her heart." Another lie. "But not half as much as-as-as-as-as— you deserve to be loved."

"I'm not sorry!" he said. "Hell, I'm only sorry I'm fifty thousand pounds out of pocket." He continued his prowl of the room, picking up objects, setting them down. She waited, breathless.

"I suppose I could marry someone else . . ."

"Yes, you could, Dove, you could, you could. And-and-and I think you should. You should marry. A man should marry. Every man should settle down and marry. And-and-and-and have *children*."

"But, hell, with my fortune wiped out, I can't marry. I couldn't, in good conscience, ask a woman to share nothing."

"Yes you could, yes you could," she argued breathlessly. "You could. A woman wouldn't mind, Dove. She wouldn't mind at all. If she loved you, a woman wouldn't mind if you didn't have a penny."

He banged down a porcelain figurine he'd picked up and glared at her. "For God's sake, I'm not destitute! I've got my investments in New Amsterdam and in the Caribbean. I'm not reduced to eating gruel and dandelion greens."

"No, no, of course not," she agreed carefully, waiting.

With those bright hazel eyes he shot her a look that was as belligerant and vulnerable as a little boy's dame-school look. Eager to be loved and admired by the teacher, but ashamed to admit to such unmanly needs.

"Cousins sometimes marry," he said crossly.

"Yes, yes, they do, Dove, they do, cousins sometimes marry, cousins do. They do. Cousins do."

"But *not*," he said, continuing his prowl of the room, "in the Roman Catholic church."

Her heart sank to her feet. "Oh."

He glanced at her, his eyes bright. "Unless, of course, a dispensation can be obtained from Rome."

"Is-is-is a dispensation diff-difficult to obtain?" She was getting dizzy, her heart constantly stopping and starting like this. She rested a protective hand on her waist, on her baby.

He shrugged without interest. "It's not difficult at all. Hell, send a tub of money to Rome and you can get anything."

She waited, breathless, praying. *Dove, ask me to marry you. Ask me. Ask us, ask me and your baby.*

He gazed at her with those bright, intense eyes, opened his mouth to speak, then shut it, opened it, shut it. Plainly in a quandary, he raked a jeweled hand through his thick golden hair and resumed his prowl. A flush crept up his tanned throat. Jericho braced her hands on the gilded edge of Angelina's settee. Suddenly, Dove wheeled around and gave her the crankiest look yet.

"Hell's bells, Jericho! If you think I'm going to stand here and court my own bondslave, you'd better think again."

"Dove, I'm not a bondslave."

"It's damned embarrassing. It's downright humiliating. Do you know how humiliating it is for a man to wake up one morning and discover he's in love with his own bondslave? His *bondslave*, for God's sake? And worse, to suddenly realize he's probably been half in love with her from the start, back when she was a scrawny brat, giving him arrowheads? Do you know how damned embarrassing that is? Do you?" he demanded.

In love with her! She felt lightheaded. Dove was in love with her. And he had been from the very first. It had never been Mrs. Verplanck. It had never even been Marguerite. It had been *her*—Jericho, Pansy Eyes, grubworm. She wanted to soar, fly.

But somehow, she managed, "Dove, I'm not a bondslave."

"Hell, when I tell Raven and Lark I'm marrying my own bondslave, they'll laugh their heads off. And my friends will laugh."

"Dove, I'm not a bondslave."

He gestured. "And when Whitehall Palace gets wind of this? Lord Dove de Mont marrying his *bondslave*? I'll be the joke of the court. I can already hear Castlemayne and Nell Gwynne giggling. I can already hear the king laughing."

"Dove, I'm not a bondslave." Her temper was rising.

He didn't even hear. But, having vented his own temper, his mood changed and he came bounding across the room with a sweet smile and took her into his arms.

"Get into warm clothes, sweeting. Aubrey or no Aubrey, I'm taking you to Arleigh Castle. We'll be married today. If the priest won't marry us, we'll marry by Protestant clergy, then marry again, Catholic, when the dispensation arrives."

"Dove, I'm not a bondslave."

"In the meantime, I'll deal with Uncle Aubrey. He's got no right to keep you from me. He might be your father, but, hell! You belonged to me long before you belonged to him. I won you at dice, and that's more than he can say for himself. You belong to me. Now get dressed, beauty." He kissed her. "Can't you see I love you? Can't you see I want you with me for the rest of my life?"

It took every ounce of Jericho's willpower to resist that sweet, bullying speech. But she managed it.

"Dove, I am not a bondslave."

"Yes, yes." Humoring her, he brushed the argument away.

"And you did not yet *ask* me to marry you."

That stopped him in his tracks. "Ask?" He blinked, his handsome mouth lax. "What do you mean, 'ask'?"

"Just that, Dove. When you betrothed yourself to Lady Marguerite, you didn't just *tell* her you were going to marry her, did you?"

"Well, of course not," he said, affronted, his smooth, tanned brow crinkling in annoyance. "I asked her."

"That's what I want. I want to be asked."

He breathed through his mouth for long moments.

"Jericho, don't be ridiculous."

"I'm not ridiculous."

"You are. Jericho, you're vexing me!"

She was a woman in love. But she was also a woman who'd learned to value herself. And if the man she loved didn't value her now, at the very moment of proposal, he never would. If she let him order her about, treat her like a lackey, she would be a lackey in his eyes forever.

"Thank you, Dove, for your kind offer of marriage. I truly appreciate it and I will think about it."

His mouth fell open. "Think about it? What the hell is there to think about? You've wanted to marry me ever since you were a snot-nosed little brat of eleven. Hell's bells, in New Amsterdam you went tooting all over the settlement with your fat friend, Martha, embarrassing me——"

"Maritje."

"——telling everyone—telling God, the whole world and all the fish at sea—that you were betrothed to me. *Betrothed*, for God's sake. I wanted to break your neck."

"Nevertheless, I want to think about it."

Her heart pounded. Denying Dove was the hardest, most frightening thing she'd ever had to do in her life.

He stared at her in utter disbelief. Then, in his lightning quick way, his mood changed. She saw the enormous flash of hurt.

"Is it John?" he demanded. "It's John, isn't it?"

"No, Dove, no. It isn't John."

"Then it's someone Aubrey has picked out!"

"No, Dove, no. There's no one. Dove, I just want time to consider your offer. Give me a week."

A week? She would die waiting a week. She longed to marry now, right this minute. The priest was still in the house. She longed to throw herself into Dove's arms and shout: Dove! We're going to have a baby. Isn't it wonderful?

He gazed at her, stunned afresh, as if he'd never before considered that she might not want to marry him. Then, like a spoiled child, he covered his hurt feelings with curtness.

"Take all the time you want," he snapped. "Take a week, take a month, take a year. Hell, get back to me on the subject in a decade or two, if you want. *I'm* in no hurry! Hell, women are more bother than they're worth."

Wheeling, he strode for the door.

"Dove, I only want to be asked."

"I *asked*! You didn't listen."

He left, slamming the door behind him. The slam reverberated through the room, rattling alabaster eggs in a silver bowl, making a log collapse in the crackling fire.

"Dove," she whispered.

She pressed her lips together and wrung her hands. She fought the urge to run after him. But if she ran after him, what sort of marriage would it be, with Dove walking all over her? A one-sided marriage. No sort of marriage at all.

"We'll wait," she told her baby. "Don't worry!"

But Jericho did worry and couldn't wait. A week? She couldn't wait even two days. On the second day, she penned a loving letter to Dove and sent it by messenger to Arleigh Castle. Then she spent the day wringing her hands, waiting for Dove to come fetch her.

But he didn't come. Instead, to her bewilderment, the

messenger returned with her own unopened letter. He also brought an accompanying letter from Lady de Mont. Jericho broke the seal and frantically tore it open.

> *My dear Lady Jericho,*
> *I regret to tell you that Dove has left England. He has gone to the New World to oversee his investments in New Amsterdam, that is, in the New York. He expects to reside in the New York for the next two years. I trust this news is as puzzling and distressing to you as it is to me?*
>
> *In Warmest Friendship,*
> *Glynden d'Orias*

Dazed, Jericho looked up and stared blankly out the window at the bleak November drizzle. She had gambled. And lost.

Chapter Twenty-Six

Jericho nagged and badgered her father for three months before Lord Aubrey finally threw up his hands and gave her permission to sail.

So it was already a fine spring day in late May before John and Jericho sailed into New York harbor, and by then Jericho was so big with child that she had to cling to John for dear life as he helped her down the ship's gangplank. When they stepped onto the old familiar wharf, John threw her a teasing smile.

"I'll give you one last chance to say yes. I warn you, I won't ask again."

Jericho grinned back at him. "You're a worse liar than Dove. You don't want to marry a great-bellied woman. What's

Jo Ann Wendt

more, I don't believe you made this journey just for me. You've been itching to get back here ever since you heard that Lizzie is now a widow.''

John shrugged happily. "That. And I confess I'm eager to see Dove. I've missed that son-of-a-bitch.''

"So have I.''

John's mouth curved in amusement. "An understatement, if ever I did hear one.''

Smiling, she let her excited anxious gaze sweep the busy wharf, the bustling familiar settlement. New York! It was all so beloved. The smell of the pine forest. The screech of the windmill. The wolfheads grinning in neat tidy rows on cottage walls. There was even a Mohawk canoe on the river, traveling gunnel deep, loaded with spring furs.

Excited, she continued to smile until her back gave a sharp twinge. Then she gasped and slipped a supporting hand to the small of her back.

"Well, it's certain I had best marry somebody. And today. If this baby is to be born with a father.''

"Good lord. Are you starting?''

She nodded happily.

"Jericho, drat you! Whyn't you tell me?''

"Because,'' she said sensibly, "you would not have let me off the ship. Now, stop fussing. These are only preliminary twinges.''

"Preliminary! Jericho—''

Brushing his objections aside, she plowed across the wharf like a waddling fat lady and inquired of Lord Dove de Mont's whereabouts from the first porter she could buttonhole.

"You're a vexing woman, do you know that?'' John said a few minutes later, as he settled her on the sunny wooden step on the stoop of Dieter Ten Boom's old tap house.

She kissed his cheek. "Please, John? Do it my way?''

He sighed and with a long-suffering look trudged into the tap house. Jericho waited in excitement. Dice cups rattled. Skittles boards banged. Men whooped and hollered and crowed. She glanced down at the old wooden step she sat on and realized with a ripple of surprise that it was the same step she'd sat on, her very first day in New Amsterdam, ten years ago. The step was worn now, concave, shaped by a decade of men's boots tramping in and out of the tap house. She stroked it. The grain was smooth as silk. Baking in the spring sunshine, warmth rose from the wood. Memories rose, too.

When a Gabriel's horn blew mellowly, the lovely sound echoing upon the canal, announcing the cows' return from pasture outside the Wall, she had the strange feeling that time had whirled backwards, that she was eleven years old again, sitting on this step—tired, hungry, scared—wondering whom she would belong to when the noisy roistering games in the tap house came to an end. The memory was painful. And so vivid, that when she glanced up and saw a dog trotting toward her, she almost cried out.

Pax!

But it wasn't Pax. It was only a homely puppy. He had the neglected look of a stray—skinny, his coat matted. He halted and cocked his head at her. When her heart stopped pounding, she held out her hand. He came bounding happily and licked it. Tail swishing, he tried to lick her face.

"Don't you belong to anybody, boy? Well, you do now. If you want to, you can belong to *me*. I'll keep you. I promise. I promise I'll keep you forever."

Stepping into the tap house, John, too, felt the queer kick of *deja vu*. As if time had moved backwards. It was almost as if he were eighteen years old again, stepping into the tap house with Dove on their birthday, eager to celebrate the day with a stolen kiss in the kitchen. Lizzie didn't serve here anymore. This was Samuels's tap house. But everything else was the same.

He swept the ramshackle room with a glance and saw Dove at the far end of the room, sitting at table, playing cards. John smiled in begrudged amusement. The beloved son-of-a-bitch. As always, Dove was as impeccably groomed as a prince. His thick thatch of golden hair tumbled to his shoulders, catching the sunlight from the window and shining. His shirt was white linen, spotless and without wrinkle. He wore a gold and ruby ring on one tanned hand.

John started across the room. He was halfway there when Dove suddenly looked up. The bright hazel eyes flashed with surprise, then with wariness. The handsome mouth tightened. Closing his fanned cards, Dove set them down warily.

John halted, wary too. Unsure of what Dove was feeling, unsure of his own feelings. For an instant, John feared it was too late. Feared they'd waited too long to mend their torn fences. But it was Dove who'd always been quick to lose his temper, quicker to forgive, and it was Dove now who sprang first. Before John could take a step, Dove sprang out of his chair, came leaping across the room and embraced him.

They embraced roughly, awkwardly, the way men do when they love each other but are ashamed to show it. They thumped each other on the back, then gripped shoulders. Their eyes met in emotion. A lot of water had gone under the bridge. There was a lot that needed forgiving and forgetting. But the overriding emotion was love. They embraced roughly again.

"What news from England?" Dove demanded, sweeping him to his table and signaling the serving girl for beer. "Is —everyone well?"

John smiled at Dove's jerky pause. "Everyone" meant Jericho, of course. He could see it. Those bright hazel eyes shone with the urgent need to know. The other card players at the table cleared out, granting them privacy. When the beer came, they settled down to talk.

"Everyone's fine, Dove. Everyone you know and love's in the best of health." John deliberately ticked off Dove's relatives one by one, giving a slow account of each, giving the news. Dove fidgeted, hardly able to sit still for the recitation. He wanted news of Jericho. Savoring it, John made Dove wait, drawing out the news, then finally said:

"Jericho's fine, too."

Dove gripped his beer tankard so tightly John listened for the wood to splinter. Dove sent him a look fraught with emotion.

"Did you marry her?" he demanded belligerantly.

John chuckled and shook his head.

"No such luck. I asked, but she wouldn't have me."

Dove relaxed a little. "Then she's not married?"

"Nay," John said, eyeing him. "But she's fixin' to be."

He might as well have stabbed him. The reaction was the same. When Dove recovered, he looked up with bright eyes.

"Who to!"

John scratched his scalp. He loved Dove like a brother, but he wasn't above enjoying this. "Damn me. Why can't I remember the fellow's name? 'Tis on the tip of me tongue. Ah, well, I'll surely recall it by 'n by." He'd known Dove all his life, and he'd never seen him so upset. Dove stared at his beer foam as if he wanted to kill it.

"Is he titled?"

"Ay. An earl's son, I b'lieve."

Shocked, Dove's blank stare went back to his beer foam then came up again, twice as fierce. "The decent sort? Someone who will treat her well?"

John took a languid swallow of beer. "There's the rub. Lord Aubrey don't think much of him. He's a handsome devil. But if you want my opinion, he's a self-centered son-of-a-bitch who'll likely lead her a merry chase for the rest of her life."

"How could Uncle Aubrey approve someone like that!" Agitated, upset, Dove scalded the room with hot looks, as if looking for a fight, looking for someone to slit from stem to stern. John hid his smile in a sip of beer.

"He didn't. Lord Aubrey stands opposed to the match. But Jericho's in love with the fellow, and what do you know? She has gone and slept with him and got herself with child."

"With child!" Dove shot straight up from his chair. He stood, sat, stood, paced to the wall and back, then sat again and slumped. "I . . . never thought . . . she would sleep with anyone but me."

"Ah, well. Women are fickle creatures, and that's a fact. There's no accounting for what they will or won't do."

If John'd had any doubts about Dove's love for Jericho, he lost them now. The man who sat strangling his beer tankard was plainly heartbroken. John let him suffer a little longer. Dove had given Jericho plenty of grief. He ought to suffer. Just a little. But when several minutes had gone by and Dove still sat there in shock, John took pity on him.

"I wonder if you would do me a favor, Dove. There is a

bondslave I brought along on this sailing. I want her to have a good master, a good home. I wonder if you would do me a favor and buy her indenture, take her in, give her a home, keep her.''

''What?'' Dove looked up blankly, stunned by his loss. John bit back a smile, repeated the request, and when he did, Dove quickly shook his head.

''I can't, John. Hell, it would remind me too much of . . . of Jericho. I can't.''

John took a swallow of beer. ''Ay, I suppose that's so. Ay, she would. The wretch even looks a bit like Jericho. With all them freckles. With that flaming red witch's hair.''

Dove lifted his head, eyes bright, alert, hot.

''Ay, you're right, Dove. 'Twould hurt. It would. Even her eyes likely would remind you of Jericho. They're dark blue. As blue as pansies . . .''

Dove shot to his feet. His chair hit the floor with a crash. He was gone in a leap, springing across the room, leaping for the door, shoving gamesters aside right and left.

Jericho heard Dove coming. She knew his step, knew it as intimately as she knew her own heartbeat. She shoved the dog away and clutched her cloak shut. She didn't want to shock him with her belly. She held her breath, her heart pounding.

The tap-house door crashed open, jumping in its leather hinges and smashing into the wall, just the way it had done on a day in May, ten years earlier. The golden Dove sprang out on to the stoop. He saw her and drew an enormous breath. Jericho drew one, too.

Does he still love me? Does he still want me?

She got her answer a hundredfold. Dove's smile blazed with love. There was so much love shining in those bright jewellike eyes that she felt weak from it. Heart banging, lips trembling, she smiled back.

''Dove,'' she cried out, leaping up the stoop step and into his arms. ''Dove, marry me!''

''Jericho, you silly little grubworm.'' He crushed her in his arms and kissed her, and then, with a jubilant laugh, scooped her up in his arms and swung her.

"Dove," John shouted. "Open your eyes."

"Dove," she gasped, dizzy.

It was then Dove suddenly noticed her bulk, noticed how heavy she was in his arms. Startled, he set her down so fast she had to catch the porch rail.

"Dove!" John scolded.

Dove took a stunned step backwards and stared. Her cloak flaps had fallen back over her shoulder. "Holy Hannah," he said, "what in hell have you done to yourself, grubworm? Is all of that *you*?" He stared at her belly as if he'd never seen anything so big and huge in his life. As if she were big as a whale. Jericho felt herself growing vexed. It was his baby, too. Not just hers.

"No, Dove de Mont! Half of it is you. *You*."

He stared at her blankly. For possibly the first time in his lordly life, Lord Dove de Mont's mercurial, lightning-quick mind worked slow as a snail.

"You don't mean . . . Wattling Street?"

She shook her head happily. "No. Not Wattling Street. The second time. That night at the inn. After the fire."

"Oh, for God's sake."

His delight was unmistakable. Shining like a golden Dove, he glowed. He was glad. Glad there was to be a baby! Bursting with happiness, she scarcely had a moment to savor it when a pain slammed her in the back, hard as a pickax. She doubled over and clutched the porch rail. John and Dove jumped for her.

"Jericho!"

"Grubworm! Oh, for God's sake." Wild-eyed, panicking, Dove scooped her up in his arms and whirled this way and that, scared and bewildered and befuddled for the first time in his life.

"Hell! Don't just stand there," he roared at John. "*Do* something. I'm having a baby!"

Jericho became Lady de Mont in bed, saying her vows between labor pains, with Dove standing at her side, holding her hand. The honeymoon was a quick kiss. Then, Dove and other unessential persons were unceremoniously shooed out of the room, and Jericho, Daisy, Maritje Ten Boom Anders, and the midwife got on with the business of having a baby.

Dove found himself not only shut out but ignored. As if he were no more than the barnyard rooster who'd performed a perfunctory and barely essential barnyard chore.

No one asked how *he* felt. And he felt like hell. His head pounded, his stomach ached, and a ball of fear the size of an iceberg had become lodged permanently in his throat.

The hours crawled by. Lonesome and more scared than he'd ever been in his life, he wandered the house alone, with only the sound of his own footsteps for company. John—the lousy traitor—had callously gone off to check out Lizzie. So whenever Daisy or Maritje came marching importantly down the stairs, going to the kitchen on some mysterious mission, he pounced on them.

"What is she *doing* up there? What's taking so damned long?"

"She's having a baby, Lord Dove."

He shook a warning finger in Maritje's face. "You just march up there and tell her to hurry. Tell her I can't take much more of this. Tell her my head hurts, my stomach hurts. Tell her I can't even swallow!"

Maritje smiled. "I'll tell her, Lord Dove."

To his vexation, Jericho didn't pay the least bit of attention. An hour later, she was still at it. Frantic, Dove pounced on Daisy when she came down.

"What is she *doing* up there," he demanded. "Having twins? Hell, *one* will do. Better yet, tell her to forget it. Forget the whole damned thing. I don't want to be a father. Hell, I don't even like babies."

"Then keep your breeches buttoned, Lor' Dove."

Dove glared at Daisy as she tramped past him to the kitchen.

"Daisy? You've a mouth as big as a bucket. And a head twice as empty."

"There, there, sir," Daisy returned cheerfully. "Don't fret. Jer'cho will be fine. You'll see. She's a strong healthy girl. Only a few more hours."

"Hours!" Dove wanted to pull his hair out. He grew frantic. He paced the rooms of his house, raking a jeweled hand through his hair while the hours crawled by. When a muted yelp rang out—Jericho's first yelp of pain—he fled the house. He sat under a tree in the backyard and covered his head with his arms. Jericho in pain. Pansy Eyes in pain. His grubworm in pain.

Glancing up to see the ugly mutt that had followed Jericho home, he grabbed a stone. Then he changed his mind and put it down. Jericho wouldn't like that.

Time crawled. Darkness came, lighted only by the swath of light that spilled out the open kitchen door. Samuels drifted into the yard from the tap house and sat with him.

"The first one be the hardest, Lor' Dove."

Dove gave him a withering look. " 'First'! This is an *only*. There's not going to be a second. I'm not putting myself through this again."

"Jer'cho'll want more. Females do."

"Then she can do it by herself, damn it. She's not getting any help from me."

Samuels chuckled and hunkered down to help him wait. Fifteen years went by. Possibly twenty. When John—that callous traitor—finally drifted into the yard, Dove looked up crossly. "Well?"

"We're going to be married."

"That was quick work," Dove said, surprised.

John lowered himself to the grass to sit and smiled wryly. "Then I haven't wasted my time, all them years in your company, watching you womanize, have I."

Dove didn't smile back. He was too sick to smile. Jericho, suffering. He covered his head in his arms and waited. Another fifty years went by. Finally—finally!—Maritje stepped out the kitchen door onto the stoop.

Dove sprang up. "What happened!"

She smiled broadly. "The usual thing, Lord Dove. Congratulations. You're a father. It's a beautiful little girl."

The news struck him as astonishing. He whirled to John and Samuels. "I'm a father!" Then he whirled back to Maritje.

"Jericho! Is she . . . is she all in one piece?"

Maritje chuckled. "She's just fine, Lord Dove. Give us a few minutes to pretty up your wife and daughter. Then you can come up and see them."

A half hour later, when he fearfully opened the door of his bedchamber and went in, he found the room in firelight. He'd expected to find Jericho laid out half dead. But there she sat in his bed, propped up amongst linen pillows, wearing one of his nightrails and looking so beautiful his heart thundered with love.

She was holding a bundle in her arms as carefully as if it were the crown jewels. It jolted him. The first time he'd seen her, she'd been holding a bundle that way. A ragged bond-slave bundle.

He closed the door behind him and stood there. She looked up, her vivid blue eyes positively shining. Her brushed hair glowed like copper in the firelight.

"Hello, grubworm."

"Hello, Dove." She spoke very softly. As if she didn't want to disturb the thing in her arms. He swallowed. He supposed he should say something. But what did a man say to a woman who'd just been through hell to have his baby? She preempted him.

"You're not disappointed, are you, Dove? That she's a daughter and not a son?"

He was. He was also a bit insulted, if he took time to think about it. De Mont men sired males, not females. But she looked so proud and happy about what she'd done that he hadn't the heart to throw cold water.

"No, no," he said quickly. "No, not at all, no. A daughter's fine. Hell, you know I like women."

Her radiant smile widened. Her bosom lifted and she drew a happy breath. "Well then. Come over here and meet her."

"I can see her from here," he assured her.

"No, you can't." She wrinkled her nose at him. "Silly. Come over here."

Dove shook his head.

"She wants to meet you, Dove."

"She does?" He craned his neck. From where he stood, it looked like she'd given birth to a cooked lobster.

"Oh, yes. Ever so much. She wants to meet her father."

"How-how can you tell?"

Jericho blinked in amazement. Lord Dove de Mont, stuttering? She covered her astonishment with a tender smile and said gently, "Well, I can tell because she's turning her pretty little head every which way, listening for her father's voice. She already knows my voice. But she's intelligent enough to know there should be *two* voices—her mother's and her father's. So, come."

Though he nearly broke his neck craning it, he refused. Jericho was mystified. What was wrong? He wanted to see the baby. That was plain. Suddenly, understanding burst through.

"Dove, are you afraid of your own daughter?"

"No! Hell, no." He denied it vehemently, then asked, "but what if . . . she doesn't like me?" He said this so plaintively that Jericho stared, astounded. Who would have thought it, Lord Dove de Mont, humbled and brought to his knees by a tiny baby. Her heart melted and flowed toward him in waves of love.

"Oh, Dove. She will absolutely adore you."

"How do you know?"

"Because *I* adore you, and she is my daughter. She will adore you, too. Together, she and I are going to love you, adore you for the rest of our lives."

The anxiety faded from his handsome features, and he came forward hesitantly. When he reached the bed, he sat gingerly and studied the baby with such intense concentration that Jericho nearly burst. "Well?" she prompted.

He dragged his eyes from the baby. "I don't mean to insult her, Jericho," he whispered, "but isn't she a slight bit ugly?"

"Dove, she's beautiful!"

"She's squashed."

"She's not squashed. All babies get a bit squashed being born. Their features plump up in a day or two. Besides—" Jericho smiled at him. "Daisy and Maritje swear she looks exactly like you."

"Like me?" Surprised at that, he looked back at the wriggling infant with eagerness. "Now that I study her, I can see she has possibilities."

"Of course she has."

The baby's tiny red hands clawed the air. Jericho held her breath as Dove gingerly extended a finger. *Love her, Dove. Love her!* The tiny hand came in contact with Dove's finger and clamped onto it like a clam.

"Look at this," Dove said excitedly. "Jericho, look. She reached right out and grabbed my finger. Hell, she *knows* me! She *knows* I'm her father. Hell, this is no ordinary baby. She's a genius."

Jericho smiled ecstatically. "Then you do like her?"

"Like her! Grubworm, she's fantastic. She's going to be the most beautiful, most intelligent young woman in the world." He added, "And if anybody says she's not—I'll knock his block off." In his excitement, he'd raised his voice. Startled, the baby began to wail. Dove's eyebrows shot up and down in alarm.

"She sounds like a crow."

"All newborns sound that way. There, there, sweetheart. There, there." Jericho cuddled her daughter and soothed her, crooning to her, telling her how wonderful she was and how much her father and mother loved her. The baby stopped crying and burrowed with her tiny head, mouth working. Dove watched in total fascination.

"What is she doing?"

"She wants to suck."

He glanced up in alarm. "Well, give her something! Don't you have anything in—in there to give her?" He gestured at her bosom. Jericho gave him a soft smile that was partly amusement. He was going to be a wonderful father. And a demanding one. Just like Lord Aubrey. She hoped her daughter could endure it.

"My milk won't come in until tomorrow. Daisy says newborns don't need anything until then."

Dove gave her a fierce look. "Jericho! *My* daughter is different. Give her something, damn it. Hell, she's starving."

To placate him, she loosed the ribbons on the nightrail with one hand and uncertainly brought the baby to her breast. With Dove watching intently, the tiny head nuzzled and rooted, then, finding what was wanted, struck like a trout.

"Ouch."

Dove turned white. "Does it hurt?" he demanded.

She shook her head. "It just feels . . . different."

Their daughter sucked noisily for a minute, then sank into contented sleep. In the quiet firelight, Dove leaned forward and with exquisite gentleness kissed the wet breast his daughter had suckled and retied the ribbons of her nightrail. Then his warm moist lips found her willing ones and clung softly.

"Grubworm?"

"What, Dove?"

"Belong to me? Be mine? Stay with me forever?"

Full of joy, she rested her cheek on his. "Oh, Dove. I *belong* to you. I always have. Didn't you know? I belonged to you heart and soul and body from the moment a scared little girl-bondslave saw a golden Dove throw her mean master into the canal. That same little girl has waited so long for just one thing . . . "

He lifted his head, his hazel eyes bright as jewels.

"For what?"

"For *you* to belong to *her*."

He gazed at her for a long time. Then the corners of his handsome mouth twitched. A smile flickered in those jewel-bright eyes.

"I suppose you would like that in writing. An indenture of sorts?"

Her lips parted in surprise. She gazed at him, startled.

"W-would you?"

"Oh, for God's sake." Smiling, he wrapped his arms around her and the baby, gathering them close and warm. "Kiss me, grubworm. And you, too, little grubworm. I've a feeling this is going to be one hell of a long indenture."

Her heart jumped with joy.

"Oh, Dove," she said, kissing him. "The very longest indenture. The longest in the whole history of the world!"

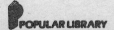